GUNMETAL
MOUNTAIN

The Cleve Trewe Westerns by John Shirley

Axle Bust Creek

Gunmetal Mountain

Blood at Sweet River (Coming in 2024!)

Published by Kensington Publishing Corp.

GUNMETAL MOUNTAIN

A Cleve Trewe Western

JOHN SHIRLEY

PINNACLE BOOKS
Kensington Publishing Corp.
www.kensingtonbooks.com

PINNACLE BOOKS are published by

Kensington Publishing Corp.
119 West 40th Street
New York, NY 10018

All Kensington titles, imprints, and distributed lines are available at special quantity discounts for bulk purchases for sales promotion, premiums, fund-raising, and educational or institutional use.

Special book excerpts or customized printings can also be created to fit specific needs. For details, write or phone the office of the Kensington Sales Manager: Kensington Publishing Corp., 119 West 40th Street, New York, NY 10018. Attn. Sales Department. Phone: 1-800-221-2647.

PINNACLE BOOKS and the Pinnacle logo Reg. U.S. Pat. & TM Off.

First Printing: September 2023
ISBN-13: 978-0-7860-4927-1
ISBN-13: 978-0-7860-4928-8 (eBook)

10 9 8 7 6 5 4 3 2 1

Printed in the United States of America

In Memoriam

Kevin Jarre, Larry McMurtry, William F. Nolan,
Robert B. Parker, Charles Portis

"Beware of false prophets, who come to you in sheep's clothing, but inwardly they are ravenous wolves." (Matthew 7:15)

Chapter 1

Chance Breen was just sitting in the saddle, he and his mustang half hidden by the gnarled bristlecone pines fringing the top of the bluff, when he spotted a man and a woman riding together far below. The riders were alone, looking small in the broad basin of windblown yellow grass below the limestone bluff. Breen took a spyglass from his saddlebag, his horse stirring nervously under him. "Hold still, you," Breen muttered.

Circled in the spyglass, the man and woman were a scruffy pair. The fellow in the charcoal Stetson was bearded, his long gray coat battered; the woman a little slumped, wiping dust from her eyes, her bonnet hanging behind on its tie. Both looked trail worn. The man rode a sorrel stallion, the woman a dappled Arabian mare. They had scarcely anything packed on their lean, weary mounts. But Breen did see that each had a saddle gun, maybe Winchesters. He could just make out an ammunition belt on the man. Likely there was a revolver to go with it.

Riding from that direction, they must have been traveling alone for a powerful long distance. There wasn't much out that way. After such a long, parched ride they'd be just about worn-out, and wondering if they were lost.

Yep, Breen figured, they'd be ready to talk to folks. Might be happy for someone to guide them along . . .

Breen grinned, put away his spyglass, and drew his horse slowly back from the edge of the bluff. Then he turned and rode back toward the camp in the small grove of locust trees.

Berenice Conroy Tucker and Cleveland Trewe were indeed saddle weary.

Cleve glanced appraisingly over at Berenice. She'd worn that same black riding habit most of the way. Her jacket was lined but not warm enough. Though tired, underfed, and dusty, Berenice Conroy Tucker never lost her wide-eyed pleasure in the countryside. A natural philosopher— what some called a "scientist"—Berry observed the world more closely than most. *She's not naive*, Cleve thought, *just recklessly brave.* She had grown up in a wealthy family and for the greater part of her life she had lived in luxury. But she had a wild streak, a fervent interest in nature, and a fierce determination.

Looking barren from a distance, northern Nevada's rough landscape teemed with life if you watched for it. Berry delighted in the snakes and lizards; in bighorn sheep clambering impossible routes across sheer cliff faces, where no track should be. Her gaze trailed hawks and eagles across the sky. She was fascinated by the instinctive strategy of coyotes in the gullies, cooperating to take a fat grouse. Passing through a dry wash, Berry and Cleve had cooly observed a wolverine driving off a puma. When they camped, Cleve sat quietly beside her, watching her make pencil sketches and notes.

He was forever keeping watch over Berenice. Cleve knew how perilous this country could be. Sometimes his watchfulness and warnings exasperated her and she would sigh and give him a wry look. But she never really complained.

Seven days back in the foothills of the Santa Rosa Range they'd run into rough weather. They kept on, riding head on into cold, bone-dry winds. When they found the trail ahead collapsed into a ravine, they were forced to detour northeast and then south, through sere, nearly waterless country. It had taken them four days to get out of the hills and down into the grasslands of Paradise Valley.

Berry didn't grumble after they were forced twenty-one miles out of their way to search for another trail, not even when they went two days without water. She was concerned for the horses when their water ran dry, but said nary a word about being thirsty herself.

Before they set out from Axle Bust, Cleve thought he couldn't admire her more. He was mistaken.

One day when the thirst got especially bad, Cleve noticed Ulysses and Suzie snuffling the air and whickering as they looked northwest. He decided to give them their head. Cleve and Berry both felt a childlike joy when the horses found a clear, deep waterhole—and the trail that ran northwest beside it.

Now they trotted their horses along a sketch of a road— merely dirt ruts in the grass. The sun was easing down before them. Their overlapping shadows stretched out behind.

Cleve pulled the brim of his hat down in front, and Berenice put her bonnet on to shade her eyes.

"There is no doubt at all we're going due west," she said, watching a slender green coachwhip snake sliding sinuously off through the grass.

He gave an exaggerated frown, pretending to be perplexed. "Now just how do you figure that?"

Berry smiled. "My hypothesis is based on this fact: the sun is sinking low and we're riding straight for it. Thus—west."

He nodded sagely. "I concur, Doctor Tucker. I'm pleased to ratify your observation."

"That is the crux of the scientific method in a nutshell—one's observations tested by peers."

"That's what I am to you, your peer?"

"Why, you're another kind of *hypothesis* being tested," she said pertly. "I *theorize* that you are suitable for mating purposes."

"Seems to me we've already mated a number of times on the way here."

"The tests must continue," she declared. She lifted her chin and put on a pedagogical tone. "A great many such experiments will be necessary."

"I sure as hell hope I confirm your hypothesis," he said. "Already made up my mind, on my end of things."

"So far, the results are encouraging." Done teasing him, she reached over and took his hand. "Are we really back on track to the trading post, Cleve?"

"I reckon we're no more than fifteen miles away."

She sighed, and unconsciously reached up to pat her windblown chestnut hair into place, tucking stray locks under her bonnet. "I must look like a scarecrow," she said. "The town women will stare and shake their heads."

"Won't be many women there to judge you. Mostly men. The men will be agog to see a pretty woman ride in at all. Those men would be pleased to see you even if you were dressed in an old feed sack."

She laughed. They rode on, and in a few minutes, she asked, "Should we not rest the horses?"

"Oh, they'll be all right. They'll be just as happy to get to town as we will. Once there, we'd best stake them well apart . . ." They'd had to work at keeping the horses from mating in the last two days, the mare having come into heat a bit late in the season. They would have a long journey, and a mare in foal shouldn't undergo such rigors.

"Suzie is looking to confirm her mate, too —with your Ulysses—but on a more temporary basis," Berry observed. "Horses, perhaps wisely, do not mate for life."

"Does Berenice Conroy Tucker mate for life?"

"She mates for life or not at all."

Cleve smiled. He hadn't proposed marriage—"mating for life" might have to be enough. Berry had told him that her only experience with marriage, ending when Mr. Tucker had died, had put her off the institution. She had come to regard it as "a ritual devised by ancient patriarchs to make serfs of women." But he already felt married to Berry, and he hoped that in time she'd accept the legalities. Convincing her might not be easy, she being as forward-thinking a woman as he'd even heard of: a suffragist, a scientist, a social reformer. He'd dallied with many a woman in his travels. But Berenice was a woman of empathy, strength, intellect, and beauty—and the only woman he'd ever truly fallen for. Settling down didn't come easily to Cleveland Trewe . . :

After serving as a Union officer in the war, Cleve had traveled extensively in Europe and England. When he ran short of funds, he returned to the States and tried working on his father's estate and clerking for his uncle. But when he wasn't traveling—afoot somewhere new—the darkest memories of the war would plague him.

So Cleve headed west. He took work as an itinerant scout, mostly for the cavalry. He found that if he kept traveling, the war receded to the back of his mind. He put in his time as a cowboy for a long drive with Charles Goodnight. After that he'd tried his hand gambling in Colorado—and when his luck ran dry, he hired on as assistant town marshal in Denver.

A few years of lawing were quite enough. He caught the gold fever and took up prospecting. He traveled from mining claim to mining claim, working feverishly but futilely around Virginia City—and then he got a letter from his uncle.

Threatened by claim jumpers, Uncle Terrence summoned him to the lawless northern Nevada town of Axle Bust. There, Cleve met Berry. And there, too, he reluctantly accepted the job of Elko County sheriff's deputy.

In time, Cleve left Axle partly to get away from his own growing reputation as a gunman, but mostly because he'd supposed Berenice, the daughter of a mining magnate, was taking up with a certain former beau.

In reality, Berenice had no such union in mind. All alone, she tracked Cleve down on the trail north, and insisted— against all propriety and common sense—on riding out to California with him. They were headed to San Francisco, and maybe farther. There was a certain valley he'd found near the California Sierras . . .

"Let's get on and see if there's room at the inn," he said. "A little canter won't hurt these two."

Cleve and Berry picked up their pace, both wanting to get to shelter, fresh water, food supplies, and the possibility of barbering and baths.

As they rode, Cleve scanned the valley: the grassy basin stretching on to the west ahead, the distant blue hills to the north, the tree-topped bluff, rising in red clay to the south. A quarter mile to the south, the bluff ended in a precipice.

Beneath the cliff, a rider swung into view, heading northwest.

"Now who could that be?" Berry asked, shading her eyes with her hand.

"Just a drifter on his way to the trading post, I expect," Cleve said.

"It appears he's coming our way."

"Could be he figured maybe it's safer to ride with us. The Bannock might be stirred up."

Cleve and Berry hadn't seen any Indians since leaving Axle Bust, though in the hills they'd noticed the tracks of unshod ponies likely belonging to the Paiute.

The rider seemed to notice them and halted his dun mustang about four hundred yards distant. He peered at them, then took off his hat and waved it. Berry waved back. The rider turned his horse, coming toward them at a casual lope.

They all reined in at the edge of an old buffalo wallow, and there the rider trotted up with a grin and a wave. He was a thickset man, dressed in beaded buckskins. He had long, uncombed brown hair and a spade beard, and wore the sort of floppy, oiled-leather hat protecting against hard weather. His bronzed, sun-etched face was round, and his gap-toothed grin jolly. On his left hip was a Remington Army revolver. A shotgun waited in a scabbard by the cantle of his saddle.

Cleve kept his expression genial, but he'd let his right hand fall to the butt of his Colt. He knew how to lay his hand loosely on his gun to let folks know it could be easily drawn, without quite making a threat.

"How do!" the stranger said, giving a mock salute. "Well say, you folks are coming from the far country. Headed for the Overland railroad? You're a long fetch from Winnemucca." The nearest leg of the Transcontinental railroad was the Central Pacific, with a station at Winnemucca, maybe sixty or seventy miles south from where they were. Cleve and Berry were both much attached to their mounts and reluctant to ship them by rail, having heard of many a horse getting a broken leg with the pitching of stock cars. Still, Cleve had suggested they head to Winnemucca for the train, since it might be safer for Berry. She refused to risk Suzie, and pointed out that the train would keep her "a considerable remove from the living abundance of the land." And she treasured a desire to meet Indians up close.

"You two goin' to Paradise?" the stranger asked.

Cleve thought of a facetious reply to that, but he said, "The trading post. They call it Paradise now?"

"They sure do, this being Paradise Valley. I'm headin' there. Mind if I ride along? Safety in numbers."

"You're welcome to," said Berry, more quickly than Cleve would have liked.

"What do they call you?" Cleve asked it mildly but kept a close watch on the man.

"My name's Breen. And you folks?"

"The lady is Mrs. Berenice Tucker," Cleve said. Still *Mrs.* because she was widowed. Her husband, a mining engineer, had died in a flooded shaft several years earlier.

Breen touched his hat brim to her. "Miz Tucker."

Cleve decided not to give his own name unless pressed.

His notoriety might have spread to Paradise Valley. "You can tag along, if you choose, Breen."

He gestured to indicate Breen should start off first. The drifter hesitated, then started out.

Cleve rode after him, keeping a few paces back. Berry caught up to Cleve and gave him a puzzled look, wondering about his coldness to a harmless stranger.

He shrugged. He was just taking commonsense precautions, a procedure Berry often set aside as uninteresting.

"Going to get cold out here," Breen said, raising his head to sniff the wind. "T'was mighty hot, and I cussed it too. Another fortnight or so comes a sharp wind from the north—Indians call it the Ice Wing. You'll feel it flyin' down through this valley. Won't snow much, but that wind's enough to make a man's nose fall off. Was me, did I have money for the fare, I'd take the train to somewhere easier."

Instinctively wanting to change the subject, Cleve said, "Last time I was through here, I saw a good many herds. Cowboys watching the beef. We've seen no one in this valley so far."

"It's the season. They get fat enough, they take them down to the Little Humboldt River, not so cold there and plenty of water. Fatten 'em up some more along the riverbanks, then drive 'em to Winnemucca for freighting." Breen looked over his shoulder at Cleve. "Where you folks headed to after Paradise? Up to Oregon?"

When Cleve didn't answer, Berry said, "Cleve wanted a look at California." She took up her canteen. "He's only seen a small part of it." She drank from the canteen, with the reins wound around the saddle horn, knowing Suzie would stay on the road. "I'm eager to see California myself. We hope to spend most of the winter in San Francisco.

In the spring, we plan to see the Yosemite. I read about it in *Hutchings' Magazine*. A wondrous place! Then there's a valley Cleve wishes to see in southeastern California . . ."

Breen was looking at her openmouthed. He wasn't used to a woman answering for a man and speaking out so boldly. He closed his mouth, chuckled, and asked, "Going to buy some land, are you?"

"We just might," Berry said airily. "There are matters yet unsettled. Life is more exciting, is it not, Mr. Breen, when things aren't quite settled?"

"Ha-*ha!* That it is!" Breen shook his head. "But it seems to me there's easier ways to get to San Francisco than what you took. 'Course, those ways cost a mite . . ."

"We did it our own way," said Cleve shortly, nettled by this prodding into their business. It seemed to Cleve that Breen wanted to know how much money they might be carrying.

Breen slowed his mustang, dropping back a little. "Ha-*ha!* Why sure! Don't mean to pry. Just talking to try out my tongue. Been so long out here with no one to jaw with but Bart here." He patted the horse and glanced sidelong at Suzie. "That's a fine mare you're riding, ma'am. She an A-rab?"

"She is a purebred Arabian, yes, and a very spirited girl too." Berry used her hand to brush dust from Suzie's mane. "One who needs a good brushing."

"How'd you come to be out here, yourself?" Cleve asked. "Business up on that bluff?"

"You could say so. I went to see a prospector friend, he's got hisself a cabin out that way. Pays me to bring him whiskey. His woman sets a good table too. But it's no more'n an excuse for the ride, you see. Then I heads out to do some prospecting, all on my lonesome. Found nothing but a piece of silver no bigger'n a booger. Run out of supplies, so I'm off to the trader. But a man like me, what keeps him going is his curiosity. And I cannot calculate how it come, you two riding out of that wilderness alone. Maybe you had a Conestoga, back along the trail? Lost a wheel?"

"Nope." Cleve said. "We rode from Axle Bust on these mounts."

"Axle Bust! Why a man would take that route at all, I don't know, if he ain't prospecting. And you ain't got the look of prospectors. Could be you needed to get out of Axle Bust right quick?"

Cleve nudged Ulysses up a little and gave Breen a cold look. "You wouldn't understand our reasons, Mr. Breen. Your *curiosity* will have to be satisfied with that."

"Why sure, sure . . . ha-*ha!*"

Cleve slowed Ulysses, to keep Breen ahead, and the three rode on in silence, except for Breen humming a drover song, sometimes throwing in a phrase or two. "When she see me comin' . . ." *Hum, hum-hum.* ". . . is you a cowboy'n has you been paid . . ." *Hum, hum-hum.*

Another three miles of the same song with many repetitions. Now orange outcroppings of dull red sandstone humped out from the grass. The wind picked up, not yet the Ice Wing, but cold enough to make Cleve shiver. It blew at them in gusts, so the grass rippled like a yellow sea.

A mile more and the outcroppings became boulders. Some were big enough to hide a man and his horse. Cleve noticed Ulysses pricking up his ears, neighing softly, head lifted, eyes searching ahead. He could feel the tension in the horse's body.

Breen reined in, and muttered something about, "I believe ol' Bart has a durn rock in his shoe . . ." He dismounted and went down on one knee, frowning at the mustang's right front horseshoe.

Ulysses stepped past Breen and a gust of wind brought the smell of horses from up ahead. Quite near. Cleve realized he'd let Breen get behind him. He drew Ulysses up short—

"Cleve!" Berry said sharply.

Cleve turned in his saddle to see Breen going for his revolver.

Berry had already drawn her rifle from its scabbard, and she shouted, "Drop it, mister!"

Surprised, Breen turned to her, his hand dropping from the pistol butt, as Cleve drew his Colt Army. Then a shot cracked past him—and he swiveled in the saddle, drawing his gun. A man was crouched by a boulder on the left. Floppy hat slanted low over his face, the shooter was aiming a rifle at Cleve's brisket.

Ulysses held just steady enough—as Cleve dropped the muzzle of the revolver and returned fire.

The outlaw jerked backward, Cleve's round cutting a deep groove through his forehead.

Breen shouted, "Davy!" and jumped on his horse, rode toward the boulder. He paused to stare a moment at the dead man. Ulysses was shifting nervously and Cleve was trying to get him back under control so he could aim at Breen . . .

The outlaw cursed and spurred his horse, riding off hard to the south.

Cleve aimed—then Breen was around the boulder, hooves thumping as he rode away south.

Berry fired her Winchester—but not at Breen. Cleve looked up in time to see a bearded man in a plug hat ducking under cover at the top of the boulder.

Spurring Ulysses, Cleve called out, "Take cover, Berry!" He rode at a canter around the big rock, past the dead man.

He saw no sign of Breen, but the bushwhacker in the plug hat was just jumping down to the grassy turf. The outlaw landed heavily on his feet, grunting, his hat falling off. He turned a dragoon pistol toward Cleve.

Ulysses was still cantering, which made the shot harder, so Cleve fired three times in under two seconds, the first shot grazing the man, the next taking him in the right shoulder, the third catching him under the chin.

The dragoon dropped from the man's shaking fingers as the outlaw tipped onto his back. Cleve drew up, glancing around, seeing no one else.

The outlaw gurgled, spat blood, tried to rise—and then went limp.

Cleve noticed two horses—a mustang and a paint pony—about thirty yards back, staked out in a cleft between boulders. There were saddles on the ground back there and a few tin cans—signs of a cold camp. The men had been waiting here for a while; Breen had set the trap, and tried to herd Cleve and Berry into it.

Cleve smiled grimly, then turned Ulysses around, patting the horse's neck with one hand. "You're a good man in a fight, Ulysses." He'd trained the stallion to steadiness around gunfire, but it couldn't hurt to praise him.

He rode back to Berry; she was down on one knee, in a shooting position, rifle in her hands, looking off to the south, the way Breen had gone.

"You think he's close by, Cleve?" Just the faintest tremble in her voice.

"He's probably gone out of range. And if I chase him, he'll set up to ambush me."

"Then please refrain."

Cleve nodded. "I was wondering about that shotgun. Most anyone with honest business out here, they're going to have a rifle. Shotgun's more something carried by road agents. I didn't give him a chance to use it, so he set up for the six shooter."

He shaded his eyes, stood up in the saddle but saw no sign of Breen—except maybe a little dust rising, a good distance off. "I don't think we'll see him again today."

Berry looked sheepish. "I was foolish to trust him, I guess."

Cleve dismounted and went to Berry. She stood up and stepped into his arms.

"You did fine," he said softly. "You're a wonder, Berry."

"The other two men?" whispering into his shoulder.

"They're dead. We'll put the bodies on their horses, and take them . . ." He shrugged.

". . . to Paradise."

Chapter 2

Cleve and Berry rode their horses at a walk into Paradise, Nevada.

He was leading the mustang and the paint pony on a lead, the dead men roped like deer over the saddles. Red-brown streaks of blood streaked the flanks of the horses.

Berry had cleaned herself up some, using canteen water. But both she and Cleve were still dusty, and the hem of her dress was tattered. Cleve's beard had grown out scraggly. Its tendency to do that was the reason he normally kept himself clean-shaven.

Cleve had passed through this valley once, a few years earlier, coming into Nevada from a played out silver field in southwest Idaho. In those days there had been only the trading post, the stables, and a few cabins.

There were but three women in the little settlement of Paradise and all came out to gawk alongside the men coming from their shops and cabins. First the stableman's wife came out. She stared at Berry, then at the dead men, then at Cleve, then back at Berry. She was soon joined by the tall, substantial, round-faced person of Mrs. Bridge, wife of Cephas Bridge, owner of the trading post. Senora Cruz, the very pregnant spouse of a silver prospector, heard the clopping hooves and came out to her porch, barefoot and yawning in her red silk sleeping gown—and stopped yawning as she saw the curious procession in the street.

Cephas himself leaned in the doorway of his trading post to watch their approach. Then the farrier in his leather apron came out of his shop to stare; next door, Grimson, owner and barkeep of the town's only whiskey bar, emerged in his stained white apron to thoughtfully stroke his side-whiskers. Beside the barkeep four moderately drunken cowboys jumped up from the bench in front of the cramped little saloon. The cowboys goggled at Cleve, Berry, and the dead outlaws—but as a man their eyes returned to fix on Berry.

The tanner came out to gawk with a hide still draped over an arm. Joining him was "Badger," the town odd-jobs man—mostly he shoveled up horse manure and swamped out the saloon. He seemed amused by the shabby couple leading the dead men in, and chortled, slapping his thighs.

An elderly Paiute and his son, colorful blankets around their shoulders, stood near the stack of furs they'd brought to sell, cawing with soft laughter and elbowing one another as they watched Cleve, Berry, and the dead men pass by.

Two thinly bearded brothers, young men who'd set up to be carpenters and had precious little carpentering to do, stared from their open-air work shed. Hiram Royce shook his head. His brother Eric snorted. "Hiram—is that the fella Davy you used to drink with?"

"It is," his brother replied. "Appears he's had his head half shot away. And that's Roy, flopped over that horse with him. I drank a deal with him too."

"You know I don't care for this town. You said there'd

be a sign from above telling us when we should leave. Hiram—this is it."

Berry gave the two ladies in front of the trading post a friendly nod. Mrs. Bridge nodded mechanically back.

Cleve saw nothing like a sheriff's office, or a jail, so he drew up at the trading post. It had a high false front, with a long, fading declaration of purpose:

C. BRIDGE, TRADING
& PURCHASES
DRY GOODS, SOAPS, FURS
BOOTS AND CARTRIDGES
LADIES' SUNDRIES
GOLD AND SILVER ASSAYED
WHISKEY SOLD UPON AVAILABILITY
BY THE BOTTLE OR GLASS
BARBERING AND BANDAGING DONE

Nailed up beside the door was a barber pole sloppily painted with its red-and-white spirals.

Cleve dismounted, tied the horses to the hitch, then helped Berry down from the saddle. She didn't much like being helped to dismount, but she understood he had to show gentlemanly ways, so that she would be respected here. Especially coming in with two dead bodies.

"Thank you, sir," she said, smiling at Cleve.

He approached Cephas Bridge, who straightened in the doorway and stepped back so Cleve could enter the cluttered trading post. At the back stood a counter and stocked shelves with notable gaps. Barrels stood along the walls. In a corner was a high-seated wooden chair that seemed built for barbering. Wearing a long white apron, Cephas was a man with narrow shoulders, wide hips, and a belly that hung over his belt. He had his rust-colored hair parted in the middle, thickly pomaded, and his beard was neatly trimmed.

"Cephas Bridge, I think," Cleve said, reaching out to shake hands. "I was through here a couple, three years back. Name's Cleve Trewe."

"I do recall you, yes sir. You bought coffee and spuds and bacon and cartridges."

"You've a fine memory, Mr. Bridge!"

"You were county deputy in Axle Bust, was you not?"

"I was, for a time. Is there a constable hereabout?"

"Why, no!" Cephas looked at the dead men. "Well, I'm the postmaster and mayor of Paradise. Sometimes I send a report to the U.S. Marshal, but only through the mail. We have no telegraph. Been seven months since the marshal was here in person. And he showed himself naught but that once. Now, sometimes folks come to me to settle disputes. We had a drunken man who enjoyed breaking windows with rocks and it was I who . . ." He seemed to realize he was wandering from more important matters. "Is that Davy Breen I saw slung over that horse, out there?"

"Might just be. Two highwaymen tried to ambush us— and a man calling himself Breen did his best to set us up for it. The bushwhackers ended as you see there—I will pay for their burial."

"*Breen* you say!"

"So he said. He got away. I heard him call out *Davy*, to one of them. He did seem some aggrieved when I shot the man."

"Chance Breen was never much for work, but I didn't know he had sunk so low as dry-gulching travelers. I cannot say I'm flabbergasted neither. His boy, Davy, was a drinker and would ride to Winnemucca after the saloon girls. Seemed to have money but no work. Well, well. Bushwhackers. Maybe that's what's happened to Jess Hopkins and his cousin Lou."

"They've gone missing?"

"They have. Jess and Lou took a freight wagon for me to Winnemucca. Supposed to bring back supplies. That was three weeks and two days ago. Should've been back before now—I thought maybe they rode off with my buying money. But that does not seem like Jess. Now, if the Breens were robbing folks on the roads . . ." Cephas shook his head sadly.

Cleve nodded. "I expect they killed your men and took the money. The wagon and horses too."

Cephas returned his nod. "Then you've done us a service. But no reward was offered for those men, I fear."

"No call for it. We're here as paying customers. We need to put up our horses, rent a room for the night. Get a bath if it's possible. We'll purchase supplies, be on our way in a day or two. I'll take care of the outlaws first— have you an undertaker?"

"Well, I do that myself, best I can, for a small fee, but as for burying—Badger does that chore, a dollar per body. He's already started drinking so he may not get them in the ground tonight. We have an old shack we store the dead in, till the graves are ready."

"I recall Badger. I'll pay him to unload those boys out there."

Cephas nodded solemnly. "Where you headed, Mr. Trewe?"

"California." Before Cephas could ask, Cleve added, "We've chosen not to take the train. We don't trust our horses to it. And we're particular about our horses. How's your stabler here?"

"He'll do. Anyhow the stable roof is in good repair, and he's got prairie hay. I just sold him thirty pounds of grain."

Berry came in then, smiling. "The lady is Mrs. Berenice Tucker," Cleve said.

"Ma'am," Cephas said, reaching up to take his hat off—then lowering his hand when he remembered he wasn't wearing a hat.

She offered her hand to Cephas Bridge. He seemed a little startled, but shook her hand as she said, "I've just met Mrs. Bridge. Agda says you can have some hot baths prepared?"

"We can, we have good spring water here, and there's a bathing house, but it takes some time to get the water warmed."

Agda Bridge came in, having finished her inspection of the dead men. Mrs. Bridge's gray-streaked blond hair was layered atop her head, and Cleve noted she was almost a foot taller than her husband. She wore a red-checked gingham apron over a puffy-sleeved housedress. "I'll get the big kettles out," she said, nodding to Cleve. "Get them boiling." Her accent suggested Agda was of Swedish extraction.

"Maybe show 'em the cabins first, dear," Cephas said. "Our little town has no hotel, but I have two cabins out back for rental."

"One for each of you," Agda said.

"One will be sufficient," said Berry, with a sweet smile for Agda. "Perhaps a meal while the water's heating? We could buy some dried meat, cheese, bread . . . and I see you have pickles. Also—I wonder if you would be so kind as to shave Mr. Trewe for me, Mr. Bridge."

* * *

With the horses stabled, watered and grained, and the corpses stored in the proper shed, Cleve and Berry saw to their own needs.

"Men are pleased to speak of the perils for women out in the wild," Berry said, stroking his smooth cheek after he got up from the barber chair. "But your beard is the greatest peril I faced in the wilderness. It is good to see you looking civilized again."

Once fed, bathed, and having imbibed a tot of Overholt, they settled into the rented cabin's little bed, spooning under a thin Indian blanket. A pot-bellied stove gave off overmuch heat at their heads and not enough to their feet. Normally the bed, little more than a cot for two, would have seemed hard to lie on, and too small. But after sleeping rough for so long, it felt luxurious. She wore her only spare dress as a nightgown, and nothing else. Cleve wore his long johns.

Drawing Cleve's arm more tightly around her, she whispered, "Cephas said there'd be no charge for that bottle of whiskey. Why is that?"

"It stands in for a reward—the men I shot likely killed his own hired boys and stole his money off their bodies."

"I did see that he made a claim on their horses, and what was in their saddlebags. But a bottle of whiskey . . . it seems a scant reward."

"You are safe and fed and lying in a clean bed. That's reward enough."

"Why . . ." She yawned. ". . . you had to pay for the cabin. . . ."

"Oh, having you safe and comfortable—that's worth any amount of . . ."

But she was snoring softly. Cleve chuckled and smelled

her hair, so close to his face, and fell into a deep sleep himself.

Close to midnight . . .

Chance Breen kept back from Paradise's only street, hugging the ink-black shadows, trying to make up his mind if he dared to go into the saloon. A full moon cast blue-white light down the street, the only light in town except for the lantern at Senora Cruz's adobe and the light from the saloon's front window.

Breen stepped out of the wind, between the saloon and Grimson's meat-smoking shed. His mouth watered at the smell of the boar meat smoking in there, and he was thinking maybe he'd cut himself some, if he could bust the lock. He was hungry, after the long circle he'd taken to evade the unnerving Cleve Trewe. Grimson sold some food in the saloon, but it could be that Trewe was drinking in there. Bragging up his killings, no doubt.

For a certainty, Breen wanted to find Trewe. But he had no desire to come upon him face to face in Grimson's place. He would find a safer setup to make Trewe pay for shooting Davy down like a rabid dog.

Breen had circled back to get Davy's body—and he'd judged from the signs, blood dripping along the hoofprints, that Trewe had taken the bodies into town. Had they buried Davy already?

Breen dropped his hand to his Remington sixer as he heard shouts from the saloon, men hooting and joshing as the door opened and someone came out. It was Badger, in his long, grimy winter coat, his ragged dungarees and down-at-heels boots, weaving toward the shack down by the cemetery. The odd jobs man must've run out of drinking money.

The cold wind tugged Breen's hat as he stepped out from the shadows to track Badger, hurrying to catch him up.

Breen waited till they'd crossed the street, and in the shadows between the farrier workshop and the carpentry works he took two quick steps and grabbed Badger by the collar. He held him fast, shoving the gun barrel through the wiry little man's long greasy black hair so it pressed on the nape of his neck.

"Who . . . ?" Badger gasped.

Breen cocked his gun. "You hear that Remington going to cock? You won't hear the shot, Badger, if you don't take me to my boy."

Still drunk, but sobered some by the gun pressed to his neck, Badger hesitated, then said, "That . . . that you, Chance?"

"It is."

"Folks, they calculate you for an outlaw now. You'd best hie for the hills!"

"What is it they saying?"

"Now I ain't saying it's *so*—but there's talk you killed Jess and Lou Hopkins and took Cephas's wagon and the buying money. They had a town meeting, about two hours ago. You'd best ride out quick. You're to be shot on sight."

"I was figuring it would take a turn that way, once Trewe got here. Where's my boy laid out?"

"Cephas's old supply shed."

"Is it locked?"

"Nope. Cephas don't keep his supplies there no more. He's built onto the back of the store for that. And ain't nobody got any use for . . ." He broke off.

Breen snorted. "For a dead body?"

"Two of 'em there are. Cephas already emptied their pockets, took their guns, took their horses. Maybe somebody'll steal their boots."

"That'd most likely be you. Now take me to see my boy."

"You going to shoot me, after?"

"Why would I shoot you 'less I have to? You can't bury that boy if you're dead. I've got other matters to tend to. Now tell me this—is Cleve Trewe in the saloon?"

"Nope. I expect he's in one of Cephas's cabins with that woman."

"Is that so . . ."

"You'd be a fool to mess with Trewe. Grimson showed us a newspaper from back in the summer. Trewe, he was a lawman out to Colorado and then in Axle Bust. He's the one who shot Buckskin Jacques, and Jug Mulvaney—and took down that Red Hills gang. A deadly gun, for a surety."

"Just my goddamn luck, runnin' foul of a killer." Breen took a deep breath and made up his mind. "Still and all, I got to get the job done. Let's go. I'll holster my gun but I'll shoot you if I have to."

They crossed into the moonlit street, Badger walking a stride ahead, only weaving a little now. No one challenged them, and they got to the shadows and walked quietly past Cephas's store. Out back, about ten paces behind the new extension, were two small cabins which he let to travelers.

"Hold here," Breen whispered, as he looked the cabins over. There were windows, covered in oil cloth. All dark.

Trewe and his woman were in one of those cabins. That presented a powerful temptation. He could bust in and shoot them dead. Take a minute to search them for money, then hurry on back to his horse. But the horse was a piece

away. And Cephas Bridge's house was about forty paces
past the cabins.

"You know which cabin they're in?" Breen asked.

"Well—"

"Keep your voice down!" Breen hissed.

Whispering now so low Breen could hardly make it out,
Badger said, "Come to think on it, I don't know if they're
sharin' a cabin or not. He treated her so ladylike and all.
She didn't have the name Trewe, do you see. Grimson says
maybe she's his sister."

Thus if Breen broke into the wrong cabin . . . she'd
scream and Trewe would hear her. It would become
necessary to take the woman as a hostage. That couldn't
end well. Not if Trewe was half the gunman Grimson
made him out. And he'd shot Davy and Roy in two blinks
of an eye.

"Let's move on to the shed . . ."

They walked quietly past the cabins, and reached the
old storage shed. The wind rose and howled through a
knothole in the door, so it sounded as if the dead inside
were crying out.

Breen licked his lips, and said, "Open her up."

Badger opened the door and used a lucifer to light the
kerosene lamp inside. It threw a ghastly blue light on two
dead men who lay sprawled close together. Davy was
awkwardly pitched over on his side, one eye open, as if he
tossed and turned in his sleep.

"So you just chucked them in like that, did you, Badger?"

"I'm paid to bury, not—" Badger grunted in pain as
Breen punched him dead-center in the face, so he fell over
the dead men. Whimpering, Badger scrambled away from
the corpses, and backed into the wall, one hand to his
blood-spewing nose. "I'm sorry, Chance, I just—"

"Shut your bazoo!" Breen hissed. "And keep your voice low! Now you *listen* to me, Badger. You straighten out them bodies and you take this—" He tossed a double eagle on the floor at Badger's feet. "You use most of that money to get Hiram to make a pine box. Lay Davy down good and gentle in it. He was the only kin I had left. Don't steal his boots neither! I want a chunk of wood set up with his name on it too! I'm going to be nigh town, so close you'll feel me watchin', and I'll send people to ask what you done—so do as I say! If I find out you didn't do it—if you drink up all that money—I'll get you alone and I'll knock you flat, tie you up, and cut off your hands! Then I'll put out your damn eyes!"

"Chance, I ain't never talked you down—"

"Say it back, Badger! What am I going to do if you don't get him that box and bury him right?"

"You'll . . . you'll cut off my hands and put out my eyes!"

Breen drew his hunting knife and waved it at Badger's eyes. "You got any doubts I'll do it?"

Badger cringed back, covering his eyes with his hands. "No, I got no doubts, Chance!"

"You going to tell anyone I was here? If you do, I'll cut out your tongue!"

"I won't say a word!"

"You be sure of it!"

With that, Breen stepped back, closed the door, and stalked off northwest, looking for his horse. Seemed he was going to have a cold camp tonight, and he had a raft of planning to do. It occurred to him that this Trewe was a self-assured man, and would let down his guard, given time. Probably Trewe never reckoned to hear from Chance Breen again.

Well now. Cleve Trewe reckoned wrong.

Chapter 3

Eight o'clock the next morning, Cleve was looking in on Ulysses and Suzie, talking softly to the horses as he combed burrs from their manes. The stableman had done nothing but feed and stall them.

Berry came in wearing a new ankle-length blue dress she'd bought from Cephas, and a new pair of white button-up riding shoes. Her bonnet had been laundered and her hair was almost coifed. "You look prettier than a catalog girl this morning," Cleve said.

"We shall keep you just as pretty, Cleve," she said, smirking. "I have bought you a supply of shaving powder. And I have a mirror. Now you will have no excuse!"

Cleve grinned. "I guess we'll find room in a saddlebag for the shaving powder."

"We would have plenty of room if we bought a pack-horse."

He liked the way she used *we* to speak of the purchase. Like a wife to a husband. "You hear of a good one for sale?"

"Cephas would like to sell us one of the horses we took from the outlaws."

"Both those nags are hammerheaded loafers, if I'm any

judge, but I expect one will do for a packhorse. It's a good thought. We'd have real traveling supplies. Might even see if we can get canvas for a tent. Unless . . ."

She came to Suzie and hugged her neck. "Good morning, Suzie. Unless what, Cleve?"

"Unless we ride to Winnemucca and take the train. We could find someone trustworthy to take the horses to San Francisco for us. I've got enough money to pay them. Local sheriff could point me to a reliable man."

"But—the railroad? Why?" Berry looked at him askance. "I am engaged in a study of the wildlife of this region! I've already discovered a new species of *Lavertilia!*"

"Ah. That peculiar lizard."

"And think of the insects! The entomological possibilities, Cleve!"

"Those too. But . . . traveling on horseback in winter! It's a rough road for a—" Cleve broke off, grimacing.

Her eyes narrowed. "You were about to say—for a woman?"

He took off his hat, and used it to thoughtfully dust his trousers. "No, no, I meant—for *anyone.*"

"Nonsense, I know who you meant. I will be as stalwart and staunch as you are! And Cleve—it is not truly the deeps of winter yet! I have consulted one of Cephas's maps. We have only to get through the Warner Mountains and then there's the Applegate Trail west."

"But—it's truly more . . . more *demanding* than you realize, Berenice—"

Berry gazed into his face—and then her expression softened. She stepped up to Cleve and slipped her arms around his waist, laying her head on his shoulder. "You fret too much about my safety. You promised me adventure, Cleve. And you well know that wildlife taxonomy cannot be accomplished from a railroad."

"I don't remember promising you adventure," he grumbled. "I think you promised yourself that." But Cleve knew he was already beaten. He could not say no to Berry.

"Oh!" She straightened up and looked him in the eyes. "Oh?"

Her eyes . . . he couldn't look away.

"I was to tell you that we are invited to breakfast at the Bridges' house! It seems you are now a celebrity in this little town. I believe Cephas wants bragging rights."

"A celebrity? For shooting two owls?"

"You shot owls?"

"Owlhoots. Outlaws."

"Oh. It's not for that, so much—apparently a Mr. Grimson has a copy of the *Axle Spinner* from August."

Cleve groaned. "Let us ride out, soon as we can decently do it. I will outride that reputation, one way or another, I swear it!"

They were not the only guests at breakfast. Mrs. Bridge's sister and her husband had arrived two days earlier—and they, too, were planning to take the trail due west. Their destination could not be approached by rail.

Having sated himself on bacon, eggs, and corn fritters, Cleve sat back at the dining room table and regarded Gil and Freja Peck, who sat across from him and Berry. Cephas and Agda Bridge sat to either side.

Gil Peck was a tall, lanky, brown-bearded man of perhaps thirty-five, in a wrinkly clay-colored sack suit. He was not talkative. His wife—Agda's sister, Freja—in a blue lace-edged dress and shawl, looked older than Gil. She seemed a more buxom version of her sister, but with her blond hair tautly coiled on the sides of her head.

The room was cozy, warmed by a crackling fireplace, with just a small cloud of smoke gathered near the ceiling.

"Got to clean that flue," Cephas observed, peering up at the smoke.

"I could do that, before I go," Gil said. "You've taken such good care of me and Freja."

Gil's Adam's apple bobbed on his long neck when he talked, Cleve noticed. He wished Leon were here. He would've goggled at the sight of that bobbing Adam's apple. Leon had been Cleve's partner in Axle Bust, and his good friend—once his enemy, in a sense, since Leon had fought for the Confederacy in the Civil War. They became friends when Leon was technically Cleve's prisoner, at Fort Slocum. Now, Leon was town marshal of Axle Bust. Cleve had promised to send a letter to Leon at the first chance.

"I didn't see a great deal in the way of ladies apparel in the store, Agda," Berry said, as she buttered a biscuit with a little silver knife. "And that seems sensible, as you are few here, but I wonder if you have a riding habit for sale?"

"You know, Mrs. Cruz has one, she feels it will always be too small for her now, after the baby is born. It might fit you. It's rather pretty."

"But is it warm?" Cleve asked, struggling to use the tiny butter knife. It was just too small for his fingers. "That's what you need, Berry. Warm clothing."

"I do have an old wool-lined cape," Agda said. "It's yellow velvet, and it's for riding in cold weather. I never felt comfortable in it, but . . . It could be my farewell gift to you."

"Oh, that would be wonderful!" Berry said, reaching for a teacup.

"You say the mail goes out once a month or so, Cephas?" Cleve asked.

"Sometimes sooner—I plan a trip to Winnemucca, with a couple of men riding shotgun. I'll take it myself."

"I'll have something for you to post for me." Cleve took Berry's hand under the table. "You could write to Teresa, and Velma Haggerty, Berry."

"Certainly," Berry said. "I can write to Leon too."

Cleve missed her point for a moment—then realized she didn't want him to suppose she could only correspond with women.

"You could deliver the mail to the Wells Fargo yourselves," Cephas said. "You could ride along to Winnemucca—we'd feel walloping obliged."

"Oh dear," Berry said. "I'm afraid we're determined to go directly west from here. Through the Warner Mountains to the Applegate Trail."

"But the snow could catch you out, in those passes!" Agda put in. Her blue eyes widened and she wrung her hands dramatically. "Do you not remember the Donner Party?"

"I know the story," Berry said. "And there is a danger of being stuck in the mountains, in heavy snow, but I flatter myself that I—that Cleve and I—could find our way out of it, without starving."

"Who's riding shotgun with you to Winnemucca, Cephas?" Cleve asked.

"Gage Crenshaw and Ira Bunse," said Cephas. "They work for the Mesa Ranch."

"I know Bunse," Cleve muttered. "We did some scouting together. A capable man. You'll be in good hands."

Freja spoke up then. "Agda—Gil and I are taking the wagon west on the Applegate here too—going to the settlement at Gunmetal Mountain. It would be so much better for us to have Mr. Trewe along at least part of the way."

Gil glanced at Freja, brows knitted.

She quickly added, "Gil is a *strong* man but in such a place . . . we all need help."

Agda nodded resolutely. "Then you will be fine. If Mr. Trewe and Mrs. Tucker are set on going on to the Applegate Trail, then it's surely God's will they should accompany Gil and Freja!"

Cleve was suddenly on his back foot. Were he and Berry to have traveling companions? He glanced inquiringly at her.

"It sounds like a *splendid* idea to me," said Berry. "We'd be pleased to have company."

Cleve nodded, and managed to smile.

The next day Cleve and Berry found an inch of snow waiting when they stepped out of the cabin. "Ah," Cleve said. "Snow already."

"Were you not raised in Ohio? Hence your first name?" she asked, tugging on some knit gloves.

"I was."

"And does it not snow in Ohio, sir?"

"It does. Well . . . not so very much, but . . ."

She tugged her bonnet on, took his arm, and they started toward the Bridges' house. "And did you not travel through snow traversing a mountain pass, in your long and storied roamings, Mr. Trewe?"

"I did. Still . . . this time of year . . ."

"It's not so very late in the season. If we're only subject to clement weather, what kind of experience is that of California? We must experience it all!"

Cleve shook his head. Must they experience it all? In his one foray into California, riding through the southern Sierra Nevadas, he'd been caught in a snowstorm. He'd gone three days without food and sleep. Once down from the mountains he'd nearly got his throat cut by a lunatic miner while sleeping by a campfire; he'd been knocked almost senseless by a grizzly, barely escaping with his life—and he'd lost his horse and nearly his life as well to some understandably enraged Miwok Indians. They thought he was with a band of ranchers who'd been laying waste to their villages.

And yet, twenty miles farther south and west, he'd come to a particularly lush, emerald-green valley, with a crystalline little river running through it—the Sweet River, it was called—and it was that valley he hoped to show Berry, come summer. There was scarcely a settler to be found along the Sweet River. He was of a mind to try horse ranching out there, with some crops too. Cleve knew farming; his father had made a great enterprise of it, hiring dozens of farmhands to become an important planter in the Ohio River Valley.

"Berenice, for the sake of your safety I truly should insist that we take the railroad," he said, as their boots crunched through the snow, "but somehow, I seem unable to deny you anything. It's unmanly of me, but there it is."

"It is *gentlemanly* of you," she said lightly. "And there's nothing unmanly about being a gentleman! At breakfast, let us make a deal to buy the mustang from Cephas . . ."

So it was that after two more days in Paradise, Nevada, purchasing supplies, taking a final bath—for a time—and getting to know their new traveling companions, they set out on a cold but cloudless morning for California, Cleve and Berry riding beside the Peck's oxen-drawn covered wagon. The road was rutted and lumpy, but fairly wide, as they trailed through the sparse pinewoods west of Paradise. The wagon rattled, and the horses had to step carefully. The packhorse, Raggy, was tied to the tailgate.

Berry was in the saddle on Suzie, between Cleve and

the wagon, chatting with Freja Peck as she went. Cleve wore a new sheepskin coat with a furred lining and Levi Strauss blue jeans, leather gloves, and leather chaps. Both women wore their bonnets and heavy woolen coats. Freja wore a long calico dress and warm leggings; Berry wore a woman's riding habit she'd purchased from Mrs. Cruz— a dark blue lady's safety dress with riding breeches—and a tight blue jacket. Swept back from her shoulders she wore the riding cape Agda had given her. Cleve thought the cape evoked Maid Marian. Her new bonnet was sky-blue, with a red ribbon.

She seemed to Cleve rather too splendid for a journey on a pioneer trail, but the sight lifted his heart every time he looked at her.

Berry said, "I hope Raggy doesn't mind the load—but I expect it's not so heavy as the man who rode him."

"You have named your packhorse?" Freja asked, with surprise.

"No," said Berry, turning back to Freja. "He was named already. Someone in town was sure that one of the . . . the *owlhoots* . . . called him Raggy. He seems to recognize the name. We see no reason to spurn a proper respect for the brave beast, simply because of his involuntary association with badmen. You do not name your oxen?"

"We named them in a way," Gil said. "North and South, so we know which one we're talking about."

"That's so," Freja admitted. "We're going west, so we keep North on the right, and South on the left."

The sky was closed with beetling clouds; cold wind, soughing between the trees, bit at Cleve's nose and ears. It wasn't cold enough to confirm Breen's claim about frostbite, but it made him shiver and pull his hat lower on his forehead. He was glad for his leather gloves. Glancing over at Berry, he saw her shoulders were hunched, her head ducked; Freja was pulling a thick woolen blanket over her legs, and Gil was squinting into the wind.

Cleve had learned a good deal about the Pecks. Freja was seven years older than her husband. Gil, an itinerant tutor and bookseller, had asked her to marry him many times before she'd consented. He'd come to the house selling books, including one by the mystic Emanuel Swedenborg. Back in West Virginia, Gil's grandfather had been converted to "the New Church" of Swedenborg by John Chapman, the traveling nurseryman known as Johnny Appleseed.

"Papa said Gil was a heretic," Freja told them. Her father also fulminated that Gil was near penniless, unsuitable, and rootless. But the house where she lived with her widower papa was quite isolated, and Freja was not resigned to being a spinster. They'd eloped, Freja taking her dowry without consulting her sternly Lutheran father about it.

Gil had felt that there was no way to know if Swedenborg had been a true prophet without meeting him, but his cousin Leman wrote him of another man—a visionary, one Magnus Lamb—who was "doing miracles" at Gunmetal Mountain, and whose "measure could be taken face-to-face." Leman had guaranteed Gil work and a comfortable house if he joined him at the Gunmetal Mountain colony.

"What makes this man Lamb so special that you cross half the nation to reach him, Freja?" Berry asked.

But it was Gil who answered, looking sidelong at Berry, his brow crinkled with irritation. "There's more there than Magnus Lamb—there's a house waiting, and there's a job waiting! I'm done selling books and tutoring. And this man—he made a town appear out of the wilderness, before anyone was there! Those who followed him, they found the town right where he said it'd be, fresh and new!"

"That's some brisk construction," Cleve said. "But it only takes money and planning."

Gil shook his head. "He's credited with many a miracle!"

"What is his doctrine?" Berry asked.

"Why, to serve the Lord with all your heart and soul, same as Jesus said!"

"I do hope he's clear who the Lord is," Berenice said.

Gil paid her no mind, and went on. "He says God told him to build a town on that mountain, and he has done it!"

"Careful, Gil, there's a hole," his wife warned him, pointing at a sinkhole in the trail about a foot deep and three wide.

He loosened the reins on North and South. The Pecks had learned the oxen would go around a hole fairly neatly, if you let them. The oxen slowed, snorted, went a little off trail, and then back on.

"Wise and sturdy beasts," Berry remarked.

"What work awaits you at Gunmetal Mountain?" Cleve asked.

"Logging!" Gil said. "There's a forest, t'the west of the mountain. The prophet logs it and sends the lumber by the Pit River, to a place called Poverty Flats. Railroad's built a terminus there. Builders for San Francisco and Sacramento buy the wood at the terminus."

"They've renamed that place Redding, I hear," Cleve said. "So you're to be a . . ." Gil's spindly frame made Cleve hesitate. ". . . a logger?"

Gil shook his head. "Leman tells me they need a man who can figure, and keep books for the logging camps."

"Gil, he's real clever with figures and such," Freja said proudly.

Cleve found the Pecks likable enough. They were decent folk, not unfriendly but not annoyingly friendly. He had hopes that once he and Berry left the Pecks at the turnoff for Gunmetal Mountain, Ulysses and Suzie could make up the time.

But on the trail with the wagon, time seemed to stretch out to a stubborn slowness. They clopped and rattled along, eking their way northwest.

The covered wagon endlessly creaking, the horses incessantly clopping, they reached an area of thick brush and black volcanic outcroppings. Here the wind was blocked for a time. Cleve spotted a small herd of mule deer, in a lea off to the north, and he thought about pulling his Winchester and going after some venison. But they had enough supplies for now. The time to supply the larder with hunting would come soon enough. He scanned the horizon, and saw an ancient lava cone rising in the southwest. "The map showed the Applegate curves a good deal, north and then south," Cleve said. It cuts by the Modoc lava beds. We're seeing some of that country already. You can see that old lava cone . . ."

"Where?" Berry asked, pleased.

He pointed it out. "This is still volcanic country. There are a good many hot springs up here. We might get a hot bath after all."

"Oh!" gasped Freja. And Cleve remembered that she could be priggish. She had seemed shocked, back at the Bridges' house, to learn that Cleve and Berry were unwedded.

Cleve changed the subject. "You know, not long ago, a year or two, was the Modoc War—it came to a culmination not far from right here. The government insisted the Modoc share land with their ancestral enemies, the Klamath, up in Oregon. Indian Affairs was not providing enough food for the two tribes, and the Indians were forced to raid stock from the local settlers. A large band of more than a hundred Modoc broke off for the hills. There was a battle along Lost River, up in Oregon, and then Captain Jack and Hooker Jim and Scarface Charley took their people south to a kind of natural fortress in the lava beds—"

"Who did you say?" Gil asked. "Scarface?"

"Captain Jack, Hooker Jim, and Scarface Charley are nicknames of Modoc chiefs," Cleve said. "Captain Jack's real name was Kintpuash. Anyhow, the Modoc retrenched in lava caves, and they knew all the trails to them—there were pitched battles with the cavalry, with the Modoc having all the advantage. General Canby himself came out to work up a treaty. But Hooker Jim and his boys convinced Kintpuash that if Canby didn't give them what they wanted, the general should be killed. When the treating failed, Hooker Jim shot Canby twice in the head and cut his throat—right there in the peace tent . . ."

"Dear Lord Jesus," Freja gasped.

"Is that renegade bunch still around?" Gil asked.

"No, the cavalry was reinforced, and the Modoc were hunted down. They hung Captain Jack and the two others, sent the rest of the band to Oklahoma and Oregon. There are other tribes in this area, but there's no trouble with them—last I heard."

They lapsed into silence. Berry seemed to ponder Cleve's account. Gil and Freja peered into the underbrush to either side of the trail . . .

The weather broke and for three days the sun edged out the clouds. The wind eased, and despite the occasional drizzle it was almost balmy during the day.

But the nights were cold. Cleve and Berry would set up their tent in the last light of sundown, placing it on high ground, well away from the covered wagon where Gil and

Freja slept. Berry seemed to enjoy helping with the small wooden poles and pegs. He set up a "dog tent," military style, naturally.

"This tent is our first try at setting up a home together," she said, the first night. She was in earnest and facetious at once.

"With a little luck I'll do better for you, someday. Something permanent to live in. Maybe a bigger tent than this."

She laughed. "I shall insist on a *palatial* tent."

Two nights later they lay in the tent belly-down, chins on their crossed arms, looking out the open flap. The horses were nearby, hobbled near to one another, Suzie being out of season now. Cleve and Berry listened to the horses nickering; they smelled pine needles and woodsmoke and watched the flames of their own little campfire dwindle. Beyond, they could see a horned owl on a tree branch silhouetted against the sky, head swiveling all the way round. The owl made a soft repetitive sound like a man blowing into an empty jug.

"*Bubo bengalensis*—how wonderfully her head swivels," Berry said.

"Like to have that ability now," Cleve said. "Keep an eye on the back trail." He'd briefly glimpsed a horseman on a hilltop, along their back trail. Nothing fearful in that, alone. But it made him thoughtful.

"Why did they call this a dog tent?" Berry asked.

"Don't know, unless they figured them only suitable for dogs. This one has the advantage of cozier company."

"Did you soldiers nestle together on a cold night?"

"We preferred shivering and misery, dear. At least in my tents we did."

Berry sighed. "You sometimes call me *dear*—which is what my father calls my mother. I'd rather you didn't."

"You spurn endearments?"

"Not at all! But we need something more personal."

"There were monarch butterflies all about, the day we met. Perhaps 'my queen of butterflies'?"

"Too mawkish and too wordy."

"My next choice was going to be 'the world's loveliest sharpshooter.'"

She laughed. "I like the sentiment of that one! Too long-winded, however. Let us seek inspiration." She closed the tent flap and came into his arms.

The next morning dawned clear and cold. Cleve woke to find Berry gone. He pulled on his pants, boots and hat, his sheepskin coat, took up his gun belt, and crept from the tent . "Berenice!" he called, standing up.

No answer. Tensing with an indefinable sense of imminence, Cleve buckled on his Colt and tied it down.

But there—he could see Freja across the clearing, squatting by the fire. He told himself Berry was helping Freja Peck with breakfast. Must be getting something from the wagon.

He crossed the little clearing between the pines, pausing only to pat Ulysses and Suzie, observing that Raggy seemed to have settled in just fine with the other horses. The three of them were champing grass in the clearing.

Cleve joined Mrs. Peck at the fire. "Morning, Freja."

"Clear skies today. Here you go."

He accepted a tin mug of coffee. Corn fritters and bacon were sizzling aromatically on an iron pan over the Peck's campfire. Gil was harnessing the oxen, clucking at the big animals. Everything seemed normal. Still . . .

"Where is Berry?" Cleve asked, looking around.

"Oh, Berenice has stepped into the brush for . . ." Freja cleared her throat.

"I told her not to do that without me standing guard!" he said, his eyes probing the hillside.

Then he heard Berry shout from the brush. "Cleve! Someone's up there!"

A bullet whined and thumped into the ground at his feet.

The gunshot cracked as Cleve dropped the coffee cup and ran toward the sound of Berry's voice, drawing his Colt as he went.

Chapter 4

Berry ran to meet Cleve as a second gunshot echoed, while the bullet thudded into the ground behind him.

The sound told Cleve the rifleman was up on the rocky hills to the east. "Get down, Berry!" he shouted, pointing at a deadfall. She threw herself flat behind the fallen fir as another shot cut close by him. He ran to her, squatting behind the big log.

"I was just standing up," she said breathlessly, "and I saw a man up on the hill with a rifle. I think I recognized that hat . . . it might be Breen!"

Cleve nodded. "I can't let him stalk us. I'm going to have to take the fight to the enemy."

"Cleve, no!"

"Breen won't quit unless I make him. He's liable to kill anyone here. We got Gil and Freja mixed up in this."

Another shot smacked into the log. Cleve looked over at the wagon, could see Gil and Freja sheltering underneath it, lying flat. Gil had a rifle and was aiming toward the hill, looking for a target.

Good man, Cleve thought. "Gil!" he shouted. "Keep him busy for me!"

Gil glanced his way, nodded, and commenced firing toward the hilltop. Cleve holstered his Colt.

"Cleve—" Berry began.

But he jumped up and sprinted to Ulysses. There was no time for a saddle—Breen could cut him down before he got the saddle cinched.

Ducking, Cleve undid the hobble, vaulted on, and rode bareback, without reins or bridle, into the screening trees between him and Breen. He guided Ulysses with his knees and a gentle grip on the horse's ears. He'd trained Ulysses for this—a man didn't always have a chance to saddle and bridle his horse.

Cleve ducked a tree branch that would have smashed him in the forehead. Twigs scratched at the back of his neck. The rushing air was cold in his face

He heard the cracks and echoes as Gil and Breen exchanged gunshots. He doubted Gil could keep Breen occupied long.

The hill rose over him, tufted in piñons and sage and cacti, studded with glossy green-black obsidian and porous red igneous rock. He glimpsed movement a little more than a hundred yards above and to the southeast. He angled Ulysses onto a deer trail, and up the hillside, squeezing the horse's ribs to keep from sliding off.

A bullet slashed by, the shot echoing, and he drew up in a little cluster of piñons on a shoulder of the hill. "Hold here, Ulysses," Cleve said, sliding off the nervous horse.

He drew his pistol and moved in a crouch behind an outcropping of the porous red rock. A bullet smashed into the rock—light, porous stuff, scarcely denser than pumice—and red dust sprayed over his head. Coughing in the dust, he slipped off to the right, behind a tall cluster of prickly pears. He caught his breath, cocked his pistol, and peered between stalks of cacti—he could just make out

Breen scrambling along the hilltop. He was moving toward Cleve's left, north and slightly west, rifle in hand. Looked to be heading for a knoll that offered good cover. From there he could cut down on Cleve with effect. But for half a second, Breen was turned away . . .

Cleve stood up, clasped the Colt with both hands, tracked Breen, and squeezed off a shot.

Breen spun, fell out of sight. Cleve started up the hillside to verify the kill—then Breen was up, moving unsteadily to cover.

Cleve fired again and saw dust spurt up where the bullet struck near the knoll. Breen slipped from sight.

Muttering a profanity, Cleve moved farther up the hill. Following the winding game trail, he got fifty feet higher, then angled a little south, trying to flank his enemy. He had a clear shot from here on the eastern side of the knoll—but Breen wasn't there.

Stones rattled, in a muffled way—seemed to Cleve the sound came from the other side of the hill.

Cleve ran the rest of the way up to the knoll, breathing hard. He spotted blood and tracks leading northeast, over the hilltop.

Hunched over, Cleve followed the footprints, his finger sweating on the trigger of his Colt.

He heard a horse whinny and looked over the narrow pinnacle—and saw Breen riding off, about forty yards down the hillside. The outlaw was bent over in the saddle, obviously wounded. The range called for a rifle but there'd been no time to get the Winchester.

Cleve fired twice with the Colt, knowing he'd likely miss.

Breen rode into a thick stand of manzanita, vanishing behind the russet tree trunks.

* * *

"I followed for a quarter mile, but I couldn't keep up afoot," Cleve said, drinking coffee by the fire, his gaze on the hilltops. "We could track him on horseback, Gil. I hate to think of that son of a bitch sniping at us all the way down the Applegate."

"We cannot forsake the women," Gil said. He was clearly in no mood to track an outlaw through the brush. "There are bears and mountain lions out there too."

Freja added, "And Indians!"

"Freja and I could come along," Berry offered. She was sitting cross-legged on the ground, eating a corn fritter out of her hand, and looking up at those same hills.

"And leave our wagon to be looted by whoever comes by?" Freja protested. "Anyway, I won't have Gil riding off into the wilderness after outlaws! Breen could surely have partners out there."

Gil nodded. "That could be."

"Do you know how badly he was wounded, Cleve?" Berry asked.

Cleve shook his head. "There was some blood but not pails of it. Might not be bad, or it might eventually kill him. I guess it will slow him down. I doubt he's got a gang out there. They'd have been here ranged against us. But could be he's dead already, for all I know."

"He's wounded sore enough he had to run," Gil said. "That tells us he's hurt plenty. Let's get back on the trail and call this business over and done."

Cleve reluctantly agreed. They broke camp and rode out, Cleve doing a fair imitation of the horned owl, looking at the back trail.

The countryside cut by the trail became even more arid

and rugged. Buzzards were seen more often than any other bird. There was water in the casks roped to the wagon, but Cleve wondered if they'd run out before they got to the Pit River. The animals had to be watered too, and not stingily—not if you expected the oxen and horses to do their grueling work on the rough, rock-strewn trail.

Twice they came across abandoned wagons at the side of the road, stripped of everything useful. They were a melancholy sight. Not long after, Raggy stumbled on a rock, dislodging a couple of pots from his load, which clattered on the trail. Cleve had to stop and check the packhorse's hooves and fetlocks, as Berry restowed the tin pots.

Late in the afternoon the right front wagon wheel banged hard into an outcropping jutting in the trail. The covered wagon jarred creakily, its iron joints complaining.

"Careful, Gil!" Freja chided him. "You about broke a wheel there and bumped me off too!"

"Nothing but an excuse-me-ma'am," Cleve said.

Berry looked at him with arched eyebrows. "A what?"

"An 'excuse-me-ma'am.'" When I was with Charles Goodnight, that's what the cook called it when the chuckwagon hit a bump."

Berry laughed.

The wagon bumped and jiggled onward; the horses whinnied and picked their way . . .

But in a few minutes, as they passed over a dried out creek bed, there came a sudden metallic squeal. The wagon shuddered as the battered wheel broke apart and fell away with a *clank*, the axle sagging to stick in the hard-packed dirt. The wagon jerked to a twisted halt, the oxen grunting and lowing as the yoke wrenched their necks. Cleve drew up and saw that the already cracked wheel had broken apart in the rocky creek bed.

"Hellfire," said Cleve. He dismounted. "Let's see what

can be done." Gil and Freja and Berry joined him to ponder the wrecked wheel. It didn't look fixable, with four spokes splintered and the iron rim twisted off.

Cleve asked, "You folks have a spare wheel?"

Gil said, "Nope. We haven't."

"We should have got a spare in Paradise, Gil," said Freja. "We knew this one was rusted through."

Gil growled to himself. "I tried to find one, but they had none to fit." He looked ruefully at Cleve. "We had a spare—this one is it. We broke the other on the way to Cephas's place."

"The farrier could've fixed one up for you, I expect," Cleve said.

"He said it'd take three days! I thought we'd be okay for this last leg of the trip. I guess I should've . . ." Gil shrugged. "I just thought the Good Lord was watching over us."

"Tribulations are the Lord's to decree," Freja said. "Not yours, Gil."

"You are not abandoned by Providence as yet," Berry said, going to Suzie. Opening a saddlebag, Berry tugged out a map and unfolded it. "I think I know where we are . . . that creek bed is marked and not so far off is a little settlement. It's called . . . if I'm reading this rightly . . . *Piswaller*."

Waking kind of surprised Chance Breen. He'd lost a good deal of blood on the dodge, and he felt his head spinning. He remembered going too weak to stay on his horse. He'd fallen, and the world kind of went down a sump hole, everything sinking into a swirl of muck and blood.

He'd figured, *Well, this is it. Cleveland Trewe has done killed me.*

But here he was. And it hurt. A pain gnawed Breen's side now. A man's deep voice urged him, "Go on, take it down!" There was a taste of beef broth . . .

The broth woke him up some more, along with the metallic taste of the spoon and the smell of burning branches close at hand. Everything spun around when he moved his head. He couldn't see much, but he could hear the fire crackling, snapping in a wind. He found he was lying on his back, his head propped on something that smelled like a sack of feed. Seemed like he was in the rear of a freight wagon.

A bearded man was leaning close to him now, a blur right at first, but he saw the spoon in the man's hand, and Breen opened his mouth for it. Someone was nursing him and that was better than being in a stinking cell, or being shot at . . .

It was certainly better than being hung.

Breen swallowed the broth and managed to say, "Thankee."

The person with the spoon leaned back and came into focus. Now Breen saw it was a man in a black coat, with big round red cheeks, a black spade beard, long ringlets of jet-black hair down to his shoulders. Glittering green eyes peering over a beak of a nose. Like an Amish elder, he had no mustache. The corners of the man's eyes crinkled, and he chortled, "Thank the Great God and his earthly sovereign, brother!"

Breen cleared his throat. "Him too. I thank him, I do. This earthly feller—he tell you to nurse me?" It wasn't so easy to talk. Breen was feeling the pain now, the wound in his side. It was hot there, burning hot.

"You could say so—that he told me to help you. I found you by the roadside, and I knew immediately when I saw you lying there. I felt His command come upon me. I knew it to be a sending from the mountaintop! *He* was testing me!"

"Testing you, was he? Say, you see my horse anywhere?"

"No, he must've run off. Gone some time. Indians will get him, or mountain lions."

"I've caught a bullet in my side . . ."

"I got the bullet out of you—I've had to pull a few bullets in my day. I cleaned it with turpentine and sewed it up good. But you've lost blood! You must take more broth marrow and wild greens, and you must rest. You shall stretch out in my wagon, as we go along."

"What's all this here in the wagon?"

"Why, grain and nails and seed and the like, which I bring to him on high, for Lambsville."

"You got any whiskey with them supplies?"

The green eyes narrowed. "No! Drinking spirits are only had by those the Sovereign appoints! And only for his special purposes! Now, how came you to be shot off your horse like that?"

"That bullet—a bad feller put that in me. He kilt my son—just up and shot him for nothin'. I went for this killer, to bring a reckoning on him, but he sneaked up and shot me."

"I see! Then the light of justice needs to shine for you!"

"Why I believe you're right!" Breen paused to cough a little. He could taste blood. "What's your name, pard?"

"I am only Brother Donahue. A servant of the great man."

Breen's head was throbbing. But he needed to know something more. "But if you're hauling me in this wagon— where you going to take me?" It wouldn't do if this Donahue was to take him back to Paradise. They'd like as not string him up.

"I shall take you up the blue mountain! It is but a few days journey to the west."

"Is it now?" Breen closed his eyes. "What you call that mountain?"

"It is called Gunmetal Mountain. Come, come . . . more broth. Then you shall sleep . . ."

A hand-painted sign, leaning over and shivering in the wind, announced the place-name as Cleve and Berry rode by it. *Piswaller.*

The settlement's structures consisted of five shacks, an open-sided shed for selling whiskey, one sizable cabin down at the end, and five privies. A few horses were tied up, down the rutted dirt road, and two mules were harnessed to a buckboard. Farther down the road, several armed men watched the newcomers from an open-air drinking shed. It was not a welcoming place, and Cleve began to regret giving in to Berry's insistence that she accompany him.

On the stool in front of a shack on the left sat a middle-aged man bundled up in a sort of parka that seemed made of varicolored scraps of old bedding. He had a jug clutched to him, its neck thrust through his long beard. Leaning beside him was a rusty two-trigger shotgun. The shotgun was the sort Cleve's father carried and talk of weapons was a good way to inaugurate a chin-wag with a stranger.

Cleve drew up, and so did Berry. He asked, "Say, friend—is that a Purdey fowling piece you have there?"

"It's a Purdey right enough," growled the man with the brown spade beard. His face was hard to see with the hood up. "But I don't keep it for birds. I keep it for liars."

"That so? Is it liar huntin' season around here?"

"Always is," the man said, and Cleve saw the flash of a

grin. "Folks ride through and say they want this and they is selling that and most likely it's all lies."

"We're here to buy something," Berry said. "And I do not lie, sir. We need a wagon wheel and we'll pay for it, if we can find the right size. Anything like that here?"

He blinked at her for a moment, then shrugged. "Frank got some maybe, ma'am. In that pile out back of his cabin." He pointed at the cabin. "He sells what he can."

Cleve asked, "Who's that buckboard belong to?"

"It's mine o'course. That's Anabelle and Dorothy, my mules."

"If we get a wheel, how's about we hire you to drive it out to where our wagon's broke down."

The man looked Cleve over doubtfully. "How do I know you don't want to steal my mules and rig, once I get out there?"

"Why . . ." Cleve was annoyed at the remark and began to think about using a rope to drag the wheel behind Ulysses, instead of hiring the buckboard.

But Berry said sweetly. "May I know your name, sir?"

"Me? It's . . . well they call me Donkey here—but it's Phil."

"My name is Berry, Phil; this is Mr. Trewe. He has recently served as undersheriff of Elko County. How about if I ride along with you on the buckboard, as an assurance of your safety?" She gave him a smile like the morning sun on a summer day.

He gaped at her—and tugged at his beard. Then, his voice hoarse, Phil said, "Yes, ma'am. That'd be fine."

Cleve noticed a pile of loose rock on the slope above the shack. Tailings, gone to weed. There was a boarded-over tunnel up above them. "Looks like there was a mine here," he said. "This a mining camp?"

"It was," Phil said, nodding thoughtfully. "I started it

too. Wasn't much silver to take out. Even less copper. Then it run dry. I got enough to keep me for a time. Most of the others, they give up and moved on. I still do a little prospectin' . . ."

"You name it Piswaller?" Cleve asked. "Some kind of local joke?"

Phil threw back his hood to show the scowl creasing his round, freckled face. "Howdya mean, *joke?* That's my *name*—Phil Piswaller! Something *funny* about that?"

"No, no," Cleve said quickly. "Not at all! Just an unusual name, do you see."

Phil glared at Cleve. Then he snorted and took a pull on the jug. He shuddered and his gaze softened as he smiled at Berry. "Say, ma'am, while your rude friend here's looking at them wheels, you want a pull on this jug here? I make it myself and it's simon-pure."

"Oh, that's a very kind offer," Berry said earnestly, smiling at him. "But I believe I know more about wagon wheels than my companion, so I'd better go with him. Cleve—let us visit this Frank. We shall be back presently, Phil . . ."

They trotted the horses toward the cabin, and Cleve said, "So you know more about wagon wheels than me?"

"Perhaps!" Berry said lightly. "I did a study of them once, in the hope of smoothing out a wagon ride. A man named Robert Thomson has developed a wheel clothed in rubber—it inflates with air, like a balloon does. But it hasn't caught on. Yet I'm sure something of the kind will replace iron rims, one day."

"A rubber wheel sounds fragile."

"Not on a good road, Cleve—you may have forgotten good roads, living west of the Rockies for so long."

They rode by the open-sided shed, where a white-haired

old man poured whiskey from an unlabeled bottle into wooden cups for three men standing at the bar plank. Two of the men were rough-looking, one young and sprucer. The drinkers stared, their gazes locking on Berry.

Cleve gave them a glance, noticing that they all had sidearms. He took in the models of guns and how they were carried. He sized up the younger man, sharper-dressed than the others. He was blond, with a tied-down six-shooter, a look of fixed defiance. He would bear watching.

Cleve looked away as if uninterested, but laid a hand on the butt of his Army Colt, in his usual "friendly warning."

As they rode toward the cabin down the row of shacks, the younger man at the shed bar followed them, just ambling but watching closely. He was blond, and clean-shaven. He had a long coat and a Remington revolver.

Reining in at the cabin, Cleve and Berry dismounted, turning to see a man of about forty carrying a Springfield rifle step out onto the porch. The rifle wasn't pointed at them. It was also just a warning. The man had long, lank hair and a pocked face. He wore dungarees, with a red undershirt and suspenders. The boots looked cavalry-issue to Cleve.

"Good afternoon," Cleve said. "My name's Trewe, this is Mrs. Tucker. We're looking to purchase a wagon wheel. You'd be Frank?"

"I am." The cabin door stood open behind him. Watching dazedly from a few steps inside was a gaunt, droopy-haired woman in a ragged calico shift. Her feet were bare, her sunken eyes downcast. There was just enough light to see that her nose was broken and her right eye was bruised. The woman swayed as she stood there.

Cleve glanced at Berry. She was staring at the woman. Appalled.

"Wheels are out back," said Frank grudgingly. "Some other wagon parts too."

"Lead the way, if you please," Cleve said.

Frank scowled. "You first."

"You really can trust him!" Berry piped up. "I was just telling Donkey that Cleve was undersheriff of Elko County. He was also a policeman in Denver."

Frank looked at her, taken aback. "Well . . . I reckon."

He glanced over his shoulder, muttering something at the girl in a threatening tone, and then closed the door with a bang.

Rifle clasped in both hands, Frank led the way to the back of the cabin. Piled near thick underbrush, they found a pile of scavenged wagon parts, with grass growing through, alongside blackened cooking pots, a tin wash-basin, sundry unidentifiable iron parts, and a broken-down upright piano. There were two wagon wheels lying next to each other, one terribly rusty and probably the wrong size. But the other looked like it would do.

"Is that wheel the right size, Berry?" Cleve asked, pointing. "You being the expert."

"I'm sure it is," she said.

"How much you want for it, Frank?" Cleve asked.

"Two hundred dollars," Frank said, with an acid edge to his voice as if he dared Cleve to scoff.

Cleve laughed softly. "Now let's try that again like two men who aren't drunk horse traders—how much?"

"You won't find another wheel inside a ten days ride! Two hundred dollars!"

"We could put a drag under the wagon, hold the axle

up," Cleve pointed out. "Slow us down but we could keep on till we get a wheel somewhere else."

Frank snorted. "Ain't no one any farther got one either. And like as not snow's coming."

Cleve growled to himself. He was sorry he'd agreed to escort the Pecks to the cutoff. It would have been better—safer for Berry—if they'd ridden on alone, so he could get her through the mountains before the snows. But he had agreed. He was responsible for the Pecks now.

He reached into a coat pocket, pulled out his billfold and counted out ten twenty-dollar bills. "I'll permit myself to be robbed, this once, if it will get us on the road and moving again."

He offered the cash to Frank, who snatched it away. "You take that wheel and get on. I got other business to see to."

"Mister . . ." Berry began, looking coldly at Frank. ". . . I don't know your last name. *Sir*—I wish to speak to the woman in the house. Alone. I have a need to know that she is well."

"What?" Frank stared at her, gripping his rifle hard, whiting his knuckles. "You stay away from her!"

Cleve put his hand firmly on the butt of his Colt.

"Is she your wife, sir?" Berry asked.

Frank gave one sharp nod. "Sure, she is! She's been here a good long piece and I have claim on her!"

"I merely need to ask her a single question," Berry said.

"Ask *what?*"

"If she wants to stay here—or come away with us. I believe she needs help. I propose to offer it to her."

Cleve nodded. "It's just a question. We'll let her make up her own mind."

Frank's eyes bugged, his teeth gnashed, and he swung the rifle around.

Cleve slapped the rifle upward with his left hand. The Springfield's shot banged into the sky as Cleve drew his Colt, stepped in, and cracked the butt on Frank's head, yanking the rifle away with his other hand.

Gasping, Frank stumbled back and fell. Gun smoke drifted from the rifle muzzle, blowing away on the cold wind.

Cleve holstered the Colt and handed the Springfield to Berry. He took the money back from the fallen man and said, "I'll roll the wheel to the buckboard."

Rifle in her hands, seeming stunned at Cleve's casualness immediately after cracking a man over the head, Berry stared dazedly at Frank. "If you don't mind, Cleve, I'd like to take a breath or two first. Is he dying?"

"No. It was just a 'Wichita love tap.' He'll come to, by and by."

She nodded. "Then I . . . I will speak to the woman in the cabin . . . I'll meet you at the buckboard."

"I'll be there soon as I can get this wheel loose from the weeds."

"Do you not propose to pay for the wheel?"

"If that woman is his wife—well, either way I'll give her the money."

Cleve stepped carefully past Frank and wrestled the wagon wheel up out of the grass and vines. It seemed intact, the spokes sound enough. He rolled it past the groaning man on the ground, past the cabin, and out to the street.

Donkey Phil was standing agape beside the buckboard, with his antiquated shotgun in his hands. "Did I hear a shot from back there?"

"Frank tried to take a shot at me. I gave him a knock

on the bean. He'll sleep it off. We'll give his woman the money for the wheel. You want to help me get this thing on your wagon?"

Phil tugged at his beard thoughtfully, then leaned his shotgun against the buckboard and helped lift the wheel onto the wagon bed.

They'd just got it in place when a gunshot came, and a shout from the cabin. Cleve's hand went to his Colt as he spun to see Berry falling back out of the cabin door, gray gun smoke drifting out after her.

Then Frank stepped onto the porch, a dragoon in his hand, snarling, pointing the pistol at Cleve.

Cleve drew and fired three shots with unprecedented speed and intensity. Three bullet holes patterned over his target's heart.

Frank spun, falling back into the cabin . . .

Before the man hit the floor, Cleve was sprinting across the road to the cabin.

He found Berry getting to her knees, looking dazed, her cheeks streaked with tears, one hand on her right cheek.

Cleve's heart leaped. *Berenice is alive.*

He holstered the Colt and helped her up, clasping both her hands, looking her over. "Are you shot, Berry?" he asked, his voice hoarse.

"No, he . . . he hit me, is all. With his fist. Nothing broken."

She rubbed her bruised cheekbone, and said, "I went in through the front door, put the rifle down." She let out a sob and went on, "I didn't want to scare her. Her name was Abigail. She told me he kept her prisoner. She'd tried running away twice. She wanted to go with us . . . He heard her say it, I guess, when he came in the back door, and he took up a . . . a pistol from the mantel . . . He shot her in the stomach, and he cocked the gun and I tried to take the gun from him and he hit me . . ."

Cleve looked through the door. The woman was lying on her back. A pool of blood was spreading around her shattered head. "Oh, hell . . ."

". . . And then he shot her again." Berry hung her head and wept.

Chapter 5

They rode through a bright cold morning, following the wagon. The trail was narrow here, and somewhat rutted. The replacement wheel was holding up.

Raggy's halter was roped to the wagon's rear gate; Ulysses and Suzie trotted along just behind him. Berry wore dungarees, boots, gloves, a bonnet, a jacket, and the winter cape.

Cleve glanced at her, saw she was hunched over the saddle horn, her face half hidden by the bonnet. He could see sadness in the set of her shoulders.

"You didn't pay for that man to be buried, the way you usually do," Berry said tonelessly.

"As far as I'm concerned," Cleve growled, "that son of a bitch can feed the coyotes and raccoons."

"Because he shot Abigail?"

"Because he hit you!" Cleve said, through grating teeth. A seething hotness rose in him when he thought of it. "But he deserved shooting, all the same, for what he did to her."

I should have gutshot the bastard, Cleve thought.

After a cold silence he added, "We buried the woman, at least. Put up a marker—"

"Her name was *Abigail,*" Berry reminded him. "Donkey Phil told me a little about her. Frank took a trip to Winnemucca and brought her back with him, saying she was a mail-order bride. She had been married, but her husband died of scarlet fever. She was abandoned, in poverty and with no family, so she answered a catalog ad. Phil thought maybe Frank was beating her, but a *man* . . ." She almost spat the word. ". . . 'does not get between another man and his woman.'"

"I don't call Frank much of a man, nor Phil either," Cleve said.

The wagon creaked along, the horses clopped, occasionally stumbling slightly on errant stones. The farrier had put new shoes on them in Paradise and he was glad of it now.

The anger in him simmered. Another gunfight forced on him. But . . . *that man hit Berry.*

Cleve knew anger got in the way of what needed doing—getting Berenice Conroy Tucker to safety. And to a better life.

We'll get there, he told himself. Let it be. What's done is done. There's a long road ahead.

A crosswind made him shudder—and another emotion seized him. A pang of regret. A bleak feeling he'd made a wrong and fateful choice in agreeing to take Berry out into this wilderness.

"I shouldn't have agreed to you coming along this way, Berenice," Cleve said. "I should have taken us both back to Axle Bust. Or at least insisted we take the train. You shouldn't have to . . ."

"No, no," Berry said, so softly he could barely hear her. "It isn't this wilderness. Cleve—*I got Abigail killed.*

I could have kept the rifle close—I could have waited for you . . ."

"Come to that, I shouldn't have let you go in there alone. I underestimated that son of a bitch's fortitude. Anyhow . . ." Cleve took a deep breath. "Berenice—you couldn't have figured it was going to go that way."

Berry shook her head. "I should have acted more . . . tactically. Thought it through."

He squinted against the wind, and said, "There was a winter's day, not much different from this one, in the war. I was tasked to send a detachment of men to destroy a Confederate battery—to kill the cannoneers and destroy the cannon. The detachment succeeded with one emplacement, and then they were overrun by the rebs. I was not permitted to leave my position to lead a rescue. I sent another detachment of five soldiers out, all I could spare. Two of them, including a good friend of mine, were killed . . . and the rescue was a failure."

She looked at him, her eyes wide. "Oh—that must have been painful for you."

"Worse for their families. But—I felt a responsibility to try to save those men. It's hard to know the right thing to do—because you can't see every side of the elephant at once, Berry. If you're going to be in the war, you've to accept the uncertainty of battle."

She chewed a lip, pondering. "At least—you understand I think of it as a battle. To save women from brutality. From enslavement."

"Abigail surely needed saving. At least she learned from you that someone cared what became of her. I doubt she'd have lived for long if we'd just left her there."

"If only I'd kept that rifle in my hands . . ."

They were quiet for a minute. Then, hoping to lead her

into a sunnier state of mind, Cleve said, "By my reckoning, we are in California now."

"Oh—are we?" Berry looked around, then shook her head, smiling crookedly. "I don't know what I expected to see. It looks just like Nevada."

They rode on in thoughtful silence. Cleve liked to ride close to Berry. But maybe he should ride out front of the oxen, to watch for trouble.

Yet danger could come from any point of the compass. He scanned the hilltops, the outcroppings, the stands of horse chestnut trees now bereft of leaves, and the evergreen manzanita. He was looking for Indians. Bannocks were roaming the area and they were likely in an angry mood. Then there was Chance Breen. Cleve wasn't convinced the man was dead.

The wagon clanked to a stop up ahead of them, and Gil came hurrying back to Cleve. "There are tracks crossing the road!"

Cleve trotted Ulysses around Gil and went ahead to look. The prints were horse tracks. Unshod. Quite a number of prints, at least ten horses—close together and roughly orderly, with an equal depth—suggesting they weren't wild.

"Unshod," he said, as Gil caught up. "Indians. They were heading north, maybe a day ago. With luck we won't run into them. All the same we'd best move on quick as we can."

Gil climbed onto the wagon and snapped his whip, shouting at the oxen to get a move on. Cleve rode beside him, figuring to keep watch ahead for a time. He thought perhaps Berry would ride up and join him, but she didn't.

Here, the Applegate wended between craggy outcroppings of volcanic rock and stands of manzanita and pine, the treetops waving in slow rhythm with the wind.

A rowdy flock of crows gave their raucous calls. A vulture soared and looked speculatively down at them.

Gil's wife wasn't at her accustomed place beside him, Cleve noticed. "Is Freja feeling poorly?" he asked.

"Lying down for a while in back. Her stomach is troubling her. It comes of a morning . . ."

Was she pregnant? But it wasn't Cleve's place to ask. "You know much about this place you're going to, Gil? How much did Leman tell you?"

"He said we'll have our own house to live in, once I take up the work for the Lamb."

"That's the . . . the prophet's name? The Lamb?"

"It is. Magnus Lamb. Leman calls him the Sovereign Lamb. *Ho there, South, steady up!* Yes—Lamb is a man who came all the way from Britain because he had a vision of this settlement in the wilderness, where the righteous could start anew."

"I wish I could know if I was righteous or not," Cleve remarked. "I have met a good many men who seemed sure they were righteous."

"You have never known if you were doing right?" Gil asked, astonished.

"I wouldn't go that far. I was sure I was on the right side in the war. When I was undersheriff, I hunted down some men who'd hung a boy without trial. I was sure I did right to hunt them then, and I'm sure now. But living a life without doubts—that I cannot do."

"Folks on Gunmetal Mountain feel in their heart that *this* man is the one," Gil said, nettled now. "I feel it myself, even now."

"I do envy your certainty," said Cleve.

They rode on, the horseman and the wagon driver, in silence. The clouds thickened, bulging darkly in the sky. A tang in the air made Cleve think of snow.

* * *

It didn't start till dusk, when they were setting up camp. Cleve had just finished hobbling Ulysses and Suzie in a narrow space between a volcanic outcropping and a dense stand of manzanita. Porous red lava stone crunched under hooves as the horses cropped at the grass growing sparsely up between rocks.

Of a sudden the wind hushed—and snow came down in lacy swirls.

"Might not stick," Gil said, as Cleve joined him at the wagon. Freja was coming back from having led the oxen to a small stand of pine trees that would give them some shelter.

"I suspect it will," Berry said, as she led the packhorse to them. "I hope it won't be enough to stall our expedition."

"Is this an expedition?" Gil asked, amused.

Cleve tugged a small canvas tarp from Raggy's pack. "Berry, if you'll take Raggy over to the other horses, and get him tied and unpacked, I'll bring that big extra tarpaulin from the wagon. This one here's going to help us shelter the fire . . ." They'd stored a few of their possessions in the back of the Peck's wagon.

Berry led the horses away and Cleve snapped the canvas open and laid it out on the ground. The snow wasn't even an inch thick yet.

"How will you use the canvas to make a fire?" Freja asked.

"The snow'll melt under the canvas, and we'll build a fire on the ground there," Cleve explained. "We build it right it won't get much wet on it. I'm going to make a quick lean-to to keep the snow off the fire." He pulled the big tarpaulin from the back of the covered wagon, along with some pegs and thin rope, then carried it all to the horses. Berry had gotten the pack off Raggy and was hobbling him, where he could reach the spare grass. Cleve clambered up onto the rocks to one side and slung the tarp over the manzanita and the outcropping, then secured it over the horses with rope and pegs, making a slanted shelter for the horses.

"An ingenious horse shed, Cleve," Berry said.

He noticed she seemed a little more cheerful now. Travel and camp work settled the mind.

"We'll gather some brush," he said. "Set up the lean-to for the fire. Best get this done before too much snow falls."

"Shouldn't we put up our tent?" Berry asked.

"We don't know how heavy the snow will be." The swirling blue-white flakes fell a little more thickly now. "Might as well sleep under the wagon tonight, if the Pecks have no objection."

Freja removed the canvas sheet Cleve had laid down, built a fire on the dirt with kindling from the wagon's woodbox, and Cleve and Berry, working together, managed to get the campfire lean-to set up before the snow could smother the fire.

Privily watching Berry intently arranging the brush cuttings on the little framework of branches he'd assembled, Cleve admired her industry, her willingness to pitch in. She had little familiarity with camp jobs, but she always looked to learn; she found a way to help, or to do the job alone if she could—setting up camp, breaking it down, saddling horses, unsaddling horses—she was always there. Cleve had taken a job, five years back, escorting moneyed sightseers laying over in St. Joseph, Missouri, who wished to see a buffalo hunt and "real-life red warriors." The genteel ladies who'd come along in an elaborate travel wagon had watched Chinese women setting up camp and cooking, for their two-night trip, toiling to keep up with caring for so large a deputation of the well-to-do, and had never offered to so much as clear away dishes. Berenice Conroy Tucker was from the same culture of educated merchant-class women, but she was of an altogether different character.

When there was a clean-enough stream, Berry washed her own clothes, and Cleve's, using Hudson's Soap powder. He suspected she put aside her objections to female servility in order to get him into cleaner clothes. She could be a frontier woman, but she liked her men to have a bearable odor. For the same reason she encouraged the use of tooth powder, applied with a cowboy-style "chew stick." A horsehair sufficed for cleaning between the teeth. Having been brought up with some gentility himself, and having been provost over a military prison for a time, Cleve wasn't unfamiliar with hygiene. But living in the dirty, rustic towns out west a man became careless of such considerations. He wondered if he were civilized enough for her, in other ways.

Returning from checking on the horses, Cleve paused to watch as Berenice crouched beside Freja at the cookfire. Berry's intentness, as she watched Freja stir the salt pork, resembled a chemist observing a colleague at work.

Freja cooked with a cast-iron pan over the camp grill brought out of the wagon; the grill was a simple framework of iron, modeled, he thought, on those used by an officer's *aide-de-camp* in the war. Just such a grill had been part of the equipage of Cleve's own aide, Charles Dunne, a Black cook who'd volunteered for the Union Army. Charles had been an amiable, patient man. He was a good cook, too, and Cleve had learned the basics of camp cooking from him. After the medical corpsman was killed, Charles had stepped in to tend Cleve's wounds, sitting up all night as Cleve struggled through fever.

More than once, Charles took up his Springfield musket to defend the camp, though it was generally not expected of an aide. He saved Captain Sterne, using musket and bayonet, when a band of rebel guerillas tried to assassinate the officers.

Charles died after a cannonball blew his leg off at the Second Battle of Bull Run. Cleve tried to stop the bleeding, but the artery was parted just under the knee, a place that could not be easily staunched. Charles had bled out, gripping Cleve's hand and calling upon Jesus to take him to Glory.

Memories of the war were coming back to Cleve frequently, of late. Might be the camp life bringing them back, or the necessity of taking lives. He'd killed two men outside Paradise—another in Piswaller. Maybe he'd killed Breen, too, he wasn't sure. And the rifle shots coming from the hilltop that day led to memories of Confederate snipers using their long-barrel, single-shot Whitworth rifles . . .

Cleve shook his head. Best not to dwell on such memories. Yet he caught himself squinting up at the snow-coated hills, looking for the enemy.

It was times like this he thought of the whiskey left in the Overholt bottle. But the Pecks did not approve of drinking, and he didn't wish to rub them wrong.

Now his feet were getting cold, right through his boots, standing there in the snow, and his hat was accumulating its own drift. When he moved his head, snow slipped off the brim. He doffed the Stetson, brushed the snow off, put it back on, and listened to the women talking by the fire.

"So you soak the salt pork in hot water, before you cook it?" Berry asked.

"It is hard as bricks if you don't," Freja said. "But that's how it keeps so long—storing in brine."

"How long to cook each side?"

"Not above a few minutes. When it's a little more than golden brown, I give it a turn. Keep turning it till it's cooked through. Venison can be some pink, but not pork." Freja took another small piece of wood she kept under the little tarpaulin and put it carefully into the fire under the grill. "You never learnt cookery, Berenice?"

"Oh, my family spoilt me with cooks and servants. I tried cooking once or twice, thinking I could be self-sufficient, and the only good to come out of it was to make Nan laugh."

"Who is Nan?" Freja asked.

"She was my cook—mine and my brother's. She still works for him. I have tried cooking on the journey with Cleve from Axle Bust too. But I tend to burn things. I've left Cleve to it, he's the cook. However—your artistry shames me into wishing to learn . . ."

"There is no artistry in me," said Freja, chuckling. "Only watchfulness, and knowing a few spices, and when a meat has gone bad and such. The making of dumplings and stews, pies and bread when I can. Baking, now, that is more of an art . . ."

Berry was listening raptly, and Cleve found himself smiling. When she glanced up at him, he suppressed the smile and looked properly solemn. But it made him feel good to think that perhaps Berry was learning to cook for him. Or was she? More likely it was to add to her store of general knowledge.

The wind shifted, diverting snowfall under the lean-to, where the snowflakes hissed in the flames.

They got their hot meal of fried potatoes and pork before the fire went out. In the last of the light, Berry and Cleve checked on the horses, found the snow had accumulated to six inches on the tarpaulin shelter. But the horses were dozing, standing close together for warmth. Cleve broke off a manzanita branch and swept the snow off their tarp.

Berry patted Suzie. "They'll be more restful than we'll be under the wagon," she said. Her eyes looked hollow in the thickening dusk.

Cleve glanced at her. It wasn't like Berry to complain.

"You all right, Berenice?" he asked gently.

"Perfectly fine, thank you," she said, shivering.

She walked back toward the wagon, hunched against the cold.

Cleve patted Ulysses, pulled three horse blankets from the roll stuck under the shelter, and put them over the horses. Then he followed Berry.

He chuckled, seeing the little tunnel she'd made in the snow to get under the wagon. She'd pushed a little drift aside and dragged their tent canvases under the wagon, to use as insulation. Cleve hunkered down, and said, "Look here, some creature has made a burrow in the snow."

"The creature wants you to bring her the remaining blankets," she called out to him.

Cleve fetched the blankets from the wagon box, knelt down, and crept through the little tunnel through the drift, into her burrow. She had a lantern leaning against a wagon wheel, and she was folding the upper end of the tents to make something like pillows, under the front axle. He took off his gun belt and slung it over his shoulder. He had to go down on all fours to get to her, tugging the blankets along.

"Our body heat will collect pretty well in here, I expect," he said, putting his Colt where he could reach it.

He lay down close to her like two spoons in a drawer, and Cleve thought he could sleep. The sun had only just sunk below the hills, but they'd set out at dawn, and after a long day's ride in the cold a man got plenty tired.

He could hear the Pecks settling in up above, unintelligible murmurs of their talk; the squeak of the boards as they stretched on the cots between their stores. They soon fell silent, and Cleve thought he could hear Gil snoring.

After a minute of listening to the wind outside, Cleve asked softly, "Am I wrong to think something's troubling you, Berry?"

She whispered, "I'm . . . there's nothing that . . ." She made a soft moan and admitted, "You are not wrong."

"It's what happened to Abigail? It truly was not your fault, Berry."

"Oh, she is part of it," Berry said. "But there was something else I'd been trying not to think about. Yet—I must. I find—I am troubled by . . . by our future together, Cleve."

He closed his eyes and felt a pit open up inside him. Berenice was thinking of leaving him. "I shouldn't have said yes to your coming along. I knew it would be dangerous. I was cruel and selfish to do it, Berry."

"Cleve—I wasn't bluffing when I said I'd go on my own if you didn't let me go with you. But . . . sometimes you frighten me."

He swallowed. That was the very last thing he wanted to hear from her. He'd have preferred to have her say she was bored with him, or he just wasn't suitable. But afraid of him . . .

"Cleve . . . I knew you were . . . something of a gunfighter. I saw some of it myself. I heard what happened at the Red Hills. I knew about those men you shot in Denver."

There were several other gunfights she didn't know about. He wasn't ashamed of them, but he was glad she didn't know. "I was enforcing the law in Denver—and they were trying to kill me."

"Yes, I know. And I know how the war has marked you. You talk about it in your sleep."

"Do I?" But another woman had told him that, once.

"Sometimes. And it tears at my heart to know what you went through. But . . . when we ran into those bandits outside Paradise. You were so fast, so efficient . . ."

"Had I not been, I'd be dead now and you their prisoner—at best."

"I know that too. And I shot at one of them myself. You saw me shoot a man in Axle."

"You stopped him from shooting me in the back."

"That's why I did it. My heart pulled the trigger. That man outside Paradise—I was trying to scare him away, not kill him. I don't blame you at all for making short work of them. You *had* to do it. But something *about* it . . . It was as if you crushed mosquitoes with your hand."

Cleve winced at that.

"Then," she went on, "that man Frank, in Piswaller. When we were looking at the wheel. The way you knocked him down—a reflex. Like a . . . a . . ."

"Like a snake striking?" he said, unable to hide his bitterness. He'd heard it said before of him.

"Well—yes. You had to do that too. And later, when you shot him—I'm *glad* he's gone. But the *suddenness* of it . . ."

"I thought he'd killed you!"

"I know you did! When I killed that man in Axle, I was glad he was gone from the world. And I was glad to have been saved from the Breen gang. But . . ."

"But the way I do it disturbs you," he said. "I expect it seems cold. I don't show much emotion about it, after."

"Why—you show *none at all*."

Cleve closed his eyes. "I'm what the war made me— that and the frontier. I can only tell you, I came to California to *get away* from gunfights. I want to make a place for us in the world, Berenice. Someplace peaceful. A ranch—and it'll be a farm too. Sweet River Valley can handle both. There's so much to see and build . . . I want nothing more than to take my gun off for good. But till then, I have to get you to . . . to safety. I have to be ready. Just now, there's a man out there—I feel it in my bones, Breen is still alive. He wants to kill me, and likely you too."

"I know, Cleve. It's just a feeling that takes me." She groaned softly. "Maybe I'm being . . . the very thing I don't respect. A woman who cannot face the realities of life. Women can be warriors, too, and I've always respected that. Yet . . ."

Yet your soul flows from a spring of kindness, my Berenice, Cleve thought.

"Berry—I don't want you to have to be . . . more like me." He cleared his throat and tried to clear his mind. There was something he didn't want to say, but he felt he had to. "Now, here's a thought." He worked to keep his voice level, to keep any hurt out of it. "I take you to the railroad, and I send you to your family."

Her shoulders shook. He squeezed her.

"I don't know," Berry whispered. "Cleve . . . I love you. But . . . I don't know. Maybe I'm too exhausted to think, just now. I can scarcely keep my eyes open."

Then, she reached out, and turned the wick down till the lantern went out.

Cleve suspected that it had been too much for her, seeing that man in Piswaller shooting a woman dead—a woman already beaten, her spirit crushed by the brute. The violence of men must seem monstrous to her. And any man using violence could seem monstrous too.

Cleve closed his eyes. *I just don't know,* she'd said.

Well, then. That was it, wasn't it? He wanted her to

know. Because the trail ahead for the two of them would not be easy.

Like as not, he'd have to release her. Take her to civilization and say goodbye. It would be for her own good.

Never would it be for his.

Cleve let out a long, ragged breath, and tried to sleep. Hours passed, and when at last he slept he dreamed of cannon fire and young men dying in the mud and wounded horses screaming. Then the cannon stopped, and he seemed to see a dark plain intermittently lit with fires. Somewhere, in the shadows, a woman was whispering . . .

He woke to Berry's whispering. "Cleve! What tribe are they?"

He lifted his head and looked past the tongue of the wagon to see an Indian peering back at him—a Bannock warrior, sporting three eagle feathers, was crouching with a war club in his hand. And his face was striped with red-and-black warpaint.

Cleve reached for his gun, but Berenice put her hand over his and whispered, "No. The wagon's surrounded. You can't shoot your way out of this."

Chapter 6

Chance Breen woke that same morning able to sit up in the back of the wagon and look around. He was atop a long crate, which Donahue had covered with blankets, to make a sort of bed. There were crates and kegs all about him. He could smell the stowed cheese and tobacco. Up front, Donahue was driving the rig's two big draft horses.

The snow had quit falling and sun had broken through the clouds to glare off the whitened hillsides. Breen's side hurt like a rattlesnake bite, and he knew he had a fever. But he was starting to think he would live. He noticed that a good deal of the snow had melted, and the road ahead was nigh clear.

"Hello up there, Donahue!" Chance called. The effort sent a pang through him. But so did every bump on the road.

The man who called himself Brother Donahue turned half around and looked at him with surprise. "I did not think you'd be sitting up anytime soon. But now you have—you see the miracle. The Sovereign has made the snow melt away around the sacred mountain!"

"Say, uh, does that mean we're nigh there?"

"We are," said Donahue. "We'll arrive tonight." He turned back to the road, to correct the draft horses.

Breen called out, "You know—I believe I had a gun on me when you found me. I can't seem to find it."

Donahue turned and nodded to him. "Oh, I have it put away somewhere. It'll be for the Sovereign to decide about that." He turned back to the road again.

"Well, how do I get my . . ." Breen broke off, and thought he ought to be slicker about this. "How do I earn your sovereign's trust?"

"Why—you must only *believe!*" With Donahue facing forward it was a little difficult to hear him over the clip-clop of the big horses and the creaking of the wagon. "You must see the miracle before you and become one of us! If you do not—we will send you away. I doubt the Sovereign will relinquish your weapon!"

Breen's side was smarting something fierce, so he lay back again and looked at the streaming gray clouds, the half-hidden sun offering little warmth, and thought, *One way or another, I will get me that gun. For I owe Cleveland Trewe double now.*

But this time, he decided to play it different. He'd fired at Trewe impulsively, up on that hill, seeing his chance to catch him unawares. Almost got him. But *almost* will get you half a pickle on half a piece of bread.

Cleve Trewe had taken something dear away from him. The boy hadn't been much use to anyone, but Davy had been his only kin. It had been clear to Breen that the woman was dear to Trewe.

Sooner or later, Breen silently vowed, he'd see them both dead.

Standing beside Berry and Gil and Freja, Cleve counted twelve braves ranged about the wagon. Three were armed with rifles, five with war clubs and sheathed knives. The other four carried bows and arrows. Their ponies were stirring in the background, snorting nervously. One man, with a chief's headdress, sat calmly on his mount. The chief was the only one with a saddle. It was of old U.S. Cavalry make.

Another Bannock, wearing a wolfskin headdress, was standing about ten strides away, looking over the Pecks' oxen.

It was a cold morning and each man's breath steamed as they spoke in asides to one another, chuckling, assessing their captives like a man assaying his gold. *What have I got here? How much is it worth?*

Cleve had his Colt in hand but pointed at the ground. Freja whimpered into a fist over her mouth. Gil was trembling, looking at Cleve with a flicker of hope.

Hope? Cleve couldn't offer much. The best outcome he could imagine would be to trade the wagon and oxen for their lives. But the way the braves were looking at Freja and Berry was worrisome. Still, none of the Indians seemed poised to strike. There was a discussion going on too. When matters were discussed, the outcome was uncertain.

The Bannock language shared some vocabulary with the Paiute and Shoshone. Cleve had spent time with the Paiute a few years back, and he'd known many a Shoshone. He'd picked up smatterings of their lingo. Now he recognized a few words passed between the two braves staring at Berry—the word for *woman*, and the word for *sundown*. Maybe a reference to her chestnut hair—which lifted in the chill early-morning breeze, as she looked brightly around, fascinated, taking in the raiment of the Bannock, the crafts they wore and carried. Her gaze roamed over their painted ponies and painted weapons. The braves with their buffalo-fur winter capes, their buckskin leggings and bead patterned shirts, their tautly braided jet-black hair, eagle feathers rakishly tilted down to the side. Cleve knew she was taking mental notes.

Most people would be looking for a place to bolt to, Cleve thought, with a sad smile.

The nearest warrior, unblinkingly eyeing Berry, was a scowling young man with a red band about his head. He had an old Springfield rifle in his right hand.

The Bannock stepped toward her, and Cleve cocked his pistol . . .

"Touch not woman," Cleve growled, in his rudimentary Paiute/Shoshone.

The warrior with the rifle stopped and barked a laugh. *"He talks like Paiute!"*

The others laughed and the young warrior pointed the rifle directly at Cleve. In English he shouted, "No gun, you!"

Tactics flashed through Cleve's mind. He could shoot the nearest warrior, probably get off two more rounds— one for the chief to weaken chain of command, one for the other brave with a rifle, perhaps fire once at the hooves of the ponies, make them rear up, create pandemonium. Then, grab Berry's hand, thrust her behind him as he emptied his gun with the others, shouting at her to run.

But he knew these men could throw their war clubs with deadly accuracy; he knew that the warriors with bows could nock an arrow in the blink of an eye. The third warrior with the rifle would get off a shot and . . . there were just too many of them.

Berry could easily be killed, along with him and Gil and Freja, in the ensuing melee.

Cleve tossed his gun at the warrior's feet.

Keeping the rifle on Cleve, the brave scooped up the pistol, turning it in his hand, admiring it. *"Ho-ahhh!"*

The chief called out to the man in the wolfskin headdress.

The man emerged from the shadows. The pelt retained the intact upper half of the gray wolf's head, so he wore the furred skull like a cap and the rest like a cape. He carried a round shield—covered in horsehide, dangling three eagle feathers—and a red-and-black spear tipped with an obsidian blade. He was a man etched by age and weather, his gaunt face lined, his nose like an eagle's beak. Ritual scars zigzagged across his forehead; unlike the others, his gray-streaked hair fell freely, draping over his collarbones. He wore a kind of long apron, figured with images of the sun, moon, and a wolf. His face was painted entirely blue. Cleve took him to be the tribal shaman, what some whites called a medicine man.

The shaman walked over to Cleve and Berry, his boots squeaking in the snow.

"Oh!" Berry murmured, her eyes lighting up. "Cleve—is he a . . . a priest?"

"Of sorts," Cleve said softly. He figured the chief had called the shaman to look the white travelers over, and counsel on their fate.

Black eyes glittering, the shaman glanced at Gil and Freja, then looked at Cleve for a long, appraising moment.

Cleve looked impassively back, careful to show no fear but no challenge either.

The shaman grunted and looked curiously at Berry—and his eyebrows bobbed when she suddenly gave a slight curtsy.

She spoke in English, perhaps hoping they understood her respectful tone and expression if not the words: "Good morning, sir. We are honored to meet you." She looked at the chief and gave him a slight bow. The braves chuckled and muttered at this.

Cleve winced. "Berry . . ."

She turned back to the shaman, and said, "We have things to trade. And gifts!"

Then Berry opened the top of her blouse—some of the braves *Ho-a ho-a*'ed at this—and she drew out a necklace of pierced opals, with a light-blue topaz in the center. Cleve had seen it before, but he'd thought it was hidden away in the luggage.

She unhooked it, and then held it up so the topaz caught the light of the low winter sun, flashing out a blue beam, which struck the snow, breaking up into countless small rainbows in the ice crystals.

The shaman rocked back a little. "Ahh!" he said. He looked at the topaz, and the rainbow, and then looked Berry in the eyes.

She looked earnestly and steadily back at him, then she gathered the necklace into the palm of her hand and held it out.

As if in a trance, the shaman reached slowly for the necklace, and she placed it in his hand. She used her other hand to close his fingers around the necklace. "A gift," she said. "From the Earth." She pointed at the ground and at the shaman.

Cleve sighed, but he translated, as best he could, saying in a mix of Paiute and Shoshone, *"A gift from the ground."* He pointed at the shaman adding in English. "To you."

"Ahhh!" the shaman said, looking into the topaz, and running his thumb over its smoothly cut facets. Then he stepped closer to Berry and looked into her face, from different angles. She kept her features amiable and returned his gaze. But Cleve noticed she clasped her hands to keep them from trembling.

Cleve noticed the shaman's knife. Perhaps he could take hold of the man, use the knife to hold him hostage . . .

Suddenly the shaman turned and spoke to the chief.

It was a long speech and Cleve heard only a couple words he knew. *Mogon*, for woman, *cugup* for earth.

The chief scowled. He looked disappointed. Then he turned to Cleve, and gestured at the oxen, then at the wagon, made signs with his hands. It seemed he wanted the oxen yoked to the wagons.

Was he going to release the white captives? Or did he merely want an easy way to take the wagon away?

Cleve took a deep breath. "Gil—let's yoke up the oxen."

Chapter 7

Cleve had to step along quickly to keep from being trampled under the hooves of the chief's horse trotting just behind him. Cleve didn't suppose the chief was trying to run him down—just that he had lost all patience for the white man.

Cleve had made to mount Ulysses when they'd all set out, but the chief had signaled an emphatic *no*. Nor was Cleve trusted on the wagon. He inferred the shaman had declared him a dangerous man.

They'd moved off the Applegate, onto a thin, fairly new trail made by the Bannock. The snow was turning to slush and mud and Cleve sometimes slipped in it. He'd been tramping for more than an hour. Now, peering ahead, he could see what looked like campfire smoke, beyond the trees ahead. They must be near the Bannock camp.

Berenice was permitted to ride her horse. But the shaman held Suzie's reins as he rode ahead of Berry on his black-and-white pony. The young brave who'd admired Berry now had charge of Cleve's horse, tugging him along behind his mount, and Ulysses was shaking his head, snorting, not taking it well.

Bringing up the rear of the procession, Gil drove the

wagon with Freja beside him, followed by braves on horseback. Gil's rifle had been appropriated, but none of the captives had their hands tied.

Stumbling hurriedly along, Cleve ran tactics through his mind. *Vault onto Ulysses, knock the brave down, spur to Berenice, take Suzie's reins from the shaman.*

And then what? Cleve shook his head. He could get Berry killed in the general melee if he tried anything.

The procession rounded a curve and moved onto a narrow track between boulders, where the snow had been stamped away by horses. There was no room for escape in this narrow passage— and up ahead he saw the Bannock camp.

The passage opened into a broad clearing, the farther side lined with wickiups sheltered from snow and wind by a row of whitebark pine and red fir. The wickiups were temporary shelters, mostly of brush and poles, some enhanced with painted hides laid over the top. There were five goodly fires set up across the clearing, with Bannock women tending them, cooking in rusty iron pots—and looking up to stare at the white captives. Smoke from the fires merged so that a gray haze brooded over the clearing.

The Bannock women wore fringed ankle-length dresses, some of flannel, some of buckskin. Blankets swathed their hips or draped their shoulders. Several wore roughly conical straw hats woven with decorative strips of bark.

Cleve tallied four sentries with rifles posted around the perimeter of the camp. They were calling out questions to the men leading the captives. A few ponies were tied up near the trees, watched over by a couple of Indian boys wearing oiled buckskin and blankets over their shoulders. Ponies and boys were all looking curiously toward the newcomers.

A white-haired elder stood up from a bear fur laid out

like a carpet in front of a wickiup and walked slowly toward them, eyeing the covered wagon coming into the camp. He had a look of authority about him. Cleve figured him for the elder chieftain. The old man spoke to a woman squatting by the fire. Though dressed like a Bannock woman, she was more light-skinned than the others and had a narrower face. She had a tattered woolen shawl around her shoulders. Her hair was graying brown. Cleve thought she might be a captive herself.

She took the old man's arm and helped him across the slushy ground. The younger chief rode up beside Cleve, signaled for him to stop where he was. The wagon pulled up short beside them.

"Will they murder us right quick?" asked Freja, her voice little more than a squeak.

Gil put his arm around her. "Freja, 'the righteous live by faith.'"

She squeezed her eyes shut. "Maybe we were not righteous."

"They seem in no hurry to do us harm," Cleve said. But he watched closely as the shaman led Suzie—with Berry still mounted—over to the woman and the old chief. The younger chief jumped down from his pony and followed the shaman.

The shaman spoke quickly in the Bannock dialect. Once more Cleve thought he heard the words for earth and woman, when the shaman waved toward Berry—who sat watching attentively, seeming strangely unworried.

Cleve noticed the shaman hadn't shown anyone else the necklace she'd given him. Maybe he didn't want the elder chief to lay claim to it.

The woman Cleve took to be a captive walked up to Berry and spoke to her. He couldn't hear what she said.

But he heard Berenice say, "Oh, I think that would be quite acceptable!"

Berry dismounted, and walked confidently over to Cleve, the woman with her. Some of the warriors scowled, but the younger chief made a dismissive gesture and no one interfered.

"Cleve—this is Claudia!" Berry said, beaming. The woman in the shawl seemed disconcerted, looking at her feet and hugging herself. Berry went cheerfully on. "She married a Klamath Indian and then he died and she fell in with this tribe—the Panati. Bannock we call them. She's the third wife of the old chief, Washakoh. His son is the war chief, Takosha."

"Her name is Claudia?" Cleve asked. "That's an Italian name, isn't it?"

Claudia nodded. She tugged her shawl closer and said, "My parents—*Italiano*. We sail from Napoli. Mama died on the . . . the boat." She seemed to stare into space, as if seeking the right English words. "Then . . . I go to school. Oregon, Point Kilchis. Papa died. The fever. I was alone."

"How old were you then?" Cleve asked.

"I was . . ." Again, she searched for the word. "Five and ten."

"Fifteen?"

"Yes. John Otter, a Klamath . . . he came to the farm, saved me when I was sick, and made me his . . . his *sposa*. Three years. Then the Army comes and he fights them, and they kill him. I took the horse and went to south and . . ." She chose that moment to break off her story, and stared down at her feet again.

"Why are the Panati here, Claudia?" Cleve asked. "They're from away to the east, no?"

She nodded. "The soldiers make us go to Fort Hall."

Cleve grunted. "Fort Hall Reservation. Idaho. I was

there for a few days—I saw some Indian folk. Shoshone I thought. And Nez Perce. Bannock, too, I reckon? Seemed like they were all hungry. Ill-fed."

Claudia looked up at him. "That is why Washakoh led the people from Fort Hall! The soldiers would no let the Panati hunt, no gather camas roots—no give us enough food. They found me alone. I knew some of their ways, and Washakoh said I would be a woman for him . . ."

Again, she stared at her boots, as if worried she was speaking too much.

"Cleve, they mean us no harm," Berry put in. "The shaman, he spoke up for us. But they demand a sort of toll—they wanted the oxen but Claudia says they will take one of them, if we give them something else. They want our horses—but I think we can bargain them out of that."

"Berry?" Cleve was remembering how she'd used the necklace. "How did you . . . I mean, why were you carrying the necklace *on* you? How did you know . . . ?"

"I didn't *know*, Cleve, but there were Indians in the area, you saw the tracks, and I thought it best to have something to bargain with, and to think of a way to . . . to appeal to them. I thought their priest was the only way."

Cleve was still puzzled. "He figured there was magic in that necklace?"

She looked at him in surprise. "Not at all! He's no fool, no primitive mind to be dazzled. He is a man of insight! That is how it seems to me, Cleve. And—he knows an object of value when he sees one. But it seems he does believe in omens."

"He is great medicine," said Claudia reverentially. "He is *Panok!* Panok says Berenice, he see her in dream, say her warrior will bring Ejupa home."

Berry frowned. "Who is Ejupa?"

"He is Washakoh's son, born from Kymana. Ejupa

goes, trade with white men at blue mountain and no come back. You—" She looked at Cleve. "Panok says you are warrior from Berenice. You will bring Ejupa home."

"The tribe has its own warriors," Cleve pointed out.

"They cannot attack the blue mountain. It has a big gun, and soldiers. That way—only death for us. You—Panok says *you* will find a way."

"Cleve!" Gil called. "What's going on?"

Cleve stepped over to the wagon and spoke in low tones to Gil and Freja. "They aren't planning to kill us. But we have to trade away an ox and some other goods for safe passage. And do something else for them—apparently. They think we're going to bring a lost boy home."

"What?" Gil frowned and shook his head. "A lost boy?"

"So it seems. Their medicine man has a powerful imagination. We've got to play it as it lays, Gil. And maybe we'll get through this . . ."

Just about noon, Brother Donahue halted the wagon. Chance Breen sat up, wincing at the pain in his side, and looked around. They'd rolled to a stop at a small, nameless shantytown—barely even that—where two meager roads met in the foothills under Gunmetal Mountain.

Gunmetal was not a big mountain, but it was far bigger than a hill. It was mostly bald of trees and shrubs, on this side. Clear enough how it got its name—in this light it sure looked like blue metal.

All in all, it was mighty barren here, just a good deal of black-and-red volcano stone with shrinking patches of snow. The snow glinted in the thin sunlight and in the spray from the creek that came bashing down the cut between two hills, splashing its way like it was descending a busted staircase. A bridge of raw logs continued the trail over the creek.

The shantytown wasn't much to look at: several shacks, a covered wagon with weeds grown up around it, and a handful of tents. Six rough-looking men stood around a grill fixed over a firepit. They were toasting meat on sticks and passing a bottle around. They didn't look like Brother Donahue's sort. More like saddle bums and prairie rats. Could be they jobbed some for the Sovereign feller up on the mountain. Maybe some did the big man's dirty deeds.

Now Breen recognized one of them—Squaw Jumper Judson. Breen knew him from the buffalo hunter camps around Fort Dodge. Couldn't miss him. The head that was too big for the lanky body, that face seeming mostly beard with a beak of a red nose sticking out of it. Judson wore a bear-fur coat, a coon cap, and knee-high buckskin boots. He was leaning on his old Sharps rifle, and his other hand was waving in the air over his head as he spouted one of his steaming lies.

Judson, Breen knew, would kill a man for ten dollars and a bottle of whiskey. Liked to poison them when he could. Failing that, he'd rush you into a bear hug and stick the knife around back.

Listening intently to Judson was a clean-shaven young man Breen had never seen before. Blond hair, long coat, striped pants tucked into Mexican boots, fancy spurs, a silver pistol set up for cross-draw.

Breen stared at the covered wagon a long moment, making sure it wasn't the one Cleve Trewe rode with. But no. This wagon was a beat-up Conestoga, with the curved top that leaned forward over the driver's bench.

"We're only stopping to get water for the horses," said Donahue, coming around to him. "There is a prodigious climb ahead." Donahue looked unblinkingly at Breen. "You have some color now, Chance. You look improved."

"Owe it to you, ha-*ha!*" Breen said, slapping his knee and nodding. "I sure am obliged to you, Brother!"

"Are you?" Donahue jabbed a finger at him. "We shall see! The *Sovereign* will see! He will look at your soul—and he will *know!*"

"Oh, I'm . . . I'm ready for him, Brother Donahue!"

"You must lay down and rest now. Do not try to talk to these men here. I will get the water for the horses. Too steep on the bank to lead them down." Donahue took two big wooden buckets from the wagon and carried them off toward the creek.

As the big draft horses snorted and sniffed longingly toward the rushing water, Breen pulled on his boots, and raised up to see if Donahue had gone off far enough. Then—grimacing with pain—he climbed slowly out of the wagon. He kept one hand on the gate and waited out the dizziness. Then he took a deep breath and picked his way carefully over the puddles of half-melted snow to the firepit. Everyone looked at him curiously. The young fella with yellow hair said, "Now where'd you come from?"

"I come with the wagon," Breen said, hooking a thumb toward Donahue's rig. He nodded to Judson, who had the whiskey bottle in hand. "Hey, Squaw Jumper."

"So that's you, is it, Chance?" Judson said, cocking his head and showing his yellow gap-toothed leer.

"You know damned well it is. I'd give two bits for a drink from that bottle. Maybe a dollar. Except you owe me a golden eagle for that race we bet on."

Judson pondered. A layer of snow on the Conestoga, responding to sunlight and the firepit, slid off all of a sudden, bashing the ground, as if urging Judson to make up his mind. "Why, I never bet on that horse," said Judson, at last. "But here's the bottle."

The other men eyed Breen suspiciously as he took a long swig of the whiskey. It masked the pain in his side some.

"What you doing with that crazy missionary, Chance?" Judson asked.

"Why, I was more'n half dead and Donahue found me and patched me up. A son of a bitch up near Paradise town shot me. Cleve Trewe is his name."

"I heard something of him. Get under his hide, did you?"

"I called him out for murdering my Davy! Trewe shot my boy dead like he was shooting a bottle off a fence!"

"How'd that come about?"

"Trewe didn't have to have him a reason!" Breen declared, taking another swig on the whiskey. The man to his left stuck out a hand and Breen reluctantly surrendered the bottle.

"Cleve Trewe," said the younger man musingly. "I saw him kill a man in Piswaller, not long ago. Fella named Frank Spaun. I will say that Frank was fixing to kill this Trewe."

"Who'd you be?" Breen asked, curious. The young man didn't seem to fit in here.

"Tha's Lightnin'," cackled Judson. "He goes by Lightnin' Crofton!"

"My name's *James* Crofton," Lightnin snapped. "But they do call me Lightnin Crofton, over in Oklahoma. I was in the Colfax County War."

"They still fightin' that, aren't they?" asked Breen. "Don't seem you got much done there."

"What of it?" Crofton asked snippily. "They didn't want to pay me what I'm worth. I killed two sons of bitches and that's my part in it."

"You saw Cleve Trewe kill a man," said Breen. "But—did you know he's wanted, dead or alive?"

"Is he?" Crofton's eyes widened.

"He is! For murderin' my boy! For killin' Davy Breen! And there's a reward on him for five hundred—no, it's a *thousand* dollars!"

"Come on now!" Judson cackled. "Which is it, Chance? Five hundred or double that?"

"I remember now—it was a thousand five hundred! You should lay for him, Lightnin! He's back down the trail a piece, on the Applegate. Maybe he'll come this way!"

"A thousand five hundred dollars," Crofton murmured. "I hadn't heard about a bounty on him. You sure?"

"If it ain't true, then Lord let the redskins lift my hair!"

Impressed by this perilous oath, the boy nodded gravely. "I'll take him on." He slapped his gun. Now all the men were chuckling and elbowing one another.

"Breen!" called Donahue, from the wagon. "Where are you?"

Breen figured it was time to make up his mind. He had no gun on him. But there was that wagon full of goods. Maybe he could get Judson here and some of the others to help him take that wagon. They could kill Donahue and sell the goods, and the wagon and the horse too. Could be Donahue had some cash on him. And he had Breen's gun.

But then—Breen was feeling mighty weak. The other boys here would like as not cut him out of the deal. He wasn't in any shape for a fight with them. And up on that mountain was "the Sovereign." Donahue could introduce him to that big man. Maybe that man on the mountain could be valuable. Who knew what treasures such a man had hidden away?

"Lightnin' Crofton," Breen said solemnly, nodding to him. "I do believe I have heard of you."

Judson snorted.

Crofton blinked. "You heard of me?"

"Why sure. You're just the man to take down Cleveland Trewe and collect that money. Boys, I've got business up on the mountain. I'll be seeing you."

Breen turned and limped to the wagon, where Donahue scowlingly awaited him.

"You should not have drunk whiskey with those fools," said Donahue.

"Oh, it's just the pain, don't you know," said Breen. "Hurts me terrible. Whiskey soothes the wound. But I'm done with whiskey now! That's all behind me."

Maybe, he thought, *that fool boy will scrape up the sense to backshoot Cleve Trewe.*

Breen chuckled at the thought and climbed painfully up into the back of the freight wagon.

Sparks rose from the fires, turning from white to red—to vanish among the stars. Bannock children were seated on blankets around Panok, the shaman, as he told stories by the center fire. Cleve and Berry and Claudia sat together near Panok. The chiefs, the old and young, sat apart, talking near Washakoh's wickiup; Gil and Freja were sequestered in their wagon.

One of their oxen had already been led away and the wagon was much lighter. Tools, a side of bacon, three bags of flour, two kegs of nails, a keg of salt pork, blankets and clothing, and a shotgun had been traded to the Bannock for free passage.

The shaman had saved them from giving up more. Cleve and Berry's horses had been fierce objects of desire. So was Berry, for several of the braves.

The Panati had given them a good feed with a venison

stew, and Cleve felt confident they were safe, for the moment, although their guns hadn't been returned. He calculated he and Berry and the Pecks were safer in the Panati camp than alone on the trail.

Cleve sat idly whittling a stick with an old kitchen knife, wondering how he could get his Colt and Winchester back. And wondering about Claudia.

Keeping his voice low, Cleve asked, "Claudia—do you want to stay with these folks? Maybe I could trade something more . . . Get them to let you go with us."

She looked at him in astonishment. "*Go?* I can go! They don't keep me. I stay! This is my family. My people."

Cleve nodded. He'd figured that was the way of it. "Sorry about your necklace, Berry," he said, tossing the stick into the fire.

She shrugged. "Oh, I brought it to trade away. My mother gave it to me to wear with my wedding dress. It was always too gaudy for me. Cleve—I've started a Bannock lexicon—Panati, I should say." She held up her notebook. "Claudia's been helping me. And she showed me how they weave. Their hats and baskets are made of bear grass—some of the baskets are so tightly woven they can carry water!"

"Will you be learning to weave baskets?" Cleve asked. "I heard something about it being used to comfort the mad."

"Are you saying—oh, you're smirking, you see fit to tease me! I wish I *could* learn to weave that way—but it takes a long time and strong hands and they do much of the weaving with their hands underwater, so the straw will be pliable. And they do that in winter too!"

"I won't be taking it up," Cleve said, "but I admire it." He listened to what Panok was telling the children. "I think I recognize some of the story Panok's telling. The Paiute tell it too." He looked at Claudia. "About the creation of seasons?"

She nodded. Berry asked, "Can you tell it, Claudia?"

She shook her head. "Not enough English still."

"Cleve—can you?"

He shrugged. "Far as I remember . . . Long ago, before the time of men, all the animals in the world were called together by Wolf. He was the big boss of the animals. He figured they should decide how the weather would go. Right then it was always pretty cold. Should it be warm or cold, wet or dry? Well, the animals with thick fur wanted cold weather. Grizzly said he wanted it cold because he had the fur for it, and he liked to go fishing. When it's cold the fish rise more in the water, easier to catch. But boars and lizards and such, they didn't want the cold. Lizard complained they couldn't come out when it was cold all the time. Then Wolf said, 'Maybe we should have it cold half of the time, warm the rest of the time.' That just led to more argument. Then the robin spoke—Robin said, 'We should have three moons for each season. Three moons cold, three warming up, three months warm, three getting cooler, back to winter. Then there's something for everyone! Those who don't like the cold season can go to sleep and come back in the spring. The bear's coat can get thinner in the spring, so he won't mind the heat when he wakes up.' Wolf said, 'That's wise talk, Robin, and that's how it will be.' And that's why we have the four seasons."

"A good story!" Berry declared. "Something for everyone. 'For everything there is a season, a time for every purpose under heaven.'"

"Ecclesiastes," Cleve said. "You know your Bible, yet you're not exactly a believer, Berry."

"Oh, as the Bible says in another place, we see through a glass darkly," Berry said, the firelight playing across her face as she gazed into the flames. "I know there's some sort of God. But there's much yet to be seen . . ."

Cleve thought this cryptic. But then Claudia spoke up. "You say the story about Wolf and the seasons, Cleve. But you not to say the part about Coyote. He always . . ." She frowned, looking for the word. "He is *interrupt* them. To make the seasons, they had to trick him so he go away."

"I'd forgotten that. They had to trick the trickster. Coyote—that missing boy's name, *Ejupa* . . . It means coyote, doesn't it?"

She nodded. "Yes. When he was born, Panok saw how Ejupa is to grow up like Coyote. One day Ejupa saw the . . ." She frowned. "Steam train. He saw a man drive it. He said that man is like great spirits."

"Ejupa admires the locomotive," Cleve said thoughtfully. "First time I saw one I was smitten too. So he wanted to be like the man with the powerful engine?"

She nodded. "He tries to be like the white men. He is not want to leave Fort Hall. But Washakoh made him to come."

"How old is he?"

She held up her ten fingers, then closed them, then opened them again.

"Twenty years old."

"Yes! Twenty."

"He went to trade with those folks on the mountain and never came back?"

She nodded. "Panok says he is on Blue Mountain." The Panati called Gunmetal Mountain the Blue Mountain.

Cleve grunted. Like as not, Panok was wrong. A young Indian brave alone among the wrong kind of whites would be up against it hard. He might well be dead.

Suddenly Panok himself strode up to them. He spoke to Claudia, and she stood. Then he pointed to Cleve, gesturing for him to come. Cleve rose and they followed the shaman to the wickiup, where the two chiefs, Washakoh and his son, Takosha, sat on blankets spread over tree fronds, to insulate them from the cold ground. A small fire burned before them.

The old chief spoke to Cleve in Panati: "Sit, friend." He and Panok sat on the buffalo skin, just outside the entrance to the wickiup, crossing their legs. Claudia stood by, waiting.

So far so good, Cleve thought. Once the Indians had traded with a man, and accepted him into their camps, he was treated with hospitality.

But would they give him his guns back?

The light from the fire was indirect here. The chiefs' faces were deeply etched by restless shadow. Panok was tamping a long, ornate ceremonial pipe, its pipe bowl cut of soft stone, its stem carved of wood and banded with red clay. A hawk feather dangled from the buckskin band holding the bowl in place. The shaman used a burning twig and puffed the pipe alight. He blew smoke into the air above them and spoke an invocation to the earth and the sky and then offered the pipe to Cleve. He accepted it, and puffed on it, not drawing much on the acrid smoke of tobacco, herbs, and red bark. That was the way, in his experience, to keep from coughing. Indians had a way of laughing at a man who coughed from the pipe.

Washakoh spoke at length. Takosha scowled and made several remarks. Washakoh turned to his son and replied, then waved his hand. Claudia translated, "Washakoh says you are a guest with great honor here. He says you are a warrior of strength. His son asks how do we know you are a warrior. Washakoh says because Panok sees it and Panok knows. And Washakoh says, 'Cleve, you must find Ejupa, to send him back to us because that is . . . that is *known* between us.'"

Cleve thought, *Tell them anything they want to hear*.

"I will seek him," Cleve said.

She translated, and Panok spoke. Claudia nodded, and said, "Panok says you must swear an oath."

An oath? Cleve really did not want to do that. He took oaths seriously. He'd figured on just keeping an eye out for Ejupa. Searching for him could mean endless delays getting Berry to safety.

He glanced at Panok and felt the man looking into him. The chief was waiting with great solemnity for Cleve's response. Panok and Washakoh were men who had led their tribe to freedom, rather than starve on a corrupt reservation—a decision Cleve fully understood. These were men who had worked hard and hunted hard and fought hard for their people, and who meant what they said. An oath sworn before such men had meaning.

"I will need my guns," Cleve said. "And our horses."

Claudia translated. Takosha's scowl deepened. He made a slashing motion with his hand. Washakoh smiled wearily and spoke to Takosha. The chief reached into the shadows of the wikiup and took Cleve's holstered Colt from the shadows, and then the rifle. He held the weapons in his arms and then he looked Cleve in the eye and spoke.

Cleve didn't need the translation. *You will vow to find Ejupa, before the sun, the moon, the stars, and the earth.*

They assuredly weren't going to give him his weapons unless he swore the oath. He needed those weapons to protect Berenice. But . . .

Cleve groaned inwardly. He knew this oath. He could feel its power. He knew he would despise himself if he broke it.

He nodded, and said, "Before the sun, the moon, the stars, and the earth, I vow to find Ejupa."

Claudia translated. Panok nodded approvingly. But Takosha growled and drew his knife. Cleve tensed—then Takosha stood, and went to the campfire. Squatting, his scowling face scarlet in firelight, Takosha thrust the knife in the red coals. He held it there a full minute, and then brought it, smoke trailing, to Cleve. He held the smoking blade out. It was red hot.

Cleve knew this tradition. He stretched out his left hand, clasped the knife blade, and as the hot steel burned the palm of his hand, Cleve gazed steadily into Washakoh's eyes and said it once more. "Before the sun, the moon, the stars, and the earth, I vow to find Ejupa."

And Washakoh gave him his guns.

Chapter 8

The covered wagon was pulled slowly through the gray morning light by a single ox throwing a horned shadow onto the Applegate Trail. Cleve and Berry rode behind the wagon, following Gil and Freja through a countryside that was more rugged than any they'd passed over before. Raggy had been left behind—Cleve had given the horse to Takosha as a gift. It seemed prudent, since the younger chief had been disappointed by the trade outcome and Cleve didn't want more enemies on his back trail. Other gifts had been given. Berry had given Claudia a silk scarf and a gold bracelet. She'd given Washakoh's younger wife a tartan wool scarf and a silver ring. Panok had given Berry an intricately beaded necklace of red and blue and yellow with a rising sun at its center. Berry was delighted with it, and she wore it even now.

A chill wind whined past them across the desolation; the rolling country was blotched black and red from volcanic rock, with only occasional patches of shrub and manzanita. Off to the southwest they could see a volcanic cone, the color of gunmetal, in the distance. Beyond it was the blue-green of a forest. Lizards flicked between the stones; the shadow of a vulture passed over them.

"How is your hand?" Berry asked.

"Not bad. Claudia's salve is doing some good."

"I asked her to describe what it was made from," Berry said, tightening her bonnet against the wind. "It sounded like a spiny cactus, the species *aloe vera*."

The wind whooshed by, blowing fallen twigs and pine needles. "It's brisk out," Cleve said, "but Panok says there'll be no more snow for a good while."

"How does he know, I wonder?"

"They live out in the weather so much, they become intimate with it," Cleve said. "A man like him is like a walking almanac of such things. Signs we would miss, they recognize." He used his left hand on the reins and grimaced as the burned place pained him.

Berry looked over at his burned hand. "Cleve—swearing the oath really wasn't enough without the knife?"

"Not enough for Takosha. But it was all part of the trade."

"And you will try to find this Ejupa?"

He made a sound somewhere between a sigh and a groan. "I will. Before the oath, I was going to kind of crawfish on that one."

"What does 'to crawfish' mean?"

"Sidestep it. I would keep my eye out for the kid but not actively search. I didn't want to make this detour to Gunmetal Mountain. But after the oath . . ."

"You take such an oath very seriously?"

"Washakoh and Panok are men I respect." He shrugged. "I'll do what I can to find Ejupa, if he's alive."

"That could mean a great many more detours."

"I'm aware of that. But that is the deal." He smiled. "I was offered another deal. Very tempting."

"What was that?"

"Takosha offered me two horses and a woman for you."

"For . . . *oh!*" She shot him a sharp side-glance. "Did you tell him that women are not to be *traded* for?"

"I believe that kind of trade is normal in many cultures." Cleve smiled.

"Oh—so you are joking?"

"He *did* make the offer. I told him it could not be. I was quite firm."

"You said it was tempting!"

He laughed. "In that, I was joshing."

"It's not amusing. It is barbarism!"

"I know it is. Still—dowries are still on offer, in many American families. But that goes the other way—a family pays the bachelor for what he's losing, I suppose."

"I sense a . . . a tone here, Cleve. This amusement of yours sounds bitter. Are you testing me in some way? Is it because I said I don't know about our future?"

That shot went home. She might be right.

"I'm sorry, Berenice, if I . . ." He cleared his throat. "I'm just sorry."

They rode on. The silence was chillier than the wind. After twenty minutes of it, Cleve said, "Believe I'll have a look at the trail up ahead." He rode up to pace beside Gil.

It was more of the same rugged country ahead. Gil was driving the wagon alone. Freja was lying down in the back again. "Sight any strangers, Gil?" Cleve asked.

"Not a one," Gil said. He seemed fairly cheerful. Gunmetal Mountain was in sight and Cleve was going to escort them there. "This is Providence at work, Cleve, us getting away with our scalps. I was sure we were to be killed."

"If they wanted to kill us, you and me, they'd like as not done it at our camp," Cleve said. "They might have taken the women. If they had, we'd have fought them, and you and I would be dead now. . . ."

"Oh, but it *was* Providence! The Lord guided Berenice to show Panok that necklace."

"Why, Berenice is a resourceful woman. She comes with her own 'providence.' How far do you calculate for the turning to Gunmetal?"

"We might be fair close, with the mountain off to the south now. Leman wrote me about a marker, a blue cross set up at the turn."

Cleve nodded and rode up ahead, looking for the turn and riders on the hilltops. Breen might be out there, or some other outlaw. From the corner of his eye, Cleve glimpsed movement and peered that way. Nothing but a mountain goat bobcat making its way up a game trail.

He rode on for a little more than two miles—and came to a fork in the road. The southerly fork headed toward Gunmetal Mountain. A wooden cross, painted dark blue and about seven feet high, marked the trail to the mountain. Cleve reined in, and patted Ulysses.

"Well, Ulysses," Cleve murmured. "That's where I've got to go, to do the damn fool thing I swore to."

Chance Breen was sitting on the front step of one of the Cabins of the Faithful, where he'd come to smoke his pipe in the sun. These one-room cabins were used to hold followers of this Lamb fella, when they'd run out of room in the fine houses down on the street below. *In time, all the faithful shall be in the Houses of God's Reward*, so Donahue said.

Breen liked it fine right here. He had the little log cabin to himself, and he was out of the wind, enjoying his smoke.

But then the Sovereign came down the path and walked

up to stand right in front of him. Lamb was outlined in
sunlight now, casting a shadow right over Breen.

Magnus Lamb in person looked just like the full-length
portrait in the settlement's chapel. Lamb was so imposing,
Breen didn't take much notice of the shotgun guard standing to the side—a tall gaunt man with long black hair and
a gray broad-brimmed hat.

Before arriving here, Breen had figured Lamb for another ragtail Kentucky preacher with a crazy gleam in his
eyes—plenty of those around. But this Sovereign Lamb
was a whole 'nother hoot 'n' holler. He was a tall, hefty
man with a broad square face, a long nose, heavy black
eyebrows, and razor thin lips above a big chin. Deep-set
blue eyes stared right at Breen. Seemed like he was about
fifty years old.

That curly white thing on Lamb's head—was that a
wig? One time Breen had been held for trial, in St. Louis,
and there were pictures of judges on the wall and a couple
of them wore those curly white wigs.

Today, Lamb wore a finely tailored double-breasted
blue suit, and a pendant held by heavy gold chains. The
pendant was of a golden lamb wearing a crown. It drooped
low over a shiny red tie with a diamond stickpin in it.
Around Lamb's shoulders was a crimson cloak, with white
fur at the shoulders. Once a trapper, Breen knew furs. This
looked like ermine.

But that diamond stickpin caught his eye. His own
grandfather had one not so different. It had been buried
with him; Breen had dug the old man up, stole the stickpin,
and the old man's coat. He sold both of them.

"Keep an eye on him, Heiler," Lamb said, to the man
with the shotgun. "But don't be in a hurry to shoot. He's
unarmed."

Heiler nodded. "Yes, sir."

"Doubtless you are the man Brother Donahue found in the wilderness," Lamb said. He had a foreign sound to his speech. That figured; Donahue said Magnus Lamb was from England.

Breen wasn't cowed by this imposing figure, but he was taken aback a skosh. Still, he knew what to do with a gent like this. You either kill him and take what you can get off his body, or you pretend he's the boss. And he'd been told that Lamb commanded a whole troop of armed men.

Breen set his pipe on the step, took off his hat, and stood up. Lowering his gaze, he said, "Yes, Sovereign Lamb, that's just who I am, a small man who was lost in the wilderness." Then he repeated a little speech Brother Donahue had given him to say: "I come to you, to ask to be part of your great plan for the world."

"Hmf! We shall see! You are a scruffy one. Brother Donahue says you have a wound?"

"Yes, sir. An outlaw shot me. I near didn't get away with m'life."

"I can see the blood on your clothing. You'll need to get yourself washed. You shall be given time to recover— and then we'll see if you can master the principles of this community. Our way is to extend brotherhood only to those who deserve it."

"Yes, sir. Thank you, sir!" Master the principles? What did that mean? He knew the word *master* but not the word *principles*.

"Now, even a wounded man can be of use. Can you work with leather?"

"Since I was but a tyke, sir!"

"We have some bridles that need repair—that sort of thing. I'll have it sent up to keep you busy as you heal."

"That'll be mighty fine, Your Honor."

Breen wanted to ask for his gun. But there was something

about the unbending gaze that made him figure it was unwise. Best to seem harmless. The gun could be had later.

"You have been fed?" Lamb asked, looking Breen up and down with a frown.

"Yes, sir, they give me beans and bacon."

"Very good. Are you a partaker of spirits?"

The tone let Breen know what answer he should make. "Why, no!" He widened his eyes in surprise. "A man cain't keep his senses if he drinks spirits!"

"Unless the man is appointed by God to imbibe liquor, and then only with moderation!"

Breen was confused. A man could be appointed by God to have a drink?

Lamb went on. "Spiritous liquors are neither sold nor distilled here! The Holy Spirit flows freely to good souls and that is all that is needed!"

"Yes, sir! I do agree!"

"Very well. Brother Donahue has volunteered to teach you our ways. Can you read and write?"

"Why, I can make out my letters so's to read a . . ." He almost said a wanted poster. Something he said in the saloons for a joke. ". . . what I need to read."

"Hmf! Donahue shall read to you! Now—do not move!" Then Lamb reached out and let his hand hover over Breen's bandaged side. He closed his eyes and intoned. "Lord, let your Holy Grace move through me and hasten this man's healing!"

Breen said, "Why, I think it's some better already!"

"Now—take your rest. In two days you shall begin your leather work. What is your name?"

"It is Breen, sir." He thought he ought to give him a false name, in case wanted circulars came through this town sometime, but he'd already told Donahue his name. "Chance Breen."

"Chance? It was not chance that brought you here. It was the will of God. Ponder on that, Breen."

Then the towering man turned on his heel and stalked off, his ermine and purple-velvet cape sweeping after him like wings. Heiler gave Breen a warning look with his beady eyes, and followed his boss.

A man like Magnus Lamb surely has some treasure hid, Breen thought. There ought to be a way to get at it, and get away. It would need patience, and slyness. Spy out the territory. Figure where the goods are and how to get at 'em.

Breen sat down, wincing at the pain—which was in no way diminished by the Sovereign Lamb's prayerful healing. He picked up his pipe, fished in his pocket for a lucifer, and recollected something Badger said when he brought supplies to Breen's camp—that the Gilbert Peck feller and his wife were headed in their covered wagon to this very place, Gunmetal Mountain. Cleve Trewe had been with that wagon on the Applegate Trail. Was there a good chance Trewe was coming here too? Seemed there was.

One way or another, Breen decided, he'd get hold of a gun as quick as he could.

The day was worn to a nub by the time Cleve rode up to the little group of shacks at the foot of Gunmetal Mountain. Cleve's left hand ached where it had been burned, and his ears stung from the biting wind. He reined in and looked around.

Gunmetal blue from an ancient coating of ash, the mountain was looming over the little cluster of shacks and tents. A narrow creek hissed and rumbled down the steep cut between the hills. Smoke rose from a firepit, where three bearded, rough-edged men stood about, smoking

pipes and looking discontented—and looking at Cleve
with suspicion. He noticed a shaggy, oddly proportioned
man with a coonskin cap and bear-fur coat was squinting
curiously at him.

Cleve smiled and nodded at them, and let his hand
drop to the butt of his gun. "Waiting on some friends,
boys," he said. "Just passing through." He glanced back
along the trail, saw the covered wagon coming over a little
rise in the trail. The Pecks' wagon was less than a hundred
yards away.

"How do you gents keep busy out here?" Cleve asked.
"Trapping?"

"We do the odd job for the settlement up yonder," said
a man with a freckled face and a red beard. He hooked a
thumb toward the mountain.

"Surprised you don't live up there," Cleve said. "Cold,
living in tents and such."

The freckled man snorted. "I was up there once. They
don't allow drinkin' and they don't allow gamblin', and
they watch your every durn move. Them women are
snooty too. Ain't no life up there, ain't no *wife* up there,
not such as I'd take! I'm saving for Sacramento."

"I wonder," said Cleve, keeping it casual, "if you gents
have seen a young Indian fella pass through? He might be
dressed different than most you'd see. He's a Bannock,
about twenty years old. His name is Ejupa but he might go
by Coyote—or something else."

The men shook their heads. "No Indians hereabouts,"
said the man in coonskin and bear fur. "They're scared of
them Apostles, with their rifles and cannon. Those boys
are good shots. You huntin' renegades?"

Cleve shook his head. "Just looking to talk to him.
Doing a friend of mine a favor."

The man in the coonskin hat seemed to make up his

mind about something. He turned toward a tent, calling out, "Hey, Lightnin'! I think this man here might be somebody you is wantin' to talk to!"

The other men at the firepit chuckled and traded winks.

A younger man emerged from the tent, a little over forty feet away. His blond hair was raggedly cut, his cheeks were freshly clean-shaven, a little red from the razor. Over his left hip was a cross-draw Remington revolver. He wore vaquero boots and pinstripe pants. Cleve remembered him from Piswaller, gawking as Cleve shot it out with Frank.

He was staring at Cleve now, too, but with his mouth closed this time, pressed to a thin line. "What's your name, mister?"

"Cleveland Trewe. I take it your mama named you 'Lightning'?"

The freckled man laughed loudly at that. The young man's mouth tightened even more. "My name's James Crofton. Some called me Lightning."

"How'd you get that nickname?"

"Why, we had a draw-and-shoot, see who could hit the target fastest—"

"Hey, Lightnin'!" called the man with the coon cap, cupping his hand by his mouth. "Them targets shoot back?"

The other men laughed at that. Crofton gave the man with the coonskin cap a venomous look. "Shut your damn mouth, Judson!"

The wagon was trundling closer. Ulysses was lifting his head, nostrils dilated, ears cocked toward the creek. He wanted water. "Well, boys, I'm going to water my horse," Cleve said.

"Cleveland Trewe!" Crofton called out, pulling his gun. "You are wanted dead or alive for murder! Surrender your weapon!"

Cleve sighed. He had suspected this was in the offing.

"Lightning, you are misinformed. I was lately deputy sheriff of Elko County. I was an officer of the law in Denver. Who am I supposed to have murdered?"

Crofton blinked. His gun wavered—then he straightened it up again. "You killed Davy Breen in cold blood!"

"Is that so! Who told you that, his pappy?"

"That's just who it was!" Judson said, chuckling.

"I have met some impressive liars in my time," said Cleve. "But after spending an hour or two with Chance Breen, before his boys tried to bushwhack me, I concluded he is the reigning king of all liars west of the Mississippi."

Judson slapped his leg and cackled. "He does know Chance!"

"We'll see what the law says when I take you to Winnemucca!" Crofton said, sighting along his Remington revolver, one eye closed.

The revolver was aimed right at Cleve's belly. Cleve looked toward the oncoming wagon and saw Berry cantering up in front of it. He raised his left hand to signal her to stay back.

"Hold up there, Berenice!" he called out.

She drew up about twenty-five feet away, looking anxious. Cleve smiled at Crofton, and said, "I'm going to keep my weapon, kid. I'm going to lead my horse down to the creek. He's fierce thirsty."

Slowly, very slowly, he dismounted. He took Ulysses's reins, keeping his hand clear of his Colt.

"Mister—I don't want to shoot you down!" Crofton shouted. "But if you don't drop that gun, I'll do it!"

Cleve turned toward the boy. "Not going to let go of my gun. But you can go ahead and shoot me, if you will. You were lied to, and you're young, so I refuse to kill you. Rather not kill anyone at all."

"You're wanted dead or alive! So . . . so if I . . ."

"I'm not wanted by anyone—except I still owe forty dollars on a poker bet I made in Tonopah." He shrugged sadly. "I won't be arrested by you, kid. You're going to have to murder me if you want to take me anywhere."

"I . . . I'll holster my gun, and we can shoot it out face-to-face!"

Calmly, Cleve said, "James—I'd kill you sure if I went along with that. I'll tell you what—you can go ahead and tell people you backed me down. I won't dispute it! You over there in the fur coat—Judson, is it? Go ahead and tell everyone Cleve Trewe backed down from a fight. I'd prefer that opinion going around. I do not wish to be known as a gunfighter."

All three men gaped at this.

Crofton's gun hand wavered. Cleve looked at him. "There's a lady over to my right, James. I prefer she doesn't see you murder me. Excuse me a moment." He glanced toward Berry. She had one hand on her scabbarded rifle. "Berenice! Go on back to the wagon, please!"

She shook her head, and sat there on her horse, watching intently. But she drew her hand back from the rifle.

He looked back at Crofton. Cleve figured he could snap sideways and draw as he did it, and probably get off a shot killing this young man, who might well miss him. But he couldn't bring himself to do it. "If you try to come over here to take me hand to hand, I'll knock you out. So go ahead and shoot me. Or—tell folks I backed off! Whatever you prefer."

Cleve wasn't sure what he preferred himself. He felt that he was standing on the edge of a cliff. He was teetering on the edge. A sharp wind could knock him off. It could go either way. He felt every inch alive and very close to death.

A darkness had welled up in him, he realized, since that

night under the wagon. Since Berenice had said, *"I don't know."*

He had no desire to die, but neither did he care all that much. And he wasn't going to shoot this kid down.

Crofton licked his lips. "You claimin' it's all a lie? You didn't kill Davy Breen?"

"Cleve *shot* him," Berry called out, "because he was protecting me from Chance Breen—and two other outlaws!" Her voice was sonorous with conviction when she added, "Cleveland Trewe is *not wanted by the law!*"

Crofton looked at her uncertainly—but then he holstered his gun.

Cleve took Ulysses down to the creek for water.

It was cold in the shadow of the mountain, though not yet sundown. The sun was lowering, ducking behind Gunmetal Mountain, as Cleve and Berry rode across the bridge. Just behind them came Gil and Freja, the covered wagon rattling noisily over the logs. The trail turned north, began to climb. Cleve could see it was curving up the mountainside. He noticed the road had been reinforced by logs carefully set into the downhill side.

He looked over his shoulder and saw that the ox was working hard to pull the wagon up the steepening grade. "I hope we won't have to add Suzie and Ulysses to the wagon team," he said. "Wagon's lighter now but maybe not enough."

"I hope so too," Berry said. "Suzie hasn't drawn so much as a buggy."

"A big strong Arabian like her would manage that wagon."

"Oh, but she's proud, you know." After a pause, Berry

added, "You're not so proud as I thought you were. I admired what you said to the boy, about not wanting to be known that way."

"Did you?" That lifted his spirits a mite.

"If we had not talked about . . . about my fears . . . Would you . . . ?"

"Would I have killed him, if not for that?" He was a little rankled she'd think the only thing that would keep him from killing a man was pleasing his sweetheart. "No, I would not have. It's not the first time I disdained a gunfight with a fool who was only going to die." The trail began to climb more steeply, so they had to lean forward a little in their saddles. "Berry—when I came back from the creek, I saw you talking to that Crofton boy. What did you say to him?"

"I told him that you saved his life. That you could have killed him even though he was covering you. He said, "'I ain't gonna say he backed down. Twarn't what it was.'"

"I wouldn't mind if he told people I backed down."

"I believe you. I was reminded of that day in Axle Bust—old Mr. Goss was threatening to shoot you with that shotgun when you went to cut Scrap's body down from the hanging tree. But you defied him. And it reminded me of Mr. Thoreau. Have you read his 'Civil Disobedience'?"

"I have read only his *Walden*."

"He said, 'I was not born to be forced. I will breathe after my own fashion. Let us see who is the strongest.' I so admire that, Cleve. If we are sufficiently resolute, we cannot be forced into a life we don't want to live."

"I would not force you into anything you don't want, Berry—if that's what you're coming to."

"I didn't mean any of that. I am just . . . I admire the spirit in which you made a choice not to kill that young man."

"I take no pleasure in killing anyone. But with Frank—I surely killed him in anger. I am no saint, Berry."

She gave a small, dry laugh. "I was afraid you might be a little too saintly—until that first night on the trail."

He had to laugh at that, himself. They rode on, gradually climbing the upsloping graveled road. The wagon was lagging a bit, the remaining ox grunting and lowing as it struggled up the mountainside. Berry asked, "Cleve—does it worry you that Breen is going about saying you're a wanted murderer?"

"There are a good many liars on the frontier. I doubt he convinces anyone of account."

They rode on in silence, Cleve starting to think that maybe there was hope for him and Berenice. He was not the kind of man to beg a woman to accept him. He would have let her go. But it would have cut him deep, and hard. Was she hinting, now, that she would not leave him? He couldn't tell. He suspected she simply had not made up her mind.

They made their way gradually up the mountain. After an hour's ride, they followed a curve that took them to the west side of the mountain. Just below, a natural vent in the rocky slope hissed out steam reeking of sulfur.

"Hot springs, here, it seems," Cleve said. "There's a lot of power coming out of that mountain. You could drive a train with it."

"Many trains," Berry said. "This is a volcanic cone, so it's not unexpected there'll be hot springs. It's only just big enough to be called a mountain. Freja said the settlement is on the other side, above the forests. So Gil's cousin told them."

"We'll rest and water the ox, soon's we get to the top of the road."

They rode slowly around the curve and took the last climb. At the road's crest, they came to a stop.

Two armed men stood in the way, and six more were arrayed to the sides, their Spencer repeating carbines at the ready. All the men wore long dark blue coats, lighter blue shirts and trousers, broad black belts, and identical broad, flat-brimmed gray hats; all were clean-shaven, and were shod with polished black riding boots. All this uniformity and their identical rifles gave them a military cast.

And their faces all had the same warning look.

Chapter 9

The wagon was still coming up behind Cleve and Berenice, the ox puffing and snorting. Berry looked at the grim uniformed men arrayed before them.

"Cleve, we seem to have arrived at a *contretemps*," she murmured, glancing at Cleve.

He shrugged and smiled at her, as if unconcerned.

But Cleve was most assuredly concerned. This was no band of outlaws—yet Cleve had no doubt that if these men got the order, they would open fire. He read it in their postures, the alertness in their eyes, the tension in the hands gripping their rifles.

"I'll wait for the wagon to catch up," said the tall, clean-shaven man in front. An officer of some kind. "And then we'll have your names and business here."

Cleve nodded. He'd noticed the man had a southern accent. Might be Alabama. He looked about forty and seemed used to command.

Cleve noticed a purple Christian cross neatly sewn onto the man's coat sleeve. The others didn't have one. Some mark of rank.

The ruddy-faced man who stood beside the commanding officer was stocky, and his lower lip was cut by a scar.

Each man wore a silver pin on his lapel. Cleve couldn't quite make out the pin's shape from here. The guards' mounts were tied up to the thin brush on the right side of the road, the horses caparisoned with a banner showing a dark blue cross on a yellow field.

Ulysses nickered, shifting his hooves nervously. Cleve pondered his next move as the covered wagon came to a halt, the ox grunting, its big horned head lowered. The ox was near played out.

Cleve was about to speak to the commander when Gil jumped down off the wagon and waved a folded paper, calling out, "Gentlemen! I am Gilbert Peck! We are here in the name of the Sovereign Lamb!"

The tall, commanding man standing in front of Cleve said, "Come ahead, Peck. Just you, mind! Bring no weapon."

"I have none to bring," Gil said. The Bannock had claimed his rifle.

Gil walked up to the tall guard, a smile of relief on his face. "I have here a note signed by Magnus Lamb!"

Gil has been expecting this, Cleve thought. *He should've warned us*.

"My cousin is a deacon here," Gil said. "Leman Peck."

"I know your cousin," said the boss guard. "I am Apostle Carmody."

"Leman has written me of you," said Gil.

"And who are these others?" Carmody asked.

"That is my wife, Freja Peck, at the wagon." She bobbed her head to Carmody as Gil went on, "Our traveling companions are Mr. Trewe and Mrs. Tucker, both recently of Nevada. Mr. Trewe has given us aid and protection on the road. We were beset by an outlaw, and Indians—and he saw us through."

Carmody gave Trewe an appraising look. Cleve looked calmly back.

Gil glanced nervously back and forth between Carmody and Cleve, and added, "Mr. Trewe was a keeper of the peace in Denver, and he was the law in Axle Bust too."

"The law on Gunmetal Mountain," said Carmody with great aplomb, "is the Holy Word. That alone."

Cleve considered reminding Carmody that California had been made a U.S. state in 1850, hence state and federal laws covered Gunmetal Mountain. But he decided against it, convinced by the eight rifles encircling him.

"We do understand, Apostle Carmody," said Gil. Speaking for Cleve and Berenice without asking. "We all do!"

Affecting nonchalance, Cleve looked out over the valley, below the mountain's west side, and the hills beyond it. The land was lusher to the west, the hillsides thick with dark-green fir, wreathed in mist. Clouds muted the lowering sun, adding a tincture of muted gold to the treetops. "A fine view from here," Cleve remarked. He noted a clear-cut area off to the southwest. He nodded in that direction. "That's the settlement's lumber operation, I take it, Apostle Carmody?"

"It is," Carmody said. "Are you skilled with a saw, Trewe? We need such men more than gunhands."

"I am a fair hand with saw and ax," said Cleve. "Berenice and I aren't sure we're staying long," he added. "We want to get a look at the settlement—and hear the Word from Mr. Lamb."

"*Sovereign* Lamb," snapped Carmody.

Cleve nodded solemnly. "Just so. Sovereign Lamb." He had to play the game, for now. He and Berenice needed to be allowed into the settlement. He had given his oath to search for Ejupa here, and Berenice wanted a hot bath, a chance to refit. They'd lost many of their supplies to the Panati. He considered asking Carmody about Ejupa, but that might complicate things—depending on what could have happened to the young Panati warrior. It might be that Ejupa had been shot down in this spot, by these very men.

"This is private property," said Carmody. "The entirety of this mountain—and thirty miles around it in every direction. Just remember that you remain here only as long as Sovereign Lamb will have you."

"I do understand," said Cleve gravely.

"You are . . . *escorting* this lady?" Carmody asked, looking pointedly at Berry.

There's that damned question again.

Cleve gave him a single brisk nod. "The lady is under my protection."

Carmody sniffed. "Very well, you and Mrs. Tucker are admitted to the settlement on a provisional basis." He handed the note back to Gil. "I and Brother Twilley will escort you into the settlement." Gil returned to the wagon as Carmody and Twilley walked to their horses and mounted up.

Following Carmody, Cleve and Berry slowly rode past the staring gunmen on either side of the road. Cleve felt a prickle at the back of his neck.

They rode not quite an hour on a flat grade along a gently curving road across the mountainside, with the sun dipping low.

"This must be Lambsville," Berry said, keeping her voice low as they trotted up past the rows of tall, turreted wooden houses shadowed by tall pine trees. A street sign read Many Mansions Way. "I heard from Freja about the 'Abodes of God's Reward.' What is the quotation? 'In my Father's house are many mansions.'"

The two-story houses, looking fairly new—three stories

if you counted the little circular room in the small turrets—
were painted in various shades of white and blue, with
scalloped detailing under the eaves. Rose bushes, looking
half dead, divided by stone walks, filled the small lot in
front of the houses. The tall pines had been here long
before men. This side of the mountain had been forested,
Cleve supposed, but most of the trees had been cut
down and used or sold. The pines had been left as wind
blocks.

On Cleve's right, a woman in a white bonnet and yellow
calico housedress, a shawl over her shoulders, was sweeping
pine needles from her walk. She was chatting to another
woman who watched two boys play with wooden swords
among the bushes. The children stopped to stare as the
guards, Cleve, and Berry rode by and the wagon rattled up.
The women looked at Berry, at one another, then back at
Berry, their expressions marked with disapproval. *Must be
that she's wearing trousers*, Cleve thought.

"Oh, look at them!" Freja burst out. "The houses! It's
all true, Gil!"

"Although there doesn't seem to be much occupancy,"
Berry said, in an aside to Cleve.

"I suppose most of them are out and about on chores for
the settlement," Cleve said. "Lots of the men will be logging, so long as the weather allows."

"I count twenty-four houses," she said. "All more or
less alike. I wonder how many live in each? Are there
other quarters? And are there shops?"

They reached the end of the street and one of her questions was answered as they turned west on a cross street.
A sign named the street, *Plentiful Avenue*. It was lined by
shops and work sheds, painted white with blue trim. There
was a blacksmith, a large general store with "sundries," a

"Shoes, Boots, and Leather Goods Store," a millinery, a feed and grain shop, a butcher's shop, and a doctor's office. None of these enterprises had the name of the shopkeeper on them.

At the other end of the street stood stables and a corral. Cleve saw no gunsmiths, no advertisements for ammunition, no liquors on offer, nor saloons. The stores varied only slightly in size and build, except the General Store with its two levels. They seemed closed for the evening, every one of them.

Heading west, Plentiful Avenue didn't actually go anywhere except along the strip of stores. It ended twenty yards past the shops—the ending marked by a large, dark blue cross rising above a row of rose bushes. Beyond the cross to the west was the south end of the valley he'd looked into earlier. Must be a pretty steep downslope beyond that cross.

"The town's almost as uniform as the guards," Berry said softly, looking at the shops. Cleve nodded.

He turned in the saddle and looked to the east—and saw that the street went to a tall fence made of iron-banded wooden poles. There was a guardhouse beside the fence gate. Beyond the closed gate, Cleve could see a sprawling white house, three stories high. Two turrets rose on its north and south sides, with stained-glass windows that seemed to look back at him like two multicolored eyes. Must be the mansion of Magnus Lamb.

Cleve turned his back on those eyes and looked west again. Just before they reached the end of the street, a narrow gravel road turned and curved sharply left to wind up a hill.

Apostle Carmody swung his horse about, and they all

reined. Closer now, Cleve could see that the silver pin the Apostles wore depicted the head of a lamb.

"Mr. Trewe," Carmody said, "there are two cottages on that hill, in those oaks, and there's a cabin as well—the cottages are for pilgrims who've come to learn about the Sovereign Lamb. The cabin is empty. You can stay there. The lady . . ." He nodded toward Berenice. "She can stay in the cottage next door, with the other two ladies—they came here on their own. Just tell Polly and Irma there I sent you, Mrs. Tucker. There is a supply of food in both cabins for your dinner. There is a horse shed out back for your mounts. The two of you are invited to the chapel tomorrow morning."

"Thank you, Apostle Carmody," Berry said blithely. "Come along, Suzie." And she rode up the hill.

Carmody turned to the wagon, creaking up to them. "Peck," Carmody called, "you and your missus, pull up over there, that side of the road. You can stay in your wagon tonight. Once you're approved by the Sovereign, you'll be able to move into a house."

Cleve sat on his mount and watched Berry ride up to the center cottage. He saw her dismount and go into the little cabin in the middle.

Berry had made no effort to insist she share a cabin with Cleve. She hadn't seemed at all bothered by being without him tonight. Maybe it was the beginning of a way out, for her.

Feeling the pit open inside him again, Cleve rode up the hill to the white-painted cottage on the west side.

It was dark out, clouds hid the moon, and this was the time to see what could be done.

Chance Breen wasn't feeling his usual manly strength. But the pain was less now, and he could walk about more easily. He slipped quietly out the front door and looked around, rubbing the sweaty palms of his hands on his trousers.

There was a bite in the cold air, but Breen was sweating. The wound in his side was still nagging and he was on edge, being in this strange place—this *very* strange place—without a gun. The seven laborer cabins were strung along in a ragged row in the pines overlooking the mountainside. He walked to the stone wall along the edge of the cliff and looked down. Maybe a hundred yards below, past the slope of pine trees, were rows of fancy-looking houses, spaced neatly on the shoulder. Yellow lantern light showed in the windows, and red glows showed from chimney pots.

Were Cleve Trewe and that Mrs. Tucker already here in the settlement, maybe warming their boots in front of a fireplace in one of those houses?

Breen turned and looked at the "Cabins of the Faithful." There were lights in the farther three cabins. He could make out someone walking along in front of them, a man carrying a rifle or a shotgun, hard to tell in the darkness.

Brother Donahue, Breen knew, liked to go down to the chapel in the evening, and take in some holy book learnin'. Likely the cabin would be deserted, and with luck, Breen's gun belt and his Remington sixer might still be stuck away in there.

Breen looked down the row of cabins, didn't see the man with the long gun now. Must have gone into a cabin.

Thirty steps took Breen to Donahue's door. Only a loop of rope on a nail held the door shut. He unhooked it and stepped softly inside, listening. No sound of anyone breathing. There wasn't much light from the window, but the place felt empty. Breen fished a lucifer from his pocket, struck it on the wall, and it flared up enough to show him a fireplace, a bunk, a satchel, a wooden box of sundries, a chamber pot, and—there, under the bunk, he could see part of a gun belt.

He crossed the room, the match fluttering, and fished out the gun belt. It was his gun belt and the Remington was in it. Grinning, he tossed the match at the fireplace and buckled on the gun belt. The belt hurt his side a mite but to hell with that.

He had the sketch of a plan. Donahue had said three men took turns being bodyguards for the "Sovereign Lamb." One was the gaunt man with the beady eyes. Another used to be a vaquero. The third was a feller named Buster, a drunk who sobered up in some so-called miracle caused by the Sovereign. That was the one. Breen thought he could get hold of some still liquor somewhere. Got to be someone in this tetched town that's got some. He'd wait till that Buster was alone and wave a jug of corn liquor under his nose. If that didn't work, he'd knock him down and pour it down him if he had to. Get him full drunk. Then he'd get the fool to kill himself, some way. Stumble off a cliff, maybe with a little help. Breen could then make out to the boss man, Lamb, that God told him to take Buster's place.

Once he was a bodyguard, he'd have access to that big house, where the riches of Magnus Lamb were most likely hidden. What then? Bag up the riches, take Lamb hostage, have the treasure put in a wagon and . . . pay someone to kill Cleve Trewe.

Not a bad plan at all.

Breen went to the door, stepped through . . . and a man waiting at his right stuck a shotgun in his ribs.

"If you don't take off that gun belt real slow, I'll use both barrels and cut you right in half." It was that beady-eyed fella, Heiler. Must have been patrolling round the cabins. The one man he'd seen.

Breen came out with some cusswords. But what could he do?

He unbuckled his gun belt.

Chapter 10

Lying on his bunk in the darkness, fingers laced behind his head, Cleve was staring up at nothing at all. He was remembering how back in Axle Bust, pondering on Berenice Tucker, sometimes he'd felt like a schoolboy with a mad crush. Now he was back in that kind of boyhood foolishness, only it was the misery end of it.

Cleve snorted at himself. He forced his mind to his main job. Find the Indian youth, Ejupa. Discharge that obligation, he told himself, then focus on getting Berenice safely to wherever she wanted to go.

Suppose Ejupa could not be found here—or anywhere? He might have gone to see those powerful, magical locomotives at Poverty Flats. He might have jumped a train . . .

He might have left the state. He might be dead, his body ravaged by scavengers.

Nothing to do but start here and find out if anyone had seen the young man named for Coyote—the trickster.

As for Berenice . . .

If she left him, he might just go to the Sweet River Valley alone. He had enough money from the sale of the mine in Axle Bust to get a good start. Why not take up the challenge? Keep his mind busy, building a life there. Buy or claim land, whichever the law allowed, build a soddy, and then start with the fencing. Have to find someplace to purchase cattle in the area. He'd need to hire some help first to move the cattle and keep them on his own grass.

It'd be lonely out there without her but if a man just kept working, doing twice what he asked his hires to do, making sure he was done in at the end of the day, he could ignore loneliness.

Could he forget Berry? *Never*. But every nail he pounded, building his new home, would drive her from his mind.

It took another hour until Cleve at last fell asleep envisioning each detail of Sweet River Ranch . . .

He was awakened by the clangor of church bells.

Cleve blinked at the morning light coming through the window, and remembered it was Sunday. There was a chapel somewhere, and it was ringing its bells to call the faithful to their Sovereign.

He changed into his one set of clean clothes, groomed himself as best he could. He hung his gun belt on a peg, and put on his hat. He went out to feed and water the horses.

Cleve communed with the horses for a minute, and then went to find Berry. The oak trees swayed and whispered in the wind, their fallen, dried-out leaves rustling by. Cleve shivered, for he had no heavy coat suitable for church.

He had to clasp his hat with one hand to keep the cold wind from tugging it off him as he knocked on the door of the cottage. A stocky chipmunk-cheeked lady in a dark blue Sunday dress and bonnet opened the door. She had a weak chin, and her lips were primly pursed. Her blond sausage curls and her dress made Cleve think of Mary looking for her little lamb. And she was on her way to the Sovereign Lamb as she said, in a British working-class accent, "I *beg* your pardon, I must get by!"

Cleve lifted his hat to her and stepped aside. "I shall see you in church, Irma!" came Berry's voice from within.

Irma bustled through the door and down the path, trailing the fragrance of bergamot and lemon oil. The bells rang again, as Berry stepped out, as if in celebration of her. She wore a sky-blue bonnet and a rose-print dress that reached to a little above the top of her high, button-up white shoes. Cleve guessed the dress was on loan from one of the ladies in the cottage.

"Good morning, Cleve," she said, tugging on white kid gloves.

"Morning, Berenice," he said. "How did you sleep?"

"Well enough."

"We truly going to that church?"

"It's prudent to do so, I think. I am interested to hear if this man's doctrine is as I suspect. Shall we go?"

She took his arm—a great relief to him. They started along the path, above the shops on Plentiful Avenue. "What is it you suspect about this Lamb's teaching?" Cleve asked.

"Only that it is based more on vanity than religion."

They came to a set of raw wooden stairs set into the hillside and descended to the gate in the high wooden fence. It was open. Two shotgun guards were posted on either side of the gate. Carmody was there, too, rifle cradled in his arms. "You're late, Trewe," he said.

"Too late for the service?" Cleve asked, hoping they were.

"Not quite. Hurry on in . . ."

Breen didn't like the look of this set-up.

Magnus Lamb, wearing that white curled wig thing on his head, sat at a big wooden desk suitable for a judge, his hands clasped on the leather top. He wasn't wearing the ermine cape—it hung on the coatrack behind him, next to a long black robe. Lamb wore a purple shirt with a priest's collar. Carmody and Heiler stood behind Lamb, their weapons in hand but not yet pointed.

Breen's gun belt, with the sixer, was lying on the desk. Not in Breen's reach. Anyhow, Breen's hands were tied up so good he couldn't operate a gun. Locked up in a cell smelling of piss, he'd spent a very poor night. Lying on the straw on the floor, just waiting to see if they were going to hang him or cut him loose.

Somewhere, church bells were going *clang-a-bang*.

"So you saw fit to break into Brother Donahue's cabin, Breen?" Lamb said, staring steadily at him.

"It weren't like that, Your Honor," Breen said, licking his dry lips. They hadn't so much as given him a drink of water. "It wasn't locked. And Donahue, he's my friend— he done saved my life! I wanted to see if he was there, so's we could talk. Then I saw my gun. Why, he said I'd surely be given my gun back so—I took it!"

"Oh, he said that did he? Hmpf!" Lamb shook his head. "I very much doubt it."

"Now out in the hills where I've been living, it's powerful dangerous, with Indians and outlaws and drunken sons of—just awful people. And a man's got an instinct to carry his iron close. Why I can't even sleep if it's not to hand. And I'll tell you—"

"That's enough, Breen! I've no time for your mendacities and prevarications! I have a sermon I must give to my people. This morning I had a meeting with a pilgrim, a new parishioner, one Gilbert Peck. He says it was well known that your gang murdered two men working for Cephas Bridge in Paradise, Nevada. And now I see the truth of it in your face! I tell you it is God's eyes that look upon you and God cannot be deceived!"

"Now that Peck told a pack of lies about me, and them lies come from that murderin' Cleveland Trewe, who shot my boy, Davy—my precious son—for nothin'! You cannot put no trust in—"

"Silence!" Lamb thundered, his face reddening. "I have newspapers brought to me here, from time to time, and Cleve Trewe was a detective inspector for the law in Colorado and Nevada, famed for his bravery! In Nevada he risked his life to save miners from certain death! And he has come here as a holy pilgrim! One close look at *you* and your actions of last night show us just who the liar is!" Lamb stood up suddenly, seeming now a foot taller than he really was, as he glowered down at Breen. "I would hang you—but it is a Sunday. And you may possibly be of use to me. Even a man haunted by demons can be used by God for His inscrutable purposes! Yes, even Satan himself is part of God's plan!"

"Yes, yes, Your Honor—I'm sure the holy Lord has a plan for me that . . . . that . . ."

"Cease your twaddle and listen! You are to *leave* here and *never return*—unless summoned!" Lamb turned to the coatrack for a black minister's robe and began to put it on. "However, Breen—there are a few men who do the unsavory tasks that are needed from time to time. They are camped at the foot of the mountain—there's a man named Judson there. You will join them, Breen, and, if you want to live, you will take a message to them for me. There is a task for you—and you will be well paid . . ."

Despite missing his breakfast and coffee, and despite the hardwood pews, Cleve enjoyed the choir. He'd always

enjoyed them, marveling at the way attuned human voices
could fit together like colors blended on a painting to make
something more. Dressed in magenta robes, and led by a
tall, full-figured young woman with long red hair, the
choir stood on tiered risers to one side of the unoccupied
altar. A pump organist played beside them.

Cleve glanced at Berry, who was gazing at the stained-
glass windows, and he wondered what her analytical mind
was seeing.

The chapel was down a brick lane from the east wing
of the white mansion. It had a steeple and a large nave,
white with natural oak trim. Dark blue-edged rugs, Celtic
patterns within, ran down the aisles to either side of the
pews. Stained-glass windows rose behind the chancel, on
the east side of the chapel. The light of the morning sun
came through the stained glass indirectly because the
upper bulk of the mountain was in the way; there was
enough to provide an eerie glow through panels formed into
the image of a lamb with a crown. The gold and rubicund
light, colored by the stained-glass windows, sent a roseate
glow over the altar, creating an air of expectation. One of
the stained-glass panels formed the image of Magnus
Lamb accepting a rose from Jesus, who seemed to be offering the blossom from a cloud. The altar on the dais, just
about five rows in front of Cleve and Berry, was finely
carved of rosewood in images of roses twined around a
lamb wearing a crown.

The silver pins on the "Apostles" coats were also of a
lamb wearing a crown. On the wall to the left was a gold-
framed portrait, about twenty feet tall, of Magnus Lamb
wearing a robe with ermine trimming and a white judge's
wig. Fitted over the wig was a golden circlet.

And here was Magnus Lamb himself, taking long, ritu-
ally slow steps up to the altar, reaching it exactly as the

choir completed a coda. Lamb wore a black surplice over a purple clerical shirt.

A charged hush spread across the room as Lamb looked around. His gaze fixed on Freja Peck. It seemed to Cleve that Lambsville's prophet was undressing Freja with his eyes. Then Lamb looked down at an open book on the altar—the Bible, or something else? With an aura of the magisterial, he placed his hands beside the book and began a call for litany, his voice deep and booming and British:

"Brothers and sisters of the Holy Crown—on what sacred day came the blessing?"

The congregation responded, *"It came unto him on the twenty-first day of June, Year of Our Lord, 1862!"*

"Whence came the rose?"

"There in the Garden of Castle Lamb!"

"Who bestowed the rose?"

"Jesus of Nazareth the Son of God!"

"What did the rose bestow?"

"The crown of the Sovereign Lamb!"

"What was the vision given to the Sovereign?"

"Many mansions for my people shall rise on a blue mountain in the American West! There, too, shall rise a chapel!"

"What did you find when you came to this place?"

"Many mansions awaited us, and the Chapel of the Lamb!"

"And now," Lamb said, in a gentler but carrying tone, "I bring you a dispatch from the Almighty . . ." He gave a rambling, seemingly interminable sermon decrying idleness, and calling for the congregation to redouble efforts and complete the holy work of maintaining the community's buildings and roads and to remember "the daily mid-afternoon kneel-and-prayer." He finished with, "Know that I am always watching, protecting each and every one of you, sending prayers for your healing. But my children, it brings me sorrow to remind you—if you decide to leave our idyll, abandoning our holy mission, I can no longer protect you. The world abounds with marauders, highway-men, and cutpurses—with misfortune and sickness! Yet two of you—two who were formerly faithful are departing tomorrow, having abandoned our cause—" Now his voice thundered out and his hands reached out as if he were sum-moning thunderbolts. "God will turn his back on Leonard Monroe and his wife, and Satan will *seize* upon his own!" The congregation gasped, and a few sobs were heard. Lamb sadly lowered his head, returned his hands to the sacred book, and went on, "Tonight, meditate upon the passage from Revelation 17:14—*These shall make war with the Lamb, and the Lamb shall overcome them; for He is Lord of lords and King of kings, and they that are with Him are called, and chosen, and faithful.*" Lamb paused to sweep the congregation with a seeking gaze. Then he went on, "I bid you now stand and open your hymnals to 'Abide with Me'."

Cleve and Berry stood, and Berry sang along with the congregation. She had a sweet, pitch-perfect singing voice he loved to hear. But Cleve was relieved when the service was over and the organ played the congregation out of the chapel.

At the door they were greeted by the deacon—Gil had pointed him out, when they'd come in. Leman Peck, Gil's cousin. An older, taller man a long neck like Gil's. He wore a gray-brown neatly trimmed beard, and a brown suit. On his lapel was the silver lamb's head pin. "Mr. Trewe and Mrs. Tucker!" he said, lisping a little. He was missing his front teeth. He shook Cleve's hand. "Just want to thank you for seeing Gil and Freja through! I hope you find what you seek here!"

"I hope so too," Cleve said, thinking of Ejupa.

Berenice led Cleve to a sunny place, out of the cold wind, where she could admire a topiary near the corner of the chapel—a juniper cut into the shape of a rose. "What is his obsession with roses?" Cleve wondered aloud.

"Irma told me about it last night," Berry said. "She's the lady you doffed your hat to this morning." Berry glanced around at the congregants coming out of the church, most of them somberly heading for the gates. She went on in a lower voice. "Apparently, Magnus Lamb is also Lord Sykes, in England. He's an earl. He had a rather large estate there, Castle Lamb, which he was in danger of losing as he had spent some time in a madhouse and had ranted something treasonous about being the rightful king of England . . . Irma said it was all a 'stitch-up job,' Satan working through Lamb's enemies. And of *course*, Lamb is also the rightful king of England." Berry couldn't help laughing a little and she covered her mouth. "She was one of his followers in England. She came here a year and a half ago and recently Lamb declared she will stay in the cottage till she is wed. *He* will pick a suitable man for her. Can you imagine? She is forced to marry the man Lamb chooses!"

"And the roses—something to do with Jesus?"

"Oh! It seems that after Lamb was released from the asylum, he went to a hybridized rosebush and found its first rose blooming, which is now called the Sykes Rose, as he was Lord Sykes, in England. This rose glowed with a holy light, and then Jesus appeared, plucked the rose and handed it to him, saying that with this blessing he anointed Magnus Lamb, Lord Sykes, the Holy Sovereign, the Lamb of God . . ."

"You were right," Cleve said, shaking his head. "The man has gone mad with vanity."

"Do keep your voice down, Cleve," she whispered. "Here, Lamb is a law unto himself."

"Sounds like he had to flee England."

"Yes. He sold everything, his manor, his property, his cattle, and family heirlooms, withdrew every cent from the bank, and came out here."

Cleve grunted. "So that's it—I wondered where he got the money to build all this. He prophesied those houses, so he had them built and then lured people here with the promise of a free house. What do you suppose he meant about followers leaving this place, and Satan seizing them—"

But he broke off hearing a boom from the mountain above. He looked up, half expecting a volcanic eruption but instead saw a puff of smoke emitting from something metallic. "That's a *cannon!*"

"It is indeed," said Apostle Carmody, smiling, striding up to them. He was in uniform but wasn't carrying his rifle. "That piece is fired as a salute to the Sovereign—given on special occasions. Of course, there is no projectile in the shell for a salute. We do have armed projectiles—should we be attacked by Indians, we can defend the manor from there on the mountain."

Cleve nodded. He knew that sometimes the British Navy fired cannon charges to honor men of high rank. "Sounded like a ninety-pounder," Cleve said. "Whitworth breechloader?"

"Very good!" Carmody said, with a supercilious nod. "But the Sovereign told me you were a Union officer. Of course, one of the disadvantages we had on the Confederate side in the late war was chiefly unrifled cannons, and often small bore. The Sovereign was able to buy this one when a fort was decommissioned . . ."

"Curious that the Army sold such a weapon, in working order—and the cartridges too."

"Oh, ha-ha—a purse of gold will often convince a purser, as it's said."

Cleve nodded. *The disadvantages we had on the Confederate side*. This man had been a Confederate officer.

Carmody turned to look at Magnus Lamb, now standing upon a balcony of his mansion, making arcane passes over a half-dozen followers below. He still wore the ermine cape, and now a gold circlet glinted on his head.

"What is the, ah, ritual he is performing there?" Berry asked.

"It is what the cannon celebrated," Carmody said, turning to gaze, awestruck, at Lamb. "When the Sovereign appears on the balcony, it's a sign he will give out healing prayers to those who are ailing." He added with verve, "The prayers emanate from his hands like rays of the morning sun! Ah—he's going in now." Carmody turned back to them, and said sententiously, "Mr. Trewe, Mrs. Tucker—the Sovereign Lamb would like to see the both of you in his study. Right this way, if you please."

A China service was set out on a low, ornate table, between four low-slung red velvet chairs occupied by Cleve, Berenice, Magnus Lamb, and his daughter, Eliza, the choir director. She sat across from Berry, but the steady gaze of her jade eyes made Cleve uncomfortable. She now wore a tight-fitting white-lace dress, daringly cut just below knee-length. Lamb was wearing a superbly tailored frock coat, with black velvet lapels, a white silk shirt with French cuffs, and a red silk tie with a diamond stickpin.

Cleve felt odd chatting over tea with a man who'd projected himself, minutes before, as the new savior sent straight from God Himself. He guessed Lamb hadn't asked him here just for a scone and a cup of tea.

"Is the tea to your liking, Mrs. Tucker?" asked Lamb, setting his cup on its saucer.

"It is," Berry said. "But I warn you that Cleve is a coffee drinker, through and through."

"I spent time in England, after the war, and learned to appreciate tea," Cleve protested mildly. "But I confess a fondness for coffee."

"I believe you'll find some in the pilgrim's cabin," said Eliza, her voice a purr. "Did you spend a comfortable night there?" She had a North England accent.

"Of late I've been sleeping on the ground," Cleve said. "It's a marked improvement, ma'am."

"Please call me Eliza." She cocked her head and gave him a look of sympathy. "It must be lonely there, in that cabin . . . all alone."

Lamb gave his daughter a sidelong glance of annoyance and Cleve wondered—how did she know he was alone in the cabin?

"'Tis my understanding that Mr. Trewe is a plainsman, a scout and 'Indian fighter,'" said Lamb. "He must have grown used to isolation in the Great American Desert. In my youth I crossed the Sahara of Africa. *There* is found true solitude!"

"I did some scouting for the cavalry," Cleve said, "but I have no desire to fight Indians—unless I must. I find most of them to be good company. In fact—I'm looking for the son of an Indian friend of mine. The boy's name is Ejupa. Bannock tribe. He came out this way to trade. Have you folks had any contact with him? He's about twenty years old."

Eliza looked quizzically at her father.

"Hmpf!" Lamb said. "An Indian? Twenty years old you

say . . ." Lamb looked at Berry, as if buying himself time to think, and said, "Mrs. Tucker—more tea?"

"No, I thank you."

Cleve ate some scone and washed it down with tea, while he was waiting for Lamb to admit he knew about Ejupa. Cleve felt sure Lamb *did* know.

Lamb leaned back, and said, "I do recall such a young red man, yes . . ."

As if his admission had freed her tongue, Eliza said, "Oh, yes! Father speaks of 'Maybe So'! We called him that because he had little English, and when we asked him if he was willing to convert to our faith, and to work hard, he would say . . . *Maybe so*." She laughed impishly, glanced at the others, and seemed disappointed no one else seemed amused.

"Yes, that's the fellow," said Lamb. "He was here—let me think about where he might be now."

"Cleve," Eliza said, a bit breathlessly, "I am informed you were decorated for your heroism in the war between the States . . ."

"They pressed a great many medals to hand out," Cleve said, breaking a scone in half, "just as many a freight wagon was filled, in advance of the battles, with crutches for the men who must lose their limbs. I was lucky to receive one and not the other."

"You were breveted several times, climbing the rungs to major," Lamb said. "That says much. And you are a graduate of West Point. I'm curious—I have read somewhere that one hundred fifty-one West Point graduates served the rebels in the conflict. Is that true?"

"It is, regrettably," Cleve said. He had learned that fact partway through the war, and he'd tried not to think of it. But some of the men he shot at were probably in his class at the Army academy. "There were a good many more graduates who faithfully served the republic."

"But you see how it is, Trewe—men without spiritual guidance are lost souls. And there is only one guidance that is without corruption."

His daughter nodded, and Cleve thought he saw the trace of a smirk on her face. "Yes! Father got his commission directly from Jesus Christ."

Lamb once more glanced darkly at his daughter. Then he sighed and turned to Cleve. "You could be of great use to Lambsville, Trewe. I need a man like you for certain plans I have in mind. The pay would be generous."

"I am not looking for work," Cleve said. He added, "But I am interested in learning more about your . . . revelation. Your spiritual vision." This was almost a lie. Cleve was curious about it, but there was not a snowball's chance in Hell he would become a Lamb follower. Still, he figured he had to keep in Lamb's good graces for a while yet.

Lamb nodded, unconcerned. "When you return to your cabin, you will find a book, along with a Bible, left on the table. We call the book the *Voice of the Rose*. It will explain much. Now—I will make you an offer. I will give you the information you require in this matter of the Indian, if you will do me a service. The right action would do great good for everyone in this part of the state." He looked into Cleve's eyes, and effused charisma. "And once you've done that service—and studied the book—you may be moved to enlist in our great and glorious crusade *to transform the world . . ."*

Must've been about half past noon when Chance Breen rode up to the crossroads on the broken-winded hack Carmody had given him. The day was gloomy with thick clouds. Breen had eaten little and slept less. His mood matched the day.

He reined in and looked back at the Apostles, four of them on their fancy-draped horses escorting him down here. At a signal from Carmody, they all turned and headed back across the bridge, for the road up to Lambsville.

"You can all go straight to the devil," Breen muttered, glowering after them. At least they'd given back his gun and belt.

He rode to the firepit, where Judson sat on an old log, huddled into his fur coat and staring into the coals. A bottle of whiskey with maybe two swallows left was leaning against the log beside him.

"Where is them other fellas at?" Breen asked, dismounting.

"Red and Snort, they're out hunting, sniffing out one of them puny goat runs about out here," Judson said, handing Breen the bottle. "Be lucky to come back with a gopher. Bix and Crimmins are prospecting. So they said. I misdoubt they'll come back. That boy, Lightnin', he rode off yesterday. You should be glad Lightnin's gone, he was fixing to shoot you if he saw you again. Didn't like you telling falsities on that gunfighter."

Breen took a swig of the whiskey. He coughed and rubbed at his aching side. "He's the one going to get shot if we meet again, that boy. And Trewe too—I'll kill him sure first chance I get, any ol' way I can. I'm in no mood to trifle. He killed my boy, Davy."

"So you said. You can finish that damn bottle, my head's already spun round with it. That's the last there is till we get some from Blasted Pine."

"You do some trapping out here?"

"Not much to trap. Not much to do. Lamb's not given us a job for a good while now."

Breen finished the bottle, and asked, "What you do for him?"

"Chased some Mormons out—they was going to settle 'round here. There was an outfit wanted to cut lumber on Lamb's property—anyhow he says it's his property. We chased them off too. Then a U.S. Marshal come through, didn't like some of Lamb's doings here. I never did hear what the complaint was."

"You kilt him?"

"You think I'd tell you if we did?"

"You calculate I'd turn you into to the law?"

"I calculate you'd turn in your pappy and your mammy, too, if it kept you from being hung your own self. But I'll say this, that U.S. Marshal, he's been real *quiet* for a time now. Just you figure that how you like."

Breen chuckled. "I saw Red had a Baker rifle. Good to knock a man off his horse from a good safe distance." Breen tossed the bottle at a boulder just to watch it bust. "How's come Lamb don't use his own Apostles and such for all that?"

"Lamb doesn't want his 'Apostles' to look dirty. We don't tell folks who we're workin' for."

Breen picked up a dried out old piece of tree limb and dropped it into the firepit. "You ever been up to that Lambsville?"

"Not a once. Never met Lamb neither. That Carmody brings us the jobs and the money. I'm about through with this, Chance. Winter's coming on, going to be ass-bitin' cold, and there ain't no women up here."

"I'll tell you something—that Lamb is rich. You should see his house! He's sure to have a pile of gold buried under there somewhere. And women—there's plenty up there."

"You gone right out of your brain hole! He has his own damn cavalry! Those boys can shoot too!"

"Was they occupied someplace else, that house would be ripe for taking. And I want to serve that Lamb outright. He's looked high-and-mighty down on me. I take that from no man!"

"You get yourself strung up—I'm not going to be hanging there on the same tree."

"I'm talking about *plannin'*, ol' Squaw Jumper! But first—we'll take on a job for Lamb. That'll give us time to figure things and it'll put some wampum in our pockets. Lamb turned me loose so's I would join up with you boys and bring you a message. He's got a job for us that's too dirty for his Apostles. Shouldn't be much trouble at all." He cleared his throat and hocked spit into the firepit, so it sizzled on the coals. "Might be a woman for you boys, if you want to keep her alive a time . . ."

Cleve was graining Ulysses and Suzie, and morosely contemplating another night alone in a cabin just steps away from Berenice, when a beautiful woman came into the small horse barn.

"Greetings, good sir!" Eliza said, in a droll tone of voice.

Thrown, Cleve managed, "Evening, ma'am. Um—Eliza."

She was wearing a hooded blue cape, and a taut green dress that looked too light and summery for the weather. With its plunging bodice, it was almost something a dance hall girl would wear. She pushed the hood back and shook her coppery hair free of her collar, and came over to stroke Suzie's neck. "You are a diligent gentleman, Cleve," she said, seeing he'd set out the buckets of water and the grain. "How do these fine mounts fare this evening?"

"They are restless," he said. "They've been penned up in here too long."

"I know exactly the feeling," she said. "I am quite of their mind. I, too, need a good . . . gallop."

She turned to him—and in the process came quite close. He could feel her body heat in the cold barn. He could smell her perfume. *Lilac*, he thought.

She was at least a head shorter, and she gazed up at him expectantly. There was something in her eyes—that *dared* him.

He looked into her green eyes, and then glanced at the bosom she clearly wanted him to see, and he thought, *This isn't fair.*

He turned to Ulysses. He patted the horse, and said, "Tomorrow morning, my friend, you and I are going to stretch our legs. It's a good ride out to the lumber camp."

"Ah yes, you will seek a lost Indian tomorrow," Eliza said, with a touch of mockery. "How colorful! You will take the direct road to the lumber camp?"

"That's the only one I know of," Cleve said, smiling at her. He kept the smile friendly, nothing more. "It's . . . kind of you to look in on our horses."

"Oh, I was looking in on you, Cleve. I was out strolling and I saw you head back here. I am something of an equestrian. Everyone in our family is raised for hunting and riding—everyone in our class, really."

"We had hoped to do away with class, in the British sense, in this country," Cleve said. "But—there are people who seem to insist on it."

Her cheeks reddened. The rosiness was not unflattering to her. Her pale skin, the snowy arcs of her bosom . . .

He made himself look back at the horses.

"You think us inadequately American, then?" she said.

"My father used to say that every man makes his own

class," Cleve said. "With his work or shirking it, his brain or failure to use it—he makes his own station."

Eliza frowned, then seemed to make an effort to banish it from her face. She moved closer to him. "Cleve . . ."

Cleve took a deep breath, slipped around Eliza and went to the lantern hanging in the corner. "I'd better let Ulysses sleep. And I need rest myself. I've got a long ride in the cold tomorrow."

"So you do. But—I wonder if you'd be good enough to escort me back to the house. It's quite dark out there now."

She looked at him innocently. Yet there was no innocence in her.

"Certainly," he said. "Step on outside, and I'll be right there."

"It does not bother me when the lantern light goes out," she said carelessly.

Cleve looked at her a long moment, then turned to the lantern, blew it out, and hurried past her to the rectangle of dim light marking the door.

Walking her to the mansion, he told himself, *Don't be a weak fool . . .*

They spoke of horse breeds, which were said to be the sturdiest and which the fastest, and then he noticed she had brought him to a side door of the big house, a longer way to go than the front doors. She took a key from an inner pocket of her cape. "Do please come in and have a glass of brandy, before you say good night," she said, unlocking the door.

"I—am abstaining tonight," he said, taking a step back. Not trusting himself. "I've got the *Voice of the Rose* to ponder. Good night, Miss Lamb."

She looked quite surprised. "Well then—perhaps . . . we might see one another tomorrow."

Cleve raised his hat to her and strode off as quickly as he could without seeming to be running across the grounds to the gate . . .

Where the two Apostles on guard watched, grinning and bemused.

Chapter 11

A brisk morning. The sun was rising on the eastern side of the mountain, and on this side a shadow and mist clung to the fir-wooded valley below. Cleve was relieved to be riding away from Lambsville. The superficially pious "settlement" made him uneasy.

He cantered Ulysses along two ruts in rocky soil, the crude road slanting north down the mountainside. Farther on, the road switched back southwest toward the forest.

Berry was with the Pecks, heading out this morning to the hot springs higher on Gunmetal Mountain, and Cleve was heading down toward the lumber camp to the west, to look for Ejupa—and to do the bidding of a man he quietly despised: Magnus Lamb.

"Now heed me, Trewe. There's a place called Blasted Pine, where resides the Red Feather gang. They're led by a white man who wears a curling hawk's feather in his hat—we know not his name. I will give you a letter for the logging boss, Wardwell, directing him to advise you regarding your Indian. And he will direct you to the trail for Blasted Pine. He can attest to the trouble these rogues are giving my laborers—selling them liquor on the sly, robbing them. And worse, their malign influence endangers the

*souls of my men! I keep my Apostles close to Lambsville.
I need a man who can find Blasted Pine and put a stop to
this vile nuisance—however he may choose . . ."*

Cleve had not guaranteed he would find these supposed
bandits and kill them. The risk would be high, too high in
the cause of a man he didn't like or trust—and he was un-
willing to be an executioner for Magnus Lamb. But once
he found Ejupa, he and Berenice could leave Lambsville.
And it might be he could do something about the Red
Feather bandits. Maybe something that needed doing. It all
depended on what he found at Blasted Pine.

He figured that Lamb had ambitions even more outlandish than stocking a town with people who thought he
was the new Jesus. He had referred to transforming the
world. Maybe Lamb was planning to hire mercenaries,
build up some kind of army. He would need men like
Cleve Trewe and Carmody to deploy that army and grab
more land. He'd probably pay well for a man with Cleve's
military background to run such a campaign. There were
state and federal laws to contend with. But "the Sovereign" was making good money with logging, so Cleve had
heard, and he might have cash remaining from selling out
in England. That gave him a power of money for bribery.
Lamb seemed like a man who would not hesitate to grease
palms, if it got him what he wanted.

Cleve chuckled and shook his head. He wasn't even
faintly interested in a lasting job with Lamb—certainly not
one that engaged in sedition. The sooner he and Berry got
shed of Lambsville, the better.

He took the switchback, and a couple of miles brought
him to the turn where the road cut due west—and then he
drew up, hearing galloping hoofbeats behind him.

Cleve turned in the saddle and saw Eliza Lamb riding
up on a white stallion with pink eyes. Even the horse's

eyelashes were white. From the horse's saddle flapped the caparison of the Sovereign Lamb. Cleve also noticed a Winchester saddle gun hanging from the pommel. The horse was sweating, breathing hard as Eliza reined in. She was wearing a tight red-and-black riding habit, lambskin gloves, and a fur-lined red velvet cloak. Her bodice was partly unbuttoned.

Kind of chilly to go half unbuttoned, Cleve thought.

She grinned at him and called out, "Well met, Cleve Trewe!"

He reckoned this was no accidental meeting. "Morning, Eliza. Bringing a message from your father?"

"No . . ." She trotted her mount closer. Ulysses turned to snort at the pale stallion with suspicion. "I am here on my own initiative," she went on, reining up beside him. Her smile had become mischievous. He could smell her lilac perfume. "I decided to find out if Galahad could catch up to you. It was quite easily accomplished—you were in no great hurry." She raised her eyebrows, her expression impish, as if his being in no hurry meant something to her. He remembered her parting remark to him last night. *Perhaps we might see one another tomorrow . . .*

Cleve badly wanted to bid her goodbye and ride away. But it wouldn't be gentlemanly nor politic. He searched for something to say. "Your fellow there is Galahad? Mine is Ulysses. We both have mounts named after heroes of myth. And Ulysses has been heroic."

"Galahad, sir, is no myth. There are many Galahads in the world, I have no doubt." She leaned a little toward him. "You could be my Galahad, Cleve Trewe—or, better still, my *Lancelot*. And I—could be your Guinevere."

Cleve was startled by this boldness. And he was made uneasy by something in her eyes—a deadness behind the playfulness, as if she were in a private dream of some kind. He suspected he was glimpsing the madness of the Lamb family. She was a beautiful woman. *And fire is beautiful, too*, he thought. But you don't take it into your arms. "Eliza—I am flattered. But I have an understanding with Mrs. Tucker." He wasn't sure the understanding was still . . . understood. But even if it wasn't, he would never entangle himself with Eliza Lamb.

Eliza stiffened; her nostrils flared. Then she said, "What does that tired widow have to offer? I can offer myself— all of myself! But also—all this!" She swept her hand to take in the land all around them. "In time, and with the right . . . maneuvers. It could all be ours."

He shook his head in amazement. "You are a *sudden* kind of woman."

She shook her head. "I suspected, as soon as I heard about you—and knew as soon as I saw you—you are exactly the one I was waiting for, Cleve!" She glanced away, remembering. "I *had* one, you know—his name was Bougainville. Very courtly and very passionate. But he was too slow to act in the important matters and . . ." She shrugged sadly but with no real grief as she said, "Father found out, and had him killed." She sighed. "Oh, Father says the man was killed by Indians. But it's a lie, you see. Father knew what I intended for this Monsieur Bougainville."

She wants a pawn, Cleve realized. A cat's-paw. And she's used to men falling at her feet.

"And does your father know, Miss Lamb—"

"I asked you to call me Eliza."

"Does he know you go about telling people he had someone murdered?"

She blinked, seeming surprised at the question. "Of course not. You won't mention what I told you about my father, to anyone? I have no proof of the murder."

"If there's no proof, then I will not speak of it."

She looked at him in puzzlement. "You seemed so shrewd—I could tell you saw right through my father. That you knew he was a man capable of anything."

"I suspected," he said.

"A suspicion that could be vindicated, and precious soon! He knows he can't trust you—he said as much after our tea. He could see it in you. He himself is a perceptive man. Father sees who he can control, and who must be eliminated. The United States Marshals have made some inquiries about him, and you are too friendly to the law."

"You saying he might have me killed?"

"I cannot be certain. But I can tell you—you must either be *his* man, or no man at all." She lowered her voice, and it became a purr once more. "I am convinced you are *quite* a man, Mr. Cleveland Trewe." Now her voice became a whisper. "You have the strength to save me from him."

"Lamb is a threat to you too?"

She looked away. "Not recently. I made him stop . . . what he was doing. But . . . he's so changeable. He can seem quite rational and then . . ." She shook her head.

"What are you saying? That he—"

"I don't want to talk about that. Cleve—last night, I knew you wanted me—and you forbade yourself. I admire the strength in you, but you are settling for something cold, and distant!"

"Eliza—"

She interrupted him impatiently. "Not far from here, down in those trees, is a cabin once used by a logging boss. Now it is a snug retreat I go to when I wish to get away from my father."

"A dangerous place for a lady alone," Cleve said.

Eliza patted the saddle gun. "I am a good shot. And I hope I won't be alone there. What matter if you go to the lumber camp today—or tomorrow? After we've come to a deeper understanding than you could ever have with that . . . that sickly, *professorial* woman—a woman who leaves you alone in that cabin at night! But in *my* cabin—there is a fireplace stocked with wood. There is a fine Scotch whiskey too—and a very comfortable bed. And *I* shall be there!" She gave him an impish smirk. "Is that *also* quite sudden, Mr. Trewe?"

Cleve gave out a short, dry laugh. "It is indeed quite sudden—Miss Lamb." He removed his hat. "I take off my hat to you. You are the goddess of temptresses. I do believe even the Pope of Rome or the most God-fearing Calvinist minister would be tempted by you! Now . . ." He clapped on his hat. "I regret, ma'am, I must ride to take care of a certain matter. I swore an oath, you see. Good day to you, Eliza!"

He heard her gasp in fury as he spurred Ulysses into a gallop and rode hard for the lumber camp.

That's the second time I've had to run away from that woman, he thought ruefully.

Little more than an hour's cantering took Cleve into the valley, through scrubland and then into the deep shadows of the fir woods. He remembered days spent rambling the forested hills near his father's estate, on the rim of the Ohio Valley. He'd sometimes strolled through a vale in those hills with a flighty young woman, Rowena, who was sure he'd marry her. After a particularly fine summer's afternoon in those shady woods, he'd told her he wasn't yet ready for marriage. She wept, and the memory of her was tinged with regret.

Two months later, she'd hurriedly married a Baptist preacher.

Now the shoe was on the other foot. He wanted to marry

Berenice—who shrugged marriage away. Maybe he should have married Rowena and accepted his father's estate in the Ohio Valley. He could have learned to be content enough there, in time. But then, he'd never have met Berenice Conroy Tucker. And whatever she decided about Cleveland Trewe, he'd had some considerable time with Berry now. Whatever happened next—it was worth it.

Berenice. Was Berry truly safe, alone in Lambsville? The place was seething like its hot springs. Who knows what could boil over there? Eliza claimed that "the Sovereign" had people killed. And Eliza Lamb hinted she'd urged her man Bougainville to take control of Lambsville. She herself just might be capable of anything.

Cleve could hear the sounds of a logging camp, now. Multiple ax blades striking, one after another, almost like an unsteady drum roll, the grinding *swish* of a two-man saw. Men calling to the horses pulling logs out of the way. He could smell the fresh sawdust, the dripping tree sap . . .

And he sensed a quick movement in the brush off to his right.

"Hold up!" barked a gruff voice. "Stop that horse right there or I'll shoot you off him!"

Cleve's right hand went to the butt of his six-gun, but with his left he tugged the reins. Ulysses whinnied, perking his ears, and stopped in his tracks.

"Step out where I can see you!" Cleve called.

A man came out of the brush, squinting along the shotgun pointed at Cleve's middle. He was a brawny black-bearded man, dressed for work, in a canvas jacket, coveralls, a blue knit cap on his head. He squinted along the shotgun pointed at Cleve's middle.

"I'm here to see Wardwell," Cleve said. "I've got a letter from Magnus Lamb. So be careful with that scattergun."

"You don't look like anyone from Lambsville I ever saw."

"You haven't been back in a while, friend. I'm on a job for Lamb. My name's Cleveland Trewe."

"Just you take your hand off that gun!"

Cleve nodded, and put his right hand on the saddle horn. "You Wardwell?"

"My name's Meeker." He lowered the shotgun. "Some of us take turns watching the trail and the road. We got some ridge runners making problems for us. Let's see that letter."

Cleve plucked the letter from his coat pocket and held it out. Keeping an eye on Cleve's gun hand, Meeker came over and took the letter.

The watchman looked at the signet ring waxen seal on the back of the envelope—the sign of the rose. "That's his mark, there. Sorry about the cold welcome. I'll take you to the boss . . ."

About noontime, Breen saw the wagon, drawn by a couple of plow horses, coming down the mountain road. There were goods in the back, covered with a canvas tarpaulin. On the driver's bench was a man and a woman, with three Apostles riding behind them. One of the riders was that bastard Carmody.

Breen wasn't yet ready to take care of this business. He was warming his hands at the firepit, and not long out of his bedroll. He had a powerful hankering for a drink, but there wasn't any in the camp nohow.

May as well get the job done. "All right now," Breen said, turning to Red. "Tell them boys it's time to git up'n mount up." His side still hurt, and he didn't want to ride but it wouldn't be a long one, he figured.

"Now when did you start calling the shots around here?" Red asked, tossing his tin mug aside.

"When? Ha-*haa!* When it came to me that you dunces had no one leading you!" Breen put his hand on his gun. "You don't like it, ride out!"

Red looked at the gun, and then shrugged and went to the row of tents. "Judson! Snort! 'They're comin' down the mountain when they come'—and they *is* comin'! Hidey-ho, let's go!" Red was prone to that sort of jabber.

Snort came out first, wearing only his red long johns. He was a man with drooping dirty-yellow hair, half his teeth missing and the others green. His face was pocked with smallpox.

He sure ain't much to look at, Breen thought, saddling his horse. *But that'll put the scare into them folks.*

By the time Carmody had sent the wagon across the bridge and led his men back up the road to Lambsville, Judson and Snort were dressed and getting their horses saddled. Breen had picked up the firewood ax, too, and tied it to a saddlebag. About the time the wagon trundled by, the driver looking nervously toward them, Breen and his riders were mounting up.

The driver lashed his horses and the wagon jolted faster up the road, heading north.

"They can't keep up that pace long, with that wagon," Judson said, pulling his fur cap down against the rising wind.

"We wait now till they're a good distance from the mountain," Breen said, shifting uncomfortable on his swaybacked horse. "That's the word from 'on high.'" He had heard that expression somewhere and it pleased him. "But we'll follow, just like we're goin' the same way."

A wind nipped at their ears and noses as they started off

at a trot after the wagon. They hung back, keeping it just in sight, for a little over three miles.

As Judson had foreseen, the wagon slowed down, and Breen said it was time to pick up the pace. They rode faster, till they were about fifteen horse-lengths behind the wagon.

Here the road cut through a stand of dusty, leafless oak trees growing up in the sere grass around black rock outcroppings. "This is it," Breen growled. "Red, Snort—you boys ride around them rocks, get out in front of them, have your guns out and hold them. Don't start nothin' you don't have to. Go on now, do it quick!"

"Quick, quick, quick, and lickety-split!" Red called out, chortling, and he rode off around the rock, Snort close behind.

"How come you sent them boys up there," Judson asked. "They're a couple of damned fools. That wagon driver's likely got a shotgun or some such."

"Ha-*haa!* That's the reason! Why risk some wise old-timers like you'n me?"

Then they heard the *boom* of a shotgun.

"Pulled their shooters too damn quick," Judson muttered, and he and Breen rode up on either side of the halted wagon.

Up front they saw the driver—a young man with a thin brown beard frantically reloading his shotgun. Snort was lying dead on the road and Red was aiming carefully, tongue caught between his front teeth. The young brown-haired woman in a bonnet next to the driver was sobbing and saying, over and over, "Leonard, Leonard . . ."

Red and Judson fired at the same time, the shots knocking and jerking this Leonard about on his seat as Red's bullet splashed open the young feller's head—Judson's cut through his neck and hit the girl. She screamed. The wagon's horses reared and whinnied.

The young woman was clutching her husband's body as she died . . .

"Well *shit*, Judson!" Red snarled. "What the doghump did you *did*? She was a purty enough piece."

"Well, she's dead now," said Breen, shrugging. "But she's still warm. You go ahead." He dismounted and took the ax from its loop on his pack. "I got to cut off the feller's head so we can show it to Carmody . . ."

Cleve rolled up his sleeves as the loggers watched. Bonfire light flickered over the blade as he picked up the ax. He tested the grip, and the weight of it. He flipped it up so it spun once overhead, and caught the handle midway, at the "belly" as the loggers call it. Some of the loggers hooted in approval.

"Seems like it'll do," Cleve said. Then he took the ax by the throat, above the knob, raised it over his shoulder— and threw it, spinning, toward the X cut on the pine ten yards away. The blade's bit sank deeply into the target, the ax handle quivering.

"Wuh-hooo!" the loggers shouted.

Wardwell clapped him on the shoulder. "Good work." The only clean-shaven man here except Cleve, Wardwell was broad-shouldered and windburned, wearing a long denim coat and knee boots. "Where'd you learn to do that, Trewe?"

"I did a power of logging for my father as a young fella," Cleve said. "Clearing land for farming. There was a hand, Cliff Bell, who showed me tricks with an ax. We had some throwing contests. But . . ." He shook his head. "I couldn't do what you men do. It's the hours you put in, doing that sawing. Never could stick it above two hours at a time."

"Two hours? That's nothing. You get your dinner?"

"I did."

The fiddle started up then. Competitions with the axes, card games, and fiddle music kept the men busy after dinner, in the absence of liquor. Cleve recognized the song as "The Arkansas Traveler." Some of the men clapped along; near everyone had a pipe lit so they kept the pipe clamped in their teeth.

Cleve peered at the hills toward the west, just visible through the trees. Too dark to make out much. But Wardwell had told him the raiders were still active.

That morning he had spent an hour looking the camp over with Wardwell, discussing the raiders. Wardwell knew Ejupa, had employed him for a time. "Don't know where he is now. Good worker, behaved well enough till those men come sneaking around with their liquor. Had to send him away, and two others besides. A drunkard will get you killed here. Had a man lose an arm because he was drunk and he got in the way when a tree was coming down . . ."

After conferring with Wardwell, Cleve scouted the area. The camp itself consisted of a clearing with a row of tents, a large central tent for Wardwell's planning, horses and oxen for pulling wagons and logs, four jerry-built three-sided sheds for tackle and tools, four log wagons, two freight wagons, a lavatory trench, and a chuckwagon. The loggers were going great guns during this break in the weather, trying to get as much done as they could before snow or sleet set in.

Sentries had been added to each point of the compass. Cleve had introduced himself to them and rode partway along the two trails that forked out northwest and southwest.

The northwest trail eventually led to the small ramshackle town of Blasted Pine. Ejupa could be there. Cleve intended to have a look at the town tomorrow and decide for himself if it was a refuge for outlaws or just another rough mining camp.

Now, off to one side, five men sitting around a small fire appeared to be having a *Voice of the Rose* study. "Everyone here is a church follower of Lamb's?" he asked Wardwell.

Wardwell looked at him sidelong, as if taking his measure. "What's your feeling about Lamb? Just between you and me."

Cleve reckoned Wardwell a decent sort and decided he couldn't lie to him. "I think he has a mania—a delusion. The man had a hallucination and he thinks he's Jesus, or maybe Jesus's stepson. I took one job with Lamb, one only, in exchange for information . . . and . . ." He looked around to see if anyone was listening. "I have started to wonder if he might be a dangerous man."

Wardwell nodded. "Between you, me, and the stumps," he said, "I'm no believer—not in him. But I *am* a believer in teetotaling, you see, because I must not have a drink—one becomes a hundred for me. And only in Lambsville can I feel safe from the liquor devil. Yet I have been having doubts about staying. Some here just go along with Lamb, because they needed work, and they were promised a house. But they're not so happy about the houses they got—and the fact that they don't get paid in actual money . . ."

"If it's not money . . . then what is it?"

"*Scrip,* good for those shops in town. Oh, he *says* there's a *cash* payment—but Lamb keeps it for them, in a church bank. That's what he tells them. He says in time it will be released to them—a time of great prosperity. But he does not say exactly when! Soon the logging will end

with the snow—but he'll have them doing other work.
Now some would run off—except they're most of them
family men. You can't just ride off and leave your family."
He paused to relight his pipe. "Last year, some folks
wanted to go to a family wedding in Sacramento. Lamb
said no. Said he prayed on it and God told him it wasn't
safe for them to go—he had to protect them, by keeping
them here. And the Apostles are always watching and
listening—no one wants to get in a fight with them. Now,
I am a man with some expertise, and he pays me in cash.
He trusts me to stay in this camp because my wife and son
are in Lambsville. Time to time I do lumber business for
him in Redding—Brother Donahue rides along to keep
me from the saloons. Would Lamb let me take my family
to Redding too? I don't believe so. He does not like to be
questioned about such things . . ." He looked over at the
men studying Lamb's holy writ. "Been kind of holding my
fire on all that—because I don't know who I can trust.
Some of them are true believers." He leaned toward Cleve
and said into his ear, "You'd best be careful what you say."

Wardwell went to talk to his foreman.

Cleve crossed the camp to check on Ulysses in a roped-
off remuda with the other horses. Patting his sleepy mount
and wondering what Berenice was doing right now, he
glanced up toward the woods.

He saw a shadow move from tree to tree, barely visible
in the scant moonlight.

Cleve's hand went to his Colt. But if he opened up on
whatever that was, he'd feel a fool if it was a raccoon or
a small bear. Might be some curious Indian too—even
Ejupa.

He looked in another direction, pretending to have seen
nothing. But out of the corners of his eyes he glimpsed a

human shape partway up the hill. A man slipping a little closer to the camp, and then ducking under cover.

Cleve strode toward the nearest sentry, which turned out to be Clark Meeker, with a lantern in one hand, watching the fiddle player and the ax-handle thumper.

"Hey there," Cleve said softly.

Meeker spun toward him, gripping his shotgun. "Oh—sorry, Trewe."

"I'm surprised you're still on guard, Meeker."

"I took Bundy's turn—he has a bellyache, or that's his story. I was feeling kinda jumpy anyhow. Couldn't sit still." He looked out at the woods. "Got me a feeling . . ."

Cleve nodded. "I think I saw someone moving out there. Those trees straight north of the corral. Maybe they're looking to steal horses."

Meeker peered toward the trees. "I don't see anything. You want to call an alarm? There's a bell we can ring, over by Wardwell's tent."

"I'd sooner try something else. You could take that lantern and head up the hillside to the west there, like you're just having a look around. Get them watching you. I don't think they'll open fire."

Meeker snorted. "You better be right about that!"

"They're hoping to sneak in and out. If they fire on you the whole camp'll fire back."

Meeker picked up the lantern. "Suppose I run into them, up close?"

"That'd be your call."

Meeker nodded and headed off, as if casually walking toward the edge of camp to the west. Cleve went east, walking past the horses, along a line of tents where men sat on logs by small fires, talking and smoking. "Good throw with that ax!" one of them called out to him, as he passed. "But can you shave with it?" The lumbermen laughed.

Cleve waved and kept on to a stretch of stumps at the edge of the clearing, and a night-shadowed stand of trees too small to harvest. Here he turned north, angling through the trees, avoiding the patches of moonlight, sometimes having to force his way through brush. Soon the ground rose and he was climbing timbered hillside.

He worked his way up the hill, ducking under branches, trying to make as little noise as possible. Now and then he stopped to listen.

After about forty yards, Cleve froze, hearing two men softly talking. They were close by.

"We got here too soon. Shoulda waited till they's all sacked out."

"They're dead tired. They'll go to bed soon enough. Hell, when I worked that camp I was in the bedroll an hour after dinner. Just too worn to do anything else. You just keep your pants on and we can get maybe four o' them horses."

Guided by the voices, Cleve peered between the trees, and in the sparse moonlight he spotted two men in overcoats squatting by an outcropping of rock, looking toward the camp. One wore a bowler hat, the other a beat-up Boss of the Plains Stetson. The man with the bowler had a rifle in his hands. Beyond them to the west Cleve saw a light bobbing slowly along. Meeker's lantern.

The man with the Boss Stetson caught the motion of the lantern and turned to look. "That some tree whacker coming up here?"

Bowler Hat leaned over a little and looked toward the lantern. "Maybe."

Cleve drew his Colt and moved a couple steps closer, while the raiders were focused on Meeker.

"Maybe we should git," one of the men whispered.

"No, he's just walking sentry . . ."

Cleve took one more step closer, opening his mouth to call for them to drop their weapons—and his boot dislodged some loose stone that rattled noisily down the steep slope. The man wearing the bowler spun around and pointed the rifle toward Cleve. "What the holy hell!"

"Drop your guns!" Cleve snapped, turning sideways to narrow himself as a target.

The raider fired sloppily toward Cleve, a bullet cracked by and Cleve fired twice, the muzzle flashes flickeringly illuminating the gunmen on the hillside. Both rounds struck the center of the raider's chest so he pitched over backward. The Boss Stetson raider was stumbling back into a scrap of yellow moonlight, raising his pistol. Cleve fired, aiming at the man's right shoulder. The raider spun around, yelping with pain, his gun discharging into air. His partner lay on his back in the motionless limpness of death.

Moving carefully on the slope, half sliding at times, Cleve made his way to the wounded man, yelling out, "Don't move or I'll shoot you again! Let that iron go!"

The gun slipped from the groaning raider's hand. Cleve walked over and picked it up. He stuck it in his belt.

"Cleve Trewe!" came Meeker calling from below. There were shouts of alarm from the logging camp.

"They're down!" Cleve shouted back. "Hold your fire and come on up! I need someone to help me carry this man . . ."

It was dark and windy when Berry came back to the little mountainside camp she shared, just for the night, with Gil and Freja. She set the lantern beside the pitted, black-stone boulders that sheltered their fire and bedding, and looked down the dark slope, faintly limned by moonlight. Far below, the windows of the Lambsville houses glimmered from the light of fireplaces and lanterns. Above, the stars showed in piercing blue-white glimpses between the speeding clouds.

"Was it really necessary for us to accompany Berenice up here, Gil?" Freja asked in irritation, as Berry hurried up to the campfire.

"The Sovereign wanted it that way, my darling," Gil said, patiently. "And we are to stay the night."

Freja, crouching at the cooking grill, looked up to see Berry. She seemed embarrassed. She hadn't realized Berry was back from the hot springs.

Berry knew that Freja was pregnant and feeling vulnerable.

"Is there anything I can do to help with dinner?" Berry asked, shivering from the cold wind despite her coat and cape.

"No, it's all right," Freja said, frowning at the fritters and beef. "How was the hot spring?"

Berry sat down on her bedroll, close to the fire. "It took a while to find one that wasn't *too* hot. It was actually a pool below the spring itself. Delightful, though I think I smell like several minerals now, especially sulfur."

"Sulfur baths are said to cure illness," said Gil, unrolling his blankets.

"Then I smell healthier now, and possibly diabolic," Berry said. "I feel parboiled, too, and sleepy. But it was fascinating—the heat I was enjoying came from deep underground. It has a connection to molten rock beneath us! The energies available under a dormant volcano make one wonder if they could be harnessed for machinery—or if the hot water could be piped to houses. The crystalline deposits around the edge of the fumaroles suggest that—"

She broke off when she heard Freja's pained sigh. The Pecks often seemed quietly annoyed when Berry waxed scientific.

Berry cleared her throat, and said, "I'll get the plates. I'd very much like to wash that pan too . . ."

She did the chores, wondering where Cleve was, and if he was safe. There were said to be dangerous men on the far side of the valley. For all Berry knew, he could have been ambushed and killed. She had left things painfully unsettled between them. She had nearly made up her mind—and she badly wanted to see him again. There was much to resolve between them.

After the chores were done, Berry was more than ready to bed down. Then they all heard a horse's hooves.

The horseman came clopping up the trail, riding a dappled-gray Irish Draught. Berry had seen that horse breed used in fox hunting when she'd visited England. And the rider, Magnus Lamb, was wearing a red-and-black fox-hunting jacket, white trousers, glossy black boots, black gloves, and a black-billed cap. His ears and nose were red from the cold as he reined in at the edge of camp.

"Sovereign!" Gil said, standing up. He had a stick in his hand he'd been about to add to the fire.

"Gilbert Peck, candidate for settlement!" called Lamb in orotund tones. "Do you and Mrs. Peck still desire to move into God's Reward?"

"We—we do, Sovereign! I'm ready to work! We need only a home—my wife is with child!"

"Then—I will speak to you privately."

He backed his horse up, onto the trail, and Gil went meekly to him. Lamb looked down from horseback and they spoke in low voices. Berry couldn't hear what they were saying. She saw Lamb point at Freja.

How had Lamb known exactly where they'd be camping? Had someone followed them and reported to him?

Berry glanced at Freja. Saw the fear on her face.

In a few minutes, Gil returned to Freja. "He wants to talk to you," he said, rubbing his hands against the cold as he stared into the fire. He seemed unnerved, uncertain of himself.

"What—what about?" Freja asked.

Gil glanced at Berry. "He'll tell you. Freja—I'm not sure—I—"

"I'll talk to him!" declared Freja, standing up and stalking back along the trail to Lamb.

She spoke to him for two minutes, shaking her hand, putting her hand over her mouth. Then she turned and, hugging herself, walked back to Gil. "What did you say to him, Gil? What was your . . ."

Gil took her in his arms. "Either we *believe* or we . . ."

She pushed him away and went to kneel by the fire, face in her hands, shoulders shaking.

Berry knelt beside her. "What did he say, Freja?" she whispered.

"I can't tell you . . . I can't . . ."

Yet Berry thought she knew. She got up and walked up the trail to where Magnus Lamb waited, sitting on his horse, smoking a pipe. She noticed he had two large, old-fashioned horse pistols hanging from the horn of his saddle. She stepped up to the horse and patted it. "A beautiful Draught, is your horse. What is her name, Mr. Lamb?"

"Victoria. She's named after the queen of England. Someday the queen will be as obedient to me as this Victoria. I was just purposing to come and speak to you, Berenice."

Berry was a little startled by his use of her first name. She let it pass. "What was it you have asked of Freja, Mr. Lamb?"

"Only that she submit to the will of God and his earthly

sovereign," he said smoothly. He pointed the stem of his pipe at her. "What will you do, Berenice? You and Mr. Trewe. Do you know his mind? Will you two be staying? I have a place for him here. A most special place."

She looked calmly up into his eyes. "If what you intend for Freja is what I think it is, I will depart as soon as I can rejoin Cleve, Mr. Lamb. And I will try to persuade Gil and Freja to go with us."

His thick black eyebrows lofted. "Indeed! You would persuade them to be heretics? Do you know how God punishes those who turn their backs on Him?"

"I heard that you exile doubters," she said. "A young man and his wife left . . ."

"Once they're out in that untamed world, Berenice, I lift my protection from them." He tapped the dottle from his pipe out, so the ashes fell on her boots. She stepped back a little, as he added, "God's punishment is swift. Sadly, the bodies of Leonard and Andrea Monroe were found about an hour ago. They were murdered by nameless highwaymen."

Berry shivered, and it wasn't from the wind. Lamb looked at her flatly, daring her to accuse him. She returned his cold gaze, and said, "Is this a cautionary tale for me and Cleve? I will give you a piece of advice—*do not threaten Cleveland Trewe*. Not with words, or actions. You see—Cleve Trewe is, whether you know it or not, the most dangerous man you have ever encountered." This was no bluff, in her mind. It was what she believed.

"Is he now? Is that a threat from *you*, woman? You are saying you will set him on me like a dog bred for fighting?" Before she could answer he leaned toward her, so close she could smell brandy on his breath, and said, "Do not suppose that you or Cleve Trewe can do me the slightest harm! If I so choose . . . and I'm sorely tempted even now . . . I can send God's wrath upon him. He is not dangerous to me—because he is not dangerous *to God*, my dear. Why, if I like, I can keep *you* as my chattel, my thrall—my evening's amusement. And he could do nothing about it. Now, I bid you good night."

With that Magnus Lamb turned his horse, so quickly she had to step out of the way, and he cantered off, down the hillside.

Chapter 12

"We want to hang him," said Meeker. "And we are going to hang Milt Dumanis right now."

"Can't let you do that," Cleve said, shaking his head.

Five men with lanterns and one with a torch stood in a circle close in front of him. Cleve was blocking the entrance to Wardwell's tent, his hand on the holstered Colt. The lanterns and torch made a circle of quivering light around them. Other loggers stood behind Meeker and the men with lanterns, some with axes in their hands, one with a shotgun. Every face he could see was scowling.

Wardwell had told Cleve to take the wounded man into his own tent. Cleve planned to keep watch there while Wardwell slept in the chuckwagon.

"You used to be a lawman," Meeker said. "But you are one no longer. You have no authority here."

"That's right," Cleve allowed.

"So you'll step aside?"

"I will not. I do not hold with vigilante hangings. This man was after some horses, but he didn't steal any. And your necktie party is not lawful in any case."

"What do you think Lamb will do, if you turn the man over to him? Lamb was a justice of the peace in England,

and he thinks he's one here. He had a man hung already, the very day he judged him."

"What was he hung for?"

"He tried to break into Lamb's home! He was a thief like this man."

"I wasn't thinking of giving Dumanis to Magnus Lamb. What did you do with the raiders' horses?"

"One of them pulled up his picket and run off. The other one we got—we're going to sit this man Dumanis on his own horse to hang him."

"I'll need that horse. I'm going to take Dumanis with me when I go tomorrow, if he lives that long. I'll find some law for him."

"No law 'round here! There was a U.S. Marshal came through, but story is he got bushwhacked. The law don't like to come up here. We got to do this ourselves, Trewe! We need to string him up where his partners can see him!"

"We already hung up the other one for 'em!" called a man behind Meeker.

Cleve grunted. "You hung a dead man?"

"That's right," Meeker said. "You don't know what it's been like, having to watch our backs all day and night with those raiders out there!"

There was a general murmur of agreement at that. Cleve saw Wardwell striding up, then. "You bringing the rope, Wardwell?" Cleve asked. His mood had turned sour.

Wardwell shook his head. "I do not condone what these men plan. But I came to tell you that I cannot stop them. I don't have the authority—and I have to work with them."

"Hell, the weather's likely to change any day now," Cleve said. "You'll be done logging for the year. You can all go home. You'll be safe from the Red Feather bunch. "

"Can't be sure of that!" Meeker snapped. "You going to make us fight you?"

Cleve slowly shook his head. "It's your decision. But if I have to fight, I'll shoot you first, Meeker, and then that man with the shotgun." His hand tightened on his gun. "Then we'll see how many more I can get." He gave them a wicked grin that made some eyes widen. "I'm ready to die, Meeker. How about you?"

Meeker clenched his fists . . . and then spat at the ground near Cleve's feet.

Cleve didn't move. He kept his gaze on Meeker, and waited.

Meeker's shoulders slumped. "The hell with it." He turned and walked hurriedly off.

Cleve's eyes swept on the man with the shotgun. "Level that Parker if you think you're going to use it," he said.

The man licked his lips—and turned away. Shaking their heads and cussing Cleve, the loggers walked off toward their tents.

Wardwell asked, in an undertone, "Would you have killed those men?"

"There was some bluff. But I wouldn't have let 'em take him. Going to need that man's horse in the morning,."

"I'll stake it out here myself."

Cleve looked after the loggers, decided they had genuinely given up, and went back into the tent. He picked up a lantern and went to hold it over the wounded man lying on a folding cot against the back of the tent.

Milt Dumanis blinked up at the light. "Where's my hat?" he asked.

"Up there on the hillside. But we got your horse nearby."

Milt Dumanis had about four days growth of beard, and long dirty black hair over his collar. His winter coat was laid over him to add warmth to the blanket. His boots had been pulled off, and they reeked.

Cleve had dug the bullet out, washed the wound with a

little of the Overholt from his saddlebag. He'd given the raider a good slug of the whiskey too.

"You hear what those boys out there said?" Cleve asked him.

"Some. They want to hang me."

"I might just let 'em too."

"You said you wouldn't. I heard you."

"Considering changing my mind. You wouldn't tell me much before. Better think about it again."

"You give me some more whiskey? Helps with the pain."

"If I think you're telling me the truth when I ask you a question, I'll give you whiskey."

Dumanis gave a slight nod. "Ask me."

"You seen a young Indian up this way? I don't know what he calls himself. His Bannock name's Ejupa."

"There's an injun in Blasted Pine. Younger'n me and I'm only twenty-three. We call him Coyote, 'cuz he says he's one."

"Where is he now?"

"Last I knew, tied to a wagon wheel. He got on the wrong side of Sedge."

"Sedge? That wouldn't be *Coop* Sedge?"

"That's him. Goes by Hawk now. Got him a red feather in his hat. Thinks it's a sign or something. He's a quarter Kiowa his own self."

Cleve nodded. "We hunted him in Colorado, once. I wondered where he'd got to. What's his fight with Coyote?"

"There's a few women in Blasted Pine. Corinna's one— if she's still alive. Coyote wanted Corinna, but Sedge figured he owned her. She gave Coyote a free poke, and Sedge got mad and the boy told him to kiss his red ass and Sedge shot at him, nicked his head. Knocked him out cold. So then he tied him to that wheel and set to beating him. Probably dead by now. The girl—no one's seen her for a while. I figured she was dead too. One of the reasons I lit out of town. Man can only stomach so much.

So Ejupa was tied to a wheel and beaten? Cleve shook his head. He'd probably have to bring a dead man back to the Bannock. But bringing the body home would still fulfill his vow.

The raider shifted a little, then gritted his teeth. "I think that bullet busted my shoulder bones."

"It didn't."

"How you know?"

"You don't have that kind of swelling. What's the population in Blasted Pine?"

"Not much over a hundred men. But it changes some. Maybe sixteen women there now. Never counted 'em, but there aren't many. Where's that whiskey?"

"Comin' up. Those men all with Sedge?"

"No, they mostly keep shop or prospect or trap and such. Sedge, he's only got a few men and they don't know what they're doing."

"And you do?"

"Hell, no. I'm no outlaw. I was just trying to get some horses to sell down to Poverty Flats. So's I could take the train south. Skeet talked me into it. He's the one you kilt."

"Didn't give me any choice. Hold on now." Cleve went to his saddlebags, and got the whiskey. He had a couple pulls on it himself and poured the rest in a mug for Dumanis.

"In the morning," Cleve said, "we ride for Blasted Pine . . ."

Berry, Gil, and Freja were having a breakfast of cider-simmered oatmeal, with dried apples and milk.

Silence reigned over the wooden table. The only sound

was the click of spoons on wooden bowls, and the sound of pinewood crackling in the potbellied stove. Freja was only toying with her oatmeal. Gil glanced at Freja. "You should eat, Freja. We need our strength. We will have much to do today, when we go to the Abode."

Freja said only, her voice a whisper, "Where does the milk come from?"

"There is a cow barn in a vale a little south of the cabins. And a pasture. Perhaps you will work there, when I'm doing the figures for the Sovereign. You always liked cows."

Freja didn't answer. She stirred her oatmeal and said nothing.

"Irma tells me that there are generally two families in each house," Berry said. "And there are people called 'Server Caste' who live in the turrets."

"There are castes here?" Freja said, frowning. "They apparently . . . are servants?"

"Yes," Gil said. "So I . . . yes I believe so. The castes—Lamb spent some time in India."

"And yet in his homeland there are already castes," Berry observed, "but they aren't called that. How many castes are there in the settlement?"

"Three—well, four really. Above the *Servers* are the *Faithful*. I and Freja will be Faithful, like my cousin. But the Servers can become Faithful if they serve a time without complaint. The Sovereign decides how long that takes. The Apostles are a high rank of Faithful—we are to obey them. Above the Faithful are the *Chosen*. Not many of those. Freja—you must eat!"

She shook her head.

Berry put her spoon down and said, "Freja. You don't have to accept what Lamb asks of you. You do not have to go to that man's bed."

She looked bleakly at Berry. "Berenice . . . Do you

know what happened to the Monroes? They were killed out there. Because they left."

"That was . . . that was *God's* doing," Gil said, not sounding like he believed it.

Berry put her hand over Freja's. "And you think if you don't give yourself up for Lamb's amusement, he'll kill you and Gil?"

"He'll exile us!" Gil said. "And then . . . something will happen. We won't get far."

"You know he had those people murdered, don't you, Gil?" Berry asked.

"I . . . I do not know. But he says it will be but once or twice she'll have to be a 'servant of God's Love.'"

Freja stared at him. "Only once or twice! And that is fine with you, Gil?"

"Well . . ." Gil closed his eyes. He swallowed hard. "I don't like it. But . . . I guess it's often done here in Lambsville. Done only for the Sovereign. Irma says in England, when an English lord chooses to, he can . . . he can just . . ."

"That happened centuries ago," Berry said. "And the Crown never approved of it. Some earls just got away with it. But here—if enough people get together and refuse Lamb, then what will the Apostles do? They can't kill everyone. If enough dissenters departed this place *in force*—they could defend each other. There are ways out of this, Gil."

Freja's lips buckled, and she covered her eyes. Her voice was muffled through her hands as she said, "They will kill us if we even *speak* of this . . . and I must do what he wants. But thereafter I will never give myself to anyone, not ever again." She lowered her hands and clenched them as she looked at Gil, her eyes streaming tears. "*No* man. No man ever."

* * *

Cleve insisted Milt shave and clean himself up some before they set out. He knew that it helped a wounded man's morale. It was going to be a painful ride for him.

But Cleve's own morale sank some when he saw the dead man hanging from the oak tree.

A small flock of crows were fighting for meat on the dangling corpse that morning. They scattered when Cleve and Milt Dumanis rode past the dead man hanging from the oak. The loggers hadn't even hooded the man's swollen face.

"Poor ol' Skeet," Milt muttered. "Me and him got drunk and he talked me into trying to steal them horses but . . . he talked himself into getting shot, and hung too, I guess." He glanced back and winced. "There go the crows, back to peck on him again. His eyes . . ."

Cleve growled to himself. "You trying to make me feel bad, Milt?" He'd taken to calling the young man by his first name, though he wasn't sure why except he kind of liked him.

"Skeet shot first. You just shot better, is all. Damn my shoulder bone hurts like a son of a bitch. 'Course, if you shot straighter at me you'd have killed me dead."

"I shot straight," Cleve said. "That's why you're not dead."

Milt looked at him in surprise. "You didn't mean to kill me?"

"Nope." He was talking mostly to keep his mind off Berry. He was a little more worried about her with each passing hour. He just did not trust Magnus Lamb. "How'd you end up with that bunch in Blasted Pine?"

"I was broke. Went to Blasted Pine because a fella told

me I could get work there. Liquor business, he said. I
thought he meant in a saloon. When I got there, come to
find out the liquor was from a still and I was supposed
to sell it to the loggers and to some other folks around
Lambsville. I knowed it was against the law—but when I
got to town, I was hungry. I had nothing to sell but my
saddle and my pistol. It was bad weather too. I needed
somewhere out of the sleet and so did my horse."

Cleve was listening closely, watching Milt's face to see
if he was making up a story. He'd heard many a piteous
and flowery story from a lawbreaker wanting to be set
free. But it struck him that Milt was telling the truth. And
likely he wasn't far along the outlaw trail.

"This saddle was a gift from my grandfather," Milt
went on. "He got it in Chihuahua."

"That's a good Mexican saddle," Cleve said. "Fine
tooling."

"I already sold the conchos off it, in Tonopah, and I was
ashamed to do it. Now the pistol . . . well I could see
Blasted Pine was no place to be without a gun."

Cleve nodded. "Where you from?"

"Kettlebough, Wyoming."

"Never heard of it."

"And I ain't heard of it since. Got tired of working on
my old man's ranch. Getting so he and I was having fist-
fights when he got drunk. And I picked up a lot of hot talk
about the silver fields in Nevada. But when I got there,
they was mostly played out."

Cleve chuckled ruefully. "I had the same experience in
Nevada."

They were riding up into the hills now, on a red clay
trail between stands of pine and Douglas fir. "How long
you had that mustang, Milt?"

"Two years. Ol' Patchy here was a wild yearling. Caught him and broke him for the saddle myself."

"Did you? Seems you're good with horses."

"My pa breeds 'em. He's too rough on a horse. That's not how you get the best out of 'em, you ask me."

"I agree with you. Seems like you could find work breaking and wrangling."

"Nothing like that in Blasted Pine. I got stuck in the butt end of the world there. You won't find any law in that burg to take me to. They haven't got a jail. Used to have a vigilance committee, I hear, but Sedge put a stop to it. Likes to call himself town marshal."

"Coop Sedge, town marshal!" Cleve gave out a short, dry laugh.

"No law in Blasted Pine. Who you going to bind me over to?"

"I doubt I'll turn you over to the law. It'd be my word against yours. And you never got hold of those horses. Maybe you can tell me the layout of Blasted Pine. Then I'll cut you loose."

"You want to get a good look from on high, we take that trail to the southwest, right up there." He pointed. "See it? It'll take us up on Ugly Joe Ridge . . ."

"You lead the way." Best Milt was where Cleve could keep an eye on him.

A cold wind picked up, whipping a rain mixed with hail at them. "Dammit, now I need my hat!" Milt said. The hail looked like rock salt, bouncing from the trail and the horses. Ulysses snorted and shook his head. Cleve could hear hail rattling off the crown of his Stetson.

The hail quit, but now the trail uphill was slicker, and the horses sometimes slipped a little.

Before long they reached the ridgetop running east-west,

and the thin trail passed along its edge. "This is Ugly Joe Ridge?" Cleve asked.

"This here's the start of it!" Milt called back to him. "Can we stop somewhere? My damn shoulder feels like there's broken glass in there!"

"You should be a stage thespian, with that drama," Cleve said. "Rein in over there under the oaks."

Dismounting, Cleve walked to the cliff's edge and saw the lower trail west below, about two hundred feet below, tracking sinuously through the rugged forestland. He glanced over at Milt who was sitting under a tree in the yellow grass. When Cleve looked back at the trail below, he saw riders coming up the trail from the east— and several more coming from the west.

Cleve drew back, took off his hat, and lay down near the cliff's edge. He crawled up a little and looked down. It brought back a memory of being on a bluff in Virginia, in command of a patrol, looking down at a regiment of Confederates coming north along the basin . . .

He banished the memory and made himself attend to the men below. Three men on the west, two coming from the east.

Cleve stared piercingly down. That floppy hat, that stubby form. The long brown hair, and beard. Was Chance Breen leading those men from the east? Looked that way.

The men met on the trail, relaxed, their postures friendly. This was an arranged meeting. The men from the west included a rider with long red hair and red beard. He waved at Breen, as if he knew him. Maybe the man who'd arranged the meeting? With Breen was a man with a furry winter hat. Hadn't Cleve seen that hat before? At the shantytown near the foot of Gunmetal Mountain— someone had called the man Judson.

The man who stood out among those coming from the direction of Blasted Pine rode a paint horse and wore a stovepipe hat. There was something red in it. A red feather?

"Coop Sedge," he whispered to himself.

Now, Cleve had a choice. He could go to his horse, get his Winchester, and cut down Breen and the others. They were all badmen, were they not? Wasn't Sedge wanted for murder—dead or alive? Wasn't Chance Breen a known killer and bushwhacker—a man who'd tried to shoot him from a hilltop?

Cleve knew he probably couldn't get them all. Still and all, there was a good chance he could bring down Sedge and Breen.

But it was just possible this wasn't who he thought it was. It was just far enough he couldn't be what his father had called "sure to the pure." His gut told him this was Sedge and Breen, and men who were just as bad.

Even if he were sure . . .

This wasn't a war. He was no Union sniper firing on a Confederate line. He wasn't even a lawman anymore. It would be killing done outside the law.

Cleve sighed. He couldn't bring himself to do it.

He watched the men who sat on their horses, jawing below, and wondered what the meeting was all about. Some skullduggery of Breen's, he figured.

The man had tried to kill him twice. And twice Breen had gotten away. And now he was letting him go a third time.

"Son of a bitch," he muttered.

Cleve crept back from the cliff, put on his hat, and walked over to Milt. "How far are we from the overlook for Blasted Pine?"

Milt rubbed his wounded shoulder and winced. "Oh—twelve, fifteen miles."

"Is there a way down to the town from there?"

"If a man is careful, yep."

"I'd like to let you go now, Milt—but I can't take the chance you've got ties to Sedge."

"Hell, the man scares me. I never wanted to work for him."

"I believe that. But just now I saw Sedge down on that trail. I need to get to town before he gets back. That'll simplify matters. You going to go with me, or do I have to tie you up and come back for you?"

Milt got to his feet, groaning. "I'm coming."

"We're going to have to ride hard."

Milt snorted. "Wouldn't you know it! You got anything to eat? And maybe some water?"

"Dried jerky, couple of biscuits, and a canteen of water."

"That'll do me."

"You'll get your victuals in the saddle. Let's ride."

Chapter 13

An hour after breakfast, Apostle Carmody came to show the Pecks the house they were to move into once "the rite of initiation, in all its phases," had been completed.

Berenice was allowed to come along to see the Abode of Reward. As she looked around, it seemed to Berry they would be rewarded with an overcrowded, drafty Abode, not quite finished—constructed in haste—and with a leak in the roof. Those in the Server Caste seemed sickly, their faces pinched with worry. Their caste was not fed as well as the others. They lived in garrets, just under the roof. The Faithful—mostly women, the men being at work—looked to be edgy from the crowding. There were already fourteen people in the house and the Pecks were to share a room with a white-bearded grandfather, who was confined to bed with a racking cough . . .

Freja reacted to all this in silence, looking miserably resigned to her fate.

When Berry took Freja aside, whispering that she should not commit herself to this home, she felt a hand on her upper arm—and turned to see Apostle Carmody looking coldly at her.

"You are no longer to sow discontent where there

should be gratitude," said Carmody. "Go now. Leave them to their own affairs."

She snatched her arm from his grip. "I will not insist on staying. Never put your hand on me again, sir."

Berry smiled at Freja. "I'll talk to you this evening."

Carmody stalked to the front door, held it open, and looked at Berry pointedly. With great dignity, Berry walked unhurriedly past him, into the windy morning, and made her way up to the cottage.

Now, as she waited for her tea water to boil, Berry was reading Emerson's "Nature," always a palliative to her mind. It was one of six books she'd brought in her bags on leaving Axle Bust. *"The whole code of her laws may be written on the thumbnail,"* Emerson wrote. *"The whirling bubble on the surface of a brook admits us to the secret of the mechanics of the sky. Every shell on the beach is a key to it. A little water made to rotate in a cup explains . . ."*

Then the door suddenly opened and Irma was there, a small book in her hand. She looked prim, and a little angry, like a thwarted schoolteacher as she swished across the boards in her long dress and sat down across from Berry. "Here," she said, "is the *Voice of the Rose.*" She pushed the book across the table. Berry did not reach for it.

"Cleve has a copy," Berry said. "I have had a look into it."

"May I ask what it is that you are reading?"

"Mr. Ralph Waldo Emerson."

"Emerson! The American paganist?"

"No, Irma," said Berry calmly. "He is not a paganist, though some have called him a pantheist . . . He believes in the Over-soul—that human souls all have a connection to God, and that God is everywhere—woven into the substance of the universe." She heard the *boom* of the cannon from the mountainside above them. "It sounds as if the Sovereign is making an appearance."

"He often takes a walk to inspect the settlement, at this hour."

Berry stood up, for the teapot water was aboil atop the potbellied stove. "Will you have some tea?"

"Yes, I thank you. The Sovereign has given us the gift of a fine oolong."

"A cup of tea is marvelous support for a philosophical debate . . ." Berry made them both tea and brought it to the table in ceramic mugs, doubting she could change Irma's mind about anything at all. Irma had followed Magnus Lamb here all the way from England.

"As for apostasy," Berry said, setting down the teacups, "is not Magnus Lamb a heretic? Would the Church of England or the Catholic church accept that he is the . . ."

"The what?"

"I take it he presents himself as the current messiah?"

"The corrupt men who lead those churches are blinded by the devil," said Irma sniffily, stirring sugar into her tea. "That is why the Sovereign was crowned—to set us free from the guidance of blind men. The Sovereign knows the true will of God."

Berry gave her a look of innocent inquiry. "And Magnus Lamb's insistence on *adultery*—at least for himself and the women he chooses . . . is *that* truly the will of God?"

Irma went very still. A mottled blush appeared across her chipmunk cheeks. "There are . . . matters that are not given to you and me to understand," she said, her voice grating. "He has his reasons—he must create more children, *holy* children—!"

"Irma, I dislike to disparage your beliefs, but in this—" A knock came on the door. "Come in!" called Berry.

The door opened, and Berry was surprised to see Eliza Lamb standing there. She wore an open ermine stole, and a tight white dress with red-lace fringes. Around her neck was a fur scarf, a fox victorine. To Berry's astonishment the dress exposed Eliza's knees. They were cream-white and dimpled.

Irma turned and gawped at Eliza's dress. "Oh!" Clearly Irma was scandalized.

Berry noted that Eliza carried something wrapped in a brown paper package. It was about the size of a brandy bottle.

Eliza's green eyes searched the cottage. "Where is Cleve?"

"You were with us when your father gave him a job to do, I believe," Berry said. She was surprised at her own snappish response. "He went to see about certain matters at the lumber camp."

"Yes but—I thought surely he'd be back by now. It's not so far away." She stamped a foot and pinched her lips. "How very disappointing! I have brought him a gift."

"Have you?" Berry made herself smile. "You can leave it for him. I'm sure he'll be back tonight or tomorrow." She wasn't at all sure of that, but the words came out of her mouth as if she were. Once more Berry was surprised at her own tart responses to this woman.

"Eliza," Irma said, "we are about to read from the *Voice of the Rose*. If you would like to join us—"

"No," said Eliza, waving a hand dismissively. "Go away, Irma, I wish to speak to Mrs. Tucker alone."

Irma drew her head back and pursed her lips. "Really! I . . . this is . . ."

"Irma!" said Eliza—so sharply that Irma jumped a little in her seat. "What caste are you?"

"I . . . I am of the Faithful," Irma stammered. "But—"

"And which am I?"

"You are . . . of the Chosen!"

"Then do not disobey me. Get out!"

"Irma," Berry began, "you don't have to go."

But Irma snatched up the *Voice of the Rose* and fled, almost running past Eliza.

Eliza closed the door after Irma and sat at the table.

"Won't you have a seat?" Berry said dryly.

Eliza put the package on the table and the sound it made convinced Berry it was a bottle of some fluid. The chances that it was not liquor seemed microscopic.

"Tell me about yourself and Cleve, if you please, Mrs. Tucker," said Eliza, frowning at the tea mug. "I am unclear on the matter. You're not married to—you keep what I assume is your married name?"

"I am a widow. I have not yet had occasion to change my surname," Berry said coldly. "I suppose it's permissible for you to call him Cleve. Even people he arrested called him that."

Eliza's green eyes narrowed. "Do you know who you're talking to?"

"If you're referring to your caste status—it has nothing to do with me. I do not believe in castes. Nor class, really."

"Ho!" Eliza said. "Are you a female Guy Fawkes, then?"

Berry drank a little tea, and said, "You *do* know there was a revolution here, already, don't you? Britain lost the war. We have a republic now."

"Do not be supercilious with me, Mrs. Tucker!" Eliza leaned toward Berry. "Clearly you will never be one of my father's—"

"Sheep?" Berry interrupted. "I certainly will not be a sheep."

Eliza's nostrils flared. "I believe I will be indiscreet—and tell you that Cleve has made it clear he desires me! In the absence of passion from you, he must turn to me! He wishes to be my lover, my husband—the hero of my hopes and dreams!"

Berry tried to show no emotion. She really did her best. But the sneering half smile on Eliza's face showed Berry she'd failed. "You are simply lying, and you underestimate Cleve," she said, aware that her voice was hoarse. "He is not so easily taken in by your sort. He has known too many women of the streets . . ."

Eliza jumped to her feet. "I have had enough of this disrespect! You shall vacate this cottage now! Get your goods, get your horse, and ride out!"

Berry toyed with her tea mug. "I think not. But I will be free to leave when Cleve comes back. If your father wants me to leave the settlement—then I will go. It is his land after all. But let him come and tell me in person."

Eliza stared stiffened as if she'd felt a chill blast of air on her neck. Then she reached out, snatched up Berry's cup, and threw it at her. The mug struck Berry between the breasts and the tea sloshed across her dress.

Berry almost stood up and slapped Eliza. It's what she wanted to do. But she gritted her teeth—and smiled. "Is that how you exhibit your higher . . . class?"

Eliza pointed a finger at Berry. "I will see my father— and he will see you *gone!*" Then she picked up her package and stalked out, slamming the door behind her.

Berry stared after her, wondering—could it be true? Had Cleve surrendered to Eliza, so soon?

The wind had died down and the late afternoon sun pierced the thinning clouds, but it was still cold up on that ridge as Cleve had a good look at the rattletrap construction that was Blasted Pine.

He was down on one knee on the edge of a chaparral, looking down at the shacks and small buildings following the wavery line of the creek. The creek ran roughly—very roughly—east to west. Cottonwoods lined its crooking bank and so did the rickety buildings, and the road. They were all on the creek side. Cleve could see a dozen horses tied up along the crooked road. Smoke drifted from shacks and one big building that dominated the middle of the stringy town. "That the general store—that big building?"

"No, that's Burton's Saloon. Top floor is whores. Burton's store is that building painted yaller about a hundred steps past the saloon."

There were clusters of men standing outside the saloon, something glassy in their hands. Probably beer steins. "Looks kinda crooked-y from up here, don't it," said Milt, coming to squat beside him.

"It does. The street's shaped like a sidewinder."

"Fittin' too. Even before Sedge got in, Bob Burton, fella that runs the only store in town, he was cheatin' people from here to Sunday."

"This a mining town?"

"The way I heard it, the town started with some gold panners who didn't come up with much, then they decided that the trail would make a good route for settlers going west, what with the creek, and a heap of game. They built it up till the settlers stopped coming—they were taking the Applegate as shorter. So Burton commenced stillin' whiskey. Then comes Sedge to horn in." He grimaced, rubbing his wounded shoulder.

"Don't rub that wound," Cleve said. "You'll dislodge the bandage and start bleeding again."

"Commenced bleeding about two miles back, with all that galloping."

"We'll change the bandage, first chance."

Cleve's nostrils twitched. "I can smell the corn liquor cooking."

"Yep. You can't see it from here—there's a building,

past the saloon, where the ridge sticks out on the south. Couple of fellas keep an eye on it."

"I can see its smoke . . ."

"Closer in, you see that wagon, part way down the road? There's a building in the way, but you can see the tongue."

"I see it. That where Ejupa is?"

"Last I knew. Can't tell from here."

Cleve nodded.

"Can we get down at the west end, close by?"

"Yep. But it's steep. Mostly it's bighorns take that trail."

"We've got good horses. They'll handle it. Let's mount up."

Ulysses and Milt's mustang carried the two men down the steep trail—Patchy leading the way—with only a few skids and nervy moments. Cleve could hear the swishing and rumbling sound of the rushing creek as they got to the muddy road. They rode into town at a walk, side by side.

"You sure you don't want to give me my gun back, here, Cleve?" asked Milt.

"Mama didn't raise any fools," Cleve said.

"Seems she raised a son that figured one gun against a dirty town was better than two."

Cleve chuckled. "That makes too much sense. Well, all right. But I'll shoot you if you crawfish me, if it's the last thing I do."

"I give you my solemn word, before my granny in heaven, I won't turn that gun on you."

Cleve leaned back in his saddle, tugged Milt's gun from his belt, and handed it over.

They moved the horses up to a trot, ignoring the stares of men at their shacks—some of the men with piles of hides close by. Trappers. Others had no clear occupation.

They seemed bored men, with some unnamed anger simmering in them as they watched the two riders.

About thirty yards before the saloon, Cleve saw the wagon. A young Indian, his bare chest streaked with blood, was sitting on the dirt with his back against a rear wagon wheel. His braids had been cut away, probably to humiliate him, and his hair hung raggedly. His broad, high-cheekboned face was marked with bruises and cuts. He wore only buckskin pants and a pair of muddy farmer's boots. His arms were raised and tied to the rim of the wheel, his head drooping limply. They could see no sign of life.

"I guess you're too late, Cleve," Milt said. "He done died on you."

Chapter 14

Cleve drew up closer to the wagon and dismounted, walked over to Ejupa—and heard the *click-click* of a gun cocking.

"Now just what the hell do *you* want?" growled a voice to his right.

Cleve glanced over and saw a bulky, bearded man on a chair. The man was pointing a Smith & Wesson Schofield at the center of Cleve's chest. He was sitting out of the wind in the cobwebbed door of a barbershop. The gunhand wore a buckskin coat and a dirty-yellow derby that seemed small for his big shaggy head.

"Just having a look," Cleve said. "You keeping an eye on him for someone?"

"That's right," rumbled the man. "You got some business here?"

"On my way to get a jug."

Milt rode a little closer and said, "Howdy, Tursk!"

The man with the Schofield glanced up at Milt. "You come back, I see. You here with this fella?"

"I am."

"Where's Skeet?"

"Shot dead. Tried to steal a horse. I'm just here to see Sedge about some whiskey."

"Sedge ain't here. He's down the trail. You can buy it from Burton or up at the store."

Milt nodded. "I was just wondering how you come to be guardin' a dead man."

"Oh, I don't think he's dead. Hope not, Sedge don't want him to die too quick." Tursk holstered his gun and walked over to examine Ejupa. "He's out, is all. I whupped him some because he spat at me."

"You whupped him when he was tied up?" Cleve asked.

Tursk squinted at Cleve. "What's that to you?"

"I think I'll take this boy with me, alive or dead," Cleve said matter-of-factly. "His folks want to see him."

Tursk's mouth dropped open. "*Take* him?" He dropped his hand to his Schofield. Then he looked at Cleve's eyes—and hesitated.

"You got a Smith & Wesson Schofield, I see," Cleve said. "That's a good gun. What do you say, Tursk, we find out how you handle it?"

"What?" Tursk blinked. "I got no time for target shooting."

"I don't mean target shooting," Cleve said. "Will you watch my back, Milt?"

"Yep," Milt said.

Cleve's hand went to his Colt. Tursk bared his teeth and pulled at his Schofield. He nearly got it clear of his holster before Cleve shot him between the eyes.

Tursk stumbled one step back—and went down like a felled tree.

"Holy God!" Milt blurted.

Cleve looked around, saw some men watching from up the street, near the saloon, but no one made a move.

They just stared. Cleve turned to look more closely at Ejupa. The young man was still breathing.

Milt dismounted and went to look at Tursk. "Dead center! If I ever get on the bad side of you—just give me room to run, will you, Cleve?"

Cleve holstered his gun and unsheathed his knife. "If I'd shot every man who got on the bad side of me the law would've hung me by now." He knelt by the bloodied captive. "*Hey-ah*, Ejupa! Can you hear me?" He patted Ejupa's face a couple times. "You in there, boy?"

Ejupa gave a slight gasp. He blinked with swollen eyes, and then squinted at the knife in Cleve's hand.

"Washakoh sent me," Cleve said. "And Panok. Hold still, now."

He sawed through the rawhide and freed Ejupa's wrists. The young man sagged with a groan.

Cleve turned, peered through the window of the closed-down barbershop, saw the chair was still set up inside. "Let's take him in there, let him lay back, clean him up some." Then he looked up at Milt. "Unless you want to ride out now."

"Oh, I'll stick with you a skosh longer. I need a rest from that saddle. My shoulder's hurtin' something fierce."

Keeping an eye on the men down the street, Milt dismounted and led the horses over to a water trough by the abandoned barbershop. He tied Ulysses and Patchy to a hitching post as Cleve picked the dazed Indian youth up in his arms and carried him to the barbershop. One hard kick and the door splintered aside. Cleve lugged Ejupa inside and put him in the dusty old barber chair. He tilted it back so Ejupa was semireclining.

"Washakoh . . ." Ejupa murmured.

"You rest right there, Coyote boy. I'll see what I can find to clean you up."

Milt came in carrying a canteen. Cleve took it and gave Ejupa a little water. "Doesn't look like he's been shot, Milt."

"Don't know how he lived through the night. But there's a dirty old blanket on the ground out there. Maybe that girl snuck it out to him."

"Could be. Wonder where she is now?"

Milt looked at Ejupa, and said, "Probably hiding . . . Sedge and them others might come back anytime, Cleve."

"I have a notion about that. Right now, I'm going trust you with some money." He took two double eagles from a vest pocket and handed the gold over. "You go on to Burton's store, get some linen for bandages, some rubbing alcohol if they have it, willow bark, lye soap, liniment, a blanket, and some cartridges. And something to make soup with . . . Maybe dried peas." He had a small pan in his saddlebags. There was a stove in the corner. He could heat up water on that if he could get some dry wood in here. He thought about asking Milt to buy laudanum for Ejupa, but he'd known men to become opium addicts from drinking laudanum when they were poorly, and he didn't want to be responsible for that.

"You don't want me to get him some whiskey?"

"Why is it you cowboys think whiskey cures everything?"

"If it don't cure you, you don't much care, I guess."

"If they have no rubbing alcohol, bring whiskey. Some beef or venison . . . and see if you can get Bob Burton to come over here."

"Burton? You want to see him?"

"Got a proposal for him. You said Sedge took the liquor concession from him?"

"Yep. It's all got to come from Sedge now. He makes Burton pay him a good price to keep it in his store."

"Then tell him I can get him his concession back. They know you here, so I figure you'll be all right. Go on now . . ."

Berry had her rifle leaning against the table, within reach of her chair. She stared at the Winchester and wondered if she would be wise to point it at Carmody, should he show up, or whoever Lamb or Eliza sent. She'd changed into trousers and a blouse, and made an attempt to wash her tea-stained dress. It was drying on a line near the stove. But it would always be blotted.

When the door opened, it was Gil, holding it open for Freja. He followed her inside and closed it after them. Her mouth quivering, Freja sat at the table. She glanced at Berry's clothes, and the drying dress. "What happened to your dress?"

"Eliza Lamb threw a mug of tea at me."

"That woman," Gil said, "isn't what she pretends to be. She acts the saint in the church, but I have heard stories about her and some of the men . . ."

Freja glanced at him. "You shouldn't repeat such things." She looked at her hands. "But it wouldn't surprise me. The apple doesn't fall far from the tree."

"Freja," said Berry, leaning toward her, "what did you think of the . . . the 'Abode'?"

"It was awful," Freja said, tears in her eyes. "It's not what Leman said it was."

"This caste thing, it doesn't feel right to me," said Gil. "These people they call Servers—they're no different than anyone else. They just didn't find the right ears to whisper to."

"Did anyone hurt you, Freja?" Berry asked, taking her hands.

"No. But that place, it's like a jail on the inside. And

Carmody! He told me that Lamb wants me to come to him tomorrow night."

"It's getting on to sunset," Gil muttered. "Best have some light . . ." He went to light the lantern over the table.

Freja whispered, "Some of those people told us they'd like to leave here, Berenice. But they're scared. And it's so far from anyplace and . . ."

"Tomorrow night," Berry said. "That'll give us time, Freja! Cleve will come back, I'm sure of it. But if he doesn't soon—we'll get out."

Freja shook her head. "I want to leave, Berenice—I don't see how we can leave at all unless it's on foot! You can't slip a wagon and an ox past them. At this time of year—that could be fearful perilous."

"Gil," Berry said, glancing at the door. "Are you willing to leave Lambsville—if we can slip away?"

He sighed and took Freja's hand. "I am," he said. "But I surely do wonder if we can do it and live."

Cleve had just finished cleaning Ejupa's wounds, using whiskey as a disinfectant on his grisly whip marks, when Bob Burton showed up. He stood in the doorway, staring at the bandaged Indian sagged in the barber chair. Burton was a stout man with a round face, receding swept-back black hair, a neat little black mustache, and small eyes like raisins in dough. He had his hands in the pockets of his broadcloth coat.

"Show us your hands, Bob," Milt said.

Burton raised his hands and waggled his plump fingers. "No gun. Only time I tried to use one I shot off a toe."

"You come alone?"

"I did. Like you said. I took a chance you weren't lying to me. You say this gent is Cleve Trewe?"

Cleve nodded to him. "I am."

"And Milt said you wanted to do a deal with me?"

"I do."

"I'll be damned. I heard of you. And there's ol' Tursk lying in the dirt out there. I don't know who's gonna be bothered to bury him, but I suppose we better do it."

"I killed him, I'll pay for his burial," Cleve said. He glanced at Ejupa. The young Indian was lying back in the chair, listening to all that was said, watching Burton closely.

"You'll pay for the burial?" Burton said. "I heard you were a gentleman, and it seems you are. Milt said you could give me back the whiskey business?"

"That's right. Only, you'll have to put up a new building."

"Well—nothing much to that."

"Your end is, you promise not to sell any more whiskey of any kind at the Lamb lumber camp."

"You working for Lamb, are you? Not too surprised. He's got some experienced men riding for him."

"I made one deal with him, and it's about to be done with, one way or another," Cleve said. "You can sell your goods anywhere but to the settlement or the lumberjacks."

Burton nodded. "You get me back that business, you have a deal."

"If you welsh on that deal, I give you my word you won't live the new year."

Burton raised his eyebrows. "I don't usually do deals under threat."

"You do with Sedge," Milt said.

"And I can see you don't have to deal with Sedge, never again," Cleve said. "Unless of course," he admitted casually, ". . . he kills me."

Burton chewed his lower lip. "Very well. I give you my word."

Cleve went very still and looked into Burton's eyes. "It's *my* word that matters here. Don't break the deal, Mr. Burton."

Burton swallowed. "I understand." He licked his lips, then pointed at Ejupa. "What's he to you?"

"That's my business," Cleve said.

Ejupa opened his eyes and spat toward Burton. Then he snarled something in Panati. Burton scowled; Cleve smiled. "Don't mind him, Burton. You'd best get back to your store."

Burton sniffed and glanced around the old barbershop. "You know I was half owner of this place. But it went bust—most of the men in Blasted Pine don't care about being bathed or barbered. Good day to you, gentlemen."

He left the barbershop, and Milt said, "Cleve—what'd the Injun boy here say, do you know?"

Ejupa's remark happened to be a Paiute Indian expression Cleve knew. "I can offer a rough translation. He said, *Kiss my ass, you fat white bastard.*"

Milt laughed. Cleve asked, "When you went for the supplies, you talk to anybody besides Burton?"

"I talked to Gizzard Jones. He's one of Sedge's boys. He saw you shoot Tursk and he didn't seem in a hurry to come and take you on."

"I'm going to go and have a look at the 'whiskey works.' You need to stay here and keep an eye on our patient."

"Suppose he tries to run off?"

Cleve turned to Ejupa. "I have to go, Ejupa. I'll come back soon. You going to run off?"

Ejupa shook his head.

Cleve nodded. "He's picked up enough English, you can talk to him. You'll want to go out and get my rifle too."

He frowned, contemplating Milt.

Milt looked alarmed. "I get on your wrong side somehow?"

"Nope. It's just I still can't figure out how come I trust you. Being as you're a horse thief who used to work for Coop Sedge—and you're here in Sedge's town."

Milt clamped his mouth shut. His jaw worked and his eyes narrowed. "I'm not a horse thief. Skeet and me were hungry. We didn't want to work for Sedge anymore and we were broke. When a man's hungry enough he'll do things that ain't natural. Anyhow—I guess we both kind of despised that Lamb fella. And those were his horses."

Cleve nodded. "Lamb is as low as he thinks he's high. He's the kind of man who brings a big crowd down with him when he sinks to Hell."

Milt said, "Him and Sedge both."

"Okay, Milt. This Gizzard Jones say when Sedge would be back?"

"Close to sunset."

"Then I'd better set the stage for him."

The whiskey works resided in an old warehouse past the saloon. It stood within a natural recess of the ridge overlooking town, across the road from a stable. An iron chimney vented gray smoke and a reek of boiling corn. Beside the shed was a considerable pile of trash—broken jugs, sodden cornsacks, a loose coil of old rope, and charred slabs of iron.

It was the bearded guards seated in front of the shed who caught Cleve's notice as he peered around the damp stone at the ridge's base—two shaggy men in winter coats and overalls, sitting on a stack of burlap bags of dried corn. The thin rainfall dripped off the tin porch roof. The man in the tilted-back Stetson, smoking a cheroot, had a rifle propped beside him; the other had a shotgun held across his lap.

Cleve drew back and glanced around. He saw no one close by. A few men were standing a hundred yards off, around the saloon, talking. He'd stayed out of sight getting here, and no one was looking his way. He glanced toward the barbershop. He could see Ulysses, switching his tail, next to Patchy—and a buzzard was perched atop the roof of the barbershop, eyeing Tursk's body.

Cleve opened his coat, stuck his hands in his pants pockets, and started whistling "My Old Kentucky Home" as loud as he could. Still whistling, he walked around into the view of the men at the whiskey works.

"Howdy, boys!" he called, before continuing to whistle the slow, mournful Stephen Foster ballad.

They stared, bemused, as he walked up to them. "No one 'lowed here 'less you work here," said the man with the shotgun, shaking his head.

"Maybe I'll just get a job here," Cleve said. "Right now, boys, I heard this is where the whiskey's made and I've got silver in my pocket to trade for it."

"Who the hell are you anyhow?" demanded the man with the Boss hat. "I ain't seen you around."

Cleve smiled. They hadn't seen the gunfight with Tursk. They'd been back here, with no line of sight to what was happening at the barbershop. "My name's Scrimshaw," Cleve declared. "Timothy William Scrimshaw. And I done run through all the whiskey I had. That Burton store's fresh out."

"Well, we ain't to sell no whiskey here. You can buy it from Sedge when he comes back."

"Now hold on, Stan," said the man with the shotgun, sitting up straighter. "Mister—how much silver you willing to lay down for a jug?"

Stan shook his head. "Galt, you gonna to get us in a storm of trouble with Sedge."

"Now let me see here," Cleve dug a brimming handful of silver dollars out of his pocket and shoved them at Galt. "This enough?" It was several times too much.

Galt leaned forward and scooped up the silver, taking his hand off the shotgun—and Cleve drew his Colt and cracked the butt over the man's head. He gasped and flopped forward as Cleve turned the pistol to Stan, at the same time cocking it.

The coins clinked onto the ground.

Stan froze, staring into the muzzle of Cleve's six-gun. His cheroot dropped from his slack mouth.

Stan blinked and said, "What'd you say your name was?"

"I confess to misleading you boys. My name is Cleve Trewe."

Stan's eyes widened. Cleve went on, "Now before Galt here comes to, I want you to drag him behind the shed. We'll see if we can find some rope to tie him up with. Then I'll ask you to lie face down, and put your hands behind your back, so's I can tie you up."

"You gonna kill us?"

"You're alive, aren't you? I had you calculated as Coop Sedge's men, and I'd have been fine with shooting you off your perches out here. You owe your lives to a lady."

"A lady?"

"Oh, yes. She has made me feel some constraint as regards precipitous killing. But I'll do it if you make me. Did I mention dropping that rifle?"

Stan dropped the rifle.

* * *

Milt was getting increasingly nervous. Sedge was most likely coming back to town any minute now. Cleve hadn't let him in on what he was up to. Said he was going to "set the stage." Meaning what? There was no stage to this town.

Cleve's Winchester in his hands, Milt was looking through the dusty, fly-specked window, watching the road from the west. Ejupa was in the barber chair, dozing, now and then muttering in his native tongue.

Gizzard confided that Sedge was going to kill the young Indian tonight. *"He wants it done up right . . ."*

Milt glanced at Ejupa.

The hell with Sedge.

Milt realized he felt different about himself now. Something about riding with Cleve Trewe.

He stepped to the door and looked over at the horses. They were restless, and Patchy was tugging his reins, trying to pull loose from the post. They were cold and hungry. Least he could do was feed them.

He turned to Ejupa. "Hey, Coyote!"

Ejupa grunted and opened his eyes, looked around. *"Hemma!"*

"I'm going to feed the horses. Cleve's got some grain, feed bags—never mind. You know—Cleve is trying to help you, yes? You know that?"

Ejupa nodded. *"Auha."*

"You won't go, huh? No go?" He pointed at the chair. "Stay?"

Ejupa nodded once more. "Maybe so!"

"No maybes about it. How about a yes?"

"Yes!"

"Good man. I'll be right back."

"Maybe so!"

"No maybe about it."

Milt hurried out past the broken door, over to the horses. "I'm gonna feed you! Don't run off now!" He leaned the rifle against the wall of an abandoned hardware store.

He got the grain from Cleve's saddlebags, strapped a feed bag onto Ulysses, and then fed Patchy by holding double handfuls of grain in his hands. A few minutes passed. He looked down the road for Sedge.

And saw three horsemen cantering up the road, coming into Blasted Pine from the east. And one of them was wearing a stovepipe hat and riding a paint horse. *Sedge.*

Where was Cleve?

Milt looked toward the whiskey works, hidden from here by a buttress of stone framing the recess in the ridge.

And then a *whump* sounded, and a rattling *thud*. Fragments of wood and metal shot out of the recess, trailing smoke.

"Holy Hell . . ."

Milt snatched up the rifle and ran back to the barbershop.

And he found that Ejupa was gone.

Chapter 15

The wreckage of the shed was burning furiously. Towering red-and-blue flames were roaring. Dark smoke roiled out.

Lying flat, peering between rusted chunks of old iron, Cleve could feel the heat licking at the right side of his face.

Seeing Sedge and two other raiders coming, Cleve had dumped buckets of the one-hundred-eighty-proof corn liquor all around the three stills in the shed. He'd set it on fire with a flicked match and ran for cover.

But the explosion had been bigger than he'd figured on, and he was thrown down beside the whimpering, bound-up guards, watching flying fragments of rusty metal from the exploding stills. If he'd been standing, one of the jagged pieces of still would've cut him deep.

Now the explosion settled, and through the murk of smoke and dust and falling ash, Cleve saw the riders coming. One of them had that Abe Lincoln hat on. It was adorned with a red feather.

Coop Sedge and his men galloped up to the flaming ruin of their whiskey works—just as Cleve had calculated.

Cleve raised Stan's rifle and aimed at Coop Sedge. As the raiders dismounted about sixty feet away, all three of them cussing as they goggled the fire, Cleve shouted, "Coop Sedge! All three of you! Put your hands up!"

Berenice or not, Cleve knew that Sedge was a man known for murder across Colorado, and he hoped the outlaw would resist. Besides the fact that Sedge needed killing, Cleve had no way to deliver a prisoner to the authorities, short of escorting him under close guard more than ninety miles through wilderness.

Sadly, Sedge put up his hands. "We're about to be shot down, boys!" Sedge called out. "Don't give 'em a reason!"

It's like he can read my mind, Cleve thought, coughing as smoke drifted over him.

"Drop your guns and step away from your horses!" Cleve bellowed.

Unfortunately—the three men complied.

"Dammit," Cleve muttered.

Then a dark, shirtless man sprinted from behind the raiders, warbling a battle cry as he tackled Coop Sedge. Sedge went down, and Ejupa, for it was he, made a slashing motion at Sedge's throat. In the light of the fire Cleve could see blood spurting.

The other two raiders grabbed at their fallen gun belts, yanking guns—and Cleve fired twice. One round hit the raider on the left, the other missed, thanks to the smoke, which now nearly hid the man. Cleve dropped the rifle and drew his Colt as a bullet cut by, leaving a trail through the smoke just beside his head.

Coughing, he jumped over the junk pile and rushed the shooter. The figure was just a gun-toting outline in the smoke. Cleve fired at the center of the silhouette and the man cried out, falling beside the dying Coop Sedge.

Wiping his eyes and coughing as he emerged from the smoke, Cleve stopped to watch Ejupa doing a victory dance while wearing the dead man's stovepipe hat. And Ejupa had a barber's straight razor in his hand.

The razor was dripping blood.

Milt came running up then, rifle in hand, shouting, "Dammit, Coyote!" Milt stared at the dead man, then came over to Cleve, waving smoke away with his hat. "Are you . . ." He coughed.

"I'm fine and dandy. How'd he get that shaving razor?"

"I just went to feed the horses—Patchy was set to run off!"

"The razor, Milt?"

"Hell—I didn't know there was one there."

"I didn't look, myself," Cleve admitted. Then he checked around for Ejupa and saw him mounting Sedge's horse.

The young Indian waved once at Cleve—and rode away to the east.

"Oh, shit," Cleve grumbled. "Now I've got to track him. Milt—if an Indian asks you to take a sacred vow, say no."

"Well . . . okay. You set that fire?"

Cleve nodded, and waved smoke away. "To get Sedge's attention." He turned to look at the roaring flames. "That corn liquor makes a powerful blaze, doesn't it?"

"It sure does. What about the fellas guarding it? Stan's not such a bad sort. Is he dead?"

"No, they're tied up over there. Better cut 'em loose. Then—" Cleve sighed. "If you're coming with me, let's get to our horses. I need to know where Ejupa's going . . ."

It was an hour after sundown. Berenice was just finishing saddling up Suzie when Gil came to the dim little barn. He was wearing his heavy winter coat, his hat and leather gloves. And he looked woebegone.

"Did you get the horses?" Berry asked.

"A mule and a horse. The horse is old but I guess she'll do. Leman's giving that stock to me, with the saddle and tackle and all. He didn't know about what would happen to Freja here. He feels considerable sorry. I told him he could come along, but . . ." Gil shook his head sadly. ". . . he's like a lame horse in a mudhole, Berry. He can't get himself to go. I guess he'll keep my ox and wagon. I just wish there was some way . . ."

Berry shook her head. "There's no possibility of getting away with that big noisy wagon and that ox. 'Slow as an ox' is not just an adage. Where are your mounts?"

"Freja's holding them, right outside. You sure that trail by the hot springs is the best one? You saw it clear?"

"Oh, yes. It's scanty but rideable."

Gil grunted skeptically. "Irma stopped me, down the way—she was asking a lot of questions. Had to think of a story to explain the horse and the mule . . ."

Irma. That was worrisome. "Was she satisfied with your explanation?"

"I guess so. She went on to the big house, they've got her helping the cook."

"Let us go. We'll lead the horses till we're away from the lights. And let us speak only when we must, and then *softly!*"

Gil nodded resignedly and went out to Freja. Berry put out the lantern, led Suzie out the door. She closed it softly, shivering in the cold.

Freja was trembling. Gil had one arm around her. Berry smiled encouragingly at them and put a finger over her lips. Then she led Suzie off into the shadows behind the cottages. They went single file after Berry, Gil leading the mule, Freja leading the old Cob.

A faint mist was falling and the wind sighed in the oak trees. The clops of the horses' hooves seemed maddeningly loud to Berry.

But she had observed the sentries that protected the settlement at night. There were four camped on the main road, two on the back road. Another two who kept an eye on the mansion, front and back. The little trail she was taking led to the place where she had camped with Gil and Freja. From there, much sparser, it went up to the hot springs. A thin game trail curved past the hot springs, southeast around the mountain's upper slopes, and then wended downward. From there, Gil and Freja could head east to Winnemucca. Berry planned another circuitous route to look for Cleve at the lumber camp. If he wasn't there, she would ask directions to Blasted Pine . . .

Suppose Cleve came back while she was gone? It was a risk Berry was taking. She was confident Cleve would find her.

They were high enough up the trail Berry could see a light from cabins, and others, just faintly, from the Abodes.

"I think we can mount up now," Berry whispered. "Quiet as we can."

They all mounted and she led the way up the trail, between two looming boulders. Was she even on the right trail? It was dark enough she couldn't be sure. Then the clouds parted, and moonlight shone through. There— the trail cut south here. She'd almost missed it . . .

"Do you hear that?" Gil called. "Horses!"

Berry reined in. "Hold here a moment." She turned in the saddle, and listened—and heard the clatter of hurrying steeds below. It did sound like they were coming up the hill. She put her hand on the rifle—

In the next moment she saw them, rounding a volcanic outcropping. It was difficult to tell in the dimness, but she was fairly certain the lead rider was Carmody. They were moving fast, on better mounts than the mule and Freja's old horse. Berry couldn't ride off and leave Gil and Freja behind. And she couldn't shoot it out with all those men. She took her hand off the rifle.

Her heart sinking, Berry said, "Remember what we agreed to tell them . . ."

Carmody and the other Apostles were quickly upon them. Carmody had a pistol in his hand.

"Are you fearful of snakes, Apostle Carmody?" Berry asked. "Why are you waving that firearm about?"

He gave out a single barking laugh, and then demanded, "Where do you three suppose you're off to?"

"The campsite, up by the hot springs," Berry said calmly. "The Pecks wanted a place to pray in the wilderness . . ."

"Lying is a sin, Berenice Tucker!" he snarled. "Irma saw how much was packed on these horses. And at this time of night—you're running! All of you!"

So Irma had turned informer . . .

"I assure you—!"

But Freja could bear it no more and burst into tears. "Forgive us!" she sobbed.

"Turn those horses, and head back down the trail," Carmody said. "Follow my men down to the settlement, back to the barn. I'll be right behind you."

"And then?" Berry asked.

"And then . . ." Carmody's smile, yellow in the moonlight, was distinctly unpleasant. "Then Gilbert Peck will be placed into custody. Locked away in a cabin somewhere. You two women will be locked up elsewhere. Somewhere quite special . . ."

"No!" Freja cried out, and she spurred her horse hard, so it suddenly ran off the trail, into a patch of scrub. A shot banged out, the muzzle flashing across the mountainside. The horse screamed and fell heavily on its side.

Berenice rode over to Freja, Carmody yelling at her to stop. Berry dismounted and saw the horse quivering as it died. The mare's blood gushed from her neck, steaming in the cold night air. Freja was weeping with pain, her right leg caught under the dying horse.

Carmody dismounted and pushed Berry roughly out of his way. "Next time I'll shoot you!" he told her.

But Berry was staring at Mrs. Gilbert Peck. Freja was with child.

Gil rushed up to her and tried to tug her free, but she shrieked in pain.

"We'll have to pull the horse off her," Carmody said, sounding annoyed.

Berry rounded on him. "You nearly murdered her! And who knows . . ." She decided not to speak of the dangers to Freja's pregnancy in front of her.

"Stand aside, woman!" Carmody snapped, shoving Berry so she stumbled into the arms of a grinning Apostle. "Hold on to her, Benjamin!"

"You men—get a rope around that horse!"

"She will need a doctor immediately!"

"We do not have a physician as such," Carmody said. "Brother Donahue can set a broken limb. She and her husband will be seen to and locked away until the Sovereign can adjudge of them!"

"And what of me?" Berenice asked numbly.

"Peck!" Carmody shouted. "Keep that woman from shrieking in that ungodly way!" He turned to Berry. "You? You'll go to a special room in the mansion."

Cleve had to stop three times on the road east from Blasted Pine, dismounting to use the lantern to check the tracks. Each time, he was pretty sure this was the same horse's tracks—the mount carrying Ejupa. But now, stopping a fourth time, he knelt by the road and frowned.

"I told you we'd need that lantern," Milt said.

"You were right," Cleve said. "But right now, it's not telling me much. We lost him somewhere on the back trail . . ."

"He cut off the road?"

"Must have. We'll have to backtrack."

"Cleve, I'm a man used to a fair day's work and then some. But I've still got a hole in my shoulder. It's not bleeding—you rebandaged it fine—but I can hardly think for the pain right now."

"How about you camp along here, somewhere. I'll go back on my own."

"No, dammit, I . . . can't do that!"

"Why?"

"I don't know. Because—you trusted me."

"I won't blame you in the slightest."

"Hell, let's backtrack . . ." Milt clucked at Patchy and turned him back up the trail.

Cleve smiled and remounted, slinging the lantern on his saddle horn.

They went back a quarter mile and Cleve noticed a scarcely visible trail through the brush on his right. A thin game trail leading up a middling slope between hills.

"Hold on, Milt," Cleve said, tugging the reins. He climbed from the saddle and took the lantern down to study the trail as Milt rode back to him. "This is it," Cleve said. "It almost worked." He climbed back into the saddle, hung the lantern up, and doused the wick. Looking up the side trail, Cleve nodded to himself. He could see, just faintly, a light flickering up there. Reflected firelight on a boulder. "Looks like he's got a fire."

"Not trying too durn hard to hide from us," Milt said.

"I was pondering the same thing," Cleve said. "There was a rifle in a scabbard on Sedge's saddle."

"You helped this Coyote out. You think he'd shoot at you?"

"Might not be sure who we are. Or he might be pretty mad at white men."

"Guess I would be, too, in his place."

"We'll ride up slow, and find a place to dismount under cover."

"Let's do it," Milt said with a dry chuckle. "One way or another, alive or dead, I want to get out of this saddle."

Cleve led the way up the trail, going slowly. After about forty yards they came to a stunted oak that had found a spot between boulders to grow, jutting beside the trail. Here they dismounted and tied the horses to an exposed tree root.

Milt drew his gun—and Cleve reached out and grabbed his wrist, whispering, "Not unless we have to."

Milt reluctantly holstered the six-gun. Cleve started up the trail, climbing carefully in the scant light.

He stopped, hearing a singsong chant in Panati. He could make out the campfire off to his right. It took a moment for his eyes to adjust, and then he saw Ejupa half lit, seated on the far side of the fire. He also saw Sedge's rifle barrel. Ejupa was holding the rifle in one hand, like a scepter. A horse dozed, a silhouette in the darkness behind him.

In the middle of the small, sandy clearing on a wide ledge was a tree log. On the log sat a bottle of whiskey, filled with the amber fluid. It glowed with firelight.

Ejupa stopped chanting. He looked to be waiting for something.

Cleve unbuckled his gun belt and set it on a rock. "Ejupa!" he called. "We're coming in! No guns!"

"Me too?" called Milt in a loud whisper

"Yeah, you too, Milt!" Cleve said. "Drop your gun and come on up—or ride off!"

"But what if we have to fight?"

"He's not my enemy, Milt—" God willing. "—now come on!" Cleve raised his hands and walked slowly into the clearing. He heard a scuffling behind him as Milt came up the slope.

Ejupa stood up, aimed the rifle, and fired. The bottle of whiskey exploded as the bullet passed through it, about three paces from Cleve. He instinctively covered his eyes and felt whiskey-reeking pieces of glass hit his face.

"Holy bejeezus!" Milt burst out, jumping back a step. "What the hell was that?"

"That was a decision," Cleve said, wiping bits of wet glass from his face. "He was thinking about drinking that whiskey. He made his decision. And he wanted us to see it."

Ejupa walked over to him, the rifle in one hand, its barrel resting on his shoulder. He looked at Cleve, and said, "Why come?"

"I told you back in town. Washakoh sent me."

Ejupa shook his head. "Why come!"

Cleve raised his left hand into the firelight. "You see that burn mark there? I swore an oath before Panok and Washakoh, and before the sun and the moon and the earth, that I would bring you to the Panati." Cleve wasn't sure Ejupa knew enough English to understand him. But when Ejupa looked at the knife mark on Cleve's hand, he nodded.

"Washakoh—where?" Ejupa asked.

Cleve pointed northeast. "Maybe two days ride. Same camp you rode out from. I'll take you there."

Ejupa shrugged. "Maybe so."

Cleve remembered Ejupa's nickname at Lambsville. "No maybe about it. I'm taking you there."

Ejupa shook his head. "I go alone."

Cleve pointed at the burn mark on his hand again. "I swore an oath. I have to bring you."

Ejupa grunted and looked at Milt. "This one?"

"He goes where he chooses."

Ejupa shrugged. "We go. You get guns, horses. We eat, we sleep."

That's just what they did. They shared what scraps of food they had in their saddlebags and then lay on the ground near the fire, using their saddles for pillows. The fire burned low, and Ejupa went quickly to sleep.

"Seems a shame about the whiskey," Milt said.

Cleve closed his eyes. "I wouldn't drink that rotgut of Sedge's. But I wouldn't say no to a glass of good brandy . . ." His mind was set on Berenice. She was intelligent and intrepid, and Cleve had figured she'd be all right till he got back.

But was she? An uneasy feeling had been haunting him. *Don't get het up*, he told himself. Berry is most likely just fine . . .

Lying on the four-poster feather bed, Berenice could hear the voices of the guards as they changed watch outside her door. One of them said something in a jocular tone and the other one laughed. She knew who the butt of the joke would be.

Berry lay there, feeling exhausted, on the red velvet

bedspread. She was fully dressed, even wearing her coat. She was locked into a bedroom in the mansion, and she had already tried the windows. She'd moved the curtains aside—and saw the iron grates affixed outside.

Glass-and-brass oil lamps on the little tables flanking the headboard made circles of quivering light. Close to the foot of the bed was a small game table on which a chess-board was set up. The board and the chess set were made from ivory, and black volcano glass. There were two red velvet cushioned chairs facing each other across the chess-board. To the right was a fireplace, stocked with wood. She had no way to light a fire, and the room was cold. The room had a closet, in which she had found nothing useful. She had been hoping for a firearm. There was only a shelf with three cut-glass decanters of some brown liquid, and two clean crystal glasses.

To her left, between two windows, was an oil painting of Christ after his ascension, gazing worriedly down from the clouds. *Well might he show concern*, Berry thought. *He must have seen some awful things in this room.*

Under the painting was a small table with a white-glass water jug in a bowl on one side. On the other was a copper bowl covered in a bell jar and containing samples of yellow-and-white crystals.

She heard a rattling at the window, coming in irregular waves of intensity—a hailstorm. She hoped they'd put Suzie in the barn as promised. Where was Cleve? Out in this storm? Or perhaps lying dead on some trail with the hail striking his staring eyes?

Stop being so absurdly morbid, she told herself.

But Berry couldn't quite escape the picture of Freja Peck, lying there weeping with her leg broken.

Where was Gil locked up? Was Freja with him? Was

she getting any help? The guards had refused to tell Berry anything.

She had never in her life been as angry as she was now. She was angry at herself too. She should have gotten Freja through safely. And she remembered Abigail, in Piswaller.

Berenice Conroy had helped many women in her life; in Boston she had convinced her father to fund a home for unwed mothers. She had helped Black women, escaped slaves settling in Boston. She'd hired an attorney to save a suffragette from being jailed. But now she seemed cursed to bring misery to those she wanted to help . . .

That is superstitious thinking, Berry told herself. She remembered what Cleve had told her about gambling odds. Sometimes you're going to lose several times in a row, because every kind of pattern arises at random.

Still—she wished Cleve had been with them, on that hillside tonight.

Fury at the Sovereign and his lackeys flared up in her again, like a fire when you heap dry wood on it. She wanted to shout through the door at the men out there—tell them what she thought of them. But it wouldn't do any good. Nor would it help to break the window and call out through the bars. No one would come to help her. She'd heard the men talking as they'd brought her in. *"No sign of that Cleveland Trewe."* She was going to have to get out of this on her own.

Then came a clinking sound, and the door opened—and there was Magnus Lamb. He was wearing a brown tweed coat, crisply pressed brown trousers, a white silk shirt with French ruffles, and lambskin slippers. Berry could tell he was drunk, as he closed the door behind him. His motions were carried out with the slow precision of a man trying to hide his inebriation.

Lamb turned to gaze at her . . .

Suddenly, Berry realized she should most definitely *not* be on this bed.

Chapter 16

Berenice clambered quickly off the bed.

"My dear, there is no need for such nervous haste!" Lamb said, with an affable laugh. "I am not going to leap upon you like some woodland satyr!"

Berry gazed back at him with all the dignity she could muster.

"And why not take off your coat, and shoes, at least," he said. "*Hmpf!* I've never seen the like. A lady reclining with her shoes and winter coat yet upon her!"

"I will keep them on against the chill," she said.

"I shall make a fire for you!"

"No, thank you."

He snorted and shook his head as if at some willful child. With a swaggering confidence she found pungently annoying, Lamb strutted across the room to the closet. He opened it, found bottles and glasses, and began to pour libations. He was turned half away from her now, and Berry thought about the lamp nearest her, and how it might be used as a club.

"This is for you, my dear!" He stalked up to her and gave a slight bow as he offered her a glass of whiskey. "You had a bit of an ordeal. This will calm you."

She was about to refuse it, then thought she might use it somehow. Perhaps she could throw it in his eyes, blind him for a few seconds, if he tried to paw her.

For she was certain it was what he intended, sooner or later.

She accepted the whiskey, and said, with a stony exterior calm, "I assume you're here to ask me for a game of chess." Berry stepped around the chess table to keep it between them. "Shall we sit down?" Then she sat behind the black pieces, looked raptly at the board, and sweetly and politely said, "You may have white."

He gave a mix of a grunt and a chuckle and then sat down across from her. "Very well, my dear. If it will help you relax."

His opening moves were instantly recognizable as a fool's mate gambit intended to quickly end the game. She knew four responses to the gambit and chose one that made it look as if she were merely defending. He smiled and moved a bishop decisively. Berry drew him into a trap, and within ten minutes checkmated him.

Staring at the board, he said, "*Hmpf!*" And then muttered, "It may be that I'm a trifle out of practice." He took a significant quaff of his whiskey. "Will you not drink with me?"

"Oh, not as yet, if you please. Quite early for me. May I ask—those minerals, in that bell jar." It was another way to keep him distracted. "What are they?"

He looked at the bell jar. "Oh yes. Your naturalism conceit. I am interested in the healing properties of hot springs. I have 'taken the waters' many times. The minerals in the bell jar came from a man who owned this property. He thought of making it a destination for those seeking cures—but it was too distant from civilization, do y'see?"

"And the minerals? Did he identify them?"

"*Hm?* Oh, he said hydrogen chloride, as I recall—and one of the sulfurs. Sulfur tri-something, what? He said one of them had uses for etching metal, in foundries . . . I kept them, finding them interesting, a . . . visual delicacy." He drank a little whiskey, staring at her the while.

Berry didn't like the hot intensity of that stare. Best to distract him.

"Do please take the white again," she said, setting up the pieces again. "It's only fair." It gave him the advantage of being first to move. But it was no real advantage, not for Lamb. Berry decided she should draw the next game out for as long as possible, giving her time to think about how to keep Lamb at bay and escape from here.

She managed to hold off checkmating Lamb for twenty minutes, as he muttered to himself and grew increasingly restive. Best to let him win, she told herself. Then she could stall him longer. But somehow her bottled-up anger got the better of her good sense, and she checkmated him.

"Oh dear," she said.

Lamb's *"Hmpf!"* had anger in it, this time.

He stood up, took a swig from his glass, and put it back down hard enough to slop whiskey on the table. He stepped close and glared at her. "Your chess is something diabolic. That should not surprise me."

"I assure you, sir, I am employing only tactical combinations well known to the—"

"Silence!" he bellowed. He grabbed her left wrist and squeezed till she gritted her teeth with the pain. "You are playing quite another game and I won't have it! You know what you are made for and why you are here! Submit, woman—to the will of God!"

She wrenched her wrist loose and leaned away from

him. "Is that how you get your women?" she asked coldly. "By force?"

"The women who choose to serve God in this room do so with sacred ecstasy!"

Berry laughed dryly. "Sacred ecstasy! Your inflated charisma, your false miracles, and the fear of expulsion to certain death—these are the only reason these women have submitted to you. But *I* am not deceived by you—nor do I fear you!"

He fisted his hands, breathing hard, and said, "*You* poisoned Freja Peck's mind so that she attempted to flee into the depravity of the outside world! And what is the result? She is badly injured!"

"And even Magnus Lamb will not force himself on a woman with a broken leg. So you turn to me! But you will not find it an easy task! I will claw your eyes and thump your testicles! I will scream at the top of my lungs the whole time! And everyone will know that it is nothing but a rape! Your guards will gossip. You will no longer be able to sustain the falsehood—!"

Lamb slapped her with the back of his hand, so hard she felt her lips split.

Berry threw her whiskey into his eyes and he yelped as it stung him and stepped back, wiping his face with his sleeve and muttering British oaths.

Berry rose and slipped behind the chair. She picked it up with the best grip she could, and shouted, "I'll smash this into your face if you come near me, you old fraud!"

Lamb roared and grabbed the chair, twisted it from her and threw it aside so it crashed into a window. Broken glass tinkled and the chair thumped and he stood there, panting and glaring at her.

Then he laughed softly to himself, and stepped back, nodding. "You have won this round, my dear," he said softly. "You will not have the honor of intimacy with your Sovereign tonight. I shall make some *special arrangements* for you, and then I will *take* my heavenly reward. We shall see . . ."

Berry's heart was thumping, her mouth dry, and she could taste blood. "Lamb—Cleve will come back. Whatever you do to me—he will find out."

"Oh!" Lamb laughed. "Him!" He picked up his whiskey glass, drained the remainder, and tossed the glass onto the bed. "I am an experienced judge of men! I gave him the chance to join me—he put off giving a direct answer. But I saw the answer in his eyes—he would never acquiesce to God. I know that he would leave here and speak to the wrong people, in the wrong places—and he would say the wrong things." Lamb's voice dripped with contempt as he added, "He still thinks of himself as 'the Law." I sent him to get something done for me—and once he's done it, he will not be coming back. A man can be as dangerous as you like, but he cannot protect himself from the shadows, my dear. In fact, by now, it's quite likely that your Cleveland Trewe is quite *dead*, his body feeding some beast of the wild."

She stared at him in shock. Lamb gave her a mocking look of pity. "You see—at the close of my conversation with your paramour, I knew that I would make you my plaything when I was done with Freja Peck. And I knew Cleve Trewe would not be alive to stop me."

Magnus Lamb strode to the door. He unlocked it and passed through without another word.

Berry heard the angry *click-click* of Lamb locking the door from the outside.

And, still ringing in her mind, she heard *". . . it's quite likely that your Cleveland Trewe is quite dead, his body feeding some beast of the wild . . ."*

* * *

It was a damp ride, that blustery day. Rain and hail took turns hammering them. The only heat rose from their hardworking mounts as they cantered along. The rain had moved on, and the cold wind made them shiver in their wet clothes. Cleve was leading the way down the easterly road, followed by Ejupa. Milt came third, quiet and thoughtful. Ejupa wore his trophy, the stovepipe hat. He'd cut holes in the brim so it could be tied to his head with strips of leather. He wore an old double-breasted coat he'd found in Sedge's saddlebag. They rode at a canter for much of the morning.

They stopped briefly around noon, ate the last of their food, and rode on until sunset began to turn the volcanic spurs around them a bloody red. Then Ejupa spotted something in the brush. The young warrior slowly reached out, drew Sedge's rifle from the saddle scabbard, brought it even more slowly to his shoulder . . .

"What the hell is he . . ." Milt began.

Cleve put a finger to his lips and Milt fell silent. Ejupa fired and a jackrabbit gave its final jump. He ran to it with the rifle—and fired again. He came back with two jackrabbits.

There wasn't much dry wood, but Cleve found a deadfall pine, and scooped dry punk from the middle of its broken trunk. He was flat out of matches, too, and so was Milt, but he had flint and steel in his saddlebags. It didn't take long to strike a spark into the punk. Dry punk wood worked so well cowboys often carried bags of punk wood in their saddlebags, for damp days.

They found some fallen tree limbs, cut the wet bark off them, and built the fire up, as Ejupa skinned the rabbits. They cooked the meat on spits made of thick twigs. With a little salt from Milt's supplies the game meat was damned welcome. While the fire was going, Cleve made coffee and they shared it around. Ejupa relished it in particular. "Ah-ho-ah!" he said, sipping it. "Ah-ho-ah!"

The wind eased, and they decided to ride long as the horses could take it. As he cantered down the road, Cleve's mind was haunted by thoughts of Berenice.

Two hours on the trail took them to a barren region of sharp-edged lava rock. It was too dark to ride in such a place, the horses could get their hooves and fetlocks badly cut. They set up camp between three rough boulders, unsaddled the weary horses, and gave them the last of the grain.

Cleve and Milt huddled close to the small flames, Milt talking of what he might find when he rode to Southern California. Cleve said, "Tell you what, you get far south enough, find the Sweet River. It's in Sweet River Valley, west of the southern Sierras. You go upriver, come next August, you're like to find me. If you want work, I'll have it for you."

"By God, I just may take you up on that." Milt seemed pleased. He glanced at Cleve. "You figure out why you trust me now?"

"Nope!" Cleve gave him a tired grin. "Still seems crazy."

Milt laughed, and Cleve's mind returned to Berenice. A resourceful woman, smart as a whip, and a good shot. But with her being flanked by the likes of Carmody and Magnus Lamb, anything could happen. Cleve had noticed the way Lamb looked at her.

She'd never submit to Lamb, he knew that. But suppose "the Sovereign" took her refusal personally? How far would he go?

He shook his head in disgust. He never should have left her there . . .

Finish what you vowed to do, Cleve told himself, *then get back to her fast as ever you can.*

Stretched out on his bedroll, trying to get comfortable on the hard, lumpy ground, Cleve finally surrendered to fitful sleep. Now and then he woke, to listen to the night. Then he'd fall asleep again—and back into the same dream:

Cleve was riding through the arid hills and rugged passes north of Axle Bust, looking for Berenice. He could hear her voice, from time to time, calling him from the distance, echoing to him with the same words, over and over. *"Cleve, where are you? I have something to tell you! Cleve!"* He would ride up a dry wash toward the sound of her voice, and never find her—only Berry's footprints, her exact boot size, on the trail. He would follow the tracks but the wind would blow them away before they really led anywhere. Then he would hear her voice echoing faintly from another part of the parched landscape. *"Cleve, where are you? I have something to tell you! Cleve!"*

But wherever he went, she wasn't there . . .

Chapter 17

Berenice had refused food the night before, and now she woke hungry, surprised she had fallen asleep at all in this luxurious prison cell. The comparative comfort of the room infuriated her. She would have preferred spartan surroundings in place of this perpetual lie.

She heard the *clip-clop* and clatter of a buggy outside. The cannon on the hillside boomed, meaning Lamb was making an appearance outside the mansion. Berry went to the window in time to see a carriage driven up to Magnus Lamb at a side door of the mansion. "The Sovereign" was wearing a long woolen overcoat, and a shiny Homburg hat. With him was a gaunt man in a gray hat and a long gray coat. He carried a shotgun. A bodyguard Berry had seen before.

Lamb and his guard got in the carriage and his driver carried him off toward the entry road.

Berry heard the lock click. Heart thumping, she turned to the door of her cell.

It opened and Twilley stepped through, carrying a silver tray covered by a white cloth. The stocky, pop-eyed Twilley was in full Apostle uniform, even to the hat. He was looking at her with something like a leer, though it might've been his attempt at a smile. He had a pistol on his hip.

"I brought you breakfast, ordered by the Sovereign," Twilley said. He had a high, hoarse voice. It sounded scratchy, as if something had damaged his throat.

"Where's he off to?" Berry asked, as he set the tray down on the bed.

"The Sovereign's off to Poverty Flats to settle a lumber deal."

Through the open door she could see another Apostle. She didn't know his name—a tall gangly man with a long neck and a vacuous grin. He had a whip in his right hand and a rifle was leaning near him on the wall. "You thinking of running?" the gangly man asked, with a sneering hopefulness. "He said if you tried to run, we could do what we wanted with you."

"It's impressive how gentlemanly and Christian you Apostles are," she said dryly. "I'm sure you're just what God wants in a man."

The flippancy dissolved from the Apostle's face. He blinked, seeming puzzled.

"Never mind Coontz, there," said Twilley. "He's missing some spokes on his wheel." He tapped his head. He added in an undertone, "He wouldn't be an Apostle but he's Carmody's son."

"I see," she said lightly. "Not up to the standards of you great men who hold women prisoner for no crime whatever."

Twilley's cheeks reddened, and his eyes narrowed. "You won't be so disrespectful when the Sovereign gets back. He's got a new place for you, a little way off. It's quiet there."

"And when does he return?"

"Tomorrow eve, like as not," Twilley said, as he started

for the door. His boots clinked on something, and he looked down to see the broken glass from the window. "Now why'd you break that window? There's bars you can plainly see!"

"I didn't break it," Berry said. Your *Sovereign* did it. His Grace, His Holiness, threw a chair and broke it."

"Did he now?" Twilley snickered. "He does have his moods."

He went to the door, muttered something at Coontz. The door was sharply closed, and the key turned in the lock.

Berry was relieved they were gone but sorry she couldn't have found a way through that open door—without being beaten, maybe even killed.

She sat down beside the tray and removed the cloth. Eggs, sliced ham, and potatoes on a China plate, bread with a linen cloth, and silverware. A small pot of tea and a cup . . . The knife for the ham, she noted, had a steel blade. That might be useful.

She was hungry—but afraid to eat. Would they not stoop to drugging her? Who knew what a man like Lamb might do?

Berry picked up a fork and knife and cut small bits off the ham and eggs. She smelled the morsels, ate a small amount, then put the utensils down. She tasted nothing unusual. But she waited. After several minutes, with her stomach growling, she concluded she'd have felt some at least minor effect of a drug or poison by now. She felt nothing but hunger.

She ate her breakfast, and drank some tea. Feeling a little better, she attempted to formulate a plan. There was always the knife. She was not trained in knife fighting. But surely, a slash to the jugular would be efficacious . . . ?

Could she even bring herself to do it?

She thought she could, yet the thought sickened her. But with two armed men—could she really kill one and still escape? There were other possibilities . . .

Berry went to the door and pressed her ear against it. She could hear a man singing softly to himself, and the wooden floor squeaking as he shifted his weight.

She went to the tray, picked up a linen napkin, carried it and the knife to the window. Pushing the broken glass on the floor aside with the toe of her boot, it occurred to her that, wrapped in a cloth, the glass shards could make a good weapon, if it came to that.

These Apostles force me to be the kind of beast they are, Berry thought. *And it is an insult to beasts.*

"Nature red of tooth and claw," she murmured, remembering the Tennyson line. But nature could be forgiven.

She busied herself removing the remaining glass from the window frame so that she could work. When it was clear of shards, she examined the iron bars. They looked to be firmly set into stone. She doubted she could find a way to dig out their bases. They were painted black and slightly decorative—they narrowed at intervals for a wavelike ornamental effect. It occurred to her that each narrowing presented a degree of weakness in the bars.

Berry wrapped the linen cloth around two of the iron bars over the window at the lower end where the bars were narrowest. The cloth was just long enough she could tie the ends around the knife handle. She tied a knot where they met over the knife grip—then she twisted the handle, turning it like hands on a clock, tightening the cloth so it squeezed the two bars. She knew that with the leverage of the torque she could increase pressure on the bars—maybe enough, she hoped, to bend the metal at its weak point, or pull a bar from its socket. She forced the knife haft to turn as far as it would go, ever tightening the looped cloth—and then it would turn no further. And the cloth was beginning to tear.

She doubted she could make it work . . . but another idea came to her. She glanced over at the bowl containing samples from the hot springs.

"I can but try," she whispered.

Chance Breen and Red were following Judson on a meager trail that zigzagged up the steep western base of Gunmetal Mountain. Breen was riding the plow horse he'd taken from the Monroe wagon. Carmody had mentioned the name to him. He'd let the old swaybacked horse go, and they used the second plow horse to haul supplies, including the few goods of value they'd taken off the wagon. The sun was down, dusk was upon them, and its gray light was fading fast.

Breen could see his breath in the gathering chill. His horse's hooves slipped on the loose rock of the game trail, and for a moment he thought it was going to take a tumble down the hillside. "You couldn't find a better trail than this'n, Squaw Jumper?"

"Stop your whinin'," Judson growled. "This is the one they can't see from up above, with all them trees and such. And we're too far off to be seen from the lumber camp."

"I think we shoulda laid for them *Aposses* and killed 'em!" Red called out. He pronounced Apostles that way, Breen noticed, seeming to think it was something to do with a posse. "We could bushwhack 'em!" Red added, chortling. "Bang, dang! They're dead!"

"Keep your damn voice down, ya fool!" Breen hissed. His wound was hurting him from all this riding. Wasn't quite healed yet. What a blessing it would be to make Cleve Trewe pay for that, and for Davy too . . .

He patted the head of the ax he'd taken to carrying, looped to his saddle.

"There!" Judson said, just loud enough for Breen to hear. He pointed at a hollow under a volcanic outcropping, up the rise.

When Breen got there, Judson was dismounted and lighting a lucifer in the recess. "This'll do us. I seen it from below, wasn't sure, but it'll do . . ."

Breen and Red climbed off their horses—Breen grimacing—and looked around. It was about seven paces deep, one wall of rock marked in red with Indian pictures. Hunters and such. The ground was blackened from some long-forgotten fire. But it had been occupied by something else more recently. He could smell the musk.

"Stinks like bear in here," said Breen.

"Brown bear, most like," said Judson, sniffing. "Mebbe a season ago. Spawned her cubs and moved on."

"Be cold if we cain't build a fire," Red observed, as a cutting wind pushed in among them.

"We'll risk a fire," Breen said. "They won't see from above."

"But why we got to stay here?" Red demanded.

Breen went to his horse and started unsaddling it. "I done told you already."

"Chance says there's treasure up there, in that big house on the ridge. Gold and greenbacks and silver."

"Even in the chapel, there's a power of silver candlesticks and such," said Breen, as he uncinched his saddle. "Why—that man in the big house sometimes wears a crown!"

Red scratched in his rusty beard. "A what?"

"Like a king has, on his head!" Judson told him. "Made of gold!"

"Well, hell and dingdong bell, let's take it from him!"

"Ha-*ha!* Now you're catching on," Breen said, as he slung the saddle on the ground. The horses snorted and looked around nervously. "There's a thicket of buckeye back down the trail. We'll put the horses in there. They can graze some scrub. Gotta water them too. We got to be ready to move quick . . ."

"We should leave the saddles on 'em then," said Red.

"Horses got to rest or they ain't no good," said Breen.

"You got a plan to get into that house?" Judson asked, taking a lantern from his pack. "I was figuring on having Sedge and his men with us . . ."

It was getting dark, so Breen couldn't make out the others' faces. "Two or three plans!" Breen said. Judson lit the lantern so the faces of the other two appeared like ghosts. Breen pointed at the flame in the lantern. "Right now, the plan I like best—is fire!"

"How's that?" Judson asked, unsaddling his horse.

"We set fire to those houses! They're all wood, them houses—they'll go up like kindling! Every man jack'll run over there to put out the fire—and we take the big house! Ha-*haa!* But first—we got to get the lay of the land . . ." He took the ax from the saddle loop and tested the edge of its blade with his thumb. "And see just who's up there . . ."

Berenice had begun on the iron bars between breakfast and lunch, using the steel knife. When Twilley took the tray away he didn't seem to notice the wear in the knife's serrations.

Now she was busily distilling hydrogen chloride in the bedroom's fireplace. She'd removed the crystals from the bell jar and the copper bowl, then set them aside, and started a low fire under the fireplace grate, using the matches she carried in her trouser pocket. She poured water from the white pitcher into the bowl and added the white crystals she'd identified as sal ammoniac—the smell was quite distinctive. It was often found in hot spring encrustations. Alongside it she placed yellow crystals, metal sulfites—vitriol, as it was called once. She scraped up copper from the little bowl and mixed it in. They weren't quite pure enough, she thought, as they began to melt down. She needed another acid to assist production of the necessary acid. Urine would provide that. There was a chamber pot under the bed . . .

Soon she was able to add urine. Now—the bellows. She inserted the tip of the fireplace bellows into the mixture, puffed bubbles into it—oxygenation was important to the process.

She smiled to herself, remembering the family outrage produced by chemistry experiments she'd carried out, at the age of fifteen, in her family's old carriage house. She had been a little too adventurous, and the really *quite* minor explosion had done nothing more than blow out a few panes of glass. It had taken a while for the hair on the right side of her head to grow back, however . . .

She drew back now, a little dizzy—she'd caught a whiff of the hydrogen halide gas, a by-product. Dangerous—but most of it went up the chimney. She went to the window, now cleared of glass, and looked out into the night. Two stories below a sentry in an Apostle's uniform was tramping by. She stepped back, not wanting to be seen at the window. When she peeked out again, he was gone.

Berry returned to the fireplace, wrapped a pillowcase around her hands and gingerly took the hot copper bowl from the fire. She carried it with exquisite care to the window. She glanced out again, saw no one below, and commenced gradually pouring little bits of the hot hydrochloric acid isomer onto the places she'd scraped into the narrows of the iron bars. The little cuts held the acid long enough to do its work, or so she hoped. It immediately began to sizzle . . .

She applied it over and over, in eight places, high and low on the bars, sweating—despite the cold coming through the uncovered window— with the effort to apply the acid as precisely as possible.

At last, it was all gone . . . and she caught a motion from the corner of her eye. Someone down below was coming around the corner of the mansion. The sentry, completing a round.

Berry drew back, and waited. When she looked again, he had moved past and was walking away with his back to her. When he'd turned the corner again, she got her knotted cloth and used a small piece of fireplace wood, thick enough to hold as the turning handle, to exert pressure on the acid-weakened metal bars . . .

It worked. Within three minutes she had broken two bars off, and there was just room to squeeze through.

Berry set to pulling the sheets off the bed and tying them together. On the trail from Axle Bust, Cleve had shown her a cowboy's knot for splicing. He had admired how quickly she'd learned it. "You'll be a better cowboy than me," he'd said.

Her eyes stung as she remembered. Had Lamb made a hollow threat—or was Cleve dead, on the trail, shot in the back?

No. She refused to believe it.

She returned to the window with the knotted sheets and waited for the sentry to pass again. He hadn't looked up at the window once—which was fortunate. He might've noticed the missing bars. Doubtless Lamb had ordered the

men to ignore the window. He didn't want them tempted
by a "damsel in distress."

At last, the sentry turned the corner. Berry dropped one
of the window bars down to the ground, then tied the
sheets to one of the remaining bars, dropped them too.
They didn't reach all the way—it was fifty feet down.
She'd have to let go partway.

Shivering with a gust of biting wind, she began to squeeze
through, feet first. It wasn't easy—she didn't quite fit. She
was very much afraid she was going to get stuck. Berry
blew all the air from her lungs, pulled in her belly, painfully
wriggled . . . and slipped through.

She dropped—and grabbed the sheet. Sliding down it,
catching the wall on the toes of her boots, she was near the
bottom when she heard the sheet rip.

Suddenly she was falling. She fell on her side into rose
bushes, gasping as thorns cut her hands, one hip, and
the left side of her face. She bit off a yell of fear and pain.
She must not be heard.

The sheet fell beside her. It occurred to her, as she
squirmed to get onto her feet, the sheet tearing was a good
thing. It wouldn't be hanging down to be spotted. She
thrust it behind the bushes and—wincing as more thorns
caught her arms and legs—she stepped out. She found the
bar she'd dropped, picked it up, looked around, and decided to run for it.

Aching from bruises and cuts, she sprinted across open
ground and to a row of topiary bushes alongside the fence.
She threw herself to the ground, panting, wincing from a
dozen hurts, and peered toward the lights of the house.
There was the sentry. He was walking by, staring at the
ground, frowning. If he looked up, he'd see a small piece
of torn sheet hanging from the window. He kept walking.

When he was gone, she got painfully to her feet, and hefted the iron bar. It was better than no weapon at all.

She had to get clear of the mansion grounds . . . and find Gil and Freja.

"Looks like we got here in time for supper," said Cleve, as they rode into the Bannock camp. They'd been spotted by scouts and Washakoh had sent three braves to escort them in.

There was whooping and shouts of greeting as the triumphant Ejupa waved his trophies, his hat and Sedge's rifle, parading around the camp on his horse—another trophy.

The fires were built up high, and pots bubbled on flat stones; grouse and rabbit were being roasted over spits. The savor of wild onion and sage was in the air. "A feast for the Prodigal Son," Cleve said, as he and Milt dismounted.

"Is he so prodigal as all that?" Milt asked, looking nervously around. He had been in Indian camps before, but never with a band of renegades.

"Here's Claudia and one of Washakoh's daughters . . ."

Claudia came up smiling to Cleve, and said, "Washakoh says *grazie*, you are now his brother!"

"I'm honored," Cleve said.

"He wish you to stay three days feasting!"

"I cannot, I regret. I must go to Berenice."

"Berry! Is she . . . well?"

"I wish I knew. My horse is played out. I'll stay till he's ready to move on—maybe an hour or two before sunrise . . ."

"But you will eat?"

"We will eat, and rest." He noticed Milt and the young

Indian maiden with Claudia gazing silently at one another. She was lithe, wearing leggings and buckskin. "And who is this young miss?"

"Pamahas," Claudia said. "Daughter of Panok."

"Pamahas!" Milt said, breathing the name. "My name's Milt Dumanis, Pam, and uh . . . Well, I don't expect you understand me, but . . ."

Cleve rolled his eyes. "Where can we put our horses, Claudia?"

"There—with Panati horses. No one touch them."

"You are the one who rides with the warrior," said Pamahas, unexpectedly, nodding at Milt.

"You speak English," Cleve observed.

"Two years in the mission school, Fort Hall," Pamahas said, shrugging. "I learn quick, they say."

"Now hold on there, Pamahas," said Milt. "Why are you saying *I'm* riding with the warrior? He's not the only fighting man around here."

"*Are* you a great warrior then?" she asked, pursing her lips to hide amusement.

"Well, I . . ." Then he shook his head. "I guess not. But I've got sand enough, when I need it."

"Milt is no coward," said Cleve. "He's a good man."

"I know he is a good man," said Pamahas. "And brave."

"Oh, how do you know this?" Cleve asked.

"I see it."

Truly she's the daughter of Panok, Cleve thought.

The drumming started then, and the dancing, as Ejupa dismounted, loudly recounting his adventures in Panati with his fellows, smiling broadly, clapping his stovepipe hat on his head . . .

* * *

Limping, shivering, Berenice slipped through the oak trees behind the cabins and cottages, stopping to watch for sentries. The iron bar felt heavy in her right hand.

There—the small horse barn behind the cabins. She took a last look around and then hurried to it, and inside, closed the door quietly behind her. It was a welcoming place, warm and smelling of horses and straw.

As she put the iron bar down beside the door, Berry heard a snort, and soft whinny. Suzie had scented her.

"Yes it's me, Suzie," Berry whispered, feeling her way down the narrow space between stalls. "Have they been taking care of you?" Coming to the back wall, Berry fumbled for the lantern. The place had no windows, but there were a few cracks in the walls. If she kept the lantern's wick low, hopefully no light would be seen. She lit it, and Suzie whinnied again. Turning to Suzie, Berry saw a bucket of water and some grain in a little wooden trough. "Looks like you're okay, but you must be terribly worried, and restless . . ."

The dappled Arabian nuzzled at her, and Berry hugged her neck. "It is good to be with a friend again, Suzie. And you're so nice and warm."

The only other beast here was the mule. Berry went to her stall, saw he had been fed and watered. She tried to pet the mule's neck, but he pulled away, seeming angry to have been left here for so long, and kicked at the wall.

"I know just how you feel," Berry whispered. She returned to Suzie and murmured. "I'm going to have to saddle you up, Suzie, in case we must ride away quite suddenly. I'm afraid I may be clumsy. I'm rather bruised, you see . . ." She opened Suzie's stall. "Come along . . ."

Suzie followed her over to the door. Berry picked up the saddle, grunting with the twinges in her bruised shoulders and hips. It took more effort than usual, but Berry got the saddle onto Suzie, and properly cinched. She bridled the mare and tied her to a stall post. "Now—I am going to find Gil and Freja so I can see how they're doing . . . I'll be back . . . then perhaps we can go and find Cleve and Ulysses . . ."

Berry picked up the iron bar, peeked out the door, and moved as quietly as she could toward the dark cabins, though her feet crunched on fallen leaves. She took the iron bar in both hands and walked up between a cabin and the "cottage of the pilgrims," where she'd stayed with the other women. She stopped at the corner of the cottage and peered around it.

An Apostle stood at the door, in a pool of light from a lantern hanging from a hook above him. His long coat was buttoned up and he was shifting from foot to foot and blowing on his hands in the cold. His rifle was leaning against the wall beside him. A young man, Berry had seen him with Carmody—who had called him Drayton.

Berry stepped back out of sight, leaned the iron bar against the wall, and untied her hair. She shook it out so it fell over her shoulders, then she knelt, letting her hair droop to cover her face, leaned forward enough to be seen, and cried out plaintively, "Apostle Drayton!" She put one hand on the iron bar, which was hidden by the corner of the cottage. "Oh—please help me! The Indians . . ."

She heard him gasp and run toward her—leaving his rifle behind. "Who . . . Indians, you say?" He reached down and took her upper arm, and she allowed him to help her straighten up—then she brought the iron bar up with her and jabbed it hard in his belly.

Drayton folded over, gasping for air as she stepped back and struck upward, the bar striking him in the chin.

He yelped "Ow!" and stumbled back. His hat fell off as he landed on his rump, clutching at his jaw.

Berry took the bar in her hands as if she were grasping an ax handle and stood over him.

"That woman! The prisoner—!"

"My name is Berenice Tucker," she said. "Do keep your voice down and listen. I am stronger than I look, and I have a good grip on this bar of iron. If you fail to do as I ask, I shall have no choice but to crush your skull." She gave him a sad smile, adding, "I will do it with regret! But—it is for the greater good, so I shall not hesitate."

His eyes widened. "*Please* don't kill me, Miz Tucker! I did not want to be here tonight, I wanted to leave a long time ago, but he kills them that try to leave!"

"I can help you, then," Berry said. "If you will turn over, and then get on your feet—and do not make a move toward that rifle!"

"I . . ." Drayton rubbed his sore jaw. "You won't . . . crush my skull, when my back is turned?"

"I give you my word, I will not strike so long as you do as I ask."

He nodded, rolled over on his belly, and then, with a grunt, stood up.

"I shall be very close behind you," Berry said. "My truncheon, if such it may be called, is at ready if you should try to pick up that rifle! Go carefully to the door and unlock it!"

He nodded and walked to the door without so much as glancing at the rifle. She followed, watching him carefully. He fumbled in his coat pocket with cold, clumsy fingers and drew out a ring of keys. Breathing hard, muttering to himself, he unlocked the door and removed the padlock.

"Drop the padlock, please," Berry said. "Then open the door and go in with your hands up."

"I'll be glad to get out of this wind!" He did as she asked.

Berry switched the iron bar to her left hand and with her right caught up the rifle. She stepped into the cottage behind Drayton. Brother Donahue and Gil Peck sat on either side of one of the beds, where Freja Peck seemed to be slumbering.

"Berry!" Gil burst out.

Berry nodded to Gil, and said, "Mr. Drayton, do sit down, over in that chair by the stove and warm yourself."

"Yes, ma'am!" Drayton sat down, rubbing his hands together at the stove.

Berry tossed the iron bar aside, turned and closed the door, and with a sigh sat down on the bed opposite Freja's. She laid the rifle across her knees. "Is Freja well? She's . . ." Berry felt a little faint.

"I broke a rule," Brother Donahue admitted, thoughtfully stroking his chin beard with one hand. "I took some laudanum from the house's stores, and I have given it unto her, and now she sleeps."

"She was in terrible pain," Gil said. "But Berenice—you don't look well yourself! You've got blood on your cheeks and face. And the back of your hand is bruised!"

"A good deal more than that is bruised," Berry said. "I managed to get out a window, where Lamb kept me in the mansion. I dropped into some rosebushes and they punished me for my impertinence. How is Freja's leg?"

"It is broken—but it's only one fracture, and I have splinted it firmly," said Donahue. "The swelling has gone down, and I believe she will recover."

"You seem to have some knowledge of medicine," Berry observed.

"Oh—yes. I was a medical student for nearly two

years. Then . . . I had an accident with some ether. And thereupon—I had a vision. I was called to find a prophet . . ." Donahue looked sadly at Freja. "It may be that I misread the vision . . ."

"No doubt, if it persuaded you to trust Lamb," Berry said.

Donahue nodded and then said, "I have a few other medicaments, in my pack. Allow me to tend to you, as well I may."

"Thank you—I will apply it myself," she said.

He brought her a salve and cleanser, and she went into the back bedroom to apply it to her hips, legs, arms, and her face. Berry had pulled a muscle in her right calf, climbing over the tall fence out of sight of the gate guards. She rubbed salve on the calf and returned to the main room. "You must tend to Mr. Drayton too. I was forced to give him a rather forceful blow on the jaw."

"Oh, I'm okay," said Drayton, rubbing his swollen jaw ruefully. "It ain't broken."

"Tell me this, Donahue," Berry said, sitting down at the table. "How soon could Freja travel?"

"Travel? Why, not for months—unless perhaps, lying on her back in a wagon. But even so, the pain . . ."

"We mustn't move her!" Gil said, taking Freja's hand.

Berry said, "Then we must act—we must persuade the settlement to turn against Lamb. He will be back tomorrow. I took it from what one of the Apostles said that you and Freja are now regarded as servants of Satan."

"That's right," Drayton conceded. "And the Sovereign is not in the mood to allow Mr. and Mrs. Peck to go on living . . ."

Cleve and Milt were called to Washakoh's wickiup to eat. They all sat inside, out of the cold, rainy wind. The fires snapped in the wind; the drummers kept drumming. It was crowded in there, with Washakoh and Ejupa and Panok and Cleve and Pamahas and Milt—Claudia was serving, and translating—but the food was hot and welcome, and festivity seemed like something Cleve could feel in the air . . .

An empty wickiup was offered to Cleve and Milt, and later on they huddled inside, tired but pensive. Milt said, "I never thought . . ."

"What?" Cleve asked, though he could guess.

"That an Indian woman could make me feel that way . . . I guess I must be too long without a woman."

"It's not that," Cleve said. "She's a fine-looking girl. And she seems bright—even though she likes you."

"Even though—" Milt frowned, and then laughed. "Guess I ain't much use to anyone."

Cleve shook his head. "My offer stands. You want to find me at Sweet River, I'll give you a job at a fair wage. I can use a man who knows horses like you do. I'm leaving early—before dawn. Their night watch is going to wake me up. But if you want to string along with me . . ."

"Now as to that . . ." Milt turned and looked out the wickiup at the sinking fires. "I got to let this bullet hole in my shoulder heal up. And they said three days of feasting. I guess I'm invited to stay a while."

Cleve chuckled. "Here . . ." He took five double eagles from his pocket and passed them to Milt. "That's an advance on your salary."

Milt seemed stunned by the gold coins in his palm. "Ain't you worried I won't show up to work it off?"

"If that's how it plays out, then I'll haunt you for it when I die. Anyhow, I'm taking the chance. That's traveling money. You see Sacramento and then come and see me in late summer—if you choose to. I'm going to roll into my blankets now. You'd best get some sleep—if you're going to spend three days chasing that girl, just be careful how you do it. You're a guest here."

"I didn't say I was going to be chasing anyone! I mean, Lordy, Cleve, I . . ."

But Cleve ignored him, took off his boots, and stretched out on his bedroll. Fatigue was overcoming his nerves. He was soon asleep.

He slept deeply. But well after midnight the dream came again. Berenice was calling to him, in the badlands. There was something she wanted to tell him. But try as he might, he couldn't find her.

He was shaken awake by the night watch. Careful not to wake Milt, Cleve pulled on his boots and carried his gun belt and rifle outside. It was still pitch dark, but the clouds had broken up and the stars were shining fiercely down. Cleve buckled on his gun and looked around. There was a small, hissing campfire near the horses. A Bannock boy sitting there nodded to him as he strode up.

Cleve soon had Ulysses saddled. He scabbarded his Winchester, mounted up, and said, "Hope you got enough feed, old boy, because we're going to ride hard this morning, and all through the day."

Ulysses tossed his head, and carried Cleve off into the cold darkness, with just starlight to show the trail and more than an hour to go before dawn . . .

Chapter 18

At midmorning, the cottage was getting crowded. Leman Peck was sitting with his cousin Gil beside Freja's bedside. She was awake, though drowsy thanks to the laudanum. She clutched at Gil's hand, looking fearfully around.

There were seven others in the cottage, two women and five men, settlers Berry didn't know by name, though she'd seen them at the Abodes. Gil had gone out at dawn, and quietly summoned them here—they were representing a crowd of others who had doubts about Lambsville.

Berry was standing in front of the fireplace, soothing her bruises and aches with the heat of the flames. She had just finished telling the story of her incarceration. "After my escape I was bruised and cut, and I slept poorly last night," Berry said. "I am not at my most intelligible. But I hope you understand me. I am telling the truth! Lamb told me that he had given orders to *murder* Cleve Trewe. He asserted the murder was quite possibly already carried out."

Berry's voice caught for a moment, and she had to clear her throat.

She went on, "You can believe me, or choose not to. But you have also heard Gilbert Peck tell you what was asked of his wife. And what became of her when the Pecks tried to leave. You have heard that the Monroes died when they took their leave—Lamb says it was by the hand of God. You surely cannot believe that. Now—we have not yet heard from Mr. Drayton"

Drayton the Apostle stood up, and said, "I have been in doubt about Magnus Lamb for some time now. I have heard Apostles laughing about 'what fools will believe.' And we were paid—when you were not. But I heard from Twilley that the Monroes were murdered by killers hired by Lamb!"

There was a general gasp at that. What was suspected was confirmed—and it was terrifying.

Drayton rubbed ruefully at his swollen jaw, and said, "When I heard that, I wanted to leave—but I was afraid to— an Apostle left about four months ago and Carmody rode him down and shot him dead! Now, because I spoke my doubts about Lamb, Carmody made me stand in the cold out here all night. He thought to intimidate me. But I can bear it no longer. I testify before you—that we must fight Lamb before we're damned to Hell for serving him!"

There was much murmuring at that. Leman said, miserably, "I have felt for some time that there was a worm in the apple. But hearing about the Monroes . . ."

Then Irma came in and scowled around at them. "Now what is all this, pray tell?"

Berry was about to caution the others to quiet, when Gil spoke up, "We have no choice—we have been deceived! We can rid ourselves of Lamb and build up a real settlement here!"

Irma stared—her eyes almost popped—and then she backed toward the door, hurried out, slamming the door behind her.

Drayton gaped for a moment and then turned to Berry.

"That one—she's a puppet of Lamb and Carmody. She'll report us immediately. I could go after her . . ."

Berry shook her head. "Do not descend to the level of the Lambs of this world. You must all hurry now to wherever you feel safest. Mr. Drayton—hide yourself! I shall ride out and find Cleve Trewe. I shall plead with him to help you. But those of you who have any way of arming yourselves—I urge you to take up those arms. And have faith in those who will do what is right."

Then Berry put on her coat, took up Drayton's rifle, and went to the door.

"Be careful, Berenice!" Freja called out. Berry smiled at her and hurried out to the small barn out back.

Suzie was waiting for her, scuffing at the floor with a front hoof.

Berry said, "Suzie—the time has come." She was talking to herself more than to Suzie. "Let us ride out, and find Cleve. Surely, he must be coming. We will meet him partway. We must hypothesize what route he might take . . ."

Berry mounted and rode hard toward the southeast.

Cleve was leaning forward in the saddle, hat tilted down against the wind, riding southwest.

The sun was out this morning, but it hardly put a dent in the cold. He had pushed Ulysses soon as the sun rose enough that he could see the road. Cleve would have liked to gallop the whole way there, but even the best horse couldn't manage a full gallop much above a mile. Mostly Cleve kept it to a canter, sometimes trotting to rest Ulysses. Partway, they stopped at a little spring that wended across the road. He got water for the canteen and the horse, and then rode out again . . .

* * *

Reaching the shanty camp near the creek crashing down from Gunmetal Mountain, Cleve reined in and glanced around. The tents were gone. Crows were fluttering inside the discarded Conestoga. The camp was abandoned.

Stiff after the long ride, Cleve dismounted and led Ulysses to the creek. Along the rocky stream bank, prismatic icicles had formed from condensation drips. What would Berenice say, looking at that? She might remark on the beauty that could be found hiding even in this harsh, craggy place.

He looked up at the mountain and wondered where Berry was, and what she was doing right now.

Then he saw the riders swinging off the mountain road. Four uniformed Apostles, coming two by two down the road above the bridge. He recognized Carmody, at the back. They were all looking his way, and the two in front had their rifles in hand, stocks braced on their knees. It was a casual posture with a rifle in some ways. But there was no reason for those rifles to be out of their saddle scabbards unless they intended to use them.

Cleve shrugged. He couldn't assume that it was him they were after. He'd left Lambsville on a job for "the Sovereign." He should still be in Lamb's good graces. But hadn't Eliza suggested that Lamb didn't trust him? You were either Magnus Lamb's man—or a dead man.

Thinking about Eliza, it seemed to Cleve she had been trying to get him to kill her father. She seemed to despise Magnus Lamb. She'd said, *"I made him stop what he was doing . . ."* Had Lamb violated his own daughter?

Cleve led Ulysses up the thin path by the crude bridge. Carmody and the others seemed to be waiting for him on the bridge's farther side. Cleve mounted up and looked toward the riders. "Apostle Carmody!" he called, making his voice loud enough to be heard over the echoing roar of the tumbling creek. "You boys are blocking the road! I've got news for the Sovereign!"

Carmody said something to his men, and they backed their mounts up. "Go ahead on around us!"

"I'll let you ride out past me!" Cleve called. He put his hand on the butt of his Colt.

Carmody shook his head. "We'll escort you up the mountain!"

"Go on up and I'll follow!" Cleve shouted.

Carmody shook his head again, more firmly. "You're not one of us yet! You ride up first!"

Cleve did not want to turn his back on Carmody. Cleve didn't trust Lamb—and that meant not trusting Carmody.

Once, Kit Carson had told him, "If you got a feeling in your innards that a man's going to turn on you, or an Indian's following you in the brush, you take special care! Don't shake off the feeling. Watch your trail close." Cleve decided he was going to trust that feeling now.

He turned Ulysses away from the Apostles, shouting, "Let's go!"

Ulysses galloped toward the remains of the camp. He heard a gunshot, then another, then swung Ulysses off the road, and up behind the derelict Conestoga. "Whoa!"

Cleve heard horses coming in pursuit as he slid out of the saddle. He took two seconds to tie Ulysses where the wagon would provide some shelter from gunfire, and then snatched his Winchester out of its scabbard with his left hand; he drew his Colt with his right and ran to the farther side of the old wagon . . . and two of the Apostles opened fire. They were about twenty-five yards off, still mounted, firing with the Spencer carbines.

Bullets smacked into the wagon, sending splinters and frightened crows flying. The big birds cawed and flapped away as Cleve fired three rounds from the Colt in quick succession, just trying to drive the men off.

But one of the Apostles jerked back in his saddle and clutched at his belly. His frightened horse turned and carried him back up the hill. Cleve holstered the Colt and knelt, partly sheltered by a front wagon wheel as he brought the Winchester into play. Carmody and the others rode into the camp, dismounted before Cleve could get a bead on them, and found cover behind a berm of dirt and rock.

They fired over the top, but Cleve was waiting for Lamb's cavalrymen to show themselves and he squeezed off a round—blood sprayed from a man's forehead. The Apostle slumped, sliding out of sight.

"Well, hell," Cleve muttered. "I'm committed now."

He had no desire to stalk these men and kill them. There were two left. Maybe the men really believed in Lamb. He'd be killing two men for their bad judgment.

Cleve ducked his head as a bullet clanged off the metal rim of the wagon wheel.

Gullible fools they might be, but it seemed he was going to have to kill them—or die trying.

There might be another way. He could see their horses behind them, stirring restlessly. Mighty nervous. He aimed the Winchester with a desperate precision and fired twice, shooting the saddle horns off.

The horses ran off in panic, and the men at the berm turned to see where their mounts had gone.

Cleve used their distraction and ran to Ulysses, tugged the tie loose, mounted and spurred, all in a handful of seconds. He flattened along his horse's neck as Ulysses galloped off toward the mountain road. A bullet whined past him, and another—and then he was over the bridge and heading up the escarpment. There was cover here from piles of rock moved out of the way by the road builders.

A few hundred yards up the mountainside, he rode past a dying man; the Apostle he'd gutshot, fallen from his horse. The man lay there squirming in pain as he died. There was no saving him, but Cleve was sorry to have hit the man in the belly. He hadn't meant to.

He rode on, fast as Ulysses could bear it, up the mountainside. He was confident Carmody and the other Apostle below would be looking for their horses for some time.

He had to get up to Lambsville in a hurry, find Berenice, and get her safely away.

Except—it was hard to say exactly where Berry would be, on Gunmetal Mountain . . .

And then a cold thought pierced him. If Lamb had sent Carmody to kill him—what might they have done with Berenice?

Berenice was glad to be in the saddle on her Arabian, and glad that the sun had shown up. The chill mountain air smelled sweet as she rode hard for the trail up the steep slope. But her thoughts were quickly clouded by fears for Cleve, and wondering if she were doing the right thing in going to look for him.

As Suzie slowed to pick her way up the steep trail, Berenice looked around, half expecting to see Apostles standing guard. But her route took her out of their line of sight.

The trail's steepness moderated and Berry rode between the two boulders, and past them, just where she'd been taken prisoner by Carmody. To her right was Freja's dead horse—something flapped darkly near it and a vulture extracted its head from a hole in the horse's side, meat dangling from its beak as it looked at her with intent, beady eyes. She looked at the vulture with scientific interest—and it was looking at her as if wondering where it would find her body.

Berry rode by, and the hill got steep again. The sun was overhead, and she was sheltered from the wind here. She could feel sweat on her forehead, and she heard Suzie's labored breathing.

They attained the shoulder of Gunmetal Mountain, and the trail narrowed. Close to Berry's left was raw mountainside; to the right was a scree of black rocks reaching to a cliff's edge. Up ahead, the thin bighorn trail rounded the upper third of the mountain.

She rode on, passing the hot springs, steaming on three descending ledges; she could smell sulfur, saw yellowish mist rising, and heard water seething. Then came the place where hot runoff crossed the trail to the bathing pools. Just five feet wide, the stream trailed hot vapor from its ripples, and Suzie shied back.

"It's not so very hot, Suzie," Berry said. "But let's go back a bit . . . back up . . . back up some more . . . there's a girl . . . and now . . . Let's take a run at it . . ." She knew Suzie had the sense to jump over a stream, if it was too rocky to step through, and she could jump this, too, if she was prepared. Berry didn't wear spurs, but she spurred Suzie with her heels, and shouted, "Go!"

Suzie quickly picked up to a canter, came to the stream—and jumped.

They made it handily and slowed to a trot as Berry congratulated Suzie—and then a bullet cracked against the steep stone rise to her left.

Startled, Berry looked back, and couldn't quite see a rider, but she heard the horse's hooves on the rocky ground. Seemed she'd been spotted by the Apostles.

Urging Suzie on, Berry looked at Drayton's rifle in its

scabbard. Perhaps if she could find a defensible position up ahead, she could stand them off, for a time. But when she ran out of bullets . . .

It mattered not. She refused to go back to anywhere Lamb could put his hands on her.

Another bullet cracked by, and Berry cringed down over Suzie. Hooves clattered as Suzie cantered around a sharp curve in the trail, with little room between her and the cliff drop-off. There was the danger Suzie could set a hoof wrong and they'd both tumble down.

Berry rode into the wind on the east side of the mountaintop. Up ahead she saw a tumble of rockfall, with scrub brush growing up around it. She turned in the saddle—and was astonished to see that the rider coming after her was Eliza Lamb, riding a completely white horse. Eliza had the reins in her left hand, the rifle in her right, its stock squeezed under her arm, roughly aimed at Berry. Eliza fired—and another bullet hummed like an angry hornet just overhead. The gunshot echoed from the mountainside.

"Woman, 'that way madness lies'!" Berry burst out.

She looked ahead, saw that the cliff edge was close—she could see, far below, the brutally rough black rocks that awaited her.

Berry eased back on Suzie, and then reined in just behind the rockfall. She pulled Drayton's carbine and slid quickly out of the saddle. "Come on, Suzie!" she said, tugging the reins, drawing her nervous horse to safety behind the rocks.

The hoofbeats of Eliza's white charger were close. Berry looked between two bushel-sized rocks in time to see Eliza's rifle fire again, the bullet ricocheting from the rockfall.

Berry muttered, "Hellfire!"—it was something Cleve said—and she fired the carbine. She prepared to fire again. Eliza was almost upon her, coming as fast as the snowy horse could go. Eliza looked strangely magnificent, her copper hair streaming behind her, teeth bared, her green eyes wild. The pink eyes of the horse looked like they were afire in this light—Berry couldn't quite bring herself to shoot—

And then Eliza seemed to realize that she was galloping too fast, and the narrow trail was quite curved, and to the right was the steep cliffside. She reined in, shouting, "*Whoa,* Galahad!"

But it was too late. The horse tried to stop but skidded over the cliffside. Eliza turned to look directly at Berry— eyes wide, mouth open. Looking astonished that this could ever happen to her .

And then she was gone. Eliza Lamb and her mount . . . simply vanished.

There was a short scream from Eliza and a longer, piteous screech from the horse. Then the sounds of meaty *whumps* and rattling rocks dislodging . . .

Berry dropped the carbine and put her hands over her face. "Oh no, Eliza . . . oh no . . ."

Cleve drew Ulysses to a halt as he rode up to Lambsville. To one side of him was a rocky hillside, on the other a screen of pines. Up ahead were "the Abodes." He drew his Colt and began to reload it.

Cleve didn't have to look at his gun when he loaded it, just as a professional gambler can shuffle the deck and deal without looking at the cards. As he reloaded, he scanned the road ahead. The turreted, two-story houses lining the road appeared to be deserted. There would be

women and a few children inside, but no one was visible.
Dried leaves and brown pine needles, fluttering down the
street toward him. He saw no Apostles either, but he knew
they patrolled here. They'd be along.

Cleve had no time to be cautious. He had to find
Berenice. He holstered the Colt and rode forward in a
walk, glancing right and left, one hand on his Colt. The
cold wind stung his nose; the sun threatened to burn the
back of his neck.

A movement to the right—he pulled the Colt and
almost shot Gilbert Peck.

Gil was coming from between two houses, mouth open
and eyes wide. "Cleve!"

Gil stopped where he was, beside a porch, looked down
the road, and then gestured for Cleve to come to him.

Cleve holstered his pistol and turned to ride past the
sickly rosebushes, up between the houses. There was
some cover here, at least. Gil stepped out of his way.
"Lord, I was just sneaking out to look in on Freja and there
you were, big as life—"

Cleve drew up in the alley between the houses. "Gil—
where is Berry?"

Gil grimaced and pointed up at the mountain. "She
went up there! She was going to take a back trail. Couple
days ago, we tried to use that trail. Berry had it all pegged
out for us, me and Freja and her, but then that Irma turned
us in and Carmody came up there and arrested us. Shot
Freja's horse. And Freja got her leg broken."

Cleve shook his head. A person could die from a badly
broken leg. "How is Freja?"

"Brother Donahue's looking after her. She'll mend.
But—"

"Wait—did you say arrested? Berry was arrested?"

Gil nodded glumly. "That's what the Apostles call it. So

was I. Lamb had Berry taken to his mansion. Locked her in a room with bars. He tried to force himself on her . . ."

Cleve's teeth ground together; his hand went to his Colt. *"Where's Lamb?"*

"He's just back from Redding. Probably at the mansion. But listen—Berry used some kind of trick with chemicals and . . . she made an acid that ate right through the iron bars—and she escaped!"

Cleve laughed with relief. And grinned at the thought of Berry's science getting her out of a barred cell. He'd never met a woman like her. "Magnus Lamb was no match for her. Did he hurt her? Is she . . ."

"She's bruised some, some cuts—but mostly from dropping from that window. She's all right, Cleve. Truth of it is—she figured out where we were locked up, she knocked an Apostle guard down with a piece of iron bar, and she got in. She's been organizing us to fight back, Cleve. Even that guard, Drayton. He's with us."

"Sounds like first Berry rescued herself—and then you!"

Gil looked sheepish. "You could put it that way. She decided we'd need you. She went off looking to bring you back."

"There's many a thing she's good at. But tracking isn't one of 'em. Where are these people who want to fight Lamb?"

He reached over and stroked Ulysses. "This house right here, and up in the cottages. My cousin Leman's changed his stripes, too, and Donahue. About eight men we know of. And a logger—he was here nursing a bad arm. He went out to the camp, says he knows men out there who will revolt against Lamb."

Cleve nodded. "A good many of them are mad they're

not seeing their pay. Wardwell has no love for Lamb either. He's feeling like a deer stuck in a tar swamp."

"Lot of folks feel the same. But—we're going to need help, Cleve—"

Cleve shook his head. "I'm going to find Berry before I do anything else."

"God help us . . ." Gil nodded toward the road.

Cleve turned in his saddle to see Apostle Twilley in the street, raising his gun. And Cleve had his back to him.

Cleve drew his Colt and—twisted around in the saddle—snapped a loose shot at Twilley while shouting, "Gil—*run!*"

Gil ran toward the back of the building, using Cleve's horse for cover. Cleve fired again.

A bullet cut into Twilley's left hip. Twilley fired blindly while backing away and the shot smashed a window out front. Glass tinkled and Cleve drew a bead—but Twilley ducked to the right, out of the line of fire. Cleve holstered the gun and rode down the alley as Gil slipped into a side door.

Cleve cut left, tugging his Winchester out as he went. He rode over rough ground and fallow vegetable gardens to the end of the row of houses and there he reined in.

He slid off the saddle and led Ulysses close behind the house, tying him to a barberry shrub. "You need to wait here, Ulysses. You're too big a target." He readied the Winchester and moved to the corner of the house. Looking east he saw Twilley with blood running down his hip, waving his arms at two other Apostles. Three of them here so far.

There'd been eight men on the road that first day. But there were others who stayed close to Lamb. Cleve hadn't asked Carmody how many there were—he didn't want them to think he had some notion of fighting them—but with two killed down at the shantytown, Carmody and another alive, Twilley here and two others . . . that was five. And he knew there were at least three others that watched the house. Had to be eight Apostles here left, maybe nine . . . and Lamb's bodyguard.

Cleve growled to himself. What an outlandish fix he'd gotten himself into.

Watching the Apostles, he noticed the one on the right, about seventy feet away, had a swollen jaw. Berry had knocked Drayton down with an iron bar. With luck, he was the rebel Apostle. *Try not to kill that one.*

Then the men turned as one toward a buggy clopping up from the direction of the mansion. The buggy pulled up by the Apostles and two men climbed out—Magnus Lamb and his cadaverous shotgun guard. Heiler.

Lamb had the ermine cape on, over his purple clerical shirt; he had a golden circlet around his neck. He looked around in fury, his mouth working soundlessly. "The Sovereign" looked crazier than ever.

Cleve was faced with another choice, like the one he'd had on the ridge overlooking the trail to Blasted Pine. Kill those men under his gun—or not?

He could take out a couple of Apostles. He could kill Lamb from here. Was it right? Had these men earned it?

Lamb had. He'd laid his hands on his own daughter— and he'd imprisoned Berenice. Imprisoned and threatened the love of Cleve's life.

The Hell with it. Lamb was going to die today.

Cleve tucked the rifle into his shoulder, laid the sights square over Lamb's heart . . .

Then Ulysses reared up, whinnying, as a bullet cut close by Cleve's neck.

Cleve turned on his heel, whipping the rifle around to point down the dirt backyards between the houses and the pines, and saw Carmody riding toward him, a pistol in his hand, and another Apostle behind him.

Carmody fired again—the bullet cracked into the wall beside Cleve as he took aim for return fire . . .

And then Carmody cunningly cornered left, between the houses, heading east toward the road. Cleve's only remaining target was the scared man who'd ridden behind his commander. The Apostle was trying to pull a rifle free of its scabbard.

Cleve couldn't risk letting the Apostle go. He aimed and fired, and the man pitched back, to be dragged by a stirrup behind the panicking horse.

The instant Cleve mounted up Ulysses made his own decision and galloped off, back north behind the houses. They thundered past an alley and someone—probably Carmody—fired at him, and missed.

Cleve reined in at the last house. "Easy!" He patted the horse's neck. "You've been through a lot today. But we've got to find Berry, whatever it takes. And *Suzie's* up there, right?" At that the horse's ears perked up. "I thought so. Come on . . ."

He trotted Ulysses up near the road, at the corner of the house. From here he had a good view down Many Mansions Way. Two more Apostles, coming from the gate to the mansion grounds, were scurrying to join Lamb at the far end of the Abodes.

Where was Carmody? There he was, with Twilley, dragging someone from one of the houses. It was a fair distance, but Cleve could see it was Gil Peck.

"Oh, hellfire," Cleve muttered. *Once more risking everything for Gil Peck . . .*

Knowing full well that Carmody might be doing this to smoke him out into the open, Cleve cantered Ulysses across the road. He was taking a chance. Several chances.

A gun boomed and a bullet struck the road just before him. Got to be a good shot to hit him at this distance. Next, they'd all start shooting.

It began, a crackling of gunfire—but he was already across the road, taking Ulysses quickly behind the closest house on the east side. He rode hard up behind the houses, hooves kicking up garden soil and wilted plants. Two houses down, then three, and he drew his Colt. Three, four, five houses more—and he saw that one of the Abodes had a fence between its lot and a neighbor. And the fence was right in front of him. There wasn't time to stop. "Jump 'er, Ulysses!" he shouted, and Ulysses leaped—and it was the highest jump they'd ever taken. A hoof struck the top of a fence, knocking free a board and then they came down beyond it, in soft dirt.

Ulysses kept on, almost galloping and spraying dirt. Cleve glimpsed the pale, aghast face of a little girl watching through a back window . . .

They rode hard past more houses, and he heard shouts and gunfire—but it was from the far side of the houses. Had they shot Gil?

Cleve holstered the Colt, tugged out the Winchester, and then they'd reached the crossroad. *"Whoa-ah!"* Cleve shouted, bracing himself and pulling back on the reins. Ulysses skidded a little and then stopped, spraying dirt, and Cleve swung out of the saddle, cocking the rifle.

About fifty feet away, in the crossroad, Lamb was waiting with a poised horsewhip as Lamb's bodyguard was standing beside him.

The Apostles dragged Gil across the street, flung him at Lamb's feet.

Lamb struck Gil across the face with the whip—and then Cleve shouted, "Magnus Lamb!" as he aimed the rifle. The two Apostles stepped in front of Lamb, blocking the shot as Lamb—seeing Cleve—turned and ran to the buggy, his ermine cape flapping behind him.

Gil sprinted off toward the cottages as Cleve tracked Lamb with his rifle—till the Apostle opened fire and Cleve had to drop to prone to keep from catching lead. He returned fire. The Apostle fell, shot through the heart. Heiler fired, but the range was bad for a shotgun and all Cleve caught was a few pellets on his right arm. It was enough to make Cleve's fingers tense—and his return fire missed.

Heiler ran after Lamb, trying to follow his master to the buggy. And the panicked bodyguard was blocking Cleve's shot at Lamb, who was scrambling into the buggy, cracking his whip and riding off. Cleve couldn't bring himself to shoot Heiler in the back.

He tried to get a bead on Lamb in the buggy, but a bullet cracked just overhead from another direction—Carmody at the farther corner of the house to his right. Cleve swung the rifle toward Carmody and fired—a moment too late, as Carmody stepped behind the house.

Yet Cleve thought he might have hit him in the upper right leg. The man was a tough old campaigner. A leg wound wouldn't take him out of the fight.

Heart pounding, a keening in his ears, his mouth dry— Cleve got up and ran toward the Abode, the last on the row, and almost ran full-on into Twilley.

Cleve fired the Winchester from the hip, point blank into Twilley's chest, the bullet taking him in the sternum, knocking him off his feet.

He looked for Lamb—the buggy was rushing toward the gates into the mansion grounds.

Two bullets fired in quick succession cracked at him from the right. Cleve ducked back, flattened down, then chanced a look—noticed a dead man on the road. It was the rebellious Apostle, Drayton, shot several times. That was the other shooting he'd heard—Drayton must've tried to stop them from dragging Gil out for a whipping, and they'd turned on him. They'd shot Drayton down for doing the decent thing.

He looked toward the road, saw Carmody favoring one leg, leaning on a horse, aiming a pistol at him. Cleve swung the rifle up and pulled the trigger—

Nothing. Out of bullets.

Cleve drew back, taking cover behind the corner of the house. A bullet cracked by. Time to find Berry, and regroup.

He gave out a loud whistle, one that Ulysses sometimes responded to and sometimes didn't. This time, maybe sensing his urgency, the horse trotted up to him. "Good man, Ulysses!" Cleve yelled, as got quickly to his feet. He swung into the saddle and rode off.

A gunshot, and something bit at his right shoulder—a graze, enough to hurt.

Then he was riding fast out of the enemy's line of sight, turning toward the looming volcanic peak. He cut across the road at the end of the row of houses, and headed at full gallop to the trail Gil had told him about.

Hoping to God he could find Berry.

Chapter 19

"You hear that gunfire, Breen?" Judson asked, coming back to the "hole in the wall."

Inside, the smell of three perpetually unwashed men now overwhelmed the musk of the bear who'd inhabited the shallow cave a season back.

Chance Breen nodded. "I heard it." He was sitting on the cave floor, back to the wall. Red was sitting crosslegged in front of him. They were playing Breen's own special variety of draw poker. Turns out Red was quite easy to cheat.

"Sounds like a small war," Breen added. "Might be good for us."

"How's that?" Red asked.

"Why, it's clear to see," Judson said.

"I cain't see nothin' from here," Red said earnestly as he tossed his cards into the deadwood.

"If they be killing each other up there, that's fewer we got to fight," Breen explained, getting up to look out the entrance. He stood there listening for gunfire. Nothing to hear now except the screech of a hawk.

"What if it's an Indian raid?" Red asked, not unreasonably.

"It ain't," said Judson. "I had a look. I could see some men up there shooting—couldn't see any sign of Indians."

"Lordy, I need me a drink," Breen said, licking his cracked lips. "Whiskey and water, in that order. We'll have us a drink today, boys. There's liquor in that mansion, I know there is, right along with gold and silver and a beautiful woman and everything a man could want. Just got to set things up right . . . and take it."

"What about the fire?" Red asked. "We don't need it now?"

"We do," said Judson. "Got to make sure whoever's up there is busy when we do the necessary."

"When we going in?" Red asked, almost a whine. "I need me a woman. I could use a drink. And I wants a get rich, son of a bitch! So when we goin'?"

"Soon's it starts to get dark," Breen said. "Got two jugs of kerosene with my saddle. The sky mostly clear, no rain clouds coming." He grinned to himself as he looked out at the sky. "Damned good night for a powerful big fire!"

Riding up the game trail, Cleve reined in to rest Ulysses and have a look down at the settlement. He saw no one and wished he knew what was happening at the Abodes.

Clearing his Colt of empty cartridges, Cleve realized he'd used every bullet he had except a handful of Winchester rounds in his coat pocket. He hadn't expected to have so much use of ammunition, and he'd given half his supply to Milt. Seemed like that was a mistake.

If the Apostles trailed him up here, he'd have to outmaneuver them, get at an isolated enemy, use his knife—and scavenge some ammunition from the body. He'd done it often enough in the war.

He peered once more at his back trail. No one seemed to be following him, not yet.

Cleve continued up the hillside, feeling a skirling gust chill the back of his neck as it tried to pry his hat off. The trail took him between two close-set boulders, and ahead he could see the sunlight glimmering in the yellow mist rising from the hot springs. Feeling a tingling of premonition, he rode a little harder, and was soon on the shoulder of the mountain. He smelled sulfur and mineral oddments, and a waft of hot steam swept over them, making Ulysses snort . . .

And then Cleve sharply reined in and stared at the steaming pool under the hot springs.

About seventy feet away and a little below him, the diaphanous form of a naked nymph rose from the seething mists. For two long seconds he thought he was seeing things . . . and then he saw the rifle standing next to the pool.

It was a woman—but her form was so distorted by the steam he couldn't make her out. It might be Eliza, he supposed. But no, not so full-figured as Eliza.

He stopped breathing and laughed. "Berenice!"

"Oh!" she cried—and she waded splashily toward the rifle, grabbed it, and turned it his way, as Cleve rode slowly and carefully down the steep trail, relief spreading through him in a wave, a feeling approaching ecstasy. *Berenice!*

But of course, he kept his appearance reserved. It wouldn't do for a man to look giddy.

He came to the edge of the pool, dismounted, and she shouted, "Cleve!"

Splashing and stark naked she hurried to him, the rifle cradled in her arms. "Oh, thank Providence!" He grinned and said a rifle wasn't much cover for modesty, but she clasped him and squeezed him to her so hard he could hardly breathe. "I'm glad to see you too—" His voice was hoarse from emotion. "Berry—I was afraid Lamb had done something awful to you. Maybe killed you—"

"I'm all right." She drew back a little and looked up into his eyes. A wisp of hot-springs steam rose from her wet, straggling chestnut hair; her cheeks were ruddy, her eyes bright. "He tried to force himself on me—I stopped him, and he said when he came back, I would surely have no choice. That very night I used some minerals from these springs—"

He grinned. "Gil told me."

"Lamb told me he was going to have you killed!"

Cleve nodded. "Eliza warned me . . ."

"Eliza?" Her face fell. She closed her eyes. He misunderstood the reason.

"She accosted me on the road west," Cleve said. "She's got the Lamb family madness."

"She tried to kill me, Cleve," Berry said, her voice breaking.

"Hellfire! Where did this happen?" He clasped her shoulders.

"Up above a little. I was on my way to the trail I'd found off the mountain—a trail that's no longer there. It's quite gone. She looked toward the cliffs. "She had some sort of obsession with you. So she tried to eliminate the . . . the obstacle. And then she followed me up here and shot at me.

It was close, a time or two . . ." Berry sighed. "She's dead, Cleve. The trail was too narrow and she—her and that beautiful white horse—"

"They fell?"

"Yes. They're both quite dead. It was horrible. Being Lamb's daughter—it's not her fault—" She broke off, staring at his right arm. "Cleve—you have *blood* on your arm!"

"A graze and a couple of shotgun pellets. Mosquito bites is all. I'm fine, my Berenice . . . my Berry . . ." There was that hoarseness again. Then—he couldn't control himself, and he kissed her, pressing her to him, and she surrendered to the kiss.

Someone shoved Cleve in the middle of his back. He heard the snort and turned to see Ulysses, staring at him from inches away. *"What?"* he asked. "Oh—"

Cleve turned to Berenice. "Where's Suzie?"

"Suzie?" She seemed dreamy-eyed, and then she blinked, and said, "Why, she's at the campsite I had with the Pecks. I noticed some sword fern growing there. Horses can eat sword fern with no danger; there are so many plants they cannot eat, but that one—"

"My peculiar darling," he said.

"I beg your pardon?"

"I was thinking that might be a good endearment for you."

"Well, there is more than one interpretation of the word peculiar . . ."

"I know!"

She laughed and socked him in his unhurt shoulder. He kissed her again and after a few long moments she broke it off. "We mustn't go on like this or I shall lose all common sense."

"I thought you had already—what do you mean bathing unclothed up here like that, Berry? Don't you think Lamb might come up here?"

"I was only going to be in the water for a few minutes, to soothe my bruises and such. The sulfur has an anti-microbial effect—and I had the rifle handy."

He stepped back and looked her over. "Oh lord—the

bruises!" The big bruises on her hip and shoulder were plain to see, along with numerous scratches, but he'd been too overwhelmed by finding her to take in particulars. "When you fell from that window—"

"I'm much better. But we must revert to common sense. I will dress, and we will look to our next strategy."

It was dusk when Breen, Judson, and Red worked their way up the hillside, Red and Judson carrying the jugs of kerosene. They had to go up a steep route, and partway Breen slipped down a full ten feet. He had to be pushed partway back up by the grumbling Red.

But pretty quick, they reached the shelf of rock under the road. They crept up on all fours and Breen peered up over the edge of the road. He knew that normally the Apostles would be somewhere close by. He had planned to spot them from cover and then figure how to get around them.

But there were no Apostles to be seen. Maybe that gunfire cleared the road for him. He hoped it wasn't some other outfit robbing the man *he* planned to rob. That could be a cruel inconvenience.

"Come on, boys," he said, standing up. "Nobody home, at this end. Let's get right quick on across the road. There's some brush along the other side, we'll stick behind that. Head to the south—and flatten down if you hear anybody coming."

"I hope to God you ain't getting me killed, Chance," Judson muttered, as he and Red started across the road.

"Ha-*ha!* If we're smart about it this'll be a party in the bawdy house, Squaw Jumper," Breen said. He crossed the street only when he saw Judson and Red hadn't drawn fire.

The three of them, hunched over, moved rapidly south

between a low ridge of rock and the scrub brush. Judson was breathing hard, carrying a kerosene jug. "Chance," he muttered, "how about you take a turn carrying this thing."

"Got to stay alert, can't be sidetracked into that. I know my way around here, more or less, but I got to watch."

"Bothers me we didn't find a way to get our horses up here." Judson broke off to catch his breath. "How we going to get away?"

"If we have to get away, we'll steal horses, there's plenty of 'em here. But I figure we don't have to get away. We do things right, we can live here like kings in that big house."

"I don't think you have any sense," Judson said. "There's too many of the bastards up here."

"They can take orders from us! Hush now!" For they'd come within sight of the Abodes. "Wind is coming from the north. That'll carry the fire from one house to the next. We'll splash a couple of them houses on both sides, and we'll set 'em afire. I got a hungry lucifer just waitin' in my pocket. Then I'll show you how we'll get to the house without running into those Apostles. I got the lay of it when they took me out of here . . . Lord, I want me a drink . . ."

Cleve and Berry were sitting close together on a hummock of dirt and rock at the camping space near the hot springs. Berry was fully clothed. Up here there was yet some scant light from the western horizon, little more than fading twilight. They'd eaten some of the dried meat the Bannock had given Cleve, and they were watching Ulysses and Suzie contentedly cropping sword fern.

"I'm so glad you found Ejupa, Cleve. What an ordeal—the way Ejupa was treated."

Cleve nodded. "He never showed he was in pain. He's a true Panati. And he evened the score with Sedge too." He looked up the mountainside. "Berry—you're sure that eastern trail is cut off?"

"It is. I tried to go that way, and I found that the ledge that had been there was gone! There were blast marks, you see. After they caught us trying to ride off that way, they went up there and dynamited the trail!"

He felt a cold mistiness, looked up to see thick gray clouds, some of them almost in reach, sweeping in from the west. "Might rain soon. But you'll have to wait here for me. I have some unfinished business. Then we'll make our way to the western road that goes to the mining camp. Find our way to Redding from there."

"And what is this unfinished business?"

He cleared his throat. "Berenice—Magnus Lamb locked you up and tried to violate you. For that—I flat cannot bear to let him live. I would never be able to sleep nights. I ask you to forgive me, and I know you think I'm bloody-minded, but—"

"No, Cleve," she interrupted. "When it comes to Lamb, I feel that—not for my sake, but for everyone here—it's *best* if you kill him."

This surprised Cleve. Perhaps with all that had happened she'd become more practical about gunwork. "He mentioned he had a set of dueling pistols, and he knows how to use them. I will call him out."

Berry reached for the canteen, and said, "Call him out with an *unloaded pistol?* You tell me you have only four rifle rounds! Is he going to let you use a rifle in a duel? I think not! Cleveland Trewe, I am astonished." She took a drink from the canteen, and added, "How could a man like *you* permit himself to run out of ammunition?"

"I am not a manufacturer of ammunition, Berenice,"

Cleve said dryly, as he picked up her appropriated rifle to look it over. "It is not always handy for purchase. I did once know a man named Jim Hickok. He was a scout for us in the war—they call him Wild Bill now—and he made his own bullets. Didn't trust the factory." He gave her back the carbine.

Berry shook her head. "How are we going to protect ourselves here with so little ammunition? I have but two bullets left in my rifle! You have but four rifle cartridges!"

"Strategy, my peculiar darling. Tactics. I . . . what's the matter?"

She was staring aghast toward the settlement, far below. "Is that a fire?"

He turned and squinted down at the settlement. The tops of a few of the Abodes could be seen—and flame licked up the side of one of them. "It *is* a fire!"

"Cleve, we've got to help them—"

But Cleve realized he'd have no chance to become a volunteer fireman, because he saw Carmody and five Apostles riding up the hill toward them, pistols in hand.

Chapter 20

The Apostles were riding single file, Carmody in the lead, about seventy yards down the hillside—as Cleve jumped up, Winchester at the ready. It was reloaded now, but with precious few rounds. He had no time for fine judgment. He tucked the rifle to his shoulder, aimed it at Carmody, and fired. But Carmody had seen the rifle pointed at him; he flattened behind his horse's head, and the shot cut by and killed the man behind him.

"That's twice he let the man behind him take lead," Cleve muttered.

The Apostle fell from the saddle and the riders behind him had to rein in hard to keep their horses from stumbling over the body.

"The horses, Berry!" Cleve shouted. He stepped in front of her, to catch any lead that might be flying her way as she ran to her horse. Carmody was still on horseback, trying for a shot at him with a pistol.

"Take Suzie down the hillside straight west!" Cleve shouted, as a shot from Carmody cracked past them.

"There's no trail down!" she said, mounting up.

"You'll have to risk that raw slope, Berry!" He ran,

ducked low to Ulysses, swung into the saddle. Turning
Ulysses toward the Apostles, he shouted, "Suzie can do it
if she has to! I'm going another way!"

The way that would lead the Apostles away from Berry.

He spurred Ulysses into a gallop, and rode at an angle to
the trail, straight at Carmody, loudly shrieking *"Hiiiii-YAHH!"*
as he came. Cleve calculated that the surprise in the ma-
neuver might throw off Carmody's shooting.

Carmody was just a few yards away when he fired his
wheelgun—a Confederate Griswold six-gun by the sound
of it. But the angle was awkward, Carmody's horse was
rearing and the shot went wild.

Cleve flashed in front of him, cutting hard, riding
roughly northeast and circling around the big boulders that
edged the trail.

Once under cover, Cleve slowed to give Ulysses a
chance to find his footing. But Carmody was coming up
behind them. A bullet slashed by, the Griswold booming.
Ulysses made his own decision, lunging up the hillside,
climbing and then galloping across a knoll to the ridge that
overlooked the mansion.

Cleve swung north on the ridge, riding toward Lamb's
salute cannon. He rode past it—and abruptly ran out of
ridge. He'd come to a sheer drop.

He cantered back to the cannon. It would make good
cover.

Cleeve jumped down, Winchester in hand. He could see
Carmody and the four surviving Apostles riding up the
trail onto the other end of the ridge, and turning his way.
They were on higher ground, that end of the ridge rising
above Cleve's.

Cleve knelt, laid the Winchester across the lower part
of the cannon's carriage, and aimed at Carmody. That's

when the predicted rain began to fall and a cloud of mist rolled over the oncoming Apostles—he couldn't see the men clearly. He fired, couldn't make out if he'd hit anybody. Told himself to stop wasting ammunition.

On the farther side of the cannon was a massy heap under an oilskin tarpaulin. He remembered Carmody telling him the cannon could be used against Indians, that they had some fully armed cartridges.

He put the rifle aside, grabbed the base of the carriage, and lifted it. It was a modest-sized fieldpiece but he needed all his strength as he swiveled the muzzle toward the enemy—who were just emerging from the cloud. They were a good distance off as yet, not quite a quarter mile.

Cleve unscrewed the breach of the Whitworth cannon. The wind seemed to scream at him to hurry as he twitched the oilcloth away from the heap of shells, grabbed two of them, hurried to the breach of the cannon, inserted a shell, closed it, and screwed it shut. Apostle bullets careened off a carriage wheel and the muzzle of the cannon. He looked up, saw the Apostles perhaps sixty yards away coming down the rocky slop of the ridgetop. Cleve pushed at a wheel, adjusting the angle of fire, then moved well to one side, with the firing cord in hand.

And he triggered the cannon.

It boomed and rocked back a few feet on its carriage. Bullets cut past—and then there came a roar as the shell struck the inclined ground under the oncoming riders. Cleve was startled to see yellow-tinged steam from an underground channel gushing up around the men. They screamed in pain and their scorched horses sunfished and bucked two of the men into the rising cloud of the explosive. Another was brutally rent by flying shrapnel and shattered stone.

Carmody was still coming, giving out a bloodcurdling rebel yell as Cleve reloaded the cannon, stepped away from recoil, triggered the shell—and the round hissed by Carmody. But two bloodied Apostles behind him, trying to stand by the shell crater, were lost in the explosion as the shell struck at their feet.

There was no time to reload the Whitworth. Cleve had only one shot left in the Winchester.

He grabbed the rifle, brought it to his shoulder, just as Carmody rode by. Cleve swung the rifle toward Carmody, who circled tightly back to ride straight at him.

Carmody's horse reared and a hoof struck out as Cleve squeezed the trigger and then . . .

He was lying on his back staring up at the darkening sky. A few stars . . . just a few . . .

Rain was splashing on his face. A shadow moved in and blocked his view. It was Ulysses, snorting, lipping his face.

"I'm fine . . . fine and dandy . . ." Cleve said. But he wasn't sure of that at all. His head rang like a bell and he felt blood oozing hot and thick over his left ear.

He blinked against the rain, sat up, took hold of Ulysses's bridle, and used it to steady him as he stood.

Apostle Carmody's horse had run off. But Carmody was there. He was lying on his back, about ten feet away, coughing and clutching his throat. Blood was gushing around his fingers. The rifle shot had caught him in the gullet.

The Griswold pistol lay near Carmody. Cleve started toward it—and then had to stop as the world spun halfway around and lurchingly swung back, all in a moment. Nausea surged up in him. He put his face up to the rain, let it wash the blood away, soothe him with its chill.

The rollicking ceased. Cleve took a deep breath and

two quick steps toward the Griswold—just as Carmody grabbed it.

His bloody hand shaking, Carmody raised the pistol, squeezed the trigger—and the gun misfired. Cleve stepped in and kicked the gun out of Carmody's hand.

"You see that, Carmody," Cleve said. "Confederate weaponry. Cheap stuff paid for by greedy slavers. Those tub-bellied plantation colonels weren't going to pay for a good weapon."

"Kill me," Carmody rasped, the words coming out with bubbles of blood. The rain washed the blood down his face, so it made pink and red puddles on the ground.

"You took my woman prisoner for Magnus Lamb," Cleve said. "You put her in a cell for his use. You can lay there and choke to death—and think about what Hell's going to be like."

Cleve turned away, found his Winchester, and returned it to the scabbard. He groaned, holding on to Ulysses's saddle to keep from falling over, as once more the world spun, left and then right. A shod hoof had clipped his head. He figured he had a concussion. But it was going to have to wait.

The spinning subsided and he looked at the Griswold pistol. He couldn't trust it, evidently. And it wasn't likely to use the same load as his Colt. He pressed the cylinder release and removed the cylinder so he could see the cartridges. The cartridges wouldn't fit his Colt.

Cleve tossed the weapon aside. If he was going to have to scavenge, there were four other dead men nearby.

He mounted up—and gritted his teeth against the pain that shot through his head. He held on, as the thinning rain washed over him. Five seconds, ten, twenty—and the pain dwindled. "All right, Ulysses, let's ride over to that mess we made along the ridge . . ."

They rode through the acrid cloud of gunpower, past the smoking muzzle of the cannon.

Cleve looked down the mountainside to the settlement. There was rain and cloud wisps blurring the view, but he could see smoke puffing up from blackened buildings. He didn't see any flame. The rain had put out the fire, maybe. That was a little luck, anyhow. The shower might have saved some lives.

Was the fire accidental? If not—who set it? And where was Berenice?

When he reached the charred craters and slid down from the saddle, the whirling and the nausea struck him again. It was a bit less this time. The rain lessened, too, and finally stopped.

Cleve took a few seconds to make sure the spell had passed, and then walked over to the mangled bodies. He lit a match, to help him see . . .

What he saw was staring dead eyes in broken heads and rendered flesh, still oozing blood. His stomach lurched. But then he saw something else—one of the dead men had lost an arm. It was lying nearby, detached. But the hand on that arm was still grasping a Colt .45. And the corpse bore a full belt of cartridges.

In the amber light of a lantern, Berry was sitting on the edge of the bed, using the last of the salve Claudia had given her on the burned arms of the little boy and his mother. They weren't terrible burns—there would be little scarring. The boy and his mother were on the same low wood-frame bed in one of the small Abode bedrooms. The woman coughed. She'd inhaled some smoke, getting her boy out of the burning house. The little boy rasped, "What will Pa say, the house burning down and all?"

His mother, a haggard, brown-haired woman now dressed only in a slip, hugged her boy, and said, "He'll say we were lucky, I expect, that we come through it And no one died—except that old gentleman. He breathed in too much smoke. But the rest of us got out."

"But we got no house now, Mama. This ain't our house."

"No, t'isn't. We're just lucky we come through. We got the help of this nice lady. Anyhow, we got each other."

"Why do you think those men started the fire?"

"I surely do not know. Bedeviled, maybe."

"What will the Sovereign say?"

"I don't know as I care," his mother murmured. "Rest now, child."

"It was Providence, the rain coming when it did," Berry suggested. She said it not because she believed the rain a special act of God, but because she wanted to ease the boy's mind.

"Yes," the boy's mother said. "Yes, it was. We're surely obliged for your kindness, ma'am."

Berry set the empty leather pouch of salve aside and looked through the window. Four houses had burned across the street. They were charred sketches of houses now, lit feebly from smoking embers. Why indeed had the arsonist set the fire?

She kept watching the street, hoping to see Cleve ride up. But he didn't come.

There were dead men leading the way into the mansion.

An Apostle lay dead by the gate. Looked like the bullet had gone through the face and out the back of his head.

Halfway to the front door Cleve found Lamb's shotgun guard dead. Five rounds in Heiler's belly.

Another Apostle lay face down near the front door. Shot in the back.

Who did this?

Cleve had a suspicion.

The Colt Army, fully loaded, was in his right hand. His vertigo had lifted, but a painful quiver passed through his head with every step. Not such a bad pain. In the war, when they were digging bullets out of him without so much as ether, he'd had pain that seemed a whole world to itself. He could manage this.

Cleve stalked determinedly to the door, flung it open— and stepped quickly to one side. No one fired through the doorway. He waited, and waited a little more, then risked a look. Inside he saw oil lamps glowing in fine sconces along the red velvet entry hall. He remembered it from his one visit here, for tea.

Pistol cocked, his senses alert though his head rang and throbbed, Cleve strode down the hallway to a marble-floored antechamber with staircases and portraits. Several stories above, a glass skylight showed a bit of moonlight through the fragmentary clouds. Under the stairs was a doorway—and here lay another body. It was a stout middle-aged man in servant's livery. Cleve had never seen the man. He lay on his back, starring into eternity. His neck was cut partway through and beside him was a wood-cutting ax, its blade bloody.

Cleve glanced around, then crossed the open space, and took up the ax with his left hand. Couldn't hurt to have an extra weapon.

Then he stepped across the dead man and up to the doorway of a room that looked like a gentleman's study.

There was a big desk, robes hanging behind it, and walls covered with books.

His own father's study had been only slightly less lavish. A small candelabra threw a symmetrical splash of light and shadow on the carpet.

He heard a voice he knew quite well. "You'll tell me where it is, or I'll cut off your manly parts. Where'd I leave that ax, Red?"

It was Chance Breen.

"Gentlemen, I have no treasure here, but what you see," said Lamb, his voice shaky. Cleve couldn't see Lamb, but he knew he was there. "My money is in two banks, one in San Francisco and another in Denver. You have found a thousand dollars in ready cash, and you have a silver candelabra, and a gold urn, and my daughter's jewelry. You must be content with that. I have sent a man for the U.S. Marshal—"

"You are a liar, mister!" Breen yelled. "Red—go get me that ax I left out there!"

"Now look here—!" Lamb shouted.

"You sit down and shut up, Lamb!"

"God will judge you and Hell will be like Heaven compared to what is coming!" bellowed Lamb. Then came a thump and a cry of pain and Judson laughed.

"You give him a good one there, Breen."

"Get that ax, Red, dammit!"

"Sure thing, Chance . . ."

Cleve holstered his Colt. He set his legs apart, got his stance as solid as he could, and took the ax into his right hand as Red came to the door and stopped. He gaped. "It's that feller! He's—"

Cleve threw the ax just as he'd thrown it in the lumber

camp. It spun to its target, and its blade sank into Red's forehead with a *chunk* sound.

There wasn't time for Red to scream. He just staggered back—and fell dead. Cleve drew the Colt.

There was a shout of consternation in the study, but Cleve was stepping through the door. Lamb, his face bloodied, was sitting on a chair against the opposite wall. Breen and Judson stood to the right. As Cleve had expected they were gawking at Red's body, giving Cleve a chance to fire the Colt at Judson, because he was nearer. He shot him in the forehead—he was only six feet away, an easy target.

Before Judson hit the floor Cleve turned on his heel and fired at Breen—who had his own Remington six-gun raised. Breen's teeth were clenched, his face rigid with hate. They fired almost simultaneously, Cleve sooner and truer. Breen's bullet cut a long groove into Cleve's right forearm.

Chance Breen sank to his knees with a bullet in his heart. Then the light in his eyes went out and he pitched over onto his face.

Cleve turned to face Lamb and saw "the Sovereign" was standing up now, his back turned.

"Turn around, Lamb!" Cleve said. The Colt felt strangely heavy in Cleve's hand. He was gritting his teeth against the rising pain in his right arm and the thudding in his head . . .

Lamb turned, a dueling pistol in his right hand. "God condemns you thus!" Lamb roared, firing the old muzzle-loaded pistol, as Cleve—his hand not wanting to work—forced his finger to pull the trigger of the Colt . . .

The guns roared at each other.

Cleve saw Lamb's right eye vanish in a splash of blood

as he felt a thud in the left side of his chest. Felt like having a pickax blade slammed into him.

Then he was falling, his right hand going numb, the world turning into liquid, swirling darkly around him and going down a hole, like rainwater going down a drainpipe, down and down; the whole world, everything he'd ever known, sinking into the earth and just . . . gone.

Chapter 21

"We'll need fresh bandages. Where is Donahue? I must have Donahue here!"

Was that Berry's voice? Was it his Berenice? Calling somewhere in the darkness to the man Donahue. Her voice echoed through a lightless cavern. *"Donahue! Quickly!"*

"I'm here, ma'am! He will need a tourniquet!"

Could anything be so dark as this place? Even a dark room had a speck of light, a little gray, something. But there was no light here. Were his eyes closed? He tried to open them. But it was like trying to force open windows that were nailed shut.

"His breathing is . . . it is erratic, Donahue!"

"Cleveland Trewe!" Brother Donahue's voice, loud in his ear. *"Take a deep breath, and another! It's all you need do, is breathe! God will provide all else!"*

Must he breathe? To breathe seemed a great weary task.

"Please, Cleve . . . !" He felt Berry's lips kissing his forehead. *"Please—for me. Breathe!"*

He used all his strength to do that simple thing that he'd done countless times without thinking. Just to take a breath.

"Thank you, my darling, my only, thank you . . . keep breathing . . ."

Had she called him her darling . . . her only? He kept breathing.

Then he seemed to float away somewhere . . . what a curious place to be . . .

Where was he? In his tent at Gettysburg? Here was Charlie Dunne, his aide-de-camp, waving a telegram at him. Then Charlie's smiling, earnest face was lost in a cloud of cannon smoke, and Cleve floated away . . . floated for what seemed like forever.

It was so hot here. He was so thirsty. Cleve was walking in a familiar, arid wasteland of canyons and hills, but this time it was much hotter. There was no shade. There were no shadows. He didn't even have a shadow himself. Nor did the rocks cast shadows. The sun was everywhere and nowhere, and it burned him pitilessly. He thought about burrowing under some sand, waiting for nightfall—but then he heard Berry's voice, calling him. "I have something to tell you, Cleve . . ." Hadn't this happened before, sometime?

"Berenice!" he called, his voice barely a rasp. He could scarcely hear it. "Berry!"

Then suddenly there was cool water at his lips. Her voice close to his ear. *"I'm here, Cleve. Take this water . . . then some broth . . . and rest . . . you must rest and get stronger, my darling, my only . . ."*

The water . . . it was as if he'd never tasted water before, never known how complex its taste was, how delightful . . .

And then he felt tired, so weary he could walk no more.

"Berry . . ." He felt himself melting into the sand . . . and then he was floating again, floating nowhere . . . forever.

"He opened his eyes, I'm sure of it!" That was Gil Peck's voice.

He tried to open his eyes. The eyelids seemed stuck.

Then he heard Berry, close by. "You sure? He looked at you?"

"I'm not sure he saw me."

"Cleve?" He felt her hand on his. Cool and yet full of life. "Two days since his fever broke . . ."

If Berenice was truly there, he *must* see her. Cleve forced his eyes open.

A blurry light. Two figures, in vague outline. One was sitting beside him. Berry's happy voice. "He heard me! He's looking at us! Cleve!"

She leaned close and kissed him, and new strength arose in Cleve. He put his arms around her and felt her warm tears falling on his cheeks.

It was another day before he could sit up without his head spinning. "Who dug the bullets out of me?" Cleve asked, his voice rough, as he took the bowl of soup from Berry. His right arm ached with the effort, but it was nothing because Berry was there, in person beside him. She wore a white nightgown, and little else. Her hair was down, flowing over her shoulders, and she was barefoot.

"Donahue was your surgeon," Berry said. "I assisted. He really is quite deft. That horse-pistol ball was lodged so close to your heart—a little twitch and . . ." She shook her head. "We'd have lost you! There was the bullet in your arm to come out, too, and some shotgun pellets, and the crack on your head to mend. You'll have a little scar, just past the hairline, where he sewed it up. How did you come by that blow?"

"Carmody's horse kicked me. Didn't connect much but it was enough I guess . . ."

"Someone fired that cannon. Was it you?"

"I did. The damned fools left live shells beside it. And I was down to one bullet. I was captain of artillery for close to a year. Did someone bury the dead?"

"Oh, yes. It's been quite a task. They gave everyone a nice burial, no matter who—Breen, and those other two—even Magnus Lamb. Some here wept over Lamb, in fact. It took a while to get to poor Eliza's body, but she's buried beside him."

Cleve ate some soup, very slowly, his hand shaking a trifle. He hoped that wasn't going to be permanent. He paused eating to gaze at her in amazement. There she was. Right there, sitting on a chair within reach. "You sure I'm not dreaming, Berenice?"

She took his hand and kissed it, a considerable kiss too. "Did that feel real?"

"Oh, yes. I feel a stirring . . ."

"You just get your strength up and mend—*then* we'll talk about your stirrings, sirrah!" Her smile was brighter than the lamp.

She'd been sleeping beside him every night, so Gil had told him, and sitting up with him during the day. Washing him, sponging him, softly talking to him while he'd been out. He had the impression he'd been under for a time.

"How long was I out? Couple days?"

"Oh," she said with dry casualness, "not above thirteen days."

"Thirteen days!"

She pulled a chair close to the bed. It was evening,

judging by the purplish sky glimpsed through the window. A wet wind lashed thin rain at the window glass. But the room was warm. There was a cheerful fire in the hearth across from the bed.

"You have been comatose, Cleve. The blow to your head, and another grazing your heart—you nearly died, you know."

"How's Ulysses?"

"The horses are well enough. I've been riding them, when the weather allows, to give them a little exercise. Ulysses once got out of the stable and tried to get into the mansion—he seems to know you're here."

Cleve smiled. He ate a little more soup. "What will folks here do without Lamb and the Apostles?"

"There is a plan! A letter has been sent to the county seat, explaining that marauders came and killed Mr. Lamb, and that the Apostles died in a shootout. I wrote the letter myself, wording it so that it does not lie about who shot Lamb. I let the county believe that Lamb was killed by the outlaws—by Breen and his gang. I did not bring your name into it at all."

He nodded. She'd known what he would want. "So the Lambsville folks are going to stay here?"

"It is now called the town of Blue Mountain! You see Lamb *did* write up papers saying they had a share in this place—I doubt he ever planned to give them any money to speak of. But he had to make it look regular enough. They can use those filings to stake a claim on this settlement. I have suggested that people from Redding could be enticed to visit the hot springs and stay in the mansion—which is to be called the Blue Mountain Hotel. A few parishioners have left, but the others have removed all trace of Lamb from the chapel. Gil has nearly convinced them to be Swedenborgians . . ."

"He's back on that, is he?" He spilled a little of the soup on his lap. "Damn me for a clumsy fool."

"Shall I not feed you the rest of the soup?"

"No, I need to do it." He concentrated on controlling his hand as he raised the spoon to his lips. "Good soup. What is this meat?"

"Mountain goat. It's a bit stringy."

"It's delicious. And you, Berenice—you are the most beautiful woman in the world."

Berry gave a small laugh. "Oh, indeed? I thought your fever had passed—evidently not!"

Several more tantalizing weeks passed, with winter deepening. Berenice was always close by, sleeping next to him but allowing him no more than the occasional kiss. "We shall discuss your carnal impulses, sir, when you are fully mended . . ."

Berry shaved him every other day and seemed to enjoy giving him sponge baths. He didn't mind it himself, seeing as it was her doing it.

Snow came, and went, and came again. When Berry was out of the room, Cleve would get up, walk around the bed, try to exercise himself as he might. It was painful, but his head had cleared, and he felt stronger every day. When Cleve heard her coming back, he would get quickly back in bed, feeling like a boy hiding mischief from his mother—and indeed she guessed what he was up to and scolded him for it.

More than once, as Cleve improved, Berenice went to the hot springs, even bathing during a snowfall—a fact that amazed some of the residents. Berry assured them that it was an accepted custom in Scandinavia, and Freja admitted it was. Freja was no longer in serious pain, and was sitting up, chatting, and sewing for anyone who needed it. Her pregnancy seemed undisturbed.

One afternoon, when he was sure Berry was at the hot springs, Cleve got up, found his laundered clothes and his sheepskin jacket, and his boots and slipped out the door, and out of the building. He felt undressed without his gun belt, but he didn't know where they'd stowed it, and Blue Mountain was safe enough now.

His arm and chest ached some, but the wounds were fairly healed, at least on the outside, and his head seemed entirely mended. His hand had ceased it's trembling too. He walked, a little slowly but steadily, out to the barn. It wasn't bitter cold and the snow was just a few coats on the ground.

Ulysses reared and kicked at the stall when he saw Cleve come into the barn. "Now is that how you say hello? All right, all right, let me saddle you . . ."

It felt good to be in the saddle again, riding around the settlement. He stopped to talk to Wardwell, who was back in the settlement with the lumbermen. On clement days they built new housing for the single men, and just now Wardwell was supervising the building of a cabin. Cleve sat in the saddle, watching. Meeker waved at Cleve and nodded. Cleve waved back.

The men didn't seem to hold a grudge against Cleve for the standoff over their plans for Milt. They were cheerful, seeing as they were finally about to get paid, the county having given the okay to the bank, and they all had a share of the lumber business. Wardwell had been elected company president.

Cleve rode on, touring the settlement. Children were playing in the snow out in front of the houses, including a little boy with bandages on his arm. Cleve showed the boy his own bandaged arm and said, "Me too, pardner!"

The boy grinned at him, pleased.

Onward and up the mountain to the area of the hot springs. He dismounted at the little campsite and tied Ulysses up near the ferns. "Ulysses—I hope this works. Wish me luck."

Cleve skulked on up the hill, as if he were an Army scout spying out the lines, and saw Berenice, her back to him, sitting in a hot spring, holding a broken piece of crystal up to see it better. He undressed as quiet as he could, silently called himself a fool for taking off his clothes outside in winter and cursed himself silently as he went barefoot through the snow. The noise of his approach muffled by the bubbling and hissing of the water, Cleve was able to slide into the hot spring beside Berry—and she gasped in outrage.

"You! You utter *reprobate!* You rogue! You shall undo all the good work we've done healing you—"

He was feeling the heat of the water—it was hotter than he'd thought it'd be—but he put an arm around her and looked her in the eyes, and said gravely, "I beg for clemency, ma'am. Do please forgive me." He kissed her— and she melted against him.

Then after a moment, breathing hard, she pushed him back. "Look at the state of you! How can we possibly . . . *no!* You must go back . . ."

He kissed her again. Then asked, "Must I go? If you insist, ma'am. Just one more kiss . . ."

"Oh, don't you dare."

But she let him kiss her again. And at last, she said, "Well . . . perhaps if you were to lean back, and I were to face you, and we remained sitting . . . and we take it all very easy . . . I suppose it might . . . it might be beneficial for your general health . . ."

Another month brought a break in the weather. It was still winter, but the sun was out and the snow eased off. Supplies were coming in steadily now for the settlement and the mansion was being prepared for guests. Cleve and Berry volunteered to take the order for posters and newspaper advertising to Redding to advertise the Blue Mountain Hotel and Hot Springs. They would not be coming back to Gunmetal Mountain.

They said their goodbyes to Gil and Freja and Donahue and the rest of the settlers the night before, left early in the morning, and set out toward the lumber camp and the road that went from there south to Redding.

It was a sunny morning as they rode south along the boisterous Pit River, the patches of snow in the shadows of pines beginning to sparkle as the sun ascended. Cleve still had some healing to do, but he felt like himself once more, and it was hard not to be hopeful.

He thought of wintering in San Francisco; he thought, too, of the ranch and farm he planned in the Sweet River Valley, nestled up against the Sierras far to the south. Without making any special declarations, he and Berry had fallen back into their old relationship, two people deeply connected. There was an unspoken understanding. From Redding, if they followed Berry's original plan, they'd trail southwest, despite the winter, as best they could. It would be a hard road to San Francisco, and that did worry him some.

"Cleve," she said suddenly, "let's rest a moment."

"I concur with that proposal, professor," he said. They

drew up beside the river, dismounted, and let Ulysses and Suzie get some water from a pool at the bank. For a while they watched an eagle preening as it sat on a pine bough above the farther side of the river.

She glanced at Cleve, and cleared her throat, and said, "Cleve . . . I . . . ."

"Yes?" He had the troubling sense that she was about to launch into a speech of some kind.

"Cleve—you are still healing—"

"I'm very well, I thank you, Mrs. Tucker," he said gruffly. "I'm right as the mail."

"Nevertheless, I think you should not live rough for a time, Cleve."

"Are you suggesting you go on your . . . your *expedition* . . . alone?"

"Not at all," she said, her eyes twinkling. "I suggest we take the train to San Francisco after all! It may be two or three trains. We shall arrange something safe for the transport of the horses."

He was relieved to hear it. "Good! There may be some delays—the snow can pile up along the tracks—but even so—"

She put a hand over his lips to stop him speaking. Then she looked him in the eyes. "It isn't just out of concern for you. I do believe I am with child, Cleve."

He stared. "What!"

"Yes. It's not so very far advanced—but I believe so. We shall rest in Redding, if that is agreeable to you, and then, if you have no other plan . . . onward by railroad to San Francisco! And Cleve—out of concern for . . . for the legalities, and the future of the child, despite the barbarism of the way marriage has been arranged in our society, I think that, perhaps . . ."

He seized her hands and pulled her closer. "You will marry me, then?"

"Have I not just said so—more or less? Really, it's just a legal arrangement. I chose you as my mate, and I may as well put up with the formality—"

"Oh ho!" He kissed her, and then grinned at her. "The experimentation is over, is it? You've come to a firm conclusion about a mate?"

"I have, Mr. Trewe. And if you are agreeable, I shall become Mrs. Trewe. We can get married in Redding, if you like."

"By God!" He seized her and kissed her again, and she pulled away, laughing at his enthusiasm—something he almost never showed. "Easy, you'll crack my ribs! There's a zygote in there—by now an embryo!"

"Lord, I—" He drew back, aghast. "Have I hurt you?"

"No, no, not at all."

"I won't touch you till . . . whenever you say is . . ."

"It's not quite like that. For a good time yet we may still engage in conjugal intimacy, Mr. Trewe."

"Yes?" He was pleased to hear that.

"But what do you say we mount up—I mean on our horses—and head for Redding now."

They mounted up, and it seemed to Cleve as if the day had gotten strangely warm for the season. They rode on, trotting slowly southward on the trail by the river, and after a time she asked, "Cleve—have you read much Robert Browning?"

"I have."

"Do you know his poem 'The Last Ride Together'?"

"Yes, fairly well—hold up now. Do you suggest this is our last ride together? Have you changed your mind already about—"

"No, no, no, I have not changed my mind! The end of the poem hints that it is *not* the last ride of the poet and his lover together. And here we are, riding along and the last lines came back to me. Do you remember it? Starting, 'What if we still ride on, we two . . .'?"

"I believe so."

Then they recited the lines together:

> *What if we still ride on, we two*
> *With life for ever old yet new,*
> *Changed not in kind but in degree,*
> *The instant made eternity,—*
> *And heaven just prove that I and she*
> *Ride, ride together, for ever ride . . . ?*

Keep reading for a special excerpt . . .

AXLE BUST CREEK
by John Shirley

From the battlefield of Shiloh to the prisoner camp
at Slocum, former Union soldier Cleveland Trewe
has seen more than enough carnage for one lifetime.
Now that the war is over he's found work as a peace-
keeper and prospector—the perfect set of survival skills
for a town like Axle Bust, Nevada,
a place seething with danger.
Cleve's uncle staked a claim in Axle Bust
only to lose it to a murderous con man partnered
with Duncan Conroy, owner of the Golden Fleece Mine
and a man determined to build an empire
by means fair and foul.
The only person keeping Conroy in check is his sister,
Berenice, a freethinker whose scientific education
benefits the family interests—
even while catching Cleve's eye.
To reclaim his uncle's mine, and bring justice to a town
under tyranny, Cleve finds himself turning the streets
into a bullet-riddled battlefield.
Conroy is about to learn there just isn't room
for both men in a town like Axle Bust.

Chapter 1

Nevada. Spring of 1874.

Cleveland Terwilliger Trewe was trying to get to Axle Bust before sundown. He kept Ulysses at a canter whenever the rugged northward trail allowed, and a trot when it didn't. He'd been told the thin trail skirting the steep hillside was prone to collapse, and rain was coming. Steady rain was rare in northeast Nevada, but sudden gulley-washers came along in April, and he had no wish to dig his horse out of a mudslide. The late-afternoon sky was closed by gray clouds, and now and then they rumbled, growling low like sleeping bears.

"Step carefully, Ulysses," he told the sorrel stallion, patting his neck. "And we'll get you to grain and rest." They'd ridden for many hours with scarce a respite. Cleve and his mount were getting tired and thirsty.

Another mile, and he reined in and got a drink from his canteen. He climbed down off the horse, knuckled dust from his gray-blue eyes, and took off his dark gray Stetson. He used the hat to slap dust from his long charcoal coat, muttering, "Yesterday it was dust, tonight it'll be mud."

Cleve got a small tin cooking pan from his saddlebags,

filled it with water from his canteen, and held it under the sorrel's mouth. Ulysses' drank it all. He patted the horse's neck. "We'd best get on. See if we can beat the rain."

Cleve ran his thumb along his jawline, feeling a thorny bristle. Better see a barber when he got to town, especially seeing as he just might have to stand before a judge.

He put the pan away, slapped his hat on his head, remounted, and nudged Ulysses into a trot. His gaze returned often to the stands of white bark pine and quaking aspen on the hills. He was alert for the long-riders said to sometimes lie in wait on the trail to Axle. They were known to pounce on travelers who might be carrying gold dust panned from a claim or cash money.

Cleve Trewe had been a Union Scout before his time as a battlefield commander, and watchfulness was ingrained. Besides bandits, it was possible that Les Wissel had learned he was on his way; for Cleve had made inquiries at the claims recording office in Elko. Wissel might purpose to waylay Cleveland Trewe before he could testify as to his uncle's claim in Axle.

He cantered Ulysses 'round a sharp bend—and slowed to a trot when he heard men talking not far ahead. The voices came from a defile opening between hills, on the east side of the trail. Cleve reined in at the gap, and peered east in the dimming light. He made out three of them, about thirty paces from him, standing in a lantern's glow just within the mouth of an old mine burrowed into the hillside. Dusty tailings lay in humps to either side of the adit. The mine's age was attested by weeds growing within its entry, the vines dangling from above, and the half-buckled state of the timbers straining to hold it open. Two horses and a mule were picketed near the opening.

Cleve knew one of the trio instantly, for the fellow had a distinct profile and voice. It was Leon Studge. He was a stocky, sandy-haired, stub-nosed man with a high forehead and small unruly beard. He was gazing intently at something glittery in the palm of his hand.

Leon had been a friend to Cleveland Trewe, despite the hard truth of their relationship—Cleve had kept Leon Studge a prisoner for half of 1865. Leon had been a Confederate prisoner of war at Fort Slocum when Cleve was in command.

Cleve swung Ulysses down the side trail.

Riding closer, Cleve heard Leon's Texas drawl, "I could not be more satisfied, sir!" His voice came clearly from the tunnel entrance, as if from a speaking-trumpet. "Ya'll have done a kingly thing!"

The other two men were wearing suits of mismatched parts, which operators of their sort slapped together in a hasty effort to look respectable. They had fresh shaves, waxed mustaches, and their hair oiled back. One was a large, swag-bellied man in a frock coat a little too small for him; he rocked on the balls of his feet as he counted a stack of greenbacks. The third man, in a checked coat and copper-colored vest, was also familiar to Cleve. This was Salty Jones, a confidence man from Virginia City. Cleve instantly knew his darting, deep-set eyes, and the strikingly large mouth, which was forever in motion.

Salty slapped Leon on the shoulder and declared, "I am obliged to you for taking this weighty responsibility from my shoulders, Mr. Studge. To let such a bounty go unclaimed would be sinful; to remain here when calamity at home calls my brother and myself to the long journey would be shameful. All the way to Boston, sir! For a mother's pleas cannot be ignored."

"Mr. Culp, I'm obliged to you for the opportunity, I surely am," said Leon.

"His name isn't Culp," said Cleve, trotting Ulysses up

close to the mine. He drew his Winchester rifle from its
saddle scabbard. He had an Army Colt revolver and shell-
belt in his saddlebags, but he rarely wore them. "Least-
ways, Culp wasn't the name he was using in Virginia
City," Cleve went on. He dismounted, and said, "He called
himself Tom Fairbanks, there. But he was known famil-
iarly as "Salty," around the benzinery he was pleased to
call a saloon."

Leon gaped wide-eyed at Cleve. "Why it's Major
Trewe!"

"No more the Major, but Cleveland Trewe I am, Leon."

Carrying the rifle in both hands, thus far pointed away
from the men, Cleve stepped up to block them from their
mounts.

"I believe you have mistaken me, sir," Salty began. "I
have that peculiar face, that mercuriality of feature, that
seems sometimes one fellow and sometimes another. I
recall one occasion in Boston—"

"I doubt you've ever been to Boston, Salty," Cleve interrupted, noticing that the other man was squeezing the
sheaf of bills in his left hand, while his right was moving
toward the interior of his frock coat.

Cleve swung the rifle to center on the man's substantial
belly. "Do not reach into that coat, mister. Drop your hand."

"You think to rob me?" asked Salty's partner, in a low-
pitched voice of outrage, as he dropped the hand to his side.

"No, sir. I am here to prevent a robbery."

"What! I am a Deputy U.S. Marshal—on leave!"

"A marshal?" said Cleve. "What is your name?"

"I am U.S. Marshal Washburn!" he sputtered.

"I doubt it." Cleve turned to Salty. "I take it that you
boys have sold mining rights to Mr. Studge here?"

"We have!" declared Salty. He was frowning, himself,

his eyes darting about, having recognized Cleve now. "All is honest and aboveboard!"

"I know gold when I see it, Cleve!" Leon said, coming over to show his glittery palm. "Just wiped it right off the rock in there!"

Cleve nodded. "That no doubt is gold dust—which is not often found in mines in its free form. Mines are worked for veins and gold-bearing quartz and the like. Gold dust, loose like that, is found in creek sand, or gravel bars. Let us have a look at that sparkling rock in the mine."

"Just as you say," grumbled Washburn. "I will not dispute with that rifle. Have your look. You will find us, when you are ready to render an apology, in the Gideon Hotel, in Axle. Goodbye, sir!" He made to go.

"No, I think we will all look at the mine together, boys," said Cleve, raising a hand. "That is to say—if Leon does not object. I do not intend to embarrass you, Leon. I ask only that you trust me for a minute or two."

"Major, you kept me alive, and you fed me when I needed it most badly," said Leon. "Come the time, you gave me ten Yankee dollars from your own purse for the road. So, I reckon I owe you at least my trust."

Cleve gestured with his rifle at the other two men. "Washburn, hand that money back to Mr. Studge. If he chooses, he'll give it back to you shortly."

"I will in no wise part with it!" Washburn declared, his piggish eyes narrowing. "We have a signed contract!"

"If it's not signed with your real name, it has no force," Cleve said. "I doubt your name is Washburn. Hand him the money."

Salty cleared his throat. "I expect you'd better give it over for now. I have seen this gentleman in action. He does not ask thrice."

The big man growled but slapped the money into Leon's outstretched hand.

"Now, Leon," said Cleve, "if you would pick up that lantern, we'll follow these two into the mine. And boys, do not try my patience."

As if deeply affronted, "Washburn" and Salty turned away, muttering bitterly.

They had not gone but fifty feet in, past cobwebs and ratholes, when Leon pointed at the clay and stone wall to the left. "There, you see it, Cleve? Gold!"

Leon raised the lantern and it set the wall aglitter with points of gold. A distinct smell hung in the air, too.

Cleve nodded. "Do you notice the odor of a shotgun charge in here, Leon?"

"I do, now you mention it."

"Ah," said Salty. "As to that, when we inspected the mine this morning, we found a rattlesnake and had to shoot it."

Cleve smiled and pointed at the black marks about six feet above the wall. "The famous 'leaping rattlesnake' was it?"

Leon laughed.

Cleve said, "Leon—are you aware that one of the common ways to salt a claim is to take a little gold dust, put it in a shotgun shell, and fire on the ground you want to sell?"

Leon stared. "I was surely not aware of that!"

"It's one way to 'salt' a mine, as it's called—an expression that may cast some light on Salty's nickname. Now normally it's done 'round about a creek, for hawking a placer claim. But these two got this mine for next to nothing, I expect, since it was played out years ago, and so they fired their charge of gold dust in here. They then told you the usual sad tale of having to rush home on a mission of mercy. I'm afraid you've been honey-fogled, Leon."

"Why, I gave them a thousand dollars!"

"They calculated that a thousand dollars for twenty dollars' worth of gold dust is a prodigious good trade."

"Why, these aspersions . . ." Salty began.

Cleve pointed the rifle at him. "Shut your bazoo, Salty."

Salty clamped his mouth into a scowl.

Leon lifted the lantern again and peered closer at the rocky wall. "It does look some . . . unnatural. The way it's all in one spot there. And I believe I see some black marks . . ."

"Yes, they stood too close to the rock, and left gunpowder there along with the gold."

Cleve was alerted by the sudden motion of Washburn reaching for a pistol. His hands responded on their own, pointing the Winchester and squeezing the trigger.

The rifle barked, loud in the enclosed space, and the ball took Washburn in his right shoulder, as Cleve intended.

The bunko artist shouted in startlement and pain; he stumbled backward and fell with a grunt. Gun smoke swirled, and made the men blink.

"He was pulling his weapon," explained Cleve. "Leon, could I trouble you to take the gun from his coat, while I watch Salty? Be careful when you do it. He may have a knife." He turned the rifle to Salty—who looked set to hie from the mine. "Do not attempt to bolt, Salty. I'll shoot you too."

"I got his gun," said Leon, straightening up over the fallen man. "It's one of those little hideaway guns. Suppose he *is* a real deputy marshal?"

"Did he show you a badge?"

"He surely did not."

"Because there's none to show."

"I'm shot!" groaned Washburn. "I'm bleeding out! Salty why'd you get me into this?"

"Shut up, Digley!" Salty snapped.

"Digley—is that his real name?" Cleve said. "I have heard that name, somewheres. I'd be obliged, Leon, if you'd come over and find Salty's gun. He's surely armed."

Salty suffered Leon to search him, and another small gun was found.

Leon stuck the two-shot into his pocket.

"Come along then, Salty," Cleve said. "You take Digley by the ankles and drag him out."

"That great oaf!" Salty protested. "I cannot manage him!"

"You do it, or you'll find yourself there beside him."

Growling to himself, Salty attempted to pull the big man toward the mine entrance. Digley set up a yelping. "That's hurting me, damn you! I shall walk out!"

Digley pulled away from Salty, then got awkwardly to his knees and struggled to his feet. "I believe a bone is cracked in my shoulder . . . I'm bleedin' like a stuck pig . . . Someone shall pay!"

"Leon, pass me that lantern and head on out, if you will please," said Cleve. He did not feel comfortable giving Leon orders, as he had at Fort Slocum. Leon Studge was a free man now, and Cleve had no authority over him.

Leon made his way out, and Cleve backed out after him, lantern in one hand and rifle in the other, keeping an eye on the scoundrels.

Cleve and Leon were soon out in the clean air. The rain had not yet commenced, but the sky was sullen and darkening as Salty came out. Digley came stumbling after, moaning and cursing.

"Cease that squalling, Digley," said Salty, gazing longingly toward the horses.

"I carry bandages and medical spirits with me," Cleve

said. "You shall have the good of them, Digley, and we will take you into Axle Bust."

"There is a man named Hull in Axle Bust who says he's a physician," said Leon. "Saw his signboard. I haven't had his ministrations, so I cain't say if he truly is. I've known men to say they were surgeons when they were but barbers."

Cleve nodded. Fort Slocum had given them both a considerable respect for real surgeons. "Sit down, Digley, and I'll see to your wound. Leon, I'll trouble you to hold the rifle on these men . . ."

Digley attended to, they were soon mounted, riding north on the main trail, all in a line: the scalawags on their aging nags, Cleve astride the sorrel, Leon on his mule Lily. On the west side was a steep valley, channeling the southern reach of Axle Bust Creek southward; on the east rose the increasingly sere, gray hills. The slopes here were flecked with scrub and stands of trees, and knobbed with boulders. The sun was dipping behind the hills beyond the narrow valley. It was dusk, and night would soon be upon them. The tang of impending rain was in the air.

"Leon," Cleve called, over his shoulder, "how far do you suppose it is to Axle Bust?"

"Not much above two miles," Leon replied. "Perhaps three."

"How's that mule for a mount?" Cleve asked.

"Lily? This mule has carried me all the way here from South Texas! She was intent on living up to her mulishness at first, but she came to like me, for I treated her well, and we had many a talk—with me doing the talking—and now we are the best of friends."

They clopped along a quarter-mile more, when they came to a narrow canyon between two hills on the right, where a rock-strewn trail branched up into the hills. The main trail continued north.

Of a sudden, Salty whooped and kicked his mount into a turn, veering down the side trail, his horse's hooves clacking on the stones.

"Damn you, Salty!" shouted Digley. "I got to go where the doctor is!"

"Where's that trail take him, Leon?" Cleve asked.

Leon shook his head. "That I do not know. I reckon he'll look for a place to turn back south. I will not chase him alone—he'd ambush me on the trail."

Cleve decided he did not have the time to pursue the confidence trickster. He needed to get to Axle Bust for the sake of the wounded man and a pocketful of other aims. "I expect he's fearful of being hung," he remarked.

"You have shot me," growled Digley, "and you propose to take me to a doctor in a town where I am to be hung? You compound your barbarities!"

"I will see that you are not lynched," said Cleve. But he said it reluctantly. In Cleve's view, men who ran confidence games on the gullible were parasites, like ticks or mosquitoes.

They rode on, and the trail widened enough that Leon could ride up beside Cleve. "Major, how long since you left Fort Slocum?"

"I resigned my commission a few weeks after the last prisoner left," Cleve said.

"That when you come out west?"

"No, I went to Europe for a time."

"Europe!"

"Oh, it was a wonder. But if I thought I was going to forget the war there—war is practically the mortar for the bricks in European history. The fine constructions, the

museums, the food, the women—now that did take me out
of myself, a while."

"And—*French* women? Is it true that they—"

"Leon," Cleve interrupted, "I am a gentleman."

"So they *do*!"

"They do. Had to go back to the States soon enough.
Tried to keep busy in Ohio for almost three years. My
uncle Terrence is an engineer, the sort for bridges and
machinery, and hired me on as a secretary. Then he in-
vented a portable steam pump—or so he thought. But it
had a tendency to blow up and scald the unwary. Terrence
is a good man, but he has a bent to . . . enthusiasms. Well,
he ran through most of his money, and half of mine,
and he caught the gold fever. He came out to the gold
fields, and I went into fur trapping and scouting, out west.
Then I went to Denver, for a rest, never intending to stay,
but a friend talked me into joining the police force. I
carried a badge—and on the side I did some gambling.
It's curious how often those two go together . . ." He
cleared his throat. "I was there for several years. Then I too
caught the bug and made my way to Pike's Peak and the
hills 'round Virginia City, trying my hand at prospecting—
and 'games of chance.' Once again, it's curious . . ." He
shrugged.

"It's surely so—those two go together as well," Leon
said, amused. "Gambling and prospecting. Anyhow, I have
read that it's so. But my prospecting experience is thin."

"And where did you go, after leaving Slocum?" Cleve
asked.

"Texas, of course. Back to Austin. Had to rebuild the
Studge Ranch, take care of Mama. Pa was sick. Two of my
brothers were dead, killed in the war . . ."

"I'm sorry to hear that." He did not ask which battles
took their lives. After a period as an Army scout, Cleve

had been elevated to captain, leading men into the battles of Shiloh, Memphis, and Devil's Backbone. It was not likely he had fired a bullet that killed one of Leon's brothers, but neither was it impossible.

Leon squinted up at the sky. "Seems like I told you, back at Slocum, the only reason I joined up was because my brothers and my best friend did—and my middle brother, poor Stanley, was killed." He rode silently for a space and then went on. "Not too long after I come back, the Texas fever killed our beeves and then Pa died—died of despair, maybe, for he had to sell the ranch. Ma went to live with her sister, and I took to building fence for folks, a time. Then I drifted west, worked in a slaughterhouse—cain't abide that job—and I did some buffalo hunting for the railroads, to feed the hammer-hands, and rode security for them too. Saved up a thousand and eighty dollars . . ." He shook his head. "I've been out here about a month, trying my hand at prospecting and finding little but skarn. There's much I do not know—that's come clear now. I owe you a debt, Major. You saved me all that money. I should split it with you—it would have been gone entirely, but for you."

"You may buy me a meal, and that's the end of it," said Cleve. "You know that fellow Mark Twain?"

"The one who told that Jumping Frog story?"

"The very same. In a book he brought out this year, he said a gold mine is but 'a hole in the ground with a liar standing next to it.'"

Leon laughed. "Today, I surely do believe it."

"But it's not always true, and I believe my uncle's claim will stand. If you want to come in on it with us, we could use the help—financially, to stake the price of timber and tools, and help with the labor too."

"A silver strike?" asked Leon.

"Why no—it is gold. There's a small vein and some more in quartz. But there's some dispute with a fellow as to the claim—and some other matters to settle with him. Perhaps I should not ask you to come in with us. There might be some risk."

Leon grinned. "I would be charmed to throw in with ya'll." They rode onward. After a while, he cleared his throat and asked. "Say, did you ever get yourself a wife? Could be you have sons and daughters by now!"

"I have no wife, no children. I came close to marrying a couple times, but it seemed too much like settling for what had wandered my way, and my heart wasn't in it. One summer I did have a live-in lady, I do confess. But marriage did not come about. Perhaps I should have asked her. Uncle Terrence says that I'm a fool of a romantic, and should give off waiting on some fairy-tale ideal. But then Terrence never did marry. And you, Leon?"

"Why, I was married, or close to it. A Mexican senorita, name of Lupe." A certain bitterness entered his tone when he added, "I sent her money every last time I got paid. Finally got back to Texas to find she'd run south of the border with a vaquero. Her pa told me she got tired of waiting on me to come home."

"Too bad. But might be for the best, if she's so flighty as that."

"I do love me a senorita," Leon mused. "Now had I done the church marrying—could be she'd have stayed, on the priest's say-so."

Digley groaned when his horse stumbled slightly on the trail. He roundly cursed them. They ignored him.

Leon lifted his hat long enough to scratch his head. "Here now, Major, you spoke of Denver—seems to me

I read something in a news sheet about an officer C.T. Trewe in a shooting affray in Denver. I thought maybe it was you."

Cleve nodded. "Two in Soapy Smith's gang. They did not wish to return the jewelry they swindled out of a merchant, whereas I did wish them to return it. The disagreement became a trifle hot."

"A trifle? You killed two men in a gunfight!"

Cleve heaved a sigh. "The shooting soured me on the job. Two men dead at my feet. Till then I brought them in with a threat and maybe a knock on the head." He thought about it and added a caveat. "However—I'm willing enough to kill a certain Lester Wissel, if it can be done legally. But on the whole—well, I saw enough killing in the war."

They rode on, in thoughtful silence, both of them pondering the years that had rolled so inexorably by.

The downpour commenced when the three riders were just descending from the hills south of town. At first the rain dropped straight in heavy, splashing drops; then it slanted, slapping at them in the rising wind. The trail soon became a slog for the horses.

But they were now within sight of their destination: Axle Bust, Nevada.

To the north rose two jutting hills of craggy stone, and from between their bases, after several falls, rushed Axle Bust Creek. A swaying pillar of mist, rippling with shards of rainbow, rose from the bottom-most pool of the falls. The creek widened, almost approximating a river, to the west of town, then narrowed as it cut to the southwest. After a long journey, it would find its way to the Humboldt River.

The rain-laden wind was swirling the gray-brown wreath of woodsmoke over the mining camp. Axle Bust was a jumble of buildings, shacks, and cabins in a basin below Beaver Peak, in the foothills of the Tuscarora Mountains. The gray and raw-wood yellow-brown shacks, the canvas tents and false-front buildings seemed as random as a tumble of rocks, so far as Cleve could make out, though a rutted, crooked passage that ran between enough of them might serve as the town's main street.

Axle Bust was hand-painted on the sign at the edge of the mining camp, but local folks mostly called it Axle. Cleve's uncle had told him what little he knew of the place. It had grown up quickly after an enticing placer strike downstream, six years back, and a hard rock mine, the Golden Fleece, was chiseled into the eastern hill overlooking the town. There were said to be several assayers here, and one of them did some banking; there were a couple of liveries, a sawmill. The few shops were greatly outnumbered by saloons and impromptu whiskey tents.

As they rode closer, and the rain eased, Cleve could see the lineaments of placer sluice flumes for separating gold from sand and soil paralleling the creek down the slopes to the north. They passed rocker boxes, used for further sifting, and an acreage studded with tree stumps. Evidently a modest forest had been cleared—the tree-trunks, sawn and shorn, had become the structures straggling with little order alongside the creek on the west side and in rough, kinked lanes extending to the east. They rode past a sawmill gushing steam and smoke, and a corral where horses bowed their heads in the rain.

The town was still growing. As they rode up to the main street, Cleve noted almost as many tents as wooden structures. One of them was particularly large; some commercial enterprise. Around the edge of the basin,

cabins were beginning to glow with lantern light, haloing
in the smoke and mist. Rising from a broad ledge upslope
from the tailings around a hard-rock mine—likely the
Golden Fleece—was the framework of an unfinished ore
mill and smelter. A partly built brick chimney jutted from
its brick foundation.

Cleve had spent nigh two years prospecting, on and off,
and learned of a mining town's life cycles. First would
come the tents of the prospectors; then, when word spread
about good placer takings, came opportunists of various
stripes: miners and those who sold goods and services to
the miners. Ever more placer miners flooded in, staking
claims and arguing over them, to pan and sluice gold flakes,
gold dust, and sometimes nuggets. When the placer gold
thinned out, the first wave of prospectors might sell their
claims to a second wave, hard-rock miners and combines.
Exploratory shafts were dug, and when a lode was struck,
a third wave of gold seekers came—agents of mining
concerns, who bought up claims and promising mines.

The work of digging a shaft from an open-cut was
backbreaking and dangerous. It took time and blood and
sweat to exploit the gold, with just a few men working
alone. But an established mining company could afford
to pay miners and set up a mill. They need not invest their
own blood and sweat.

To Cleve's eye, Axle Bust was in transition, shifting
from a period of feverish prospecting to the systematic
takeover of big Eastern Money. Such a transition could be
rowdy.

This was Elko County, but they were far from the
county seat, and Cleve thought it likely there was little
law here apart from miners' courts—which were often
as not run by the local bullies. Sometimes a "constable"
was brought in by a mining concern, like as not a hired

gunman with some history as a deputy. He had once heard James Butler Hickok say, "Any jackass can be a deputy and some of 'em decorate wanted posters." Wild Bill was right: Cleve had encountered deputies, in Colorado and Arizona, who'd turned out to be wanted for killings across territorial lines.

As Cleve, Leon, and their prisoner rode down into town, Cleve heard a double *crack*. He at first thought it might be lightning. But when it recurred, he realized it was gunfire. It might be a drunk shooting at the sky or at another drunk.

The sky to the west reddened, the sinking sun stretching shadows over the basin; the smoke over the town was tinged by the sunset light, and it became the color of diluted blood.

Maybe they could locate Les Wissel this very night. But first they must rid themselves of the wounded Mr. Digley . . .

Look for **AXLE BUST CREEK** *on sale now!*

Visit our website at
KensingtonBooks.com
to sign up for our newsletters, read
more from your favorite authors, see
books by series, view reading group
guides, and more!

Become a Part of Our
Between the Chapters Book Club
Community and Join the Conversation

Betweenthechapters.net